# Drinking Saké
# All Alone

# Drinking Saké All Alone

## Geri Bennett

iUniverse, Inc.
Bloomington

# DRINKING SAKE ALL ALONE

iUniverse books may be ordered through booksellers or by contacting:

iUniverse
1663 Liberty Drive
Bloomington, IN 47403
www.iuniverse.com
1-800-Authors (1-800-288-4677)

ISBN: 978-1-4620-4068-1 (sc)
ISBN: 978-1-4620-4069-8 (ebk)

Printed in the United States of America

iUniverse rev. date: 07/27/2011

FOR

ROLAND W. BLAHA

AN HONORABLE MAN

AND

LOUISE BOWERS BLAHA

AN EXTRAORDINARY WOMAN

No blossoms and no moon
And he is drinking sake
All alone

Matsuo Basho
1644—1694




In the void is virtue, and no evil.
Wisdom has existence,
Principle has existence,
Spirit is nothingness.

Shinmen Musashi
(known as Miyamoto Musashi)
1584—1645

# THE PLAYERS

## The Japanese

Sunao Tokumura, Vice Minister of the Ministry of International Trade & Industry
       Otsu, his wife
       Mineo, his son
       Sachiko, his daughter
Satoshi Yoshida, billionaire industrialist
Stan Mitsunari, financial news editor
       Akiko, his wife
Hideki Watanabe, Minister of Finance
Nobuya Saito, Vice Minister of Finance
Sumio Masabe, timid chemist

## The Americans

Maggie Davidson Stuart, daughter of Michael Davidson
       Victoria Davidson, her mother
       Michael Davidson, her father, founder of The Davidson Hotel
       Group
Charles Stuart, Maggie's husband, economist
Bill Stuart, Charles' father, Chairman of the Federal Reserve Bank
Ken Williamson, San Francisco banker

Grant Williamson, Ken's father, Secretary of Commerce
The President and The First Lady
Victor Buchanan, former president of the U.S.
      Pamela, his wife
Reston (Rusty) LaFarge, governor of Tennessee
      Anne, his wife
Zach Templeton, Tennessee congressman
      Marge, his wife, former Miss Tennessee
Diane Manchester, computer genius
Bill Morita, aspiring yakusa
George Hagura, California labor leader born in WWII detention camp
Buzz Craddock, general manager, Davidson Chicagoan
Allison Jennings, Davidson Hotel Group Public Relations

# CHAPTER ONE

The stars that twinkled in the sky above Tokyo Bay paled in the shimmering light that glistened aboard a luxury yacht that drifted gently on the water below. The sounds of cocktail conversation wafted lazily into the otherwise silent harbor as American politicians and their wives enjoyed the lavish hospitality of 82-year-old billionaire industrialist, Satoshi Yoshida. The star studded guest list included not only the popular former president of the United States, Victor Buchanan, and his wife, Pamela, but the current president and his wife as well. Ostensibly, the illustrious gathering was a celebration of friendship between Japan and America.

Yoshida's company had recently delivered a two-hundred-million-dollar cruise ship to Honolulu to be christened, then sent on to San Francisco where it would take on its initial passengers. In what was described to the press as a joint venture between Japanese and American interests, the ship had been built by Yoshida's Nippon Heavy Industry Corporation, would be owned by a subsidiary company, and only its operations would be under the direction of the Americans.

"How is that library of yours coming along, Victor?" Yoshida asked of the former president.

"Very well, thanks to your generosity to the foundation. As you know, we have acquired the land, and construction is scheduled to begin next week," Victor replied.

Yoshida nodded his grizzled head. "Good, good. Such a distinguished presidency should be remembered. I'll never understand why your government will pay for maintenance of a presidential library, but won't put up the funds to build it. This could not happen in Japan. What is good for the country is good for its citizens," he murmured, somewhat pompously.

Pamela Buchanan smiled woodenly. She gazed up at her husband's still handsome face. His broad smile made it seem that he was enjoying himself immensely, but then, it always did. That's what had made him so popular. But to watch him suck up to their elderly host made her slightly ill. The old man had spent three years in prison after World War II, convicted of collusion with the Axis powers!

Pamela turned to watch the current American president who held tightly to his wife's hand. There couldn't be much more in the way of differences between her husband and The President, she mused. Where Victor was outgoing and jovial, a true politician who basked in the limelight, The President was introspective and a bit shy. A recently retired army general, The President had been swept into office following his heroic and well documented actions on the battlefield. Though he was formidable when it came to military action, he was painfully out of place in politics. And where Victor took her presence for granted, in fact, probably wouldn't notice what she was wearing unless she showed up in a bikini, The President hardly noticed anyone *but* his wife.

For that matter, the two women were as dissimilar as the men were. Pamela was a no-nonsense kind of woman who preferred tweed skirts and bulky sweaters to evening attire. The First Lady had delicate features and a tendency to dress in soft, filmy fabrics that made her seem slightly fragile, even a bit ethereal. Her behavior had been a bit peculiar in recent months and speculation on her mental health had begun to arise in the media. It was clear to anyone who looked at them however, that The President was devoted to his wife.

Sunao Tokumura, the Japanese Vice Minister of International Trade and Industry, sat quietly at the end of the bar, watching them as well. He paid close attention to each of the Americans, mentally assessing their personalities as he tried to keep his hostility from appearing obvious. That he, the descendent of an old and honorable samurai family, should be forced not only to associate with these people, but to treat them with deference was beyond distasteful. He couldn't help but wonder what Yoshida's motives might be. Surely, there was a reason why the old man would so lavishly entertain representatives of his former enemy, no matter what their status might be.

Tokumura's attitude stemmed from the memory that had tortured him since childhood. The image of his father's tears as they listened to the radio broadcast of Japan's formal surrender aboard the American battleship, USS Missouri, in 1945, burned on the inside of his eyelids. Tokumura had been only ten years old, but had vowed even then to avenge his samurai heritage. That goal had kept him studying diligently and pursuing his objectives until he had achieved the position that had made him one of the most powerful men in Japan, if not the world: Administrative Vice Minister of the Ministry of International Trade and Industry—MITI—the bureaucrat who made the rules that the politicians followed.

The ministers themselves were political appointments. It was common knowledge that the administrative vice ministers were the real power holders. The men who made the decisions. And of all the ministries, that of International Trade and Industry was the most powerful.

"Beautiful, isn't it?" The voice belonged to the distinguished Minister of Finance, Hideki Watanabe, who placed the crystal goblet he had been holding on the bar where it was immediately refilled by the steward. The minister's abundant white hair and strong jaw were set off handsomely by his finely tailored clothes. Men found him intimidating and women found him irresistible. Barring the unforeseen, he would probably be the next prime minister.

Startled, Tokumura realized that Watanabe meant the glittering harbor. "Yes, it is inspiring," he responded. "If you close your eyes and listen, the hum of the city almost becomes the beat of samurai marching along the road long ago. Ah, to have been among them!"

"It must be rewarding to know that your ancestors were part of the illustrious Tokugawa era," Watanabe commented politely.

"Sometimes I dare to hope that I am the reincarnation of one of them," Tokumura admitted modestly, concealing the fact that he not only hoped, but truly believed that he was, indeed, a reincarnation of the great seventeenth century warrior, Miyamoto Musashi.

He practiced The Way of the Warrior daily, even as he made love to his wife, Otsu. In the strategy called the Three Shouts, the first shout signaled the start of the battle, the second the attack, and the third celebrated victory. Otsu had been terrified the first time he shouted during their lovemaking, but had grown accustomed to it, hiding the tension that crept into her body as she anticipated first the shout as he entered her, then another as his sword did battle, and a final yell at the moment of triumph.

The two men watched as Satoshi Yoshida moved slowly among his guests, tilted slightly forward and appearing much younger than his 82 years. His cropped hair made him look bald from a distance and the pockets of his coat bulged with scraps of paper accumulated as he made notes that only he could decipher. His mind was still exceptionally sharp and he was completely cognizant of all that went on around him in spite of his advanced age.

"Americans," he muttered under his breath as he approached the bar where Tokumura and Watanabe stood, "with their lofty commitments to international goodwill. It's all rhetoric to excuse their laziness and the inability of their workers to sacrifice for the greater good of their country! They reached their peak fifty years ago and have been in decline ever since!"

Their expressions carefully impassive, the three men surveyed the American guests who mingled on the deck beyond the bar. It may have been noticed, but not commented upon, that the only Japanese wife at the party was that of Finance Minister Watanabe, and her presence was tolerated, if not encouraged, by the fact that her husband was a politician. Yoshida had been a widower for many years and Otsu Tokumura was far too traditional to appear in such a situation. Secure in their own beliefs, the Japanese men were unaware of the hostility that lurked among the wives of the American politicians.

Anne LaFarge, wife of Tennessee governor, Reston—'Rusty' to his constituents—LaFarge, stood at the rail trying to hide her disgust behind the smile that becomes a habit with wives of professional politicians. Anne was tall, with the air of one who would be more comfortable on a horse than making small talk among people with whom she had little in common. She had somber dark eyes that sometimes seemed like those of a large dog that had outgrown its dreams of being a lap dog.

"What a crock!" she murmured, watching her husband in conversation with Zach Templeton, a Tennessee congressman.

Pamela Buchanan joined Anne at the rail, asking, "What's a crock? Not that there isn't a qualifying abundance to choose from."

Anne gestured toward where her husband and Zach Templeton stood. Ignoring Pamela's question, she said, "The worst of it is that they think of it as political maneuvering, perfectly respectable. They've got their heads together over the automotive plant the Japanese are proposing to locate in Tennessee. It will be a 'screwdriver' operation with the parts manufactured in Japan, shipped to the U.S., and only assembled in Tennessee. The cars will then be considered made in the U.S.A. and save the Japanese company an enormous amount in import taxes! In return for fifteen million dollars worth of land, roads and power lines, Rusty and Zach will be able to announce that they were personally responsible for the creation of twelve hundred new jobs in a depressed region of Tennessee."

She went on, "Zach has his eye on moving from congress to the senate. He figures the fifteen million is a small sacrifice, and he'd be the first to insist that his intentions are of the highest moral fiber."

Anne paused as both she and Pamela noticed Zach's wife, Marge Templeton, in conversation with Japanese Vice Minister of Finance, Nobuya Saito. The former Miss Tennessee was obviously gushing at the opulence of the yacht. Saito's short stature put his eyes at the level of Marge's chin, his hands clasping and unclasping nervously as he did his best to avoid staring at the beauty queen's cleavage.

"I do hope his glasses don't steam up," Anne said solemnly. Pamela turned quickly toward the railing, unable to repress a giggle.

Tokumura, Watanabe and Yoshida also noticed Saito's distress and repressed the urge to snicker as well. All three knew how uncomfortable the little man was in social situations, but the rivalry between their two ministries made it a particularly enjoyable moment for Tokumura.

Everyone's attention was suddenly diverted as The First Lady began to move gracefully, swaying from side to side. Her hand slipped from her husband's grasp as she circled him playfully, dipping to pick up her long, full skirt near the hem with one hand. The other guests fell silent, mesmerized by the unexpected display. Tossing her head and oblivious to the stunned expressions on the faces of those around her, she began to fling herself about the deck, weaving in and out among the other guests.

Spinning faster and faster, she leapt suddenly onto a lower rung of the railing of the yacht, her arms outstretched toward the moon. Appearing from nowhere, a Secret Service agent's arm went around her waist as he plucked her from near disaster. The president hurried to her side. Since his back was to the others, no one saw the tears that filled his eyes. A collective sigh of relief arose as the moment ended.

Satoshi Yoshida was the first to recover his wits. "Well, my friends, what a dramatic conclusion to the evening," he announced. "The boats are available to transport you back to the dock whenever you may be ready."

Victor and Pamela Buchanan were the first to respond, their own experience as previous occupants of the White House coming in handy when unexpected events rendered a situation difficult.

Anne LaFarge linked arms with Marge Templeton, leading the suddenly speechless beauty queen toward the tenders that awaited them. Rusty and Zach followed obediently, leaving The President and his now docile wife to the Secret Service agents entrusted with their care.

Always cognizant of propriety, the Japanese bureaucrats bowed respectfully to their political counterparts and began to make their way toward the exit. Yoshida beckoned discreetly to Sunao Tokumura.

"If you have a moment, please join me for a little private conversation," he said.

When the guests had all departed, the two men retired to Yoshida's private quarters below. As he made his way down the passageway, Tokumura wondered what might be behind the doors to the guest staterooms. It was rumored that there were even fireplaces in some. The yacht was so huge that it was really a ship rather than a boat. Yoshida welcomed him, closing the door firmly and gesturing toward a table set with lacquered trays that contained sake cups and small but sumptuous delicacies, special treats not found among those on the deck above.

"As I get older," Yoshida began, "I have realized that westerners may have the right idea in using tables and chairs rather than our traditional Japanese floor cushions. Getting down isn't difficult, but getting up again is often a strain on my old bones."

Leaning back in his chair, his elbows on the arms, the fingertips of his hands tapping gently against one another, Yoshida said slowly, "I think we have a great deal in common, my friend."

"It would seem that we might," Tokumura answered carefully.

"The Americans from Tennessee are eager to have a Japanese assembly plant in their state, and the former president is so grateful for the money for his library that he nearly drools." Yoshida laughed and added, "Mrs. Templeton's cleavage may contribute to his salivating glands, however. Such simpletons."

Tokumura smiled carefully in agreement. "Their attitudes toward international business relationships are myopic at best, and fixated upon free trade ideology. They are so committed to the idea that they don't seem to notice that every other competitive nation in the world protects itself against trade imbalances."

Yoshida stared at an imaginary point of interest in space and commented, "You must find it difficult to endure the Americans and their presumptions of superiority."

Tokumura hesitated, unsure of what response might be expected. To say the wrong thing to such a powerful man could put him in a very uncomfortable place. A word of criticism from Yoshida could seriously damage his career.

Yoshida hid a small smile, recognizing the strength of his position. "As you might suspect, I have harbored significantly hostile feelings for many years. I have spent a great deal of time gathering information on those who appear to share my hatred of our former enemy. Am I right in suspecting that you are among those who consider the Americans inferior and undeserving of their outrageously superior position in the world community?"

Tokumura still hesitated, then said, "I was just a boy in those last terrible days in 1945. My mother was determined that my education should not suffer because of the war and we ran through the streets of Tokyo, dodging the bombs, to get to my classes. On the day of the formal surrender, my father and I listened to the radio broadcast together. Tears fell from my father's eyes as he whispered, 'We are shamed. Our samurai heritage must one day be avenged.' Those words and the vision of his tears are burned on the inside of my eyelids."

"I thought as much," Yoshida said. "Perhaps the time has come to fulfill your mission."

Tokumura waited, his breath slightly ragged in anticipation.

"It has occurred to me that the time may be right for a little encouragement in the devaluation of the dollar," Yoshida began. "Do you think the Americans can be convinced that Japan can import twice as much in the way of American products if the dollar is worth half as much in yen?"

Tokumura adjusted his weight, playing for time before he answered. "There are some economists in their Department of Commerce who might argue that their real estate would be obtainable for fewer yen as well, but I think a little pressure from American manufacturers who wish to sell their products in Japan would go a long way toward making them forget that. We have the best lobbyists in Washington, and though only Americans can contribute directly to the election campaigns of sympathetic candidates, our leverage is extensive through what they call political action committees."

Yoshida's next words startled him despite his growing suspicion that the day he had dreamed of for so long had arrived.

"It is 1992 and the war has been over for nearly fifty years. I have waited too long to retaliate against the Americans for the shame I suffered, and I am getting too old to wait any longer. Japan has outsmarted them in every field, has improved upon their technology and outwitted them in the international marketplace. We are now in a position to bring them to their knees. Can I depend upon your support in this effort?"

Though he had been quick to undermine the perception of friendship between the United States and Japan whenever the opportunity presented itself, Tokumura had not spoken openly of his hostility. Now the commitment had to be made or lost. He looked into Yoshida's steely eyes and said, "Most assuredly."

# CHAPTER TWO

Yoshida grunted as his smile hardened. He picked up a file that lay on an otherwise empty chair next to his. Handing it to Sunao Tokumura, he said, "You may already be aware of some of the information in this, but my sources are well paid to make sure that I'm kept informed of potential allies, their interests and affiliations."

Opening the file, Tokumura noted a list of names that began with that of Stan Mitsunari, a vice president of Nihon Keizai Shimbun, the Japanese financial newspaper. His innate distaste for the American first name made him grimace.

"How can one so westernized be advantageous to your plan?" he asked.

Yoshida's lips curled in an expression that could be either amusement or agreement. He studied Tokumura's scowl for a moment, then replied, "You are a student of The Way of the Sword. 'Know the Ways of all professions. Develop intuitive judgment and understanding for everything. Perceive those things which cannot be seen. Pay attention even to trifles,'" he quoted from Musashi's Book of Five Rings.

"The boy was named for an American serviceman who assisted the family during the occupation," he went on. "His education in the States may provide insights otherwise overlooked."

"Traitorous," Tokumura muttered. "But you are right, of course. His knowledge and experience could be useful, and his influence in Japan's financial community is substantial. His cooperation in manipulating the American economy would be extremely helpful."

"It is nearly time for the Nihon Keizai annual publication of notable promotions and you are certain to be allotted an amount of space proportionate to your prestigious position. An informal visit with Mitsunari-san would not be considered out of the ordinary."

"Yes, my photo and biography will no doubt be featured." It was difficult to appear modest when the facts were so obvious.

The old man's scrutiny was disconcerting, however. Tokumura adjusted his sturdy frame once again, his double chin sinking into the collar of his shirt. He had the feeling the interview was coming to a conclusion, but to rise before his elder would be a breach of etiquette.

"We are both nationalists, Sunao-san," Yoshida mused, deliberately using the bureaucrat's first name. "It is no secret that I supported a Japanese alliance with the Axis powers and supported military aggression against the United States as well. I paid for my decision, but I would make the same decision again. Global economic conditions have initiated another crisis in international diplomacy and an alliance of industry and government such as ours is only natural."

Pausing to be sure that he had the younger man's full attention, he said softly, "Does it not seem unusual that a man with an American university degree and offers of highly paid positions in that country would choose to return to Japan where he could not hope to live as comfortably as he might have in America? Perhaps there are reasons we are not yet aware of . . . ?" Yoshida let his voice dwindle thoughtfully as the significance of the words became apparent to his bureaucratic ally.

One of Sunao Tokumura's greatest pleasures was driving through the gates that concealed his ancestral home on the outskirts of Tokyo. The original portion of the home had been built several centuries before in what was then farmland. As the city expanded and began to surround the farm, crops had diminished and eventually disappeared as the value of land appreciated to unheard of heights.

As it was inherited by future generations, each one added to the original structure. Plumbing and electrical wiring had been installed by Sunao's grandfather and updated by his father. Sunao, Otsu and their children now occupied the home that was the envy of nearly everyone but the emperor himself. Only a portion of the house was visible from the drive, making it impossible to know what lay ahead. As in a Japanese garden, its secrets were revealed one by one as the visitor explored.

Small stones, set in a bed of rock and gravel two feet deep held the posts of the foundation in place. Tongue-in-groove polished beams supported much of the house, allowing it to rock gently in an earthquake, should one occur. A stone basin with a ladle stood in the curve beside the front door, a reminder of the purifying ritual that directed all who entered to leave their anxieties outside. Each wing, connected by passageways of black cherry wood and shoji screens, hid treasures that had remained there throughout time. Sunao never tired of strolling through the rooms that held pieces of history.

A rather nondescript man, he often wished that his physique was as imposing as his government position. Over the years, his natural enjoyment of good food had added more pounds than he cared to acknowledge, but when he smiled, his wife thought him the handsomest man in the world.

Removing his shoes as he entered the house, he was not smiling as the raucous sound of rock music rattled the floorboards, creating a very real threat to the well-being of a fifteenth century camphor wood carving of a Shinto goddess that stood silently on a rosewood stand.

"Mineo!" he boomed, repeating his seventeen-year-old son's name when he received no reply. "Mineo!"

Striding toward the source of the music, Sunao threw open the door to Mineo's room and stood glowering at the scene that met his eyes. The boy was absorbed in strumming an imaginary guitar, his head thrown back as his body contorted in moves that his father thought might well cause his bones to dislocate.

Suddenly aware of his father's presence, Mineo dropped his pose and hurried to lower the volume on the stereo.

"Hi, Pops. Sorry, I didn't expect you home so early."

"Pops? Is that the way you show respect for your elders? Why are you not studying, you lazy oaf? Your exams are coming up in only a few months and if you fail them, you will not be admitted to Todai and your future will be dismal at best! I did not dash through the streets of Tokyo to study classes as a child, bombs falling all around me, to watch my own child throw away his life!"

"Yeah, yeah, I know." Mineo threw himself onto the bed, slouching in defiance. "You spent whole nights at cramming classes, crawling into bed as the sun came up. I've heard it so many times, I could recite it along with you. That was a long time ago, Pops, and times are different now. Rock music is where it's at."

Sunao's face turned purple with rage. "You dare to mock me? It is because I studied, then played the game according to the rules, that I am successful! And soon I will be a great hero to my countrymen. My dream is a noble one!"

"What dream is that? Working in a dreary office day in and day out so that you can retire to some elite club and talk about the good old days with all the other drones? Not for me, Pops. So the exams aren't all that important and neither is Todai."

"Todai, the University of Tokyo, the greatest in the world, is not important?" Sunao could no longer stand to look at Mineo. He turned and fled from the room before the urge to strike his son became too strong to resist.

Crossing the garden outside the wing he shared with Otsu, he entered the small, round teahouse where he spent time each evening in meditation and contemplation. Made of rustic timbers with plaster walls by some long-dead ancestor, the little room was lighted only by the moonlight that crept through its round windows or by candles on dark nights. It was here that he found solace as he withdrew from the often chaotic world of Japanese politics, or searched for solutions to personal problems.

What miserable god had given him such a son? Had the gods been looking the other way and mixed up his son and daughter? Sachiko had done well in school and now badgered him relentlessly to allow her to attend graduate school in the United States, or even worse, get a job. He shuddered at the thought of his lovely child in the work place. Though he knew it was considered acceptable in some circles, it would be perceived as a blemish on her character by the most suitable men in search of wives.

The timing could not be worse for his children to provoke such distress. His mind must be free to sort through the possible ramifications of the commitment he had made that evening. The revenge he had dreamed of was within his grasp, but the dream now frightened him. He had worked long and hard to get where he was. He must be very careful not to appear 'different' or cause too much dissent among his peers, thereby losing power. Could it be done?

Ah, but as he had told Mineo, the dream was a noble one and he would emerge a great national hero in the end. What would Musashi have done? The ancient warrior's own words came to him quickly.

"Strategy is the craft of the warrior . . . the warrior's is the twofold Way of Pen and Sword, and he should have a taste for both . . ."

Yes, strategy was the key. Sunao closed his eyes and began to concentrate on breathing in and out, thinking only of filling his lungs with the energy of life and releasing all his fears.

Soon he was at peace once again.

A world away in Chicago, Maggie Davidson Stuart hurried up the seven steps that led to the front entrance of the Davidson Chicagoan Hotel. She knew there were seven steps because she had been climbing them since she first learned to walk.

"Hi, Miss Maggie! Don't you look lovely today!" exclaimed the doorman who had been ushering her into the lobby since she'd been a young child.

"Thanks, Bert. Is my mother here yet? Our reservations in The Pub are for one o'clock and I think I'm running a little late."

"She came in just a few minutes ago, Miss Maggie. I think she went up to your daddy's office."

Maggie loved the lobby of the hotel. Wood paneling shone in the subdued elegance of soft lighting, and deep upholstered chairs were clustered cozily, inviting hotel guests to enjoy a cup of tea or a cocktail served by observant, but unobtrusive waiters. Sometimes when her mother was busy, Maggie had spent afternoons there, curled up with a book or watching people come and go. Sometimes she pretended that she was a fairy princess in an enchanted kingdom where she could be invisible if she wanted to be. The magic had never worn off; it was still a special place.

Foregoing the elevator, Maggie took the staircase that led to her father's office suite on the second floor. The Davidson Chicagoan was the flagship property in the Davidson Group of mid-sized hotels founded by Michael Davidson. A mainstay in local society, the Chicagoan was a tradition among those who wanted their parties written about and remembered. And visitors to the heartland of America who insisted upon taste and distinction would lay their heads only upon Davidson pillows.

Michael's secretary greeted her as she came through the door of the outer office. "Go right on in, Maggie. Your mom and dad are waiting for you."

"Don't you look stunning!" exclaimed Victoria Davidson, her manicured hand reaching toward her daughter's hair to tuck a stray curl back into place, then brushing a non-existent hair from the collar of Maggie's black silk jacket. "Of course you always look wonderful, dear, though I wish you'd wear something more colorful now and then."

She always spoils the compliment, Maggie thought, but never so obviously that it warrants complaint.

"I think you look wonderful in black, Maggie. It sets off your blonde hair so beautifully," said her father, always the peacemaker in the family.

"Can you have lunch with us, Daddy?" Maggie asked.

"I'm afraid not today, darling. I'm meeting with Buzz." The general manager of the Chicagoan, Buzz Craddock was also Michael's right hand man and had been for many years.

"Well, say 'hi' for me. Maybe next time?"

Maggie and Victoria headed back downstairs to The Pub, a landmark restaurant that was a meeting place for celebrities. Anyone who was anyone knew just where to be when someone said, "Meet me at The Pub at seven."

"Martini, Mrs. Davidson?" asked their waiter.

"Why, yes, thank you, Mark," Victoria replied. "Extra dry, please." She glanced at the menu briefly, then put it down and looked at Maggie. "How is Charles, dear?" she asked.

"I guess he's fine," Maggie said. "I hardly talk to him anymore. He's gone so much to the west coast and when he is here, he stays at the office until all hours and then brings work home with him."

"You want him to be ambitious, don't you? All of this didn't happen without a lot of hard work on your father's part." Victoria waved her hand in the air vaguely.

Maggie glanced around the elegant room. Crystal chandeliers hung from high ceilings and tall, narrow windows were covered by diaphanous curtains that allowed the daylight to filter in without letting the hustle and bustle of the city disturb the ambiance. Velvet valances hung across the tops of the windows, draping graciously to the floor on either side, absorbing any residual noise from diner's voices. As children, Maggie and her friends had loved Saturday afternoon visits to The Pub where they were treated to ice cream and gooey cakes, often pestering her daddy till he laughingly gave in.

"Charles has been the fair-haired boy at the bank ever since he started there, Mother. Success is practically a given. We have a beautiful home that's far too large for the two of us and way too suburban to suit me. I have a closet full of clothes that would keep half of China outfitted for life, I'm bored stiff by the 'ladies who lunch' and I hardly ever see my husband anymore. When we do go out, we don't have any fun. So what good is all that success?"

What Maggie didn't mention was that she and Charles didn't have any fun in bed, either. Charles Stuart apparently had no idea that sex might be something more than satisfying physical needs occasionally, and in the dark at that. But then, Maggie's own experience prior to her marriage to the man her parents thought suitable had been limited to heavy breathing in a parked car with Stan Mitsunari in college.

Now and then she considered having an affair, but couldn't think of any available men with whom to have one anyway.

"If you had children, the house wouldn't seem so big and you'd be too busy to care how late Charles stays at the office," Victoria was saying.

"Well, Mother, children aren't hatched, you know. It takes two people who spend time together other than at charity dinners. What we need is a little romance in our lives."

"Well, if it's romance you want, San Francisco is about the most romantic city in this country. Why don't you go with Charles next time?"

Maggie's eyes widened as an idea occurred to her. "Why don't I get on a plane and surprise him on *this* trip?" she said excitedly. "A sort of second honeymoon?"

"Are you sure you should surprise him?" Victoria frowned. Surprising her own husband was the last thing she'd have done. "Why not phone him so he can meet your flight?"

Maggie tilted her head, thinking. "Yes, I think something spontaneous might be just what we need to spice up our lives."

# CHAPTER THREE

Charles Stuart hurried past other passengers who paused in the waiting area to greet friends and families there to meet the plane upon its arrival in San Francisco. Descending on the escalator that led to the baggage claim area, he waited impatiently for his luggage. Normally, Charles traveled with only what he could carry, but Ken Williamson had suggested a drive up to the Napa Valley to do some wine tasting, making it clear that Charles' usual ivy league attire would be inappropriate, and urging him to loosen up a little.

Charles was looking forward to the excursion. Ken was in the correspondent banks department of the west coast bank that Charles' Chicago bank used for many of the transactions requiring the services of a California financial institution. Both men were on the corporate ladder to success and though they had spent quite a bit of time together in the office and over lunch, this would be their first purely social outing.

"What a glorious day!" Charles exclaimed, turning his face upward to bask in the warmth of the late summer sun that shone down on Ken's convertible. The top was down and Charles peered over his shoulder at the crystal clear skyline of San Francisco as they sped north across the Golden Gate Bridge. Exuberant, he threw up his arm, hand in a fist, and shouted, "Yes!"

"It isn't always like this," Ken said. "There are more days in the year when you couldn't see the bridge towers above us than there are when

Tony Bennett's 'golden sun will shine' for us." He finished the sentence singing the line from the best-selling song.

"Yeah? Well, give me one day like this and I'll be happy to put up with a lot of dreary ones!"

Ken laughed. The temperature was crisp, but not cold, and the hills of Marin County were etched against the sky like cardboard cutouts ahead of them. Just north of San Rafael, Ken took the Highway 37 off ramp from the freeway and headed east. It wasn't long before signs began to appear announcing that they were nearing a winery, then another and another.

"It looks like there's a winery on every corner!" Charles noted. "How long would it take to stop at each one and sample every wine made in the whole valley?"

"I think there's a Napa-Sonoma wine country map in the glove compartment," Ken responded. "I couldn't tell you how many wineries there are, but I'd guess it would be several hundred. Even if you could stay sober enough to visit them all, it would take months, maybe years."

The road narrowed to one lane in each direction as they drove through the town of Napa, heading north on Highway 29. Fields of grape vines laden with fruit began to appear along the side of the road. Workers prowled among them checking clusters for ripeness, their multi-colored garments flashing among the leafy plants.

"What a scene!" Charles exclaimed. "Like something right out of a movie. How do you know which wines are the best? How do you choose which winery to visit?"

"It isn't really a matter of 'best' or 'worst.' It's more in the variety of the grape, the soil and weather conditions in which it was grown, and the processing," Ken said. "Many of the growers sell their grapes to the big name wineries rather than doing the processing themselves and a lot of the wineries have converted to high volume, stainless steel production that's more cost effective than the old wooden casks. The purists would tell you that the smallest detail can affect the wine—like picking the grapes a few days too soon or varying the temperature a degree or two during the aging. So a particular wine, say a cabernet sauvignon, from a particular winery might be great one year and not so great the next."

The castle-like fortress that was Christian Brothers Winery appeared on the left and Ken turned into the parking lot. Charles swung the car door open and jumped out, running his fingers through his windblown hair absentmindedly as he gazed up at the old building where monks had once tended fields and lovingly cultivated the grapes.

Ken was as dark as Charles was fair, with broad shoulders and a muscular physique developed during his years of playing football at Stanford University. His all-American football hero look complimented Charles' boyish smile and aristocratic bearing, creating a magnetic impression.

The young, female tour guide smiled brightly as they approached, resolving to give them special attention. After all, guys this good looking and obviously well off, didn't grow on trees and a girl had to make the most of the opportunities she's given. Her efforts went unrewarded, however, as they left without so much as flirting, never mind asking for her phone number.

The afternoon passed amiably as the two men sampled varieties from chablis and chardonnay to pinot noir and cabernet sauvignon. Charles ordered several cases to be shipped to Chicago and Ken bought two cases to take home with him as they went from one winery to another.

Charles was happier than he could remember being in a very long time, and offered no objections when Ken suggested that they stop for a drink on the terrace of the Alta Mira Hotel in Sausalito. As they were seated at a table under a colorful umbrella, he was once again stunned by the view of San Francisco across the bay from the tiny town that clung to the hillside at the north end of the Golden Gate Bridge.

"I cannot thank you enough for this unbelievable day! I knew there were an abundance of great places to see around San Francisco, but we've always been so busy trying to cram the workload into a couple of days, that I'd begun to despair of ever getting out of the financial district," he told Ken. "I thought we might be great friends if we got to know each other, but I really don't know much about you at all. Have you always lived in California?"

"Not only have I always lived in California, I've always lived in or near San Francisco," Ken answered. "I was born at the University of California Hospital. My dad was a partner in one of the big downtown law firms before he retired and since he went to Stanford, it was assumed I'd go there, too. I had a football scholarship, and with the family prestige as well as the attention that goes along with being a jock, there didn't seem to be any reason to leave the area."

"I graduated from my dad's alma mater, too. Dartmouth." Charles said. "I doubt I'll ever quite measure up to his success, however. He went from small town banker to Chairman of the Federal Reserve Bank."

"Oh, my god, you're Bill Stuart's son? I should have known that, shouldn't I? I'll bet our fathers know each other. My dad is a fanatic fundraiser for the Republican Party. He and the president are good buddies and there's been some talk lately about a cabinet post."

"The over-achiever generation," Charles said, grinning. "I'll bet they do know each other."

By the time they pulled up in front of Charles' hotel, both men were more than a little intoxicated. Reluctant to end such a perfect day, Charles suggested that dinner in the hotel dining room would be a fine conclusion and it was to be his treat.

"After all, our palates are already conditioned to excellence. It would be a shame to waste the effort," he said in mock seriousness.

A tall, leggy blonde, stunning in a red suit with a very short skirt, was speaking to the maitre d' as they approached. Her conversation ended and she turned to leave, nearly running into Charles and Ken. All three of them murmured apologies and the blonde allowed her eyes to look both men up and down slowly. Nodding her approval, she drawled, "All right!" as she left the room. Ken and Charles looked at each other in amazement and burst out laughing.

"I thought only men did that," Charles remarked in astonishment.

"Not anymore," Ken chuckled.

They lingered over coffee after dinner, then decided that it wasn't really all that late and a touch of cognac in Charles' room sounded like a jolly good idea. It was after midnight when Ken looked at his watch and stood up to leave, weaving slightly as the excessive amount of alcohol took its toll.

Grasping Ken's hand, Charles looked into his eyes and said fervently, "I don't think I've ever enjoyed a day more than this one. Thank you, dear friend."

"Nor have I," Ken replied. They swayed drunkenly together, holding each other up, and fell toward the bed.

Maggie Stuart stared into the darkness outside the window of the plane, doubts beginning to form in her mind. Maybe it hadn't been such a good idea to surprise Charles in San Francisco after all. He wasn't really the kind of person who responded well to the unexpected and there was every chance that he might even resent her intrusion on his business trip.

It was just beginning to get light outside as her taxi pulled up at the hotel entrance. She straightened her shoulders and told herself that it was too late to change her mind. Lifting her chin, she stepped purposefully toward the front desk and was soon walking down the hall toward Charles' room.

She giggled as she inserted the key into the lock. Maybe they'd have time for a quickie before Charles left for whatever appointments he might have. Ha! She thought immediately. Fat chance. Only if he undergone an overnight metamorphosis!

The drapes were closed and it was dark as Maggie tiptoed across the room. She was about to turn on the lamp and tap the shoulder of the sleeping form on the bed when she realized that the head on the pillow was far too dark to belong to her husband. Backing away hurriedly, she left the room, closing the door as quietly as possible, and ran toward the elevator. Every instinct told her to get as far away from that room as possible before she was discovered.

Reason reasserted itself as she realized that no one had seen her. She dropped into the chair beside a table that held a house phone across from the elevator. She took several deep breaths, then picked up the receiver to call the front desk.

"Yes, Mrs. Stuart, your husband's room is number 1016. Isn't that the number on the key you have?"

Maggie held up the key. "Yes, but . . ."

"Is there a problem, Mrs. Stuart? Doesn't the key work properly?"

"No, that is, yes, it works, but . . . never mind. Thank you. I'll try it again. I must have made a mistake." She replaced the receiver quickly and sat staring at the key in her hand. Who was in that room? Charles couldn't be having an affair with a woman in San Francisco. It was unthinkable. Or was it? Could that be why he was so uninterested in her? She had to know.

She stood in front of the door to room 1016, gathering her courage, then knocked gently. There was no response, so she knocked again, harder this time.

A voice called out, "Just a minute," and a moment later, Charles opened the door, disheveled and groggy. His mouth dropped open in shock as he recognized his wife. They both heard the groan from the bed at the same time and turned toward it.

"Oh, God," said Charles.

Ken's head rose from the pillow, his eyes only partially open. He glanced around the room, looked at Charles and Maggie standing in the doorway and moaned, "Oh, God."

"Oh, dear God," Maggie cried softly before she turned and ran out, stumbling back to the elevator as tears blinded her.

# CHAPTER FOUR

Akiko Mitsunari heard the key in the lock and adjusted her position in the bed, making sure that her long dark hair fell across her face so that she could watch her husband as he tiptoed into the room and undressed. In the early months of their marriage, she had greeted him eagerly, but time had made it apparent that he thought of her with the same kind of affection he might have felt for a pet and that he'd prefer to believe she was sleeping soundly so that he wouldn't feel obligated to make love to her.

It had been an arranged marriage. It was a matter of tradition for the daughters of middle ranking politicians to form alliance with the sons of influential businessmen. Stan's father had been a noted journalist, so his foreign education was discreetly overlooked, as was the fact that though Akiko was a very pretty girl, her father's position did not offer much in the way of assistance to Stan's career.

Stan removed his suit jacket as he came into the room, his shoulders and the muscles in his back straining against the fabric of his shirt as he reached for a hanger. Akiko shivered involuntarily, longing to run her fingers over his magnificent body. Donning western style pajamas, he drew on a kimono, tying the sash carelessly, and went back to the living room. It wasn't long before the mellow sounds of the Four Freshmen singing, "the things we did last summer, I'll remember all winter long" began to drift into the bedroom. Tears slid down Akiko's face. How could she possibly compete with his memories of the beautiful

American girl with the pale skin and blonde hair whose photograph was hidden between the pages of Stan's university yearbook? Her name was Maggie.

Stan poured a hefty measure of scotch into a tumbler and stood listening to the music. Most of the time he avoided the old albums, considering them counter-productive to mental well-being, but his earlier meeting with Sunao Tokumura had provoked one of those old self-destructive cravings for introspection that tested his resolution.

The bureaucrat's obvious hostility toward Americans had recalled his own bitterness the summer after graduation from the University of Missouri's School of Journalism. The old cliché about sticks and stones might be useful in the face of playground taunts, but words could be the cruelest weapon known to mankind. They could injure the soul.

"Surely you realize that marriage to Maggie is out of the question?" Michael Davidson had said. Stan had expected some resistance, but to be told outright that he was unacceptable had stunned him.

"Perhaps it would be best if you accept an offer from a Japanese firm that would be, after all, more culturally advantageous to your career," Michael had continued. Stan's vision of his future had been thoroughly demolished at that moment.

Vice Minister Tokumura had probed, asking about Stan's years in America and affecting an interest in the difference between American and Japanese higher education.

"There's more independent study for one thing," Stan had told him. "American professors encourage students to search for the information they need on their own rather than simply giving it to them."

"Is this because they lack this knowledge themselves? It would seem that such a policy delays the learning process," Tokumura had said.

The comment made Stan pause. "No, it really isn't that," he said thoughtfully. "They believe that it teaches the student how to locate sources of information and accumulate useful data that can be applied to problem solving. The instructor is the guide. Japan's system depends more on memorization of pre-established fact, which may account for the ability of the Americans to create new products and the Japanese ability to refine and perfect them."

In an effort to draw him out, Tokumura had pursued the idea that studying with the Americans must have been difficult for Stan. "There was an American professor in my office last week," he said. "A very irritating man, associated with the planning of another of those intellectual conferences that they are so fond of presenting as pathways to mutual understanding."

Stan had laughed aloud. "Actually, I enjoyed the university very much, but I agree that Americans can be annoyingly eager in their pursuit of noble ideas."

"This one was more like an ill-mannered dog," Tokumura had observed dourly. Sipping at his drink, he had begun asking about career opportunities in the states, triggering the memories of what had turned out to be Stan's last day in the country he had hoped to make his permanent home.

"I had several offers of positions when I graduated, but I decided that I preferred to remain Japanese," he had said abruptly, changing the subject.

Maggie Stuart huddled in the window seat that had been her childhood refuge, willing herself small again. She had very little recollection of the hours between the time that Charles opened the door to his hotel room and the moment her mother opened the door that admitted her to this safe haven.

She knew she had scurried from the hotel as quickly as her feet would carry her, but the flight from San Francisco back to Chicago was only a blur. Getting to the one place that represented safety had been the only thought that kept her from hysteria.

"Maggie, darling, please tell me what's wrong," Victoria Davidson pleaded. "Are you ill? Has something happened to the house?"

"Nothing happened to the house and I'm not ill, at least not in the way you might think," Maggie had managed to say.

"Why don't I call Charles for you? Which hotel is he at in San Francisco?"

Maggie's head jerked as she cried, "No!"

"Has something happened to Charles? Is that what's wrong?" Victoria couldn't imagine why her daughter was being so difficult.

Maggie's stomach turned at the question. "You might say that, Mother," she said bitterly. Too tired to cry anymore, she could only rock back and forth wretchedly.

Becoming more annoyed than anxious now that it had been established that Maggie and her house were apparently safe, Victoria decided that the problem must have something to do with Charles. Perhaps Maggie had called him after all and was upset because he had rejected her plan to join him in San Francisco. She decided it was time to summon Michael home. He had always been closer to the girl than she was, a fact that bothered her only when she thought of it as a reflection on the quality of her mothering.

Michael held his only child in his arms as the tears fell once again, but was unable to elicit any more information than had Victoria. The phone rang and Maggie shuddered, sure that it was Charles. A moment later, Victoria was holding the receiver toward her in confirmation.

"I don't want to talk to him," Maggie said dully.

"Why on earth not? Don't be silly, darling. He probably just wants to apologize for telling you not to join him."

Both Michael and Victoria were astonished to hear Maggie wail, "I *did* join him! Tell him I never want to see him again!"


"Maggie, please say something. Say anything. I can't stand the silence," Charles begged later that evening when he arrived at the Davidson's home on the Near North side of Chicago.

"What would you like me to say? That I understand? I don't. Is that why you're so uninterested in me? Or are you revolted by me? When you *have* made love to me, were you wishing I was someone else?" Maggie's voice broke. "Were you wishing I was a man?"

Charles sank into a chair, his elbows on his knees, his head in his hands. "I swear to you, Maggie, nothing like that has ever happened before! For that matter, I'm not at all sure that anything *did* happen. We'd been drinking all day, for Christ's sake!"

"All the alcohol in the world wouldn't make me fall into bed with someone I didn't want to be with," she responded. "Apparently, I'm just not the right person for you."

"It has nothing to do with you, Maggie. It isn't your fault so please don't beat yourself up like this."

"Who should I beat up, Charles? You? Okay, you son of a bitch, I'd like nothing better than to keep hitting you until I can't hit anymore." She raised both arms and pummeled him with her fists for a moment, then fell back and sobbed. Her initial shock had turned to anguish, then self-doubt, and then anger. Sometimes all three emotions got mixed up until she didn't know *what* she felt.

"What are you going to do?" Charles asked.

"What am I going to do? What am I going to do," she repeated. "More to the point, what are *you* going to do? Do you want to be with him? How long has this been going on? Is he the reason you've been going to San Francisco so much lately?"

Tears rolled down Charles' cheeks as he said, "We've been friends, Maggie. That's all. Until now. I don't have any idea what to do. I'm ashamed and yet something inside of me asks why. Am I ashamed because I may have been unfaithful to my wife, or am I ashamed because it wasn't with a woman? Such a thing has never occurred to me before. I don't know how to handle it. I've always assumed that I just didn't have as strong a sex drive as some men do. I have *never* looked at another man in that light. *That* I swear to you, Maggie."

"Are you looking at him in that light now?"

Charles cried miserably, rubbing his eyes with the heels of his hands. "His name in Ken, Maggie, and he's a great guy. He's educated, witty, fun to be with. You'd like him!"

"You make me sick! How could I like that man after what he's done to my husband?"

"Don't blame him, Maggie. He didn't do anything more than I did. We didn't really talk, except that we both said we'd never done anything like that before. Hell, I'm not even really sure we actually did anything!"

"Oh, God, Charles, I can't take any more of this," Maggie said wearily. "You go back to the house tonight. I'll come up and get my things tomorrow. I can stay here with Mother and Dad for the time being."

"We can't just end our marriage! Please, give me time to figure out why it happened! Other than that we were both pretty drunk."

"I don't plan to see a divorce lawyer just yet, Charles, but I want you to understand. I went to San Francisco to be with you and to bring some romance into this marriage. I wanted us to talk about why we were just sort of muddling along, why we didn't have fun together—you and me. I wanted to make you happy!" She broke down again. "And there you were, being happy with someone else. I need time to sort out my feelings, too. Maybe we never really loved each other at all." The thought was almost too much to bear.


"Maggie, you can't mean that!" Victoria Davidson was horrified. "A week ago you were talking about rekindling the romance in your marriage and now you tell me that you're going to divorce Charles? What could he possibly have done that was so dreadful?"

"You really don't want to know, Mother, and I don't want to talk about it. Not now, probably not ever. You'll just have to trust me and believe me when I say I can never live with him again."

Maggie had searched her soul for answers, but could find no other way. If Charles had been able to explain somehow, or even lied about it, she might have been able to overcome the revulsion she felt for him. But he had not. Quite the opposite, he had defended his actions and told her repeatedly what a fine fellow Ken was until she finally realized that what he was really saying was that he had made his choice and it wasn't her. She wasn't sure he knew it himself.

She tried to put up a brave front for the benefit of her parents, but at night when she closed the door to the room that had always been hers, she cried herself to sleep. As the days passed, she began to realize that losing Charles wasn't what she was crying about. It was that her value as a woman had been challenged and she had failed. It was not the first time the man she loved had made another choice. Stan Mitsunari had not valued her enough to stand up to her father's objections and had chosen to leave her as well. Her anger dissolved into depression.

Victoria couldn't accept her daughter's non-answers. "Was it another woman?" she persisted. "Many men stray now and then, but you can get through it. It just takes time to forgive."

Maggie sighed. "No, Mother. It wasn't another woman."

"Well, the only other reason I can think of for such drastic action is some kind of dishonesty, and I find that difficult to believe in Charles. He's from a fine family and could never do anything illegal. Why, his father is Chairman of the Federal Reserve Bank, for heaven's sake!"

"He didn't embezzle funds from the bank or anything, but it was a form of dishonesty nonetheless, Mother. Please don't ask me any more questions."

The phone rang and Victoria rose to answer it. It seemed only a moment between the time that Maggie heard her say 'hello' and the bloodcurdling scream. She raced into the den, her eyes wide with terror and saw Victoria standing rigidly, the phone dangling loosely on the floor.

"Your father collapsed in his office. He's dead." The words were like knives in Maggie's chest.

# CHAPTER FIVE

Stan Mitsunari frowned as he stared at the paper he had just torn from the telex machine. The item that had caught his attention was a short one, only a few wire service lines telling of Michael Davidson's sudden death. He knew that while Michael's death would be a serious loss to the company he had founded, it probably would not cause much of a ripple in the financial world. Still, he couldn't help but wonder who might take over management of the Davidson Hotel Group.

It wasn't a large company, only four hotels in all, and was a family owned corporation for the most part. The only shares held by non-family members were those that had been acquired by a few trusted corporate employees through stock options granted by the CEO himself. Of those, Buzz Craddock, the general manager at the Davidson Chicagoan, held the largest number, an amount equal to just under five percent of the total shares outstanding. Bob Mattheson, general manager at the Davidson New York, and Van Carducci at the Davidson San Francisco, each held another two and a half percent. All three of these men had been with the Davidson Group for many years, and all three were practically members of the family.

The fourth hotel in the company, the Davidson San Diego, had seen turnovers in management several times over the years and was the only one not represented by partial ownership. It was also the only one to be appreciably different from the others. Chicago, New York and San Francisco catered to corporate and city travelers, but the San Diego property was a full service resort, offering golf and tennis, and beachfront rooms.

Stan stared at the telex for several minutes, then carried it to the desk of a researcher where he dropped it with a request for follow-up on successor management. The phone on his desk was ringing as he re-entered his office. He was surprised to hear Sunao Tokumura's voice on the other end. It was the second time in recent weeks, again with the suggestion that they meet.

"It has occurred to me that the time might be right for Japanese investors to move into U.S. government bonds," Tokumura said later. "Recent years have seen an increasing amount of direct investment by Japanese businesses in American properties. The value of these acquisitions has jumped from three and a half billion dollars to around fifteen billion dollars, resulting in significant cash flow from high rents. American economists are concerned that this money will be diverted out of the country."

"Hmmm, yes," Stan responded, wondering where this might be leading and why the man responsible for the well-being of Japan's trade and industry was consulting a journalist.

The vice minister went on, "The U.S. industrial sector has slowed down long term investment abroad and the gap between U.S. wealth overseas and foreign ownership at home has swung from a six billion dollar surplus to a forty-one billion dollar deficit in only four years. Their government is competing with the industrial sector for a share of the available capital and savings, making high interest rates on government bonds and inevitability."

Stan responded cautiously. "Yes, with rates at twelve percent and still going up, the return looks favorable," he said.

"Perhaps it would be advantageous to Japanese investors if they were made aware of the opportunities arising in the U.S. bond market."

He's asking for cooperation from the paper, Stan thought. That isn't uncommon, but he could have had someone in his office phone. Why the personal touch?

"I see that you are wondering why I have not used the usual channels of communication," Tokumura commented. "It occurs to me that your experience in America allows you an insight that warrants respect." He watched Stan's face for a reaction and was not disappointed.

Stan's harsh laugh betrayed him. "My experience in that country was instrumental in my career choice. It seems that an American businessman noticed the cultural differences between his daughter and me that I had chosen to ignore." Instantly chagrined at his undisciplined response, he said quickly, "Forgive me. The man was on my mind. He died quite recently, leaving his company without his leadership."

So that's it, Sunao Tokumura thought. "Is your interest merely a financial one or is it more personal?"

"A little of each, I guess. The Davidson Hotel Group is not a major player in the international market place, but its four hotels are upscale and Michael Davidson was a hands-on executive. Just curiosity on my part."

The vice minister made a mental note to find out more about the Davidson hotels. The storage of information was often as expedient as the warehousing of a valuable commodity.

The following day, a survey appeared in the Nihon Keizai Shimbun, indicating the rising interest rates on U.S. government bonds over the past year on a graph. The day after that, officials from the Ministry of Finance met with high level representatives of Japan's six largest banks. By the end of the week, Japanese bids at the U.S. Treasury auction had increased significantly.


About fifty miles northeast of Tokyo, in the Tsukuba district, Japan's 'science city,' Sumio Masabe was bent over a microscope. Only in his spare time was he allowed to conduct the research that had begun accidentally and now filled him with excitement. In breaking down the DNA sequence of a protein called amylin in connection with a study of diabetes, his computer database had suggested another protein molecule known as amyloid. There did not appear to be any similarities in the two codes, but he had noticed that the amyloid code was very close to that used by other genes that acted as ion channels.

What made this fascinating was the apparent connection of amyloid to Alzheimer's disease. Unlike cerebrovascular dementia which occurs when nutrients and oxygen fail to reach brain tissues, Alzheimer's dementia apparently resulted due to atrophy of nerve cells and tissues in the cerebral cortex. The precise cause of this degeneration was unknown. If he could discover the secret of balancing neurotransmitters and activating the energy metabolism in the brain, it would be a major breakthrough.

When he was engrossed in his work, he was able to forget his mounting debt to the sarakin, a salary loan company. Unable to establish credit, he had assumed what he thought would be a short term loan, but the outrageous interest rates were causing him to sink deeper and deeper into debt. He had heard the horror stories of gangsters demanding to be paid and destroying the reputation of the borrower. They had already alluded to the possibility that his pretty wife might earn the money through prostitution, a thought that drove him wild with fear. In the back of his mind, he held onto the thought that his research might save him through the prestige and subsequent increase in salary that would come with an outstanding discovery.

He was so close. He studied the synthetic cell membrane and watched as the calcium channel allowed ions to penetrate. It wouldn't be long before he solved the mysteries and discovered the secrets that would eliminate the deterioration that caused Alzheimer's. He was already fairly certain that he could slow it down.

Checking his watch, Masabe was astonished to see that it was nearly midnight. He put away his research reluctantly and left to go home to his wife.

As soon as he opened the door, he sensed something was wrong. Then he saw her. She was seated on a straight chair in the center of the room, her arms tied behind her, her legs spread wide with her ankles tied to the back legs of the chair. Her face was painted a ghostly white with vivid red lips and she was naked.

Unable to move at first, he stared in horror, then turned and staggered back outside to retch. When he could stand again, he went in and removed the bindings and the gag in her mouth without actually looking into her eyes. She fell forward in a dead faint and he carried her to the bedroom.

The message was abundantly clear.

Across an ocean and half a continent, Buzz Craddock tapped his fingers impatiently on his desk. He had left several messages for

Victoria Davidson, but she had yet to return his calls. He had just learned that Michael Davidson had provided options in his will for Buzz and the other two managers who held shares in the company to secure an amount equal to their current ownership. This meant that Buzz would control ten percent and Van and Bob would each hold five percent, for a total of twenty percent.

Victoria still ran the show, however, and Buzz had no idea what she might have in mind regarding the future of the hotels. If she intended to sell out, it could be a whole new ballgame. Maggie might be the key, he thought. Maybe he should be calling her instead.

Maggie was at her wits end. Her mother seemed to believe that Michael Davidson would walk through the door at any moment, alive and healthy. Busying herself with an arrangement of flowers for the dining room table or directing the twice-a-week maid to clean out a cabinet, Victoria refused to acknowledge Maggie's questions regarding anything connected with Michael's death, saying only, "Do as you think best, dear."

Maggie contemplated the telephone answering machine and wondered if she should get tough and insist that her mother return Buzz Craddock's calls or just call him herself. He surely would know that Victoria was not up to any discussion of the hotels, she decided, and dialed the number.

"Buzz? Maggie Stuart. Mother isn't feeling well, as you might imagine, so I thought I'd better check in with you."

"Thanks, Maggie. I was just wondering if I shouldn't be calling you instead of Victoria. Is there anything any of us here can do to make it easier for you?"

"I don't think so, Buzz, but thanks for asking. Just knowing that you're there to run things is comforting."

"The hotels practically run themselves, Maggie. But we do need to get together to talk about the future. Is it too soon for Victoria? Or could you and I chat informally? I hate to bring it up, but Michael left stock option provisions that I'd like to act upon and that requires some paperwork."

"Of course, Buzz. Could you ask Dan Levinson to give me a call?" It occurred to Maggie as she was speaking with Buzz that the man in charge of the Davidson legal department might be the one to consult regarding her mother's inability to cope.

A few hours later, Dan Levinson had come and gone, and Victoria had agreed that she hadn't the slightest interest in taking charge of business decisions. She had signed a power of attorney authorizing Maggie to act on her behalf. A meeting had been scheduled for the following morning with the lawyer, the corporate treasurer and Buzz Craddock.

Maggie reflected on the radical changes that had taken place in her life in a matter of a few weeks. Charles had moved out of their house and then, in a surprise move, had left Chicago to accept a position as an economic advisor in the San Francisco office of the Federal Reserve Bank. As Chairman of the Board in Washington, Bill Stuart had assisted his son in this career move, but was still reeling at the suddenness of it. No amount of long distance phoning had brought forth any explanation beyond a firm, "because it's what I want to do, Dad."

# CHAPTER SIX

A few hundred miles east of Chicago, Diane Manchester was completely engrossed in her work as a systems analyst in research and development at IBM. Diane loved her job. The project she was working on was one that could mean a lot to the company in terms of profitability in increased sales and increased stock value.

Diane was not a beautiful woman, but she was pretty. Her short brown hair was always neat and her very dark brown eyes flashed with enthusiasm when she was happy. She was exceptionally intelligent, a quality that had been a bit of a cross to bear as she was growing up because she was smarter than anyone else her age, and most adults as well. Promoted twice to higher grade levels, she had always been the smallest one in her class and that, combined with her quick mind, got her into a lot of trouble, including more than a few physical confrontations. In her adolescent years, she had assumed that all human beings were endowed with comparable mental abilities and that assumption had led to repeated disappointment in the people around her.

She had finished college in three years, graduating with honors and a double major in math and computer sciences at the age of twenty. Fascinated by the development of computers since her teen years when she read about them being used in an Apollo space mission, she had spent much of her free time reading anything she could get her hands on about improvements and new technology in the industry. By the time she left the college campus, she had amassed far more knowledge than her degree indicated.

Diane's brilliant mind was no help at all, however, when it came to relationships with men. To make matters worse, she had grown up accepting the premise that men were naturally superior to women, though she was not exactly sure what it was that made them that way. She had a vague idea that it must have something to do with a generic ability allotted to them at birth that included a divine right to rule. After all, they were bigger. The notion caused her a certain amount of confusion when a concept she understood with ease was seemingly obscure to older, taller and bigger males.

Now thirty-five years old and an assistant vice president at one of the world's most prestigious corporations, Diane was more or less content with her life. She had plenty of money because she didn't waste it on clothes and didn't want the responsibilities that came with the ownership of property. She slept well and awoke eager to get to the office.

She was close to concluding the work on an important design to revamp the Multiple Virtual Storage (MVS) operating system. The modifications would make it possible to store and retrieve information four times faster and more efficiently, thereby reducing the processing time for main frame customers. The anticipated savings in employee time would create a popular product that generated credibility as well as profit.

Diane was impatient. Going through proper channels to have her group's projects thoroughly tested and released for general use often took far more time than she considered necessary. She had worked in quality assurance and had been instrumental in putting procedures in place for testing, so she knew how long testing should take when done by a competent, motivated employee. It was for this reason that she created a user ID with a security level that allowed her to do anything she wanted to do on the system.

This had been fairly easy to accomplish in a visit to the system's security office, ostensibly to share a cup of coffee with the man in charge, her buddy. Knowing, or at least pretty sure that he would have no reason to distrust her, she created her new secret ID by using his ID, carelessly left signed onto the system as he went to refill his coffee cup. She didn't often use her 'back door' option, but it came in handy now and then when she encountered a glitch that was a simple error she could fix and move out herself.

At the other end of the corridor from the room in which Diane was working, Harry Cesnick, Executive Vice President of Research and Development, was trying to steady his hands. His hangover was worse than usual and had held on into the afternoon. He pulled open the center drawer of his desk and reached far back to grasp the bottle of valium he had hidden there. Just half of one would make him feel better, he reasoned, and he needed to present himself as the executive that he was at a meeting coming up in fifteen minutes with the board of directors.

It was Harry's intention to tell them that he planned to fire Diane Manchester the next day. She was doing a fine job—too fine. She was making him look bad. He knew that she was close to completing the new project and if he got rid of her now, he could take all the credit for it.

Harry had problems and he couldn't afford to lose his job. His wife spent money faster than he ever imagined it could be spent; his daughter was enrolled in one of the most expensive private schools in the country and he'd had to pay an outrageous amount in damages to keep his teenage son from going to jail following a joy ride in a car stolen from the country club parking lot.

Nobody could blame him for drinking. He needed it. He dropped the cap from the bottle of pills and bent to retrieve it, bumping his head on the desk as he straightened. Frustrated and angry, he popped a whole pill in his mouth and swallowed it quickly. He leaned back in his chair and forced himself to relax until he felt calmer, then left the office.

Maggie was fuming and getting more aggravated by the minute as her taxi crept through Chicago traffic. Impulsively, she pulled a bill from her purse, handed it to the driver and told him to keep the change—she'd walk the rest of the way. She hardly noticed his grin as he thanked her for the handsome tip.

"Those arrogant bastards!" she exploded, slamming the door as she entered her mother's apartment.

"Maggie, dear, such language," said Victoria. "What would your father say?"

"He'd agree with me, or at least I hope he would," Maggie told her. "But since he isn't here, I guess it doesn't matter very much."

Victoria looked over her shoulder a little nervously, as though she expected Michael Davidson to be standing behind her. "Darling, please don't talk that way. Your father would be very upset."

"Mother, you have to start accepting the fact that Daddy is dead. He isn't coming back and he can't hear what I'm saying."

Tears threatened to slide from Victoria's eyes as she turned to leave the room. Maggie knew she'd been harsh and should probably apologize, but it was beginning to drive her crazy. Victoria couldn't seem to accept that Michael was really dead. She spoke of him as though he might be in the next room, or at the office, or out of town. On the phone, she said he had 'left us,' or that he was 'gone,' but never 'dead.'

The meeting with Buzz Craddock, Dan Levinson and Nelson Croft, the company treasurer, was the source of Maggie's irritation. Buzz had been terribly kind, ordering coffee for her and even bringing her a glass of water himself. Dan Levinson had been businesslike and Nelson Croft had avoided looking at her. All three of them talked around her as though she weren't there. She had nodded her head when it seemed they expected her to agree with what they were saying until she realized that not only did they not respect her opinion, they didn't expect her to have one.

They had discussed the future leadership of the Davidson Hotel Group as though she were not in the room. Apparently, it had not occurred to any of them that Michael Davidson's daughter might want to participate in the management of the company. She hadn't really thought about it herself. But why not? She was smart, she'd been around the Chicagoan nearly all her life, and no one cared more than she did about the company.

"Mother," she called out. "We need to talk about the hotels."

Victoria came back into the room. "What about them, dear?"

"I met with Buzz, Dan and Nelson today and there seems to be a sort of tacit agreement that Buzz would be the one to take over. I'm not sure that's a good idea and it occurred to me that I might spend some time in the office myself. Any thoughts on the matter?"

Victoria looked at her daughter in amazement. "Maggie!" she exclaimed. "You don't know anything about running a business! What possible objection could you have to Buzz? He's been like a big brother to you for years."

"Yes, he has. And he treats me like a little sister. I'm sure he'd be as surprised as you are. But they brought up a number of things this morning that I'd like to know more about before they proceed with any major plans."

"What kind of things?"

"Things like closing one floor at a time in New York for renovations that sound like they're going to be very costly. And taking out the golf course in San Diego to build a high-rise with a parking garage. I think we should review the estimates ourselves before any contracts are signed. After all, it's our money they're spending and while I trust Buzz, that is, I don't think he'd deliberately do anything he didn't believe was in the best interests of the company, I think Dad would want us to be cautious."

Victoria frowned. "These must have been plans that your father approved or they wouldn't be discussing them," she said.

"From the way that they were talking, I think Dad had authorized exploration of the ideas, but that nothing had been settled. It's my impression that Buzz is moving too quickly. You wouldn't have any objection if I spend some time looking into things, would you?"

The next morning, Maggie was in her father's office before anyone else arrived. She was going through his desk when Buzz Craddock came through the door.

"Decided to clean out the desk, Maggie? We didn't want to disturb anything until you or Victoria had had a chance to pick up anything personal that you wanted to take home."

"Actually, Buzz, I thought I'd like to know more about the business. You don't mind if I use Dad's office, do you?" Maggie smiled brightly.

Buzz' eyebrows went up reflexively, though he was quick to say, "Of course not, Maggie. Is there anything in particular you wanted to know about?"

"Now that you mention it, I was wondering about the San Diego high-rise plans that you talked about yesterday. Could I see the files on that?"

"Is there something you don't understand about it? We've been considering the project for quite some time now," Buzz said, speculating to himself on Maggie's motives.

"I'm sure there's a great deal I don't understand about it, Buzz. It seems like such a massive undertaking that I thought it might be wise to know more about it, that's all."

"I'll have the files brought in right away. Let me know if there's anything else I can do to help you out." Buzz left the office deep in thought. Maggie had always been Michael's little girl to him, but today she had begun to take on a new image. She wanted files instead of ice cream and she had spoken with an apparent confidence that he had failed to notice before. He had assumed from her silence at the previous day's meeting that she and her mother were prepared to let him run the company. Just how deeply did she intend to get involved?

Maggie took a break a couple of hours later and went down to the coffee shop where she asked the startled hostess to show her around a little before she ordered anything. Following a quick tour of the short order kitchen, she took her coffee and went through the hallway that led from the rear of the kitchen to the reservations office behind the front desk. Introducing herself to the personnel there, she asked a few questions about their jobs and then went out through the lobby and back up to her father's office.

Closing the door behind her, she stood in the middle of the room for a minute, then walked around the perimeter checking the titles of the books on the bookshelves, touching the heavy draperies that hung on the windows, noting the drabness of the furniture. She had seen it all many times, but today she looked at it from a different perspective. If it was to be her office, she'd have to make some changes.

# CHAPTER SEVEN

In a conference room within the rabbit warren of corridors at the Japanese Ministry of Finance, the discussion was heating up. Vice Minister Nobuya Saito sat rigidly, his eyes downcast, as Sunao Tokumura rotated the pencil he held round and round between his fingers. Tokumura had agreed to the meeting at the rival ministry office in a calculated move to appease Saito. He hoped to secure endorsement of the economic moves he had planned.

Saito raised his head. "By encouraging investment in U.S. Treasury bonds, we are creating a climate whereby capital is leaving the country," he said, his voice brittle.

"Much of the invested funding will come from the high rents collected on property already owned by Japanese interests," Tokumura pointed out. He had explained his position regarding the growing trade imbalance. It included a call for the appreciation of other currencies against the dollar. In exchange for the devaluated dollar, his proposal offered the promise of import growth, an appeasement to the aging American president who was committed to increasing exports to Japan.

"If the Japanese yen is worth more, he argued, "Japan can afford to buy more from the U.S. At the same time, the yield on U.S. treasuries is significantly higher than that on Japanese bonds, so investors will still see better returns on their investments even if the dollar falls by fifty percent. The timing is crucial. The U.S., United Kingdom, France,

Germany and Japan will be discussing the link between international trade and monetary policies at the upcoming G-5 meeting."

"What makes you think the Americans will agree to devaluate?" Saito asked.

"I am convinced that we may have allies in high places within the U.S. government who will support this strategy," Tokumura began. Deploring the American bureaucracy, he reminded his colleague that the U.S. had not just one approach, but dozens when it came to foreign policy.

"They must obtain agreement from the Departments of Commerce and Treasury, and probably the State Department, not to mention the U.S. Trade representative, the Office of Management and Budget, the Council of Economic Advisors, the Import-Export Bank, and committees and subcommittees in both the senate and congress! The politicians walk a fine line between satisfying their special interest groups and their big contributors. They consume too much and save too little. They are committed to moving money around rather than manufacturing products!" Saito's agitation was growing.

Tokumura nodded, hiding his own growing impatience.

Saito went on, "What about banks holding dollars in their reserve funds? And American branches of Japanese banks?"

"In cooperation, the Finance Ministry will suggest that bank customers such as insurance companies will be able to acquire American real estate at lower prices when the value of the yen is increased, and further, we will jointly recommend that American branches expand their U.S. operations by directing credit toward U.S. owned commercial and industrial firms, thereby eliminating the need to convert dollars into yen at a loss."

Saito was still not convinced. Any mistakes on his part could cause the Minister of Finance, Hideki Watanabe, to lose credibility and subsequently, his bid for the post of Prime Minister. And if that happened, Nobuya Saito would lose his coveted position as Vice Minister of Finance as well. He must be *very* careful.

"What about Foreign Affairs? Have you consulted with them?" he asked, thinking to deflect responsibility.

Well aware of the perpetual joust for supremacy, Tokumura said, "The Finance Ministry is most knowledgeable in international monetary principles, so it seemed wiser to consult with you first. When we have agreed, we will solicit the approval of Foreign Affairs."

Saito sighed, then removed his glasses to clean them with a handkerchief he pulled from inside his coat. "Sometimes I wish we didn't have to deal with the West. We should be considering imports from other Asian countries before we think about conciliatory moves toward western nations."

"Asia for Asians," Tokumura remarked. "You are a patriot, my friend, as am I. We must cooperate with each other in the interests of our country. After all, we Japanese are unique and we must be careful to maintain the purity of Japanese nationals."

In San Francisco, Charles Stuart crossed Market Street and entered the brown granite building that housed the Federal Reserve Bank. He strode through the lobby to the bank of elevators and pushed the button that would take him to his fifth floor office.

Charles was a happy man. So happy, in fact, that he felt guilty. His Midwestern, Christian background had conditioned him to believe in a pattern for life, with pieces that fit together properly. If the pieces were sewn incorrectly, the end result was unacceptable. The dreary pigmentation of his silk blanket had turned into a riotous patchwork quilt that made him glad to be alive.

He had moved into a stately old apartment building on Russian Hill that had a stupendous view, if you leaned forward and squinted a little, of the Golden Gate Bridge. It was a comfortable apartment, one bedroom, a small study, and a fireplace in the living room. But the best thing about it was that Ken Williamson lived just across the hall.

The two men spent most of their evenings together and found that they enjoyed being together even in silence as they watched television or read. They shared passages of magazine articles and tossed good natured barbs at each other over college football games on Saturday afternoons. Neither of them was entirely comfortable with their physical relationship as yet, and they had not spoken of it directly. Certainly, they had not admitted it publicly, being careful to maintain the image of eligible bachelors about town.

Charles was also very happy with his new job. He had always been good at research and found that predicting economic trends gave him a great deal of satisfaction. He had been assigned to a study of international currency that would be the basis for U.S. policy at the upcoming G-5 meeting in New York. There had been pressure recently to appreciate other currencies against the strong dollar, calling for growth oriented adjustment combined with International Monetary Fund reform programs.

Shortly after five o'clock that afternoon, Charles met Ken at the English pub in Maiden Lane that offered hearty hors d'oeurves to the office crowd in San Francisco's financial district.

"You aren't going to believe this," Ken said as they took seats at the bar. "Remember when I told you that there might be a cabinet post in store for my dad? Well, it came through and he's headed for Washington! It seems the Secretary of Commerce is suffering from lymphatic cancer and wants to leave as soon as possible. Dad's as eager as a pup to accept it."

"Commerce, huh? That means he'll have some heavy input in the study I'm working on," Charles said.

"Yeah, I guess so," Ken replied. "He's been in commercial law for so many years that he's familiar with damn near every trick invented and probably a few that haven't surfaced yet. I imagine if they haven't met before, he and your dad will be working together on the G-5 summit agenda."

"Has he said anything to you about what the administration has in mind?"

"Nah, it's too soon. He won't be confirmed for at least a week or more, though it seems to be a foregone conclusion. But you know The President keeps pushing for open-door trade policies and talks a lot about a substantial reduction of the deficit. The big deal is getting American products into Japan, so appeasing the Japanese in some way will probably figure into the scheme of things."

"Their P.M. mouths a lot of promises to deregulate their financial markets and encourage import growth, but you know how evasive they can be. Each one of them says oh, yes, he's in favor of importing more American products, but he must secure agreement from some other ministry before he can commit to anything specific."

"Hmmmm. The never-ending story. When's the conference again?"

"In September." Charles leaned back in his chair, accidentally bumping the man seated next to him. He turned to apologize and was startled to see a bespectacled Japanese man. Glancing at Ken, he rolled his eyes in concern that the man may have overheard his comment and taken it as an insult.

But if the man had been listening, he gave no indication of it. He smiled and said, "No problem! You guys work in the financial district?"

Both men nodded and Ken asked, more to be polite than in genuine interest, "You?"

"Yeah, the S.F. branch of Yamasu Securities. Mergers and acquisitions, but mostly I research and leave the merging and acquiring to somebody else. Bill Morita's the name." He introduced himself, holding out his hand to Charles.

Morita joined in the conversation as naturally as if he'd been invited to do so. His genial attitude was disarming as he spoke knowledgeably about securities and, after inquiring about the businesses that Charles and Ken were in, asked their opinions on economic trends. When they stood to leave, he asked, "You come here often? Maybe we'll run into each other again sometime."

An hour later, he was on the phone in the efficiency kitchen of his small apartment. He tucked the receiver between his ear and shoulder and poured three fingers of scotch into a glass as he waited for his connection.

"I met the two guys. I followed them after work and arranged to bump into them. What's next? You want 'em to have an accident or something?"

The man on the other end of the line in Tokyo concealed his irritation at Morita's attitude and instructed him to continue friendly surveillance, reporting back in another week.

"Okay. It's your money." Morita hung up and added more scotch to his glass. American born of Japanese descent, he had been fascinated by secret societies and ninja tactics since childhood. But for the diligence of his mother and the fact that he had been a sickly child, not to mention near-sighted, he would have been an ordinary thug.

As it was, he possessed a moderate education that had allowed him to get a job that occupied the time not devoted to daydreams of glory. The friends he did have had heard him speak time and again of the feats he accomplished in his fantasies, and though he was considered something of a loose cannon, his extra-curricular employer counted on the allure of clandestine operations to keep him in line. They needed someone who could associate with Charles Stuart and Ken Williamson without attracting attention.

# CHAPTER EIGHT

The sun was blazing in the California San Joaquin valley. George Hagura wiped the sweat from his brow and gazed at the foothills in the distance. His work gave him a sense of accomplishment and he was proud to do it.

He didn't often think about the past, mostly because he was a busy man, but when he did remember, his eyes blazed with the fury and determination that had filled his entire being for many years. His parents had come to this valley from Yokohama as newlyweds in 1938. They worked hard, saved their money, and two years later made the down payment on a small farm of their own. George's sister was born there in the spring of 1941.

Early in 1942, the family was forced to move to the detention camp where George was born. The barracks where they lived in one small room was often very cold at night and George's sister was frail. She didn't survive the first year. His parents were determined to make it through the war and take their son back to the home they had made for him, but when they were finally allowed to leave the camp, they discovered that their property had been repossessed because the loan payments had not been made.

George's mother died of a broken heart and his father managed to make it back to Japan with his young son just weeks before his spirit broke and he, too, passed away. Little George was sent to live with cousins who ran a slaughterhouse on the outskirts of Yokohama. He was too young to know that those who did such work were considered unclean and known as burakumin—outcasts. It was years before he discovered that he would be forever tainted by his background if he stayed in Japan.

Since he was an American citizen by birth, he returned to the United States when he was nineteen years old, vowing to be someone of importance. He found work on the biggest cattle ranch in the valley and within a few years, he was spokesman for the rest of the workers in labor disputes. By the time he was thirty-five, he was a respected leader in the United Farm Workers Union of California, his name recognized throughout the industry. At forty-three, he assumed the position of vice president of that organization.

But however respected he might be, happiness had eluded him. Still burakumin in Japan and a Japanese laborer who got lucky in California, he would never be accepted by the people who mattered in either society.

The heat was stifling and at times like this George wished he had chosen to be a fisherman. It would be the cool, salt water of ocean spray instead of his own salty sweat that he'd be wiping from his face as he inspected the new housing provided by a coalition of ranchers and growers near Fresno. The buildings were far from luxurious, but they were clean and offered a healthier environment for the children whose parents worked the fields.

His inspection completed, George went back to the battered white pickup truck he'd been driving for many years. He was surprised to see a shiny white Lincoln parked beside it and noted ruefully that the pickup looked even shabbier by comparison.

A well-dressed Japanese man opened the door on the driver's side of the Lincoln, got out and held out his hand as George approached. Introducing himself as a business acquaintance of the Hagura family in Japan, he suggested that they have lunch at a nearby restaurant. The thought of relief from the heat in an air-conditioned building was appealing and George accepted the invitation gratefully.

Sunao Tokumura entered the building in the Marunouchi business district that housed Yoshida's executive offices and crossed the marble floor of the sumptuous lobby to the elevator. He stepped in and immediately felt as though he'd been wrapped in a velvet cocoon. The motion was nearly undetectable as his cocoon rose soundlessly to the top floor.

Yoshida greeted him warmly, urging him to make himself comfortable. A kimono-clad a woman of indeterminate age appeared through an interior door carrying a tray laden with refreshments. Glancing in Tokumura's direction, Yoshida nodded slightly, directing the woman to pour tea for each of them, then dismissed her with another small nod of his grizzled head.

Tokumura began by filling Yoshida in on the conference with Saito, adding that it was his intention to double Japanese investment in U.S. government bonds before the Americans realized that Japan was financing a sizeable chunk of the national debt, then pull the rug out from under them as the nation fell into chaos. Further, he explained, advising American branches of Japanese banks to direct credit to American owned industries would put them in a position to control much in the way of commercial enterprise.

"Japanese banks will be encouraged to create capital by over-loaning to their clients who buy U.S. real estate," he went on. "Tax breaks for these businesses, such as insurance companies, will be instituted and investors will not only command high rents on their commercial properties in high profile American cities, they will benefit through government support at home. Japan will control much of the American private sector as well as the government." He smiled at the prospects ahead, then mused, "Now if we could find a way to manipulate the New York Stock Exchange . . ."

"Perhaps 'sabotage' might be a more appropriate word," Yoshida suggested softly.

Tokumura looked up, startled, and Yoshida laughed.

"You are an honorable man, my friend. I, on the other hand have been on both sides of the fence and find that it is not difficult to adjust to a lack of scruples when the objective is an honorable one."

"Of course," Tokumura said matter of factly.

Yoshida continued, "I believe you are aware that my resources are very nearly unlimited when it comes to achieving my goals. I have learned that Stan Mitsunari's relationship with the American girl was a serious one, and that her father, who recently died, left a provision in his will for three of his trusted employees to obtain stock equal to the amounts they already own, should they so desire.

"It has occurred to me that a well hidden offer to the man who owns the largest percentage would make him a rather wealthy man should he accept and be able to fulfill the terms of the offer. Significant ownership of stock in the company that was Michael Davidson's life work might be an appealing reward for his services should Mitsunari-san choose to be of assistance in the execution of our plan—a small satisfaction for any previous insult to his heritage."

He stopped speaking and reached into a pocket to extract several crumpled notes. Smoothing the scraps of paper on his desk, he squinted at them through his glasses.

"Further, my contacts have arranged for surveillance of Charles Stuart, the husband of Mitsunari-san's university alliance, and his new lover, Ken Williamson. Their relationship came to light during an investigation into Mitsunari-san's connection to the Americans. Their fathers, interestingly enough, are very prominent men. Charles Stuart's father is Chairman of the Board of the Federal Reserve Bank and Ken Williamson's father is the newly appointed Secretary of Commerce. It is my belief that the sons are not anxious for their relationship to become known to their very public fathers. Charles Stuart's position in economic research with the Fed may also provide us with some, shall we say, leverage, should we need it."

Sunao Tokumura squelched a slight revulsion at the thought of blackmail, which was what it was even if it was called 'leverage,' but as Yoshida had said, the honorable objective made it easier to justify whatever might be required.

Yoshida shifted slightly in his chair and went on, "My associates in the states have also located an American born Japanese labor leader who is desperately looking for respect. Apparently, he was born in a detention camp in California during the war. His mother and older sister did not survive and his father brought him back to Japan after the war. The family here is burakumin. The boy returned to the states when he grew up and realized his status here was hopeless. I can see by the look in your eyes that you are wondering why this man is of interest to us." He grinned maliciously.

"Burakumin?" Tokumura asked. "Why would an outcast be useful to our cause?"

"For just that reason. He is an outcast in Japan and even though he is a leader of men in California, he will never be accepted by the owners of the land on which the men he leads find work. Let me explain."

Yoshida paused to pour more tea into their cups. There was a gleam in his eye that suggested to his friend that he had something up his sleeve that might be even more treacherous than the blackmail he had already proposed. His cunning was admirable, however.

"Did you ever see any of the survivors of Hiroshima?" Yoshida asked rhetorically. "They were pitiful, hardly human. Parts of their bodies were hardly recognizable. And those who could still function had to make a choice between eating food that had been contaminated by radiation or starving to death. It is my desire to let the Americans find out how it feels to be without sustenance. No, no, I don't propose to bomb them. What I do suggest is that a serious labor problem might deprive them of commodities that they take for granted."

Tokumura's eyes widened in amazement. He knew that the old man possessed a nefarious past, but he had not suspected the extremes to which he was prepared to go in the name of retribution.

Yoshida stared back. "No one knows of our alliance, Sunao-san, and no one need know unless one of us speaks of it. We have agreed that we have a common goal, and that together we will restore the honor of our nation by effecting the collapse of our enemy. To do that, we may have to resort to tactics you find distasteful. It is not enough to ruin them economically. To achieve a full measure of justice, we must destroy them in the same manner that they destroyed our cities when they dropped those bombs—physically as well as monetarily, and that requires not only your brilliant negotiations, but my resources among the yakuza, the underworld that you know is there, but that you rarely have to acknowledge." Yoshida spoke softly, his eyes steely, demanding that their union be absolute and that the commitment be unqualified.

Tokumura returned his gaze, nodding in agreement.

"Well, then," Yoshida said amiably, breaking the tension, "we must find a way to sabotage the stock market, banking and even computerized records. It can be done, I'm sure. We will find someone with the appropriate motive and talent."

That evening as he sat in contemplation in the teahouse that offered quiet refuge, Sunao realized that the roads had been drawn on the map of destruction. As in Musashi's Book of Five Rings, the warrior's path was the twofold Way of Pen and Sword, and he must have a taste for both. He must assure that his mental attitude was in tune with his dedication to this noble cause and undistracted by misplaced scruples.

A pilgrimage, he thought. Meditation on The Way in the cave that had provided inspiration to Musashi himself.

# CHAPTER NINE

Sunao sat alone in his room at the ryokan, a traditional inn near the Kumamoto Castle, facing an open shoji screen that led to a lush garden beyond. Leafy shadows played on the white surface of the screen as a tiny stream gurgled in accompaniment to the twitter of fluttering birds. Azaleas framed the bathing pool that was fed by a gentle waterfall. He lifted the cover from a lacquer bowl on the low table in front of him and savored the aroma of the bamboo shoots that lay in clear broth.

His spiritual journey had begun upon his arrival at the inn only hours before. He had been shown to his room by the kimono clad young woman who would be his attendant during his stay. Changing into the cotton kimono in the room for his personal use, he had slipped across the shiny black stones that surrounded the bathing pool and lowered himself into its soothing warmth. In such tranquil surroundings, it was not difficult to begin emptying his mind of the anxieties of daily life.

As he prepared to eat, he admired the presentation of the food. Each bite that he put in his mouth offered a unique sensation—a different texture, or flavor, or temperature. He focused solely on the meal, his attention only on the now. Between the courses brought by his attendant, he closed his eyes to concentrate on breathing in and out. When his mind wandered, he acknowledged the thought, then dismissed it as his attention returned to the breath that was the source of life.

The next morning he rose early, bathing again in the pool, and left the ryokan to continue on his journey. His first stop was at Kumamoto Castle where Musashi lived for several years as the guest of Lord Hosokawa before his final retirement to the cave called Reigendo.

He stood gazing up at the stone foundations of the castle. The peaked roofs that sheltered the living quarters above inspired a joyful reverence as he visualized his warrior hero teaching and painting behind those walls.

He began to circle the castle in walking meditation, raising each foot slowly, feeling the change in pressure as his heel left the ground and his weight shifted from the ball of one foot to the heel of the other. Every tenth step, he paused, his eyes closed, to listen to the sounds of the castle . . . the rustle of leaves, the mysterious sound of empty air.

The sun was high in the sky as he reached a walled rock garden. Composed entirely of stones and white sand, the patterns that directed the viewer's eyes from one design to another were carefully raked each morning. Far from the neon confusion of Tokyo, it was not hard to imagine the ghosts of another era—aristocrats and warriors, emperors and shoguns.

The shadows of the trees were growing longer as he made his way up Mt. Iwato toward the cave. Coming to a pile of stones that were the only marker of a grave, he read the inscription on the wooden post beside it: 'The grave of the teacher, Miyamoto Musashi.'

Sunao's meditation had failed to prepare him for the overwhelming sense of humility that made him fall to his knees. Chipped and weather-beaten, the stones seemed far too humble to mark the final resting place of this magnificent swordsman. Unable to stop himself, he wept.

Recovering, he contemplated the life of the man who had killed his first opponent at the age of thirteen. The man who survived a three day battle in which seventy thousand people died. The man who took part in the massacre of Christians prior to the closing of Japanese ports to foreigners for more than two hundred years.

And then he asked Buddha for the strength and courage to carry out his mission against the Christian world that was still an enemy. And for the strength and courage to end his own life should he fail.

In Tokyo, Stan Mitsunari's eyebrows raised slightly as he read another announcement torn from the telex. A new IBM operating system technology that proposed lower costs and increased international main frame market share, lowering the threat of competition from Japan, had already pushed IBM's stock price up one and a half points, and it wasn't even available yet. Stan wondered if Sunao Tokumura was aware of this development.

Allison Jennings burst through the door into Buzz Craddock's office and began speaking at once.

"What the hell is she doing in there? I thought you said she'd be bored and go home in a few days! She's been going through files for two weeks, and now the maintenance crew is in there painting Michael's office! What's next? Fabric samples?"

Buzz stared at her, then sighed. "Your guess is as good as mine, but it's beginning to look like she's planning to stick around."

"What's she *doing*? She doesn't know diddly shit about the business, does she? Can't you keep her in line? I thought *you* were the one who was running the company!"

"I thought that myself, but it looks as though that was an assumption I shouldn't have made quite so quickly," Buzz spat out angrily.

Allison had been Michael Davidson's administrative assistant for many years. Actually, she'd been an extremely competent and valuable executive secretary, but administrative assistant sounded more important than executive secretary, and since Allison had assumed the duties of marketing director as well, her power in the company was significant, and she now had her own secretary.

She was approaching forty, but still turned heads, possibly because she was not bothered by the distractions of a husband and children. She'd had an understanding with Buzz Craddock for almost as many years as she'd been Michael's assistant. It was an agreeable arrangement given their very different preferences. Allison loved to spend a romantic evening with the lights low, listening to the lament of a tenor saxophone while Buzz found that to be better than a sedative. His idea of a great day was sitting on the bench at a Chicago Bears game, and gloating over each tenth of a cent that increased the value of his investment portfolio in the evening. There were two things that both of them were passionate about, however: good food and the Davidson Hotels.

Well known in Chicago social circles and the sports world, Buzz was considered something of a bon vivant. He didn't look much like a bon vivant, being a little short with a barrel chest and wooly hair. It was more a matter of style. Allison liked being the woman on his arm. Women envied her glamorous and independent life, and men envied Buzz.

Maggie's presence in Michael's office was beginning to create problems in their well-ordered lives. She was reviewing the cost estimates for Buzz' pet projects and causing delays that he considered unnecessary. A city boy, Buzz looked at space as a commodity and valued it according to the revenue it brought in per square foot. A high-rise hotel was obviously more profitable than a golf course and he was eager to begin construction in San Diego. Michael had been sidestepping a decision, claiming to be exploring some 'other possibilities' that he had chosen to keep to himself. Now that Michael was gone, dollar signs had begun to spin round in Buzz' head and he chafed at the further delays that Maggie was causing. If only Victoria had given him the power-of-attorney instead of Maggie, and named him Michael's successor as she should have done . . .

Maggie leaned back in her chair and stretched, flexing her arms, then shaking her wrists to loosen up her fingers. She was using the large file room with its round conference table while her father's office underwent the renovations she had decided upon.

She stared at the file she had just come across on an old public relations campaign designed by the beautiful Sarah Fremont who had vanished from a cruise ship off the coast of France many years earlier. Seeing the name brought back memories of the one time Maggie had met her. It had been in New York just months after Stan Mitsunari had gone back to Japan.

Maggie found herself thinking about Stan a lot lately. Now that her father and her husband were gone, there were no further obstacles on the path that might lead her back to him. With one glaring exception. She had not heard from him in all that time. She allowed herself the tiniest daydream, imagining running into him—where?—at a restaurant?—on the street? He'd take her hand, look into her eyes . . .

She shook her head to dispel the images and sat up straight, forcing her attention back to the files. Picking up the one that lay next to the public relations campaign file, she wondered at the label: Prospective Property Acquisitions. Prospective property? Acquisitions? Had Michael been planning to expand the company by acquiring another hotel? Her interest piqued, she opened the file, snatching up the colorful brochures that tumbled from inside.

The Kaimana Surf and Sand, she read on the first one. In Hawaii? Shuffling quickly through the others, she was astonished to see that they were all in Hawaii. Under the stack of brochures lay a series of financial reports, one on each of the properties. Three of them had red check marks in the upper right-hand corner, but the fourth carried a black exclamation point. It wouldn't be unreasonable, she thought, to reach the conclusion that the three red marks meant unprofitable, while the black exclamation point indicated profitability. It turned out to be on the one headed with the name Kaimana Surf and Sand. Turning back to the brochures, Maggie retrieved the one on the apparently successful hotel that her father must have been considering for purchase.

It was located on the edge of Kapiolani Park, just a short distance beyond Waikiki at the foot of Diamond Head. The cover showed a couple dancing in the moonlight under a banyan tree. Romantic, she thought. Not like the pictures you usually see of suntanned nymphets lying in the sunlight on a beach. She tucked the brochures and financial reports back into the file and carried it with her to Buzz Craddock's office down the hall.


Damn her! Buzz thought. He had spent the past two days in one meeting or another with Maggie as she dug deeper into her father's files, questioning each entry on the financial sheets. She had finally approved the renovations at the New York Davidson, but his pet project, the San Diego Davidson, had been put on hold indefinitely. Now she was planning a trip to Honolulu to scope out the property that had attracted Michael's attention.

"I'm going to take a look at the Kaimana Surf and Sand in Hawaii, Buzz," she'd said, cool as a cucumber. "Who do I talk to about plane tickets?"

It wasn't just that she was interfering. He simply couldn't think of her as anything but Michael's little girl. It looked as though he might have to make some sort of move.

He pulled an envelope from the inside pocket of his suit jacket and tapped it thoughtfully against the edge of the desk. He was still a little confounded by its contents—a written offer for his shares in the Davidson Group. It had been hand delivered that morning from a local brokerage firm. The astounding part was the provision for an additional hundred thousand dollars for every one percent over his own that he could deliver. The bonus alone equaled a million dollars if he could get Bob Mattheson and Van Carducci to sell. The prospect of instant wealth was infinitely more appealing than retiring on his social security and the earnings on his current portfolio.

Who would make such an offer, he wondered. The Davidson Group was solidly established and profits were acceptable though not exceptional. It couldn't be the start of a hostile takeover because the majority of the company shares were held in family trusts and twenty percent wouldn't be enough to allow an outsider the control that would normally be assumed by the kind of money he'd been offered.

Buzz was torn between his love for the hotels, his loyalty to Michael and Victoria, and the prospect of being rich enough to thumb his nose at anyone who got in his way. He picked up the phone and dialed the number of the brokerage firm.

No, he was told, they didn't know the name of the party making the offer. It had come through a bank in the Caribbean with only a bank officer as primary contact. It was definitely a bonafide offer, however. Did he plan to accept? Buzz told the voice that he hadn't yet made a decision and hung up.

# CHAPTER TEN

The vice president of the United States strode purposefully through the corridors leading to the conference room where high level advisors would determine American positions at the up-coming G-5 meeting. Head high and posture erect, the wide grin that had made him more popular than any vice president in recallable history bestowed upon staffers who happened to be passing by, he maintained the carefully cultivated image of a man in charge. The American public had been easily cajoled into voting a loveable buffoon into office in the last election and he'd had to settle for second place—for the time being.

The Secretary of the Treasury, the U.S. Trade Representative, the newly appointed Secretary of Commerce, and the Chairman of the Federal Reserve Bank were already seated at one end of the large conference table as the vice president entered the room. Their respective assistants were seated on chairs against the walls behind them. The vice president took his seat at the head of the table and suggested amiably that they begin the meeting.

The U.S. Trade Representative was quick to point out that the U.S. could approach the conference with renewed hope due to the gala opening of the Japanese automotive plant in Tennessee that had been celebrated just recently. She commented enthusiastically that it was her belief that the Japanese had finally gotten the message that America would protect the welfare of its labor force and that the plant would employ several hundred people, thereby adding that number of jobs to the economy.

Grant Williamson pointed out that those new jobs didn't sell many American made cars in Japan.

"It does indicate that they're trying to cooperate," retorted the trade representative, going on to say that the plant manager had joined the U.S. Trade Association with instructions from the home office to participate to the fullest extent. "They are providing a quality product that Americans want to buy and providing employment in a depressed community at the same time!"

"You're buying into their propaganda," Bill Stuart said quietly and without malice. "They hope to divert attention from the trade deficit by creating a false economy. The real issue is one of opening up the market for American products abroad."

The vice president nodded sagely and directed a glance at Grant Williamson who cleared his throat and said, "If the yen had increased purchasing power, the potential for sales in Japan would increase proportionately."

Bill Stuart responded by suggesting that to do so would also increase the potential for acquisition of property in America by foreign investors. He was not convinced of the benefits heralded by proponents of devaluating the dollar.

The vice president tapped his pencil gently on the table and spoke with conviction. "You all know that The President is committed to an open market economy. He believes that the dollar no longer reflects fundamental economic conditions and that an orderly appreciation of other currencies would be timely. That is the position he would like the U.S. to take at the conference." What the vice president did not mention was that it had been his own suggestion to The President in the first place. The others at the table looked down at the files in front of them and nodded in agreement. It was clear that U.S. attitudes had been pre-determined despite the growing suspicion that pressure from abroad was responsible and that this meeting was mostly just for show.

Bill Stuart caught up with Grant Williamson in the hallway outside as the meeting concluded, saying jovially, "I understand that our boys are acquainted with one another."

"So Ken tells me," Williamson responded. "Charles, isn't it? Moved to San Francisco a couple of months ago?"

"Right. I guess the tour he got from Ken made The City irresistible. His mother and I were more than a little surprised that he and his wife split up and that he was determined to make such a drastic career move, but from the sound of things, he couldn't be happier than he is in San Francisco. Speaking of moves, you made a pretty big one yourself. I haven't had a chance to say congratulations yet, so congratulations on your appointment. If my wife and I can be of any assistance, please call on us."

"Thanks. You know, The President has been a friend of mine for many years and I thought I knew him pretty well. Such a strong position on economic policy doesn't sound like it's coming from him."

"You catch on quick," Bill Stuart responded. "He's a great man, a hero in the minds of most people, but the vice president is the one who does most of his thinking when it comes to anything other than military budgets and the like."

"A career politician, I know. It was pretty common knowledge that we could win the election with The President running for the top slot, but we needed somebody with Washington savvy in the second slot if we hoped to hold onto the next election. It isn't any secret that the veep has his eye on being head man. He's the ultimate career politician. He made the decision when he was in college that he intended to be president one day. He actually researched the political climates in a number of states and deliberately chose Ohio as his entry level residence. I've heard he rejected California as too flamboyant, New York as too corruptible, and Texas as too hokey. Ohio had the air of homespun honesty along with a lot of electoral votes that would be cast for a favorite son candidate."

Bill laughed. "Yeah, he actually told me once that Americans tend to spread the wealth, so to speak, and the last president from Ohio was Warren Harding and nobody remembered him anyway. I wonder if his middle-of-the-road image is as carefully planned as the rest of his career."

"He doesn't let it show, but everybody knows he's pretty bitter about losing the presidency to the general just when he thought he had it all sewn up," Grant said. Looking pensive, he went on, "The general was ill prepared for the demands of the office. His knowledge of military tactics is staggering, but beyond that, he's a babe in the woods."

Neither man spoke of the potentially serious problem in The President's life that had surfaced only weeks earlier. It seemed his wife, the woman on whom he doted, was showing signs of mental instability. Not only was her impromptu dance on the yacht in Tokyo being talked about, but apparently she had risen in the middle of the night recently, evaded the Secret Service and been discovered frolicking amid the sprinklers on the White House lawn as the sun rose.

The President was playing a game of tag with the shadows that danced on the tabletop in front of him as moonlight stole through the partially drawn drapes. He glanced toward the bed where his beloved wife lay sleeping so innocently and a tear slid down his cheek.

The long blonde hair that she wore in an elegant French twist lay loose on the pillow, a few strands curled around her chin. Her face was peaceful now, but only hours earlier she had cried in his arms as the despair brought on by her failing memory threatened to overwhelm her. She knew that it was only a matter of time before she would no longer remember even her friends and family. She had begged him to help her die before that happened.

How could such a thing happen to someone so good, he wondered miserably, just as they had arrived at almost inconceivable heights, with love, respect and even adulation lavished upon them wherever they appeared. She had spent so much of their marriage alone as he traveled around the world, making it a safer place for free people. Now that they were together at last in the United States White House, why had God given her this evil sickness?

A short and popular war halfway around the world had made his name a household word. The gruff expressions that hid his shyness, the receding hairline and portly body, the sly sense of humor—all of these things had endeared him to the American public that loved a hero.

They had been swept along in the joyful surge until they woke up one morning as the The President and The First Lady. They had giggled all through breakfast. In the early weeks, it had been exciting as he maneuvered his way through the intricacies that guided the political world. But as time went by and he was called upon to make decisions in areas where his knowledge was sketchy, the initial thrill began to sour.

He had discovered that the bureaucrats who inhabited the labyrinth of government were of a different cut than the military men whose lives often depended upon the loyalty of a comrade. Even the vice president, so genial and cooperative during the months of campaigning, was often barely able to hide his impatience with the bumbling warrior.

The illness of his beloved was the final straw. The President was losing interest in his lofty office though in fairness to the people who had elected him, he tried his best to do the job. He longed to take his lady back to the peaceful lakes of Minnesota to live out what was left of their days together listening to the chirping of the birds at sunrise and sipping martinis on the porch as the red glow of sunset sent small creatures scurrying for shelter from the night.

His moonlight game of tag with the shadows forgotten, he watched The First Lady's chest rise and fall ever so slightly as she breathed. Did she dream, he wondered. Were they happy dreams? He hoped so. There had been no further incidents like her impromptu dance aboard the yacht and her frolic in the sprinklers a couple of weeks ago. She had been led back to their bedroom and had fallen asleep with no recollection of her escapade in the morning. His heart cracked at the thought that she had to be watched, even discreetly.

In a world where men could walk on the moon, it seemed so damnably unfair that there was no medicine that could stop the disease that crept insidiously into the brains of people who had spent lifetimes storing up knowledge and memories. The White House doctor had explained that the dementia was caused by the degeneration of nerve cells and tissue in the brain and that as yet no one seemed to know why this happened to some people and no one seemed to know how to make it stop. The President of the United States could blow up the world with the push of a button, but he was powerless to save the woman he cherished. He would do anything, anything at all, to save her.

As The President agonized in the darkness of Washington, Sumio Masabe was bent over a microscope in his beautiful new laboratory on the other side of the world. Finally, someone had been impressed with his research, though it nagged a bit at the back of his mind that he wasn't sure just who it was. He had gone to the sarakin and begged, blubbering about how close he was to discovering a cure for the dementia called Alzheimer's. He had rambled on about how he would be rewarded, even honored for his work.

They had given him a reprieve of seven days, but on the third of those seven days, a man in a dark suit and very dark sunglasses had walked into his laboratory, dismissing his immediate agitation at a visitor during working hours.

The man had been brusque, informing Sumio that he would work off his debt in the new laboratory, created just for him and stocked with equipment and supplies from a list he would make up himself. He had been so grateful that not only would he be able to continue his research and repay the loan without further harassment, but his wife had been saved from prostitution. He could not have borne that and she could not have done it. The only alternative would have been suicide.

Now his life had taken a miraculous turn. Whenever doubts arose in Sumio's mind, he found it quite easy to dismiss them. After all, his research was important to all mankind and, when revealed, would bring honor and glory to Japan. How bad could anyone be who supported him in his pursuit of such a noble cause?

# CHAPTER ELEVEN

A kiko Mitsunari had been dreaming. At least she thought it must have been a dream. She hovered between sleeping and waking, afraid to open her eyes and find that her dream had ended. She moved her shoulder a little, then her fingers, edging them toward her husband's side of the bed. His arm twitched and she withdrew her hand hastily. But wonder of wonders, instead of pulling away, he reached toward her, drawing her into the circle of his arms.

Her eyes flew open to find that it had not been a dream at all. The sliding glass door to the balcony was open, allowing a soft Hawaiian breeze to steal into the room. Akiko was sure she had never been as happy as she was at that moment. She closed her eyes again, taking only shallow breaths in order not to awaken Stan, and began to relive the previous night.

It was amazing. They had boarded their flight very early on Saturday morning and arrived in Honolulu in time for dinner on Friday night. Moonlight shimmered on the water that lapped against the sand just beyond the railing beside their table in the outdoor dining room. Stan had ordered a fruity white wine that made her giddy with joy.

It had been a fairytale week for Akiko that began when her husband asked if she'd like to accompany him to a conference scheduled to begin the following Monday in Honolulu. Would she like? Did Amaterasu, Goddess of the Sun, bring light to the world? The days that followed had seen her in a flurry of indecision as she scorned the clothes that hung in her closet, shopped for new ones, and was sure that she would bring nothing but disgrace and humiliation to her husband if she were to be seen on his arm.

She had been handed a key to the door to her wildest fantasies, but she was afraid that her hand would tremble so that she'd be unable to insert it into the lock. But here she was in this luxurious room at the foot of Diamond Head, still tingling from the ecstasy of her beloved's touch. She could almost believe that he loved her after all.

As the sun crept higher on the other side of Oahu, light began to steal further into the room like a puppy creeping toward its master. Akiko squeezed her eyes shut, recalling the lovemaking she so desperately craved and so often went without. She pushed aside the doubts that still lingered around the edges of her mind. Did Stan have a lover? Was that why he hardly ever touched her? Why now? Why was he treating her so well, so romantically? No! She would not let those thoughts ruin it!

There had been only one imperfect moment the whole evening. Stan had cupped her chin with his hand, forcing her face upward toward his. When she demurred, her eyes downcast, he had pulled away angrily.

"Why do Japanese women have to be so damned coy?" he had demanded wrathfully. "For that matter, why do *all* Japanese refuse to look you in the eye? It's so deceitful!" His years in America had taught him the American way of looking directly into the eyes of whomever he was speaking to, and he now found it irritating that even his wife avoided looking at him. He could understand it to some degree in business dealings. It kept your opponent from reading anything into your expression. But your wife? He wanted to see passion in her eyes. But then, he feared that perhaps there was none and he had said as much.

If he only knew, Akiko thought, how much I want him. But it would be thoroughly improper for a Japanese wife to let her husband see her desire so shamelessly. She could show him, however, by her response to his touch, his kisses, and she had tried to do that in the darkness. Since every inch of her skin tingled at his touch, it came naturally. But since she wanted so desperately to please him, she could not hide the tension that crept into her body whenever he came near her. Her conflicting emotions were a constant presence, try as she might to ignore them.

He began to stir slightly as she lay quietly beside him. His head moved lazily and she felt his lips against her hair. His hand moved to her breast, his fingers playing with her nipple. It responded by growing hard and she gasped audibly in her eagerness. Abandoning whatever embarrassment she might feel at making love in broad daylight, she clung to him, surrendering her soul to the man who was the center of her universe.

Dawn became morning and the breeze from outside was no longer cool. Stan got up and closed the balcony door, then turned the thermostat on the air-conditioner to a cooler temperature. He sat on the edge of the bed briefly to phone room service for breakfast before disappearing into the shower, oblivious to the fact that his wife lay trembling under the sheet as she sought to hide the pounding in her chest.

They ate buttered croissants and drank coffee at a table on the balcony, listening once again to the waves that lapped against the sand. They dressed without haste and left the room to stroll through Kapiolani Park toward Waikiki and the shops that lined Kalakaua Avenue.

Returning to the hotel late that afternoon, they sat at a corner table in the lobby cocktail lounge to share the sweet, cooling taste of a huge mai tai. Akiko peered into one of the shopping bags that held the treasures Stan had insisted upon buying. She rummaged through the tissue paper intent on finding the purple silk scarf that had caught her eye in the Royal Hawaiian gift shop, and failed to see the shock and disbelief on her husband's face as he watched a familiar figure emerge from a door on the other side of the lobby.


Maggie Stuart was engrossed in conversation with the general manager of the Kaimana Surf and Sand Hotel as he accompanied her to the elevator, and did not even glace toward the table where her old beau sat with his Japanese wife. She had fallen in love with the hotel and had already made up her mind that it would be a great addition to the Davidson Hotel Group. She was doing her best to hide that bit of information from the GM, however, and stifled the smile that was on her lips until she was safely gliding upward in the elevator to her suite on the eighth floor.

Maggie had metamorphosed over the past couple of months from wife and daughter, subservient to the men in her life, to self-assured hotel executive. A woman confident of her place in the world. She couldn't have given anyone a specific date on which this had happened, and in fact, hadn't really noticed the change. She only knew that she felt great and was enjoying every moment of every day. It showed in the way she walked, the way she spoke, and even the way she dressed. She no longer even thought about her mother's attitude toward her hair. She was too busy.

While she would have been happy to sign the papers that would make the Kaimana hers, she knew it would be only prudent to consult with her Davidson Group associates, Buzz Craddock in particular. Since Buzz was already unhappy with her decision to postpone construction at the San Diego property, Maggie had been mulling over the problem of his increasing antagonism. It was only natural, of course, that he would feel that he had been shafted when she took her father's place in the company. But she was finding it more and more difficult to work with him. His alliance with Allison Jennings added fuel to the fire.

Just what was their relationship, Maggie wondered. She was certain that they had what would be known as an 'arrangement,' but how serious it really was was the unknown element. Unlike Buzz, Allison had no stock in the company, but she had been with Michael for years, so it could be assumed that she had a serious interest in the hotels. If she left, would Buzz leave as well?

Buzz was no longer a young man. He could retire anytime he wished. It was almost a sure thing that Allison would leave with him should he decide to do that—or was it?

The other two stockholders were also unknowns. So far, neither Bob Mattheson nor Van Carducci had indicated any opposition to Maggie, but Van might consider retirement as well. He had run the San Francisco hotel for as long as Maggie could remember, and was getting on in years. Bob was the youngest member of the team, having begun his career as sales manager at the New York property, but even he was middle-aged.

Would the Davidson image suffer without the men who had been Michael's associates for so many years? That was something to think about. Would Chicagoans or New Yorkers defect if the hotels changed leadership? It shouldn't make too much difference in the rooms divisions, but the public rooms and catering business might decrease since they depended upon local socialites. San Diego wasn't a problem, since occupancy there was dependent upon the tourist industry.

After some consideration, Maggie decided that Bob and Van probably wouldn't defect, but Buzz, who had expected to head up the firm, probably would. What would he do with his stock? She'd have to work out an offer to buy back his shares. Perhaps it would be a good idea to have it ready before confronting him with her decision to buy the Kaimana Surf and Sand.


Akiko Mitsunari's dream was turning into a nightmare. Stan had suddenly stopped talking to her and even seemed to be completely unaware of her presence as he retreated into some silent place of his own. She was the mime on the street, arms outstretched, palms forward, patting the empty air in search of an opening in the invisible wall that surrounded her husband. She could see him there, but his spirit had gone to a place so far away that even the tears she tried to hide without success went unnoticed anyway. It was almost as though she had ceased to exist, no longer had substance and had become invisible. She had dried up, evaporated. If she screamed, would he hear?

She racked her brain trying to think what she might have done to cause the change in his attitude. They had enjoyed the sun on their faces, the breezes that made the Hawaiian heat bearable, and the shops where he bought her present after present, smiling at her pleasure. He didn't seem angry, just far away. He sat on the balcony, unmoving, staring out at the ocean, alone in the dark. Akiko crept into the big bed that had been such a happy place to be only that morning. Finally, she slept.

Had Stan's mind not been otherwise occupied, he might have noticed the article in the evening paper. The finance ministers from the G-5 countries had issued a public statement following their meeting in New York. The dollar was too strong. Within twenty-four hours, the dollar had fallen by more than four percent.

# CHAPTER TWELVE

The American Secretary of Labor sat at his desk staring at the glossy newsletter in front of him. The cover story rambled on about the need for unity among blue collar workers. Turning it over, he scanned the back page for the name of the publisher and found a small box at the bottom listing only the title, The Wage Earner, and a post office box in Fresno, California. There had been an unusual amount of dialogue in recent months concerning labor practices around the country, with a number of strike threats from unions representing a variety of unrelated trades and occupations.

At first, there had been no reason to believe that it was anything other than labor-management contracts up for renewal, and the usual demands made by labor leaders who meant to maintain the power they wielded by making that power felt. Each week brought new disputes, however, until it had been impossible not to notice as senators and congressmen from states with high blue collar populations began to call for government mediation.

It had fallen to the labor secretary to lead an investigation and come up with some initial suggestions as to possible solutions that would satisfy nervous legislators. Responsibility for researching the issue had been delegated to an aide who found that many union representatives were pointing to instances of unfair practices that had been publicized in the pages of the newsletter that the secretary held in his hands. Coincidence? Or was someone deliberately instigating something?

Frowning, he pushed a button on his phone and spoke into the receiver. "Sally? See what you can find out about a labor publication called The Wage Earner that's coming from Fresno, California. Like who's behind it, how long it's been around—that kind of stuff."

In Fresno, George Hagura smiled as he gazed at the same issue of The Wage Earner that had come to the attention of the Secretary of Labor. The office that George now occupied was a far cry from the wooden barracks of his birth. He leaned back and stroked the leather arms of the chair, then ran his hand over the top of his desk. Real wood, not laminated fiberboard. He no longer wore the faded cotton work shirts that had been through the wash so many times that he'd been hard pressed to find one without a frayed collar. He had bought a new suit earlier that week, and though it hung in his closet, unworn as yet, it gave him great pleasure just to know that it was there. In his air-conditioned office, he wore new chinos and plain shirts with soft sweaters that felt wonderful against his skin. Anyone who visited him there could see that he was a man of importance, a man to be respected.

Sometimes he felt a little guilty at the pleasure he felt just sitting at his desk. Life was much better for migrant farm workers than it had been twenty years ago, but there was still a long way to go. Migrant workers still followed the crops from southern California to Canada, uprooting their children every two of three months, just when the little ones had begun to make friends. The tents that used to be set up in the fields had been replaced by wooden structures on many of the farms, but there were still too many people occupying them, and often the electrical wiring was faulty and the plumbing inadequate, forcing worn-out parents and children to carry water in leaky buckets at the end of the day. The Chicano diet was still mostly beans and tortillas, often cooked over open fires, and a hot bath was something only dreamed about.

The money was better and the hours weren't quite as long, but it was still a dead-end street because so many of the children couldn't speak English well enough to learn much during the little time that they were allowed to go to school and would more than likely end up following in the footsteps of their parents, becoming migrant workers themselves.

There was one unexpected benefit to the lifestyle, however. The camps were generally too far from town for the kids to be influenced by gangs or drugs, so at least their fingers were calloused from work rather than stained by nicotine or pot.

The Wage Earner promised to be a tool for communication among blue collar workers all over the country, bringing hope to those who were isolated. It was George Hagura's responsibility to coordinate the articles that were sent to him from union representatives in places like Chicago, Detroit and Pittsburgh, getting them to the printer in time for deadlines.

The man from Tokyo who had come to him with the idea for the newsletter had also been very helpful with guidelines as to how to feature the problems faced by industrial laborers as well as the relationships between farm labor and industrial labor. In fact, the man often supplied entire articles himself.

The current issue featured the trucking industry. George had been surprised to learn that truckers often faced hours of waiting time before they could load their trucks—sometimes as long as twelve to fifteen hours, and sometimes in freezing weather. The trucking companies didn't charge the shipper for waiting time—called 'demurrage'—and the driver didn't get paid for a lot of lost time. A wildcat strike in the late '60's had brought about some changes, but the average driver still put in a far longer day than he should. At least that's what the article said.

Long distance drivers spent days at a time in their cabs, unable to get a decent night's sleep. If they paid for a hotel room every night, they'd be bankrupt in no time. Plus they were away from their families for weeks at a time, picking up a load here, delivering it there, deprived of companionship.

Other articles had told of the never-ending struggle for benefits like health care and insurance, something beyond the imagination of the migrant farm worker. It seemed there were physical problems associated with nearly every job. Back breaking field work brought on arthritis; sitting for hours in the cab of a truck brought on hemorrhoids, shoulder bursitis and hearing defects.

Though he had been surprised at first by the somewhat inflammatory ideas and not too subtle suggestions that strikes might be in order, George Hagura was beginning to see that the publication could play a significant part in improving the lives of working men and women everywhere.

In San Francisco, Charles Stuart brooded in the dark. Ken was out for the evening and Charles suspected that he was with a woman. In fact, he was almost certain that it was a woman. Ken had been spending less time sharing the quiet evenings together that they both enjoyed so much. Sometimes they watched television, sometimes they played Scrabble, sometimes they worked on one of those maddening puzzles, and sometimes they just caught up on their reading. It didn't matter. Charles had begun to believe that he had discovered the purpose of life itself.

Admittedly, their relationship was complicated if it were to be examined. They had yet to come to terms with any form of commitment, but Charles was sure that it was only a matter of time. After all, Ken was accustomed to being a super stud; it wasn't part of his image to love another man. Charles had certainly never considered it either. He couldn't recall even knowing anyone who was gay and had taken his own sexuality for granted, unsatisfactory as it may have been up to now.

They went so well together. They seemed to be almost a matched set. The weaknesses of one were the strengths of the other. Charles had a tendency to get absorbed in whatever he was doing, forgetting the mundane. Ken was always on top of things and had begun making lists for Charles when there was the slightest chance that he might forget something. If he'd been aware of the term, Charles might have said they were soul mates.

It was strange, Charles mused. He'd thought that Maggie Davidson was the most perfect example of a life companion when he first saw her. She'd had a sort of Grace Kelly look, with soft blonde hair, intelligent eyes, and a smile that fell like summer rain on everyone who came near her. He'd known instantly that she was the girl he wanted to marry.

Marriage meant a partnership with clearly defined roles. A man chose a wife who would be an asset in his portfolio of life. It had to do with transporting charming, well-behaved children in the air-conditioned comfort of a luxury station wagon while the dog snoozed beside the fireplace and the cat purred on a window ledge.

It also had to do with having a woman on your arm who was pretty enough for the men to admire, but not so beautiful that she was perceived as a threat by their wives. A woman who read the headlines in the newspapers, but could swap recipes with Betty Crocker at a cocktail party.

Of course, Charles had never *consciously* thought any of those things. It was just the way things were. Elusive concepts like joy, happiness, anxiety and fear were just that—concepts. Love was just a word. You loved your mother, you loved your dog, you loved your job, you loved your wife. Until now.

Now he genuinely loved another human being. On evenings like this, he felt as though he were swimming in an ocean of emotions, pulled into murky depths and struggling to stay afloat. He didn't want to believe that Ken was drawing away from him. He couldn't believe it. But a little nagging doubt had crept in despite his efforts to ignore it. If Ken was with someone else, a woman, who was she? Where had he met her? Where did they go together?

Oh, God. Was this what jealousy felt like?

Charles racked his brain trying to remember if Ken had been talking to anyone or sitting with anyone when they met after work at the bar on Maiden Lane. The only person who turned up on a regular basis was Bill Morita, the mergers and acquisitions guy from Yamasu Securities. But he was just a pest. Getting pretty nosy about their personal lives and making some grandiose, though vague, claims about being on the inside track with powerful people in an apparent effort to impress Charles and Ken.

He'd begun to make suggestions regarding the availability of Japanese funds for loans to American businesses, and even hinted that Charles' father might use his influence as Chairman of the Fed to promote these funds. Charles had dismissed it as the machinations of a little man yearning to be a major player.

He looked at his watch. Nearly midnight. Hating himself, he turned off the lights in his living room so that it would look like he'd gone to bed, then settled down on the sofa to listen for Ken's footsteps in the hall, the sound of his key in the lock on the door across the hall.

# CHAPTER THIRTEEN

Sunao Tokumura rose from his desk and crossed the room to a mirror on the opposite wall. Closing his eyes, he drew in a deep breath through his nose, held it for a few seconds, then exhaled slowly through his mouth. Repeating the process several times, he willed his spirit to the place where only he could go, the place where he dwelt as the reincarnation of Musashi.

His eyes flew open, blazing with the fire that burned in his belly, and he saw not the short, stocky vice minister, but the wiry warrior of four centuries earlier. Staring at the image in the mirror, he practiced the Twofold Gaze of perception and sight. The gaze should be large and broad in order that one may see distant things as if they were close and take a distanced view of close things. Closing his eyes again, he took several more breaths as his spirit returned to the present, prepared to meet the challenges of the day.

Stan Mitsunari, just back from a conference in Hawaii, was on his calendar for later, but his immediate attention was directed toward a file on Japanese banks doing business in California. Recent discussions in committees representing MITI, Finance, and Foreign Affairs had resulted in agreements concerning proposed loans to contractors and developers. Nobuya Saito's conservative attitude and annoying caution had to be circumvented again with appropriate reassurances. Tokumura was not looking forward to his morning meeting with the little man from Finance.

"Why concentrate on California banks?" Saito asked.

"Because that's where the most significant development is," Tokumura replied patiently. "And five of the eleven largest banks in California are Japanese owned. I'm sure you're aware of the assets, around sixty-three billion in dollars that are held in our California banks, agencies and subsidiaries, an amount equal to approximately twenty-one percent of the total assets held in California institutions."

"But if you use the statistics, seven out of ten of the *world's* largest banks are Japanese. Why not diversify and reduce the risk?"

"Fifteen years ago in the late 1970's, not one Japanese bank was among the ten largest worldwide," Tokumura said doggedly. "Japanese savvy has made us leaders in the international financial community. Our growth rate in California is cause for concern, however, among Americans intent on Japan bashing, and contributes to the arguments put forth in trade negotiations. If they were to be convinced that deposits held in California would be inserted back into the state economy in the form of loans, rather than diverted to interests *outside* the country, the Japanese image might be greatly improved. Additionally, the higher interest rate on investments by bank stockholders will support trickle down benefits here at home."

Tokumura smiled inwardly as he began to see agreement in Saito's unspoken response. He moved in for the kill. Already aware of the probable answer, he asked, "Have you suggestions for a public relations strategy that will inform the American business community of the Japanese commitment to a harmonious monetary policy?"

"As a matter of fact, I met recently with the U.S. ambassador and proposed that he might want to submit an article to one of the major publications in his country reiterating the importance of cooperation between our countries," Saito said thoughtfully.

"Perhaps he might be instrumental in convincing California bankers of the benefits to the economy of their state and their nation through Japanese largesse in the form of industrial loans."

"Yes, an excellent idea. Then they will recognize that Japanese banks are crucial to their prosperity."

It was so easy, thought Tokumura. He grinned conspiratorially, sealing the pact. He looked forward to reporting his latest success to Yoshida.

Stan Mitsunari rose to greet the vice minister as he approached their table in the semi-dark cocktail lounge, bowing slightly in respect. A copy of an article that would appear in the next edition of the Nihon Keizai lay on the extra chair. A second telex on the heels of the first had told of the firing of the assistant vice president in charge of IBM's new operating system enhancements and Stan had recognized the implications immediately.

Though IBM stock had dropped in response to the announcement, the CEO had been quoted as saying that the new project would be released as planned and that the unfortunate loss of the project leader would not alter expectations. The project leader was a woman and it had occurred to Stan that she might prove invaluable to a Japanese company seeking to duplicate the IBM technology.

Sunao Tokumura seemed different somehow. Stan couldn't put his finger on it right away, but within a few minutes he decided that it was because the older man was carrying himself with even more determination than usual, which was considerable in any case.

"You seem particularly fit today, Tokumura-san," he remarked cautiously.

Tokumura was caught slightly off guard. "I do? Well, thank you, I think. It must be that things seem to be falling into place and an old dream may soon be realized."

"Oh? What dream is that?" Stan asked politely.

Tokumura was silent for a moment, wondering just how much he might confide in the journalist.

"You do not remember the war, of course," he began, "but I remember the sound of the bombs as they fell on Tokyo many years ago. Everyone was stunned that the Americans had been allowed to get so close to Japan itself. We believed that our navy and our soldiers were winning many victories and that the Americans were cowards who would surrender at any time. How could they have established an air base close enough for the planes to fly over Tokyo?

"I don't know to this day whether our leaders had lied so effectively to us or whether we chose to see only what we wanted to see. Perhaps it was a little of both. My father became more and more silent; he spoke only when necessary. I began to think that he didn't love me anymore, so I stayed away from him. Then the atomic bombs were dropped on Nagasaki and Hiroshima and I saw my father cry. On the day that the Japanese surrendered to the Americans, his anguish was nearly unbearable.

"I had been taught the samurai traditions. My grandfather's swords still hung on the wall of our home. They hang there to this day, kept shining and sharp. According to the code, death was preferable to dishonor." Tokumura's voice had dropped to barely a whisper, his anger evident.

"My father died soon after that. My mother said his heart got sick and stopped working. I was still a child and did not understand just what it was that had made his heart sick, but I made a promise to him that when I figured it out, I would make it right."

Stan stayed silent, waiting for more of the story that was so obviously distressing.

In a few moments, Tokumura continued, "It seems that opportunities may have arisen that will make it possible for me to fulfill my old promise." He stopped abruptly, then changed the subject as he recalled that their meeting had been at Stan's suggestion.

Hiding his curiosity, Stan retrieved the article from the chair and handed it to Tokumura.

"This will be the lead article in tomorrow's edition of the paper," he said. "I thought you might be interested in a preview. I noticed a telex a couple of weeks ago that said IBM had developed a new technology that would increase their main-frame market share by at least twenty-five percent. I wondered about it at the time, but had other things on my mind. Another telex came through yesterday saying that they had fired the assistant vice president in charge of the project, a woman by the way, but indicating that the project would be released as planned in spite of the 'unfortunate loss of the project leader.' It occurred to me that an unhappy former employee might not be adverse to an offer from a Japanese company."

"A woman?" Tokumura was astonished. "How could a woman achieve that level in a company of such stature?"

"It appears that she's some sort of genius. While it wasn't germane to the article, I was curious about why someone at that level would leave or be let go, so I did a little checking. I think it's probably some sort of rivalry within the company rather than a question of competency. This Diane Manchester finished college in three years, having skipped a couple of grades in her early years as well. She's not married and apparently had fed her addiction to computers through devotion to her work for the past ten or fifteen years. If this development will do what IBM claims it will do, she'd be in a position to do the same thing for a Japanese company."

"What Japanese company would consider a woman for such a responsible position? And an American woman at that!" Tokumura was dumbfounded.

"A company already established in the States, like Habatsu," Stan responded.

"Ah, yes. Sometimes I forget how many Americans we hire, but a woman? At that level?" He could taste it, maybe even swallow it, but digesting it was difficult.

Stan smiled at the obviously traditional point of view. "It just so happens that one of the fellows I went to school with in Missouri is now with Habatsu in San Francisco. He is more than likely already aware of these developments, but I might suggest to him that he look into it with the idea that she could be extremely valuable in offsetting any anticipated loss due to the technology gap."

"Hmmmm. Yes, an excellent idea. An American concept, refined by Japanese ingenuity once again."

It was remarkable how things began to fall into place once the thousand mile road had been mapped out and the strategy had been established. 'Injure the enemy by injuring the corners. Mingle and separate as on a winding mountain path. Do not rely upon one technique—the long sword is of no account when called upon to fight in a confined space.' Musashi's words of long ago held constant relevance, Tokumura reflected.


Yoshida replaced the telephone receiver on its base and leaned back in his chair. He was extremely pleased by the information he had gotten from Vice Minister Tokumura and had already moved ahead with the plan. A word or two in the right places and it was done.

The Sunday editions of the San Francisco Chronicle, the L.A. Times and the San Diego Union would each carry a glossy special supplement with a lengthy article by the American ambassador to Japan called, 'Outlook on Cooperation—the U.S. and Japan.' Paid for by advertisements touting the advantages of Japanese products, it would carry the usual line on correcting economic distortions and eliminating trade barriers, but with subtle suggestions on the availability of operating capital from Japanese banks.

The issue of hiring Diane Manchester, distasteful as it may be, had been even easier. A corner office was already being prepared for her, complete with a full set of hidden cameras that would pick up every move she made. The executive who had been on the line moments ago was probably speaking to her now.

Stan moved across the living room and into the bedroom where he undressed quietly as Akiko slept. He closed the door behind him as he left the bedroom and went into the tiny kitchen where he opened the cupboard that held their liquor supply. Filling a glass to the rim with ice, he poured scotch over it and paused, leaning against the kitchen counter, lost in thought as he sipped the whiskey.

The shock of seeing Maggie again after all these years had not lessened. She had changed from the naïve college girl he remembered. The purity that had shone in her young eyes had become the shrewd gaze of a career woman. What would she look like if the pins that held her perfectly coifed hair were to be removed? If he ran his fingers through her curls would they be sticky with hairspray? Would she be soft in his arms as she once had been, or would she be as unyielding as the business woman he'd seen at the hotel appeared to be?

His questions about the leadership of the Davidson Group of hotels had been answered. It was apparent that Maggie had assumed the reins of power. A discreet inquiry had provided the information that she was there to discuss the addition of the Kaimana Surf and Sand to her small empire.

The sight of her as she strode across the lobby had struck a blow to his midsection and the old bitterness that had softened over the years now threatened to consume him once again. Had she adopted her father's prejudices along with his title after his death? Or had that happened when she married the fair-haired banker? His anger made it easier to bear the pain of seeing her again.

Poor Akiko. Stan knew that she had no idea what had happened to make him withdraw so abruptly. Though her face reflected the hurt, she had covered it as best she could in the tradition of the Japanese wife. He didn't deserve her, he thought. He had fallen into the typical mode of most Japanese men, maybe men everywhere, and took her for granted. It was easy to do, especially in Japan where women still had their place and most stayed in it.

That was why he had taken her with him to Hawaii and made an effort to love her as he knew she wanted to be loved. It had been working, too. Her obvious happiness had lapped at him like the gentle surf beneath their balcony, curling around his toes and bathing him in its warmth. He vowed silently to make it up to her and headed toward the bed where she lay sleeping.

A fleeting thought crossed his mind. What had Sunao Tokumura meant when he spoke of opportunities that would fulfill his old promise? How did he plan to 'make it right?' Obviously he had some sort of retribution in mind . . .

# CHAPTER FOURTEEN

Charles sprawled on the sofa, the Sunday papers scattered around him overflowing onto the floor. He picked up the magazine supplement that pictured the American ambassador to Japan on its cover along with the title, 'Outlook on Cooperation—the U.S. and Japan.' A professional looking, glossy publication, it was lengthy, twenty pages, with advertisements on copiers and the like. The text spouted the usual propaganda calling Japan the junior partner in a bilateral relationship and the need for eliminating trade barriers. Charles wondered if the Japanese were in agreement with the 'junior partner' designation.

It went on to say that Japanese companies had directly invested more than $53 billion in the U.S. and employed about 250,000 Americans in plants such as the one recently opened in Tennessee. Tennessee Governor Reston LaFarge and Congressman Zach Templeton were praised for their efforts to bring about this effort at joint prosperity through cooperation.

Charles' attention was suddenly riveted on the next paragraph. In a spirit of unity, the Japanese ministry of Finance had announced that Japanese banks in California would make a significant amount of capital available to American business, notably in construction and land development. Californians could be sure that deposits on record at these banks would be reinserted into the local economy. The fear of American money disappearing into the Japanese economy had been eliminated, and the Japanese had proven their desire for a mutual participation in an improved economic atmosphere on both sides of the Pacific Ocean.

Charles stared at the page. Bill Morita's words on the 'availability of funds to American business' sprang into his mind. Nearly the same phraseology! Coincidence? Or had he been too quick to dismiss the little man as a bit of a bantam rooster? If he did have the connections he claimed to have, just what were they and with whom?

In Tennessee, the plant manager was beside himself. The plant had been open less than a year and he'd just been told to lay off two hundred employees. He couldn't believe it! He'd seen the figures and knew that the plant was making money. Why then was it necessary to lay off sixteen percent of the workers?

He grabbed the phone and punched in the three-digit number that would put him through to the accounting office. The moment he heard the senior accountant's voice, he began shouting.

"Goddammit, Ray, what's going on here?"

"Tommy? What's going on where?"

"I'm holding a memo in my hand telling me to lay off two hundred employees due to unexpected promotional costs! Advertising? The press couldn't be more favorable, locally at any rate, and the need for 'promotional costs' of this magnitude escapes me! What the hell is going on?"

"Don't get your shorts in a bunch, Tommy. I'll be there in a minute. I think this is something we should discuss privately."

"Make it fast. And don't call me 'Tommy.' It's *Tom!*"

"Be right there, *Tom.*"

The day wasn't starting out well. Tommy Durand paced the floor as he waited for his old friend. He grabbed the profit and loss sheets from his desk and waved them above his head as the door to his office opened to admit the accountant.

He got right to the point. "Well?"

"Have you ever heard of a political action committee, Tommy?"

"*Tom!* No, what the hell is that?"

"They're called PAC's for short. I wasn't really familiar with them either until I noticed the term on the adjusted P & L's from the home office. I called Congressman Templeton's office to ask about it and it seems they're a legal way for foreign owned companies to contribute to American political campaigns. Since our esteemed congressman was pretty much responsible for getting the plant located here, the company thought it would be a nice way to say thank you."

"Are you telling me that contributions to Zach Templeton's election are costing an amount equal to the salaries of two hundred employees? No way!"

"I couldn't say the whole amount is going directly to Zach. There's no way to trace it unless the home office wants us to know, Tom."

"Well I'm damn well going to find out. They can't do this to us. Production at current levels is doomed if we lose that many people."

The day didn't get any better, and by late afternoon Tom was gobbling Maalox like it was candy. A junior staffer in the congressman's office had declared that contributions had definitely not been excessive and suggested that it was common practice for funds to be allocated to sympathetic associates in congress to assure passage of favorable legislation, not to mention administrative costs. When pressed for an explanation of just what constituted 'administrative costs,' the staffer had told him about lobbying firms in Washington that existed solely for the purpose of promoting the interests of their clients.

"You mean they buy votes in congress?" Tom had asked angrily.

"No, no, of course not," the staffer had said quickly.

"That's what it sounds like to me," Tom had insisted. "Who are these people?"

He was told that most were former members of congress or high level former staffers and lawyers. Insiders who knew how to get things done in Washington.

"Holy shit," Tom said to himself later. How could his relatively small plant, hailed the biggest boon to the local economy since the invention of the automobile, play such a role in partisan politics? It was mind boggling.

He was just about to leave for the day when his phone rang.

"Tom? Rusty LaFarge here. How's the fishing down your way? I hear this is the time of year to catch the big ones." The exaggerated drawl was unmistakable.

"Governor? Well, this is an unexpected pleasure. And something of a coincidence, I might add. I've been on the horn to Zach Templeton's office half the day. You know anything about the cutbacks that have been ordered here?"

"That's why I'm calling, Tom. I know it's inconvenient for you to lay off a few people, but it'll all come out in the wash when you increase production again and can hire even more than the layoff calls for. Look at it as a temporary situation."

"A few people? You call two hundred men and women with families to feed a few people? What do I tell them when they remind me of the promises we made just a few months ago?"

"Tell them that the costs were higher than anticipated and that they'll all benefit from resulting higher production," the governor said soothingly. "Now isn't the time to make waves, Tommy," he added quietly. "It really wouldn't be good for anyone."

The plant manager rolled his eyes. Would he never escape his childhood nickname? Why couldn't southerners talk like grownups?

"Let's run away and do some fishing one of these days," the governor went on as though the veiled threat had not been spoken. "I'll have my secretary check my calendar and give you a call."

It wasn't until later that evening that Tom realized the implication in the governor's statement and wondered if he'd really heard it right. He pictured himself lying in a pool of blood in some dark alley and then dismissed the image as ridiculous. "Nah, that kind of thing doesn't happen anymore," he said aloud to the half empty beer can in his hand.

Settling into the recliner chair that was his favorite spot, his thoughts turned to how he could best protect the jobs of his employees. He made a promise to himself that he'd do whatever it took.


In San Francisco, Diane Manchester was nearly overcome by the luxury of her new penthouse apartment. The view was breathtaking. Lights twinkled on both bridges. The hills of Marin County were a dark outline against the horizon beyond the Golden Gate Bridge and Coit Tower was swathed in light a short distance away from her windows. At the far end of the Bay Bridge, the shoreline that was Berkeley shimmered as the sun slipped into the sea. It was more than Diane could believe was real.

She'd had no idea that her knowledge of what was the most interesting thing in life to her could be of such stupendous value to someone else. The penthouse had been a bonus, the touch that made Habatsu's offer impossible to refuse, not that she'd really wanted to refuse it anyway. Her salary was twice what IBM had paid her, and three weeks a year in Hawaii went along with the whole package. Since she truly loved her job, she was sure she'd died and gone to heaven.

She wouldn't have believed it possible to be so completely happy such a short time after being unceremoniously fired. That bastard, Harry Cesnick, knew she was smarter than he was. Diane recognized the truth: Harry had to get rid of her before she got credit for the new technology enhancements. She was still a little bitter, but San Francisco sure made up for a lot of it.

She knew that Habatsu wanted her to provide them with the program enhancements and she was happy to do it. She had confessed that she had a 'back door' user ID and could probably even improve on the system with a little time. Unwilling to compromise her personal ethics, however, she'd made sure she was alone when she entered her ID. It was one thing to access the IBM system herself, and quite another to let anyone else do it, no matter how much money they threw at her.

Very late that same night, when the offices had been closed for hours and only a couple of guards were sipping coffee in the first floor security office, a nondescript Asian man sat in front of a panel of black and white screens viewing video tapes of Diane's first week on the job. Four cameras had picked up every move she made, one of them focused on her computer keyboard. The man stopped the film as he saw Diane enter her user ID, and created still photographs as she pressed each key by touching a button on the side of the console. He tucked the photos into a manila envelope, wrote on the front of it and left it in the inter-office mail box outside the door before he left the building by way of a staircase that was unscrutinized by security cameras that kept guards informed of movements nearly everywhere else in the building.

The next day, a diplomatic courier boarded a non-stop JAL flight from San Francisco to Tokyo. In the briefcase he carried was an envelope addressed to Sunao Tokumura, Vice Minister of International Trade and

Industry, marked 'PERSONAL AND CONFIDENTIAL' in large red letters. Inside that envelope was another addressed to Satoshi Yoshida, also marked 'Personal and Confidential,' though in smaller letters.

The day after that, Yoshida met privately with a computer specialist in his employ who was known for his hacking ability. In a matter of minutes, that employee was back at his terminal, busy creating a virus. He had been told only that his expertise was required in view of the mounting possibility of existing viruses that may need to be circumvented at a future date and that the company wanted to be sure it had the proficiency to avoid any major problems.

Within a few days, a second man entered the IBM mainframe using Diane Manchester's ID and inserted the virus that would erase all data on the system as a specific date was rolled over on the new systems installed by mainframe customers when the enhanced technology was released. A vaccine had been created as well, with a suitable explanation that would be distributed to Japanese companies in advance of the activation date. There were still a few glitches to be ironed out, but unless IBM got anxious and released the system early, there was time to consider all the possibilities.

Yoshida was delirious with joy. It was beyond his wildest dreams. Not only would the American stock exchanges be in chaos as year-end transactions were recorded, but payroll data, criminal records, insurance records, bank deposits, government data, and nearly anything of importance to the American way of life would cease to exist in the storage system. It could take months to find the source of the problem and restore the information. By that time, the American economy would be beyond repair. Revenge was the best medicine in the world.

Force the enemy into inconvenient situations.

Seize upon the enemy's disorder and derangement.

Do not let him recover.


The Wind Book
Book of Five Rings
Miyamoto Musashi

# CHAPTER FIFTEEN

Buzz Craddock lay beside Allison Jennings in the king-sized bed. His arm was around her, with her head on his shoulder. She was sound asleep, her blonde hair fanning out to tickle his skin. He wasn't exactly uncomfortable, but on the other hand, he wasn't very comfortable either. The bed was too soft, his arm was starting to cramp and it itched. He had too much on his mind to sleep anyway.

He had made up his mind to sell his shares in the Davidson Hotel Group if he could get the other two minor shareholders to agree. He was pretty sure that if he offered both Van Carducci and Bob Mattheson a bonus of twenty thousand dollars for each one percent they held, one fifth of what he'd get in the end, they would agree. After all, that meant an additional hundred thousand each over and above the stock price and Buzz would come out with eight hundred thousand instead of a million, plus the dollar value of his stock. He could live with that.

He hadn't decided what to tell Allison, however. She might be a problem. He was sure that she wouldn't stay with Davidson if he left and she might get demanding about a permanent arrangement, like marriage.

I'm too old to have another person under foot night and day, he thought, limiting my freedom to do as I like whenever I like. On the other hand, I've grown accustomed to her face as the song says, and the sex is certainly good. She looks good and I don't have to make small talk. Who else would have me anyway? What the hell, maybe it wouldn't be such a bad idea after all.

Now that he'd decided that marriage might work after all, Buzz had to think about what to tell Maggie Stuart. If he could get away with it, he hoped to tell her only that he was retiring, and be gone before she knew he'd sold his stock. But either Van or Bob might spill the beans the minute he made the offer to them. They hadn't had to deal with Maggie on a daily basis since she'd taken over a few months ago, so their loyalty no doubt remained intact. Maybe he should present his case in person by paying each of them a visit. That would probably be more effective.

Allison's arm moved on his chest, her hand ending up near his groin, and he responded involuntarily. God, even at his age, he never got tire of making love to her, he thought, as he turned toward her. He put his hand on her breast, moving it gently until the nipple hardened and he could suck on it comfortably. He began to stroke her skin all over, poking his fingers into the little crevices under her arm, at her elbow, then down to the best one of all—between her legs.

She stirred, waking just enough to adjust her position so that he could enter her easily. She moved with him slowly and he lost himself inside her, letting it happen without the need for even working up a sweat. How sweet it was. As climax neared, he pumped a little faster and they came together as only lovers who know each other very well can do.

The next day, Buzz bypassed his secretary and made his own arrangements to fly to New York for two days, and then to San Francisco for another two days. He didn't want word of his departure to leak until he was ready to leave. A last minute explanation for the trip would be easier than to allow Maggie time to question his motives.

He spent the evening alone concentrating on the presentation he would make to Bob Mattheson. Bob's agreement was crucial to the deal. Van would probably be fairly easily persuaded to retire on the substantial profit he'd receive.

By the end of the week, Buzz was back in Chicago with approval from both of the other men. It turned out that Bob was glad to get the money. His young son was in need of specialized medical treatment for a heart murmur, and Bob and his wife were desperately seeking funds. When told that Buzz and Bob would both be leaving the hotels,

Van had agreed that he'd like to retire and take his still beautiful wife, Sabrina, to Italy to visit relatives they hadn't seen in years.

In no time at all, Buzz' resignation was on Maggie's desk and the brokerage firm had been notified of the intent to sell shares equaling twenty percent of Davidson Hotel Group stock according to the offer put forth by their client. Buzz felt little or no remorse. He wasn't betraying Michael Davidson, he was giving Michael's heir the freedom to take the company in new directions.

Very soon after that, Allison Jennings submitted her resignation as well, along with the announcement that she and Buzz would be married in Las Vegas prior to a trip around the world on one of the most luxurious cruise ships ever built. In fact, it had made its maiden voyage only a few months earlier following its delivery from Japan to Honolulu where it was christened among a great deal of hoopla from the press who called it a joint venture between Japanese and American interests.

Maggie heard her mother's voice calling her from the dining room. "Oh, God," she said aloud, "I've *got* to get my own place."

Victoria Davidson was driving her daughter crazy. She had transferred her need to be needed from her husband to her daughter following Michael Davidson's untimely death, and had yet to accept the fact that Maggie had taken over as CEO of the hotels. She simply could not believe that her little girl was not only all grown up, but had executive qualities as well.

At first, Maggie had found it easy to stay on in her old room after Charles left for San Francisco, telling herself that her mother needed her. Then she said it was more convenient to the office a few blocks away. Her most recent excuse was that she was much too busy to look for a place of her own. She realized now that if she didn't move out soon, her mother would grow more and more accustomed to her presence and come to expect it. There were any number of fine old buildings on Chicago's Near North Side where she'd have privacy and still be close to the office, and by extension, her mother. She made a mental note to bring up the subject at dinner that evening. She was about to leave for the office when she heard the phone ring and then her mother's voice calling out that Dan Levinson wanted to speak with her.

"Yes, Dan?"

"You'd better get down here fast, Maggie. I've just opened the mail and the news couldn't be worse," said the corporate attorney.

"I was just on my way out the door, Dan. What is it?"

"I think you should see for yourself, Maggie. Should I wait in your office or would you prefer to stop by at mine? You might want to be unavailable until we've had a chance to talk."

"I'll come directly to your office, Dan." She checked her watch and added, "I should be there in about ten minutes."

Luck was with her. Not only did she get a taxi right away, but traffic up Michigan Avenue was light and she was inside the Chicagoan in less than ten minutes. She pretended not to notice a frantic wave from the front desk manager and walked briskly up the stairs rather than wait for the elevator. Dan Levinson's secretary handed her a cup of coffee as she passed through the outer office, and she saw the worried look in his eyes as she approached his desk.

"What *is* it, Dan?" she asked.

Wordlessly, he handed her a letter that was on top of several others in front of him. She read for a moment, then looked up and said, "I don't understand this. What does it mean?"

"It means that somehow, somebody bought twenty percent of the Davidson Hotel Group stock, which means that Buzz, Van and Bob must have sold out," Dan said grimly.

"Sold out? No, that's impossible. They'd have offered to sell it back to my mother and me if they wanted to sell. And why would all three of them sell at once? This can't be right!"

"That was my reaction, too, so I phoned the broker whose name is on the letterhead. It's real all right. And it gets worse. I asked who the buyer was and was told that it was a corporation with a Caribbean charter, simply called 'M & D, Inc.' and all mail is to be addressed to them care of the broker. In short, whoever bought the stock wants to remain anonymous. We can probably find out who it is, but it'll take time."

"Get Van on the phone," Maggie ordered.

"There's more, Maggie," Dan said. He handed her two more letters.

"Resignations? From both Van and Bob? What the hell is going on? I can't believe Van would just sell out and leave after all these years.

Bob either! I knew Buzz wasn't happy when I took over. He expected to get the job himself, but I had hoped he might cooperate. When he and Allison decided to get married and go on that extended cruise, I realized that our differences were too great for him to stay on, but to sell out without a word to me? I just can't understand it. He must be behind the decisions from the others. How could he do it? And why didn't Van let me know? He'd *never* do a thing like this." Maggie shook her head in wonder and dismay.

"Still want to talk to Van?"

"Yes, of course. More than ever. I have to know what this is all about!"

In minutes, Maggie had learned that Van had been under the impression that Buzz wanted the stock for himself as an investment for his retirement. He'd had no idea that Buzz had sold out and left without a word to Maggie.

"He offered Bob and me each a hundred thousand dollar bonus, Maggie. We thought he figured the investment was worth it, and we each had our reasons for taking the money. I'm not getting any younger and Sabrina has been talking about seeing her family in Italy for years. The extra money would mean we didn't have to scrimp when I retired.

"And you must be aware of Bob's problems with his son," Van continued. "The money was a godsend for medical expenses that aren't covered by insurance, and it meant Bob could be with the kid more. If I'd known that Buzz wasn't going to hold onto the stock, I'd have let you know right away. I hope you know that. Your father was very good to me for many years and I'd never have betrayed him that way."

"Did you know that Buzz was resigning?" Maggie asked.

"Yes, he said he wanted to retire, too. But he didn't say a word about selling the stock, Maggie. You've got to believe that. I guess I was so happy to get that hundred thousand that I didn't want to see any problems. I phoned your office late yesterday afternoon and left a message with the switchboard. I wanted to talk to you personally before you got resignation, but even after all these years, I still forgot about the time difference. I feel terrible about this."

"What am I going to do without you, Van? How am I going to replace three GM's all at the same time?"

"Don't worry about San Francisco, Mags. I'll stay until you can get New York and Chicago handled. That is, if you want me to stay after what I've done."

"I'd be very grateful if you'd stay on for another few months at least. Buzz must have resented me more than I knew."

Maggie hung up the phone and said, "Get on this right away, Dan. Find out who this M & D company is. A list of their corporate officers has to be on file somewhere. I'll get in touch with Bob Mattheson, but I'd venture to say his story will be the same as Van's. If I go to New York, can you handle things here without Buzz?"

"Sure, Maggie. We'll just go on a rotating assignment basis with each of the major department heads taking one-day turns as acting manager until you get back."

A short time later, Maggie had spoken to Bob Mattheson in New York and heard the same story that Van had already told her. He had no idea that Buzz had sold the stock without a word to Maggie and her mother. He, too, agreed to stay on as general manager in New York until a suitable replacement had been found. He suggested that his secretary begin an immediate search in the area, as well as to contact the local headhunter agencies. When a list of candidates had been made up, he'd inform Maggie and she could make the trip for interviews at that time. He felt that a few weeks should do it.

Just after lunch, Dan Levinson rang her to say that he had obtained the names of the corporate officers of M & D, Inc., and had reached a secretary who told him that her boss was a licensed real estate planner who often served as a figurehead for clients who wished to remain unidentified. She had further indicated that her file contained instructions that proxies were to be assigned to Mrs. Stuart until further notice.

Maggie was perplexed. "Why would anyone want to buy twenty percent of our stock and then give me the proxies?" she asked.

"I have no idea, Maggie. Can you think of anyone who might want to get their fingers into the pie for some reason? Would Charles have done it?"

"I can't imagine why Charles would do such a thing. He doesn't really have that kind of money, anyway. And I'm sure he wants as little to do with me as I do with him! Once the house is sold, we'll have no reason to be in touch at all. As far as I know, he's happy in San Francisco and has no intention of ever coming back into my life."

"I don't suppose your mother would know anything about it?" Dan didn't want to say it, but they had to consider all the options.

"Oh, Dan, she knows almost nothing about the hotels except that they're very comfortable and they keep her very comfortable as well. She certainly wouldn't know anything about setting up dummy corporations in the Caribbean! And why would she want to do it anyway?"

Dan nodded in agreement. Maggie frowned as something she hadn't thought of occurred to her. "I have to ask this, Dan. Did Daddy have any business dealings that might have caused this?"

"I've been with the Davidson Group for ten years, Maggie, and I've never heard so much as a whisper in regard to your father's integrity. That's one reason I love my job. I've never had to lie to anyone or cover up anything shady. No, I don't believe it could be anyone out for revenge."

"Well, how about the reverse? Someone who appreciates a good company and wants a piece of it?"

"Why would anyone like that be so secretive about it? And why would Buzz agree to it? Whoever it is must have offered Buzz a sizeable bonus to deliver all of the outstanding stock, and since it was all done through a broker, Buzz probably doesn't know who it is either. That would account for his secrecy and the way he left. He didn't want to answer questions."

"Could someone be trying to take over the company?" Maggie knew the answer to that question, but asked anyway.

As she expected, Dan said, "Anyone who knows enough to do it would also know that you and your mother hold the balance of the stock, so there wouldn't be any point to acquiring only twenty percent. No, it has to be someone who has a lot of money, and I do mean a *lot* of money, and has some motive other than control of the company."

"Hmmm . . . ," Maggie said, "that leaves us right back where we started, doesn't it?"

"At least you know that you have even more authority than before since you don't have to consult with the others even as a courtesy. You have the proxies." Dan stared at her as another thought occurred to him. "Could someone be hoping you'll fail?" he asked incredulously.

"I'm not going to fail, Dan, and I can't think of anyone who hates me enough to want me to fail. I may not be the most popular person in the world, but I don't think I've ever done anything that would make me an enemy like that. I need to have a talk with Mother tonight about moving into my own place, so I'll find out if she knows anything. Hopefully without having to actually tell her that twenty percent of the company stock has slipped through our fingers somehow!"

At dinner that evening, Maggie toyed with her food trying to decide whether to bring up the subject of her own apartment before questioning her mother about the stock, or do it the other way around. She concluded that the hotels might be more neutral and approached it through the back door by saying that the acquisition of the Kaimana Surf and Sand was going nicely and that she hoped to have a grand opening by Thanksgiving, celebrating the new addition with a holiday party and special promotions in each of the hotels.

"I hope you know what you're doing, Maggie. I know Buzz must have been very unhappy or he wouldn't have left so quickly. Your father would be distressed to know that you've ignored Buzz' advice."

Maggie sighed. It wasn't going to be easy no matter what she said.

"Mother, I've told you that I found files that indicated that Daddy wasn't in complete agreement with Buzz, and that he had already researched the acquisition himself. I think he'd be very happy with the way things are going."

"That may be true, but I also know that he never dreamed you'd take over his job and leave Buzz out in the cold," Victoria said somewhat imperiously. "How are you ever going to find someone to replace him?"

'The Davidson Group has a fine reputation, Mother. There are any number of well qualified people who would love the job." Maggie paused, then plunged in. "You might as well know that both Van and Bob are retiring, too. Van and Sabrina want to spend some time in Italy, and Bob wants to be with his son during the medical procedures. It seems they've both been considering this for some time."

Victoria looked up from her plate in astonishment. "You mean all three of our best men are leaving at once?"

At least she doesn't seem to know about it, Maggie thought and went on to say that both men had agreed to remain in their positions until suitable replacements had been found.

"Oh, Maggie, how can you run the company yourself? And without the men who've been at your father's side for years? What if you ruin us?" Victoria's voice had risen to a wail.

"Your confidence in me is overwhelming, Mother. I'm sure that not only will I not ruin us, I may take us to new highs. I'm not Michael Davidson's daughter for nothing and I'm certainly not stupid!"

"Of course you're not stupid. You just don't have the experience or the knowledge to do the job!"

Maggie fought to keep her anger under control, and concentrated on chewing her food for several minutes. When she could breathe again and was sure her voice wouldn't betray her, she brought up the subject of moving to her own place. Her mother began to cry.

"You can't mean that you're going to leave me here all alone! How could you, Maggie?"

"If Charles and I were still living in Lake Forest, you'd be even more alone than if I get a place nearby, Mother. We can have lunch together at The Pub and dinner together often. We just won't be tripping over each other, and we'll each have more privacy."

"Privacy? You need privacy from me, your own mother?"

"I'm a grownup now, Mother, and I need my own space and my own home. With the hours I'm keeping and the traveling I'll be doing for the next few months, I won't interrupt your schedule if I come and go at odd hours."

Victoria sniffled and nodded, then rose to pour each of them a glass of brandy, ending the conversation. As soon as Maggie felt that she could reasonably retire, she said goodnight and carried the evening newspaper with her to her room.

The next day, she made several phone calls, setting up appointments to see apartments, and by the end of the week had found one that suited her perfectly. It occupied the entire to floor of an old brownstone and had a fireplace in the master bedroom as well as one in the living room. It was on Astor Street, a stone's throw from the cardinal's residence, and five minutes by taxi to her mother's home at Oak and Michigan.

On Tuesday of the following week, she was unable to get a taxi. The drivers were staging a sympathy strike. In sympathy for just what, she wasn't sure.

# CHAPTER SIXTEEN

Bill Morita stood in the entrance to the little noodle shop that was located in an alleyway a few blocks from the high profile restaurants frequented by tourists to the area known as Japantown. He watched the retreating back of the yakusa who had just left and wished he could dress the way they did. Their dark blue double-breasted suits, white ties and sunglasses made them easy to spot if you knew what you were looking at. His job made it impossible, however, as Yamasu Securities would never permit it. Maybe if he fulfilled the promise he had just made, he might be accepted into their ranks as a full-fledged member, with induction at a secret ceremony that established blood ties through the sharing of a sake bowl. The mere thought of it sent shivers of anticipation up his spine.

Only the Japanese people were reasonable enough to recognize that since crime inevitable, they might as well make use of organized crime to control unorganized rabble. The shoguns of the sixteenth century had been the first to delegate responsibility to the forerunners of those who maintained order today. In Bill's mind, the yakusa were a far more admirable group than the samurai warriors whose main function was the acquisition of territory for their daimyos. Yakusa had originally protected travelers from the highwaymen who plied the famous Tokaido Road between Edo and Kyoto.

They still protected people today. Some even served as bodyguards to very important people, which gave them something in common with the samurai, but the reward was cold hard cash rather than some altruistic sense of honor.

Morita felt sure that the instructions he'd just received had originated from someone very powerful. It really wouldn't be difficult. All he had to do was put a little pressure on his new friend, Charles Stuart.

He left the alley and walked over to his favorite bar on Geary Street. Calling out to the bartender for a double scotch neat as he passed the bar, he went into a narrow hallway in the back where the pay telephone was located. He pulled Charles' business card from the inside pocket of his jacket, inserted a coin and dialed the number.

"Charlie!" he said jovially. "We need to speak privately. Let's get together later."

"And just what is it that we need to discuss privately?" Charles asked, annoyed by the suggestion that they had anything at all to discuss, let alone privately.

"How about your relationship with your good friend, Ken? Or is it a secret that the two of you are really more than just good buddies?" Morita could tell by the silence at the other end of the line that he'd made his point.

"Where?" Charles asked abruptly.


Charles paced the floor as he waited for Ken. It seemed he did that a lot lately. But this time it went beyond a little jealousy. He was on his third drink since returning home from his meeting with Morita when he finally heard Ken's footsteps on the stairs.

"Where the hell have you been? It's nearly ten o'clock!" he began angrily.

Ken sighed, remaining silent until he reached the landing where Charles stood. "You're starting to sound like a jealous wife, Charles," he commented.

"Sorry. It isn't that. We have to talk."

"Can't it wait until I've had a chance to fix a drink and relax a bit?"

"You won't want to relax when you hear what happened awhile ago. Come on in here and fix your drink. You're going to need it." Charles strode back into his apartment.

It didn't take long to relate the basics of Bill Morita's threats: that in exchange for keeping their secret, he proposed that they put pressure on their fathers to encourage favorable treatment of Japanese interests in the international marketplace.

"What does he have to do with international trade? I thought he was mostly a researcher in mergers and acquisitions." Ken was puzzled.

"Haven't you noticed how often he shows up lately?" Charles began. "And he's been making noise about the powerful people he's associated with. I thought it was just wishful thinking on his part until just the other day when he told me that Japanese banks that do business in the States would be making funds available to American companies. And that's just the wording he used, 'making funds available.' Then last Sunday there was a magazine supplement in the Chronicle with a lengthy article written by the American ambassador to Japan that said the same thing, in nearly those same words. It struck me as coincidental at the time. I didn't really believe that he knew the kind of people he's hinted at knowing."

"How does he know so much about our personal lives?" Ken wondered. "And what does he expect? Who does he plan to tell other than our fathers?"

"Beats me. He must have followed us or something. But he was very specific. He knows we're more than friends, Ken. The way he said it was, 'Do your fathers know how close the two of you are? I bet they'd be shocked, wouldn't they?' He knows that you were an athlete at Stanford; he knows that I went to Dartmouth, and he obviously knows that your dad is a cabinet member and that mine heads up the Federal Reserve."

Ken frowned. "You're sure he's serious and not just grandstanding?"

"If you'd heard him and seen the look in his eyes, you'd know that he's serious. It was almost evil. It *was* evil. He said if we didn't believe he could bring us down, we should watch for developments over the next couple of weeks in treasury bonds. Then he went on to say that patterns in the movement of short term government bonds are ultimately reflected in long term bonds, and that together they influence the prime lending rate, mortgage rates, time deposit yields, and a lot of other things in the American economy. When I asked him to be more specific about what kind of developments, he just smiled and said we'd know when we saw it in the papers."

"I can't risk my father finding out about us, Charles. Maybe it's time we end it. I don't think that I was cut out for a permanent relationship like this anyway. I still like women too much."

Charles was shocked. He knew that Ken had been going out without him, but had convinced himself that he was just making sure of his feelings. It would pass. They loved each other.

"You can't mean that, Ken," he said. "I know we haven't actually said it out loud, so I'll say it. I love you. I need you. You're my life!"

Ken stared at him, then turned away and fixed himself another drink. He didn't want to hurt Charles, but he realized now that he'd never meant it to go this far. Charles was the one who'd had a wife. It had been a more or less pleasant experiment, but that was all. The danger of being found out had made it more exciting, but now that the danger was real, it had to end.

"Charles, I never meant to hurt you," he began, "and I'm certainly not your life. You have a great job that you like a whole lot better than you liked climbing the corporate ladder in Chicago, and I know you like San Francisco."

"Because *you're* here!" Charles exclaimed. "I left my wife, or I should say that she left me because of you, and I left everything I'd grown up believing, everything that was familiar and everything I'd worked toward, to move out here to be with *you!*"

"But you love it here! If you've decided that you really are gay, San Francisco is the best place in the world to live. If you're bisexual, it's still the best of both worlds, and if you really want to go back, you can. No one, with the possible exception of that scum, Morita, knows about us, so we can just be the friends we've pretended to be all along with no one the wiser. Come on, Charles, you're an intelligent man. You can do whatever you choose."

"*I chose you!* You can't say you didn't love it, too. You can't just abandon me!" Charles' voice rose.

"I'm not abandoning you, Charles," Ken responded patiently.

Charles refused to be appeased. "No! No, you can't do this." In spite of himself, he began to cry. Reaching out, he grabbed Ken's wrist and pulled him into an embrace. Repulsed, Ken pushed him away and shuddered. Charles sank into a chair and sobbed helplessly.

"Get hold of yourself, Charles. I'm going to my apartment. When you can talk rationally, we'll discuss what to do about Morita and his threats."

Darkness had settled over the city as Charles cried, his mind numb. He had no idea what time it was when he finally got up and crawled into bed where he clung to his pillow in despair.

Two days later, the office was in turmoil when Charles arrived. The heavy buying of the previous treasury bond issue had driven interest rates down and climbing interest rates in Japan had made investment at home more attractive. The economists at the Federal Reserve office in San Francisco were speculating on rumors that Japan might pull out of the U.S. bond auction that was coming up soon. One of them was on the phone to Yamasu Securities, the firm known to be one of the world's premier bond trading operations. If the Japanese stopped buying U.S. bonds, America would be hard pressed to support its current lifestyle.

Everyone stood watching as the economist put the phone down, each face saying silently, "Well?"

"Nothing. You know how they are. They just say they have no information and that Japanese investors wouldn't be a part of any kind of deliberate scheme. To suggest that they would is highly insulting."

"They control more than nine billion dollars in 30-year treasury securities. Let's face it. The U.S. bond market is hostage to Japanese activity. They've got us by the balls and we'll have to raise interest rates to keep them interested," said another man.

"Can you imagine the depression that would result if they pull out?" asked still another.

Charles felt ill. He sat down at his desk and put his head in his hands. "Oh, dear God," he muttered. His life was falling apart. How could the relationship that brought him the most happiness he'd ever known be used against him in a scheme to manipulate his country into economic cooperation on such a scale? It was incomprehensible. What did they want from him?

In the days that followed, articles appeared in publications throughout the financial world.

"Bond Prices Take Tumble as Investors React Coldly to Treasury Note Auction," said the Wall Street Journal.

"The U.S. Gets Foreign Aid," declared Newsweek in a write-up that went on to tell of legislation before the House of Representatives that would require foreigners to register with the U.S. government if they planned to invest more than five million dollars in an American company. The investment of foreign capital was vital to the U.S. in returning dollars lost due to the massive trade deficit.

Charles and Ken talked of nothing else. Bill Morita had been strangely out of touch and never seemed to be at his desk when his phone rang. Apprehension and anxiety became Charles' constant companions. Finally, one week before the scheduled Treasury auction, Morita called.

"Heard the rumors about the bond boycott?" he asked, the smugness in his voice making it evident that he knew full well that there had been little else on their minds.

"What is it that your people want from us?" Charles could not hide the fear he'd lived with for the past week. If they went to his father with the information about his relationship with Ken, his father would disown him, his career could be ruined, but most devastating of all, he knew he'd never see Ken again. He'd do anything to prevent this.

"Relax, Chuckie. A word or two from people in the right places shouldn't be too hard for you to manage. If the Chairman of the Federal Reserve were to speak out against protectionism and unfair trade barriers, and the Secretary of Commerce were to put a little pressure on congress to eliminate unfair legislation, it would go a long way toward eliminating the need for retaliatory action. As a player in international economic trends, you ought to have some influence, right Chuckie-boy?"

Ken's reaction to the demands frightened Charles even more than he had been before. He blamed Charles for putting him in an untenable position, angrily asking how the hell he was supposed to tell his father that he had to pressure members of congress. What if Grant Williamson turned out to be an isolationist? He wouldn't change his mind just because his son asked him to. Ken had no idea what his father's attitudes were when it came to the Japanese, and it infuriated him that it was necessary for him to care.

"Maybe you won't have to ask him. He and my dad must know each other by now and they must have exchanged viewpoints on this kind of thing." Charles was desperate to make peace.

"Just how the hell does anybody pressure members of congress, anyway? I know that bribery is out of the question."

"Morita said that an official letter urging cooperation and signed by a cabinet member as well as the Fed would go a long way toward stopping the passage of legislation that they consider prejudicial. And press coverage, some sort of editorializing."

Charles was in luck. In a phone conversation with his father, he indicated that economists in his acquaintance were gravely concerned by the possibility of a Japanese boycott of U.S. treasury bonds and that everyone agreed that congress was over-reacting to the trade imbalance by proposing restrictive legislation. He discovered that not only did Bill Stuart and Grant Williamson know each other, they had discussed that very issue just the day before. The Chairman of the Fed was impressed by the suggestion from his son that he and the Secretary of Commerce write a joint letter to congress.

In a matter of days, a letter addressed to the House of Representatives was read into the record. It said, in part, that legislation of the sort that had been proposed would have a chilling effect on the excellent cooperation the U.S. was experiencing with the Japanese on behalf of an improved balance of trade.

Shortly after that, the Chairman of the Fed was interviewed by a reporter from the Associated Press and wire services throughout the country picked up his comment that protectionism was not the answer to free trade with Japan.

Interest rates increased to attract buyers as bids came in slowly. Traders and economists watched their computer screens anxiously and at the last moment a surge of bids came in from the big four Japanese bond traders. Not only was participation significant, it reached record highs as nearly eighty percent of the issue went to Japanese investors. The crisis had been averted and Americans could relax, their continued affluence assured.

Alone in his apartment, Charles wept with relief. His personal crisis had been alleviated in that his father thought highly of his ability instead of being disgusted by his lifestyle. Ken remained distant, but

Charles lived with the hope that he would realize that it was their destiny to be together.

A week or so later, a pair of very expensive leather attaché cases were delivered to the apartments of the two men. A card enclosed with each read, "For a job well done."

# CHAPTER SEVENTEEN

Though the news was sadly received by those who knew him, it didn't even make the papers in Memphis and went completely unnoticed by most of the world.

> "Friends and relatives of Tommy Durand, General Manager of the Nippon Auto plant near Jackson, were saddened to learn of his death in a boating accident. An avid fisherman, Durand had apparently gone out alone last Saturday. When he failed to report to the plant on Monday, officials began a search that led to the discovery of his overturned boat. Durand's body was found soon after that, and cause of death is listed as drowning by authorities who stressed the importance of not going out on the water alone. Tommy Durand was extremely popular among employees of the plant, many of whom cited his efforts on behalf of the nearly two hundred who were laid off recently."

Even in death, Tommy Durand could not escape his childhood nickname.

In Illinois, just outside of Chicago, Dan Whiting switched on the lights in his office. Refrigerated trucks used in long distance hauling of fresh produce were beginning to crowd the company yard. As drivers finished their runs, they were coming back empty and many had already gone home to their families, leaving their trucks behind. The yard could turn into a real traffic jam if somebody didn't get out there to establish some order.

Dan had been a driver at one time, but had moved into the office as a dispatcher several years ago when his arthritis made it impossible to sit in the cab of a truck for long hours. He had assumed the post of president of the local union a couple of years later and took his position seriously.

The publicity surrounding the layoff of two hundred auto plant workers in Tennessee had incensed drivers who serviced the area. The mysterious death of the plant manager had put a damper on efforts to reestablish jobs and many of the truckers now urged support from their union. It had been a snowball effect as interstate drivers carried the message, and Dan knew it wouldn't take much to turn the current slowdown into a full blown strike.

The United Auto Workers unions in Michigan had had several slowdown days in recent weeks and word was spreading that an all-out strike was imminent there as well.

Dan had been surprised by the silence on the part of the Japanese plant owners. Union membership was usually discouraged by Japanese companies that promoted the idea that the well-being of the worker depended upon the well-being of the company. As a rule, loyalty was a primary quality. What was their strategy? You never could figure out what went on in the inscrutable oriental mind.

Sympathy was on the rise for farm workers in California, too, which was another reason the produce drivers were thinking in terms of strikes. It hadn't been too long ago that the Teamsters and the United Farm Workers had been at odds when the Teamsters tried to organize farm labor in the early seventies. Bitter disputes on recruitment had finally resulted in an agreement with farm labor leaders in 1977.

Being expelled from the AFL-CIO in 1957 when the membership refused to oust reputed mob leaders had not slowed Teamster growth. The decade from 1964 to 1974 had seen a gain in membership that exceeded every other union despite the continuing controversy over its leadership. Only recently had it been allowed to rejoin the AFL-CIO when its bargaining power was acknowledged as unquestionable due to the significant portion of all goods that are moved from factory to store by truck, giving Teamsters power over employers unequaled by any other union.

With a membership of nearly two million, if the Teamsters don't move, nothing moves. The thought gave Dan Whiting an adrenalin rush.

It was dusk in California as George Hagura climbed up onto the rickety platform to address the hundreds of migrant families that had gathered there. His eyes misted as he looked out over the sea of sunburned faces—faces aged beyond their years by long hours in the fields and the never-ending struggle to earn enough to put food in the mouths of children who would only grow up to do the same thing.

Hands that were rough and often bleeding from the work began to clap as cheers filled the air. Cheers for him, George Hagura, child of a Japanese burakumin family, shunned by his own countrymen and now a source of hope to these tired laborers.

The lettuce boycott ahead would be the biggest event in the effort to achieve labor contracts since the legendary boycott of California table grapes led by Cesar Chavez in 1968. Already workers were beginning slowdowns in the fields. Each morning at eleven o'clock, field hands sat down wherever they happened to be, refusing to pick over the noon hour when the sun was at its peak. Soon there would be an all out strike against growers who refused to negotiate.

George could hardly wait to announce his upcoming meeting with the former California governor, Jerry Brown, who was an ardent supporter of human rights for the migrant workers. They would be discussing the march on Sacramento that was planned for the following month. Governor Brown had promised crowds of marchers that might well number in the hundreds of thousands. Growers would be forced to capitulate when produce began to rot in the fields.

Victor Buchanan, former president of the United States, looked around the White House dining room at the faces of the dignitaries invited to eat with the Japanese prime minister. He pasted a slight smile on his lips that made it seem he was listening intently to the ramblings of the elder statesman at his side and allowed himself a moment to reminisce.

Whatever happened to the lovely young woman who had been his administrative assistant for a time, he wondered. Perhaps he could slip away later and give her a call. Such silky skin. Such supple arms. She'd be older now, of course, but no doubt more experienced as well, offering more scintillating caresses than she had as a nubile ingénue.

Victor's close ties with the Japanese had been responsible for the invitation to this evening's dinner. The current president was such a klutz in foreign policy that he needed all the help he could get.

Victor looked for Pamela, his wife, and saw her across the room speaking to The First Lady. Thank God for Pamela, he thought. She's a pro. Knows just what to say to everyone, and God knew it was a crapshoot with The President's wife. Talk of The First Lady's escapades was escalating. The story of her romp on the White House lawn, eluding the Secret Service and generally causing them a great deal of grief, was spreading around Washington, and had more than likely spread far beyond as well.

Satoshi Yoshida, the old scoundrel, was present this evening, too, acting like he was the best friend America had ever had when everybody knew about his years in the hoosegow after the war. But he's one of the richest men in the world and we all want a piece of it, thought Victor, and I'm no different from the rest. Makes it easier to ignore his past.

Yoshida was leaning his grizzled head toward The President, apparently fascinated by whatever he was saying. The ever present scraps of paper began to appear as he pulled one after another from pockets. The President waited for whatever it was that Yoshida was searching for, then took his arm and led him through a door that Victor knew led to a study used for last minute briefing before the arrival of invited guests. What was *that* all about?

Yoshida, too, knew about The First Lady's problems and had told The President about a laboratory near Tokyo where a brilliant young Japanese scientist was inches away from establishing a cure for Alzheimer's disease. He stressed that it was Alzheimer's rather than senile dementia.

"Such a terrible disease," Yoshida said, shaking his head in sympathy. "It strikes even the greatest of human beings without warning." He conveyed the idea that no one would think that The First Lady could be senile, just ill with a terrible disorder.

The circles under The President's eyes were evidence of his distress and Yoshida wanted to help. Obviously a very caring man.

The Vice President was concerned as well. The situation was really becoming impossible. The First Lady seemed to be all right, for the moment anyway, but who knew when she might take it into her head to invite all the guests to join her for a dip in the sprinklers? And where the hell was The President going with Yoshida? He should be keeping an eye on his wife, not vanishing with the one guest he should keep at a distance.

American diplomatic relations were headed for disaster if this kept up. The Vice President could hardly wait for the next election. Another few months and maybe his candidacy would be public knowledge—if The President would admit that he did not wish to run again, that is.

In the anteroom, The President took the crumpled piece of paper offered by Yoshida, stuffed it into his own pocket and then grasped the old man's hand in gratitude. As they opened the door to rejoin the others, The President heard the string quartet in the corner playing a medley of songs that had been Mario Lanza favorites from the fifties, songs that he and his wife always asked to be played at these gatherings because they held so many memories of the early days of their romance. The music began with 'Be My Love,' then melted into 'Because,' and finished with 'The Loveliest Night of the Year.'

The President's eyes met those of his lady as she moved toward him, swaying a little in time to the music. Conversations in the room ceased as she crossed the room. The sound of cello, bass and violins became an overture in anticipation of a love scene as the curtain rose on a romantic opera.

The fifty or so guests were transfixed as The First Lady reached her husband and wound her arms around his neck. The smile on her lips as she looked into his eyes recalled all the sweetness that their love had known from its beginning. His right arm circled her waist as his left arm guided her slowly into dance position.

The guests held their collective breath lest they interrupt the exquisite vignette being played before their eyes. They were witnessing a very special moment between lovers and each was careful not to be the cause of distraction. It was one of those moments to be treasured and recalled over and over as they told friends and family of their evening at the White House.

Yoshida remained in the doorway to the anteroom and thought to himself that his discovery of The President's Achilles heel was fortuitous indeed. The old warrior, master strategist on the battlefield, would be the slave of anyone who promised help for his beloved wife.

# CHAPTER EIGHTEEN

It was mid-morning of the next day in Tokyo. Sunao Tokumura was at his desk reviewing the file labeled 'Nito Ryu,' or Two Sword School, and marked 'TOP SECRET' in large letters. The smile that it brought to his lips as it grew thicker with each passing day was one that he kept hidden until he was alone.

The term Nito Ryu had a double meaning. Musashi used the words to describe the style of fencing that used a sword in each hand when all of one's resources were required. In this case, the two swords also referred to Sunao Tokumura and Satoshi Yoshida.

It was astounding how much could be accomplished when two of Japan's greatest minds pooled their resources in a joint effort. The vice minister tried not to think about how Yoshida had brought about the developments under his direction. It was enough to know that the results would be devastating to the Americans. Tokumura was impatient to reach the culmination point of the plan that was so rapidly falling into place.

As for his own achievements, the Ministry of International Trade and Industry provided him with the power to bring about the devaluation of the dollar and the heavy lending to American business. It also offered a forum for manipulating Japanese business into cautious investment in U.S. treasury bonds. The initial slow response to the offering, followed by increased bond purchases would lull America into a false sense of security prior to the ultimate disaster that lay ahead when future bond issues failed to raise funds that they had to have in order to make the interest payments on existing issues. Very soon, America would not only be dependent upon Japan, it would be at her mercy.

The rumor of a bond boycott had been a temporary ploy to remind them of their place. Somehow, Yoshida had managed to find the key to maneuvering both the chairman of the Federal Reserve and the new Secretary of Commerce into siding with the Japanese. The spirit of economic partnership had been confirmed and the strategy was fully operative. Tokumura did not want to know the details of Yoshida's actions.

The union strikes that loomed would cripple the country when crops rotted in the fields and those that made it to trucks were left at the side of the road by striking truckers. Now they must prevent intervention by The President in the name of national emergency. Tokumura made a note to bring up that possibility with Yoshida upon his return from Washington.

The computer virus was pure genius. At a crucial moment, as the country was preoccupied with empty shelves in grocery stores, all transactions on the New York Stock Exchange would be wiped out. Bank deposits would disappear, rendering it impossible for the American public to pay for goods that they couldn't get anyway. And, given the American code of justice, committed as it was to 'inalienable rights,' criminals whose records vanished from the system would be free to roam the streets. It awaited only the determination of a specific date for activation and the now imminent release of the new IBM MVS system.

Sunao Tokumura's only regret was that the emperor, a direct descendent of Amaterasu, goddess of the sun, might never know who had brought about the destruction of the Rising Sun's greatest enemy. The recognition that he deserved might lie unclaimed.

Akiko Mitsunari took her time walking from the Kabukiza Theatre in Tokyo's famed Ginza District. She headed toward Hibiya Park across the moat from the emperor's palace where she intended to catch the subway home. She could have gotten on in the Ginza and then transferred, but she enjoyed the hurly burly, polychromatic confusion of the crowded sidewalks.

She stopped often to gaze at window displays of sensuous fabrics, sybaritic paintings and elegant antiques. Going to the kabuki theatre always gave her a heightened appreciation of the beautiful She had been fascinated by the world of make believe from childhood and had delighted her family with small productions of her own which she based on fables told to her by her grandmother.

She had played all the parts herself, rushing behind a curtain to make costume changes. Though her formal education had ended with high school, she had collected theatre programs and books on kabuki and noh plays for years. Most of her collection remained at her parent's house, but she spent much of her time re-reading the plays and pouring over the programs that she kept hidden under the bed she shared with her husband.

Whenever she managed to save enough money from her household funds, Akiko treated herself to an afternoon of escape. Stan was only vaguely aware of her love of the theatre and, she thought, probably wouldn't care much anyway. He was much too busy and had little interest in how she occupied her time.

The earliest noh plays had been rustic performances in fields or exhibitions by jugglers and acrobats in the thirteenth century, featuring comic servants who played tricks on their daimyos. Kabuki had been established in the sixteenth century by the merchants of the day who, though wealthy and powerful, were still considered commoners.

The players then were principally women and the spectators were often more interested in their beauty than in their performances. Authorities, concerned that this would lead to demoralization of the public, officially banned the appearance of women in 1629. Since that time, all female parts had been played by males known as onnagata. Many of the noh plays had been adapted for the kabuki theatre which places primary importance on the actor rather than the literary aspect of the drama.

One of Akiko's favorite plays was the story of the beautiful Komachi, who had been cruel to her many lovers in her youth, mocking their ardor. One, a young man named Shosho, came many miles to see her. She had told him that she would not listen to his pleas until he had come on a hundred nights from his house to hers, and had cut a hundred notches on the bench of his chariot. Shosho had come through rain, hail, snow and wind for ninety nine nights in a row, but on the hundredth night he died.

As Komachi grew old, her beauty disappeared and she wandered in destitution, a tattered and crazy beggar-woman, often possessed by the spirit of her lover, Shosho.

Sometimes Akiko stood in front of her mirror reciting her favorite lines from the play:

"Crowned with nodding tresses, halcyon locks,
I walked like a young willow delicately wafted
By the winds of spring . . .
Westward with the moon I creep
From the cloud-high City of the Hundred Towers."

She sometimes wondered if she could be a reincarnation of the cruel Komachi. Perhaps it was her karma to do penance for Komachi's pitiless behavior, receiving no reward for her devotion to her husband. She had waited night after night, far more than the one hundred nights of Shosho's journeys, for any small kindness, any loving gesture. Her heart had soared until she thought it might crack under the weight of her happiness when Stan took her to Hawaii, but she had been thrust back into the void where she lingered. Would her beauty vanish as had Komachi's? Was she, too, doomed to lose her faculties and drift, possessed by her love, through her days?

Could Stan be Shosho come back to spurn the attentions of the one who had caused him so much pain so many centuries ago? Akiko knew that Stan was not intentionally cruel, merely unmindful of her at all. Was she doomed to love him as poor Shosho had loved Komachi, until she died? That would be the cruelest joke of all.

Akiko wore the scarf that Stan had insisted upon buying in Honolulu. She loved the rich colors—blues and purples that melted together. She loved the way it felt around her neck and fingered it constantly. Sometimes she peeked at her image reflected in store windows, tossing her head a little so that the fabric fluttered gently. It gave her hope that her husband really did care for her and was only distracted by the pressure of his job where deadlines were critical. He had been so kind, so generous, and yes, so loving in Hawaii. Surely that meant something.

Her mind wandered back to that lovely first day. She could still taste the croissants that melted in her mouth, the butter that had dribbled down her chin. She could still feel her husband's hand in hers as they strolled through Kapiolani Park to the Waikiki hotel district. And if she concentrated, she could still see the expression in his eyes as he made love to her.

She was concentrating very hard as she stepped off the curb. The big bus that carried a full load of American tourists had no chance of stopping and hit her squarely. The scarf around her neck caught on the bumper guard and she was dragged for several feet before the huge vehicle came to a stop.


Stan was in his office, his work finished for the day. He sat back in his chair and rubbed his eyes. There was certainly a lot going on in the States these days, what with so many of the unions going on strike. Many of the issues were cloudy at best. It seemed to have begun with small grievances that took on added importance as workers in other unions walked out in sympathy.

He had been in constant attendance on the wire services communications for several days. That was probably why he noticed the short paragraph noting the sale of twenty percent of the Davidson Hotel Group stock to an unknown company with a Caribbean charter. Odd, he thought. Why would Maggie sell such a significant portion of her stock? It wouldn't matter much in the overall picture since she still controlled eighty percent, but she must have some sort of cash flow problem or she'd never have let an outsider into the company. Had acquisition of the Hawaiian property put the Davidson Group in jeopardy?

The blurb ended by noting the retirement of three executives with longtime service to the hotels. Another surprise. Three top management people at a time. Trouble in paradise? Stan's attitude was one of ambivalence. Part of him wanted to pick up the phone, call Maggie, and offer to help her out in any way he could. Knight to the rescue.

But another part of him said she was perfectly capable of running her own company, and if she wasn't, she deserved whatever she got. She certainly looked like a confident executive these days, if that was any criteria for judgment. The two women in his life couldn't be more different, he thought. Maggie's soft blonde curls and delicate face had sometimes made him afraid to touch her for fear she might break. In contrast, Akiko's long dark mane lying on a snowy white pillow made him think of the lush and shadowy clouds that sometimes hid the sun on a late summer day.

His guilt had been increasing with each day that passed since their return from Hawaii. He had had such good intentions. He really meant to treat Akiko with the love and respect that she deserved. It had started out so well. He had actually looked at her and realized how lovely she was. Any man with eyes could see that she was beautiful. Although he had done his best to ignore it for the past ten years, he knew in his heart that she loved him and that it would take very little to make her happy.

It dawned on him suddenly that he had no idea what she did with her time when he was away from her. Their apartment was small so he was sure she didn't spend much time doing housework. Since he was hardly ever there for meals, she didn't spend much time in the kitchen, either. What did she do? Perhaps if he spent more time with her, he'd find out.

There were times when he regretted having gone to college in the States. Though the University of Missouri had a fine school of journalism and the learning experience had given him advantages he otherwise would not have had, it had clouded his nationality, often presenting conflicting loyalties. He saw the world through eyes that were sometimes Japanese, sometimes American, and that left him perched on the lip of a cauldron, teetering precariously. It would be so much easier to be one or the other.

He straightened in his chair and looked at his watch. It was not quite six o'clock in the evening. After a moment's reflection, he made a sudden decision and rose quickly, putting on his suit jacket and hurrying through the office to the elevator that took him to the lobby. It was time that he took note of Akiko and of what gave her pleasure. It was a sure bet that she'd be responsive to any suggestions he might make regarding his own pleasure. Didn't he owe her at least the same consideration?

The scarf that he'd bought her in Honolulu had made her happy, he recalled. He'd buy her another gift, something really special. He looked up and down the street for a taxi, then concluded that the subway would be faster.

The jewelry shop was located on the third level of a building in the heart of the Ginza, and was owned by an old friend of his father whose father had built a fine reputation by specializing in cultured pearls. The son carried on the business and would know just what Stan should buy for his wife.

A short time later, he was standing before a tray of pins fashioned in gold scrolled around the most perfect pearls in the shop. Some had gemstones that glittered in the light. He picked up one in the shape of a lotus blossom, its petals made of pearls with a center of amethyst and rose quartz. The Buddhist symbol of perfection that grew out of the mud. Like many Japanese, Akiko adhered to a combination of religious ideas. She visited Shinto shrines to honor her ancestors as well as Buddhist temples to pray for access to the secrets of nirvana. The lotus blossom might please her.

Holding the pin in one hand, he ran the index finger of his other hand over the pins that remained in the tray. Another caught his eye. It was a tree with jade leaves and a garland of pearls woven through the branches. In a burst of romanticism, it occurred to Stan that he might write a short poem telling Akiko that he would be her tree, sheltering her from harm and protecting her from injury. He was, after all, supposed to be a writer.

Either one would be lovely fastened to the scarf. He held them, looking from one to the other, then carried them to the window that overlooked the street. A flash of color in the street below caught his eye and he recognized Akiko wearing the very blue and purple scarf that he was thinking of as he chose a pin to hold it in place. It must be a sign!

He tapped on the window to attract her attention even though he knew full well that she would never hear him. The tap became a frantic pounding as he saw the tour bus headed straight at her and realized that she was unaware of its presence. What could she be thinking of? He screamed her name as she stepped off the curb, but even had the window been open, she would not have heard his voice above the screech of brakes and the din of other traffic. He watched in horror as the scarf caught on the bumper of the bus. A burst of bright red mingled with the blue and purple of the scarf as she was thrown beneath the wheels and dragged along.

He would be unable to remember how he got from the shop to the street, nor would he know that horrified spectators parted, allowing him to reach her as she lay on the pavement. He gathered her bloody form in his arms, trying frantically to separate the tattered fabric and long dark hair from the shredded skin of her once lovely face.

She moaned almost inaudibly and opened her eyes to stare into his, the corners of her mouth turning upward just the slightest bit as she recognized him. Her strength gone, she went limp as he held her and her eyes closed one final time. Panic and fear rose in his throat, but no sound came from his mouth. A hand grasped his arm, pulling gently in an effort to make him let her go, but he held her close to his chest, rocking her lifeless body.

In the blur of the next few days, he would remember the faces that looked down at him—the faces of American tourists from the bus. He made a decision. He would be Japanese and only Japanese from that day forward.

# CHAPTER NINETEEN

"**A**re you sure you can trust him?" Yoshida asked. He turned from the window of his penthouse office, his fists digging into the pockets of the raggedy sweater that he wore.

Sunao Tokumura spoke quietly, but firmly. "His wife was killed two weeks ago by a tour bus full of Americans. If he had any doubts about where his loyalty lies, they were dispelled by the sight of her lying in a pool of blood surrounded by gaijin faces. Added to the insult to his heritage by the family of the American girl, his wife's death left him with nothing but loathing for Americans."

"Hmmm . . . ," Yoshida murmured, turning back to stare out the window once more. "It might be wise to keep his knowledge of Nito Ryu limited for the time being. The power he wields in the financial world has already been of great value without his knowledge, but let us see how well he uses it to stoke the engines of revenge. We have come too far and we are too close to our goal to allow anyone to stop us."

"The new IBM system is ready for distribution. It has been released to a small test group and should be fully operative soon. You are sure that the virus will be introduced as planned?"

"Yes." Yoshida's affirmative answer boomed. His aging body acquired renewed vigor at the thought and he moved from the window to his desk where he stood grinning at his bureaucratic counterpart in the plan. "I await the day with more gladness in my heart than I have felt in many years!"

"What is the date selected for activation?" Tokumura asked.

"December 28th," replied the older man. "As mainframe users of the system prepare to close their books at year end, every transaction will be wiped out. As soon as the date rolls over automatically, the virus kicks in. Since this will occur during the traditional Christian holiday week, many key personnel will be unavailable to reload the systems, adding to the chaos."

Tokumura smiled at Yoshida's enthusiasm. "That's only a little over two months from now," he said. "Is everything else going as planned?"

"The strikes are already crippling transportation and selective violence will escalate in coming weeks, further diverting the attention of the general public. Once these laborers get a taste of it, they seem to develop an addiction to it—momentary power, I suppose. The threat of a bond boycott was another effective diversion. Their economic dependency on us was reinforced and the Japan bashers in congress were silenced, at least temporarily, by the Federal Reserve chairman's comments regarding the destructive effects of protectionism. When the boycott becomes a reality, added to the effects of the computer failure, the ultimate blow will have been delivered. In the interim, we must continue our efforts to manipulate American opinion in our favor and encourage the elimination of unfavorable legislation.

"A series of articles by Stan Mitsunari, suggesting that criticism of Japanese trade policies is spawned by racism would keep the American bureaucrats anxious to placate the country upon which they depend so heavily. Do you think he would react favorably to such a series?" Yoshida finished.

"The timing couldn't be better. I'll meet with him as soon as possible," Tokumura responded.

Yoshida thought it best not to mention the purchase of twenty percent of the stock in Stan Mitsunari's former American girlfriend's hotel company. The reward for his services would be presented to him at the proper time. A hint might be in order, however. Everyone had his price.

"Tell him discreetly that he will not be sorry."

The following Friday, an editorial by the vice president and editor, Stan Mitsunari, appeared in the Nihon Keizai. Urging cultural unity, it supported the viewpoint that the success of Japanese electronics companies proved that Japan could succeed in any industrial undertaking, and that Japan was doing the United States an enormous favor by refining technology in the field of telecommunications satellites and semi-conductors.

On Tuesday of the week after that, another editorial suggested that Japan had the technology to change the world balance of power if she were to sell Japanese semi-conductors to the Soviet Union, denying them to the United States. The importance of strengthening Japan's geopolitical influence was stressed in a discussion of joint development of the FSX, a new fighter plane. To buy the F-16 from the Americans rather than developing their own model would not be in the best interests of the Japanese people, the column said. Japanese industry would be better served through the development of an indigenous plane. Military technology leads to civilian technology.

By the end of that week, editorials urging cooperation with the Japanese and warning against a policy of U.S. protectionism had begun to appear in the financial pages of nearly every major U.S. newspaper. Economic nationalists must end the Japan bashing and obsessing over the trade deficit. Import barriers had been falling in Japan, evidenced by their willingness to buy parts for the FSX from American manufacturers who were eager to bid on supplying them. Since the strengthening of the yen, Japan had been restructuring its economy toward a greater reliance on domestic demand as opposed to export performance as a stimulus to growth. Imports had increased by nearly forty-seven percent, proof that "Protectionism is no friend of the United States."

No one mentioned the acquisition of prime real estate across America that was also a result of the strong yen. Nor did anyone mention the fact that increasing percentages of stock in American financial institutions were being acquired through the strength of the yen. The relief that followed the averted bond boycott was relegated to the deepest recesses of the minds of gluttonous American consumers.

Bill Stuart stood on the curb in front of the Federal Reserve building in Washington, D.C., trying in vain to find a taxi. It was really getting to the point where The President should take steps to end the strikes that were plaguing the country, he thought. His wife had told him just yesterday that they would probably have to cancel a dinner party next week because she'd been unable to confirm her grocery order. People were starting to hoard, making it more and more difficult to find the little luxuries that made it possible to entertain well.

Bill had an uncomfortable feeling stirring in his gut. He couldn't quite put his finger on it, but there were so many odd things happening at once. It was almost as though there was some kind of conspiracy afoot. He shook off the idea immediately. It smacked of paranoia. Conspiracy required plotting of some sort and that was too absurd to consider.

Not far away from where Bill Stuart stood ruminating on the state of the states, Grant Williamson was frowning at the pile of letters on his desk. They were all from U.S. aircraft manufacturers, and without exception they were complaints that American commercial interests were being ignored in the debate over the Japanese FSX. As Secretary of Commerce, it fell to him to see to it that American businesses received priority treatment in the international market place. He was beginning to understand that this job was not going to be the piece of cake he'd thought it would be. Proper management was all that any government agency needed, he'd thought. Something often lacking in bureaucratic institutions that he was prepared to remedy.

He'd been so sure that the devaluation of the dollar would increase the purchasing power of the international community, and that American products would benefit. It seemed that there might be another, more complicated agenda on the board. The increased purchasing power was being put to use on a grander scale than automobiles and food products. Maybe it was time to re-evaluate his convictions.

He pulled out a yellow pad and began the rough draft of a letter to the Secretary of Defense regarding the manufacturer's complaints, suggesting that in their haste to provide the Japanese Air Self Defense Force with an up-to-date airplane, they were not adequately addressing the effect on American industry. The letter went out the following day and was soon on a desk in the Department of Defense. A harried aide who screened correspondence and kept the secretary's appointments book was just about to leave for lunch with a former White House staffer who was now lobbying for the Japanese defense industry. The aide was looking forward to a martini and the best meal he'd had in weeks, given the problem of empty shelves in grocery stores. It couldn't hurt to let the lobbyist know that the Secretary of Commerce was beginning to balk at the concessions being discussed at the FSX talks. It wasn't as though it was a matter of national security or anything.

A copy of the letter to the Secretary of Defense was sent to the Secretary of State along with a short cover letter indicating that the Secretary of Commerce thought that State should be aware of industry concerns as well, and should consider these concerns at the negotiating table.

The deputy secretary who read the letter had just finished going over the daily file of newspaper articles relevant to the ongoing trade talks with the Japanese. The discussions on the costs involved in similar programs in the U.S. and Japan were stalemated over use of the terms 'co-development' versus 'self-development,' with the Japanese delegation claiming that American designs did not meet Japanese parameters. Now was not the time to introduce the complaints of American manufacturers. The deputy secretary made an executive decision and slid the letter into a file. It was addressed to Defense, after all, and if they wanted to bring up the complaints, let them.

"Be neither insufficiently spirited

Nor over spirited

An elevated spirit is weak

And a low spirit is weak

Do not let the enemy see your spirit."

The Water Book

Book of Five Rings

Miyamoto Musashi

# CHAPTER TWENTY

That evening, Bill Morita received a phone call from a man in Washington, D.C., who did not identify himself, but who made it clear that the attitudes of the Fed chairman and the Secretary of Commerce were not as cooperative as they had been in recent weeks, and perhaps this unfortunate situation could be remedied through the use of further intimidation of their sons. The man had gone on to say that Bill's cooperation had not gone unnoticed by insiders on the international scene and hinted that a champion of justice such as he had proven himself to be was sure to be remembered by the organization. Bill was too elated by the words to notice that the man failed to specify just which organization he meant.

Bill was beside himself with happiness. He couldn't stand those two pompous faggots anyway. It would be a pleasure to lean on them some more. And he'd just heard that his acceptance into the society that had been his life-long dream was virtually assured. He allowed himself a few minutes of joyful reverie before picking up the phone to dial Charles Stuart's home number.

As Charles' phone rang, Ken Williamson was dialing his parent's number in Washington to tell them that he had met the girl of his dreams and planned to marry her on Thanksgiving weekend. He had not yet told Charles and was dreading the moment. He had been avoiding Charles for several weeks, during which he had spent much of his free time at his fiancée's home in Los Gatos where they rode horses, played tennis and golf, and soaked up the late summer sun beside a kidney-shaped pool.

"That's great news, son!" his father exclaimed.

"Where did you meet her?" his mother asked, listening on an extension.

"At an alumni fundraiser at Stanford," Ken explained. "She was a couple of years behind me in high school and graduated from Stanford a couple of years behind me as well. She remembered me from both football teams. I didn't remember her, but you might know her parents—the McDonalds from Los Gatos?"

"Know them well!" said Grant Williamson enthusiastically. "Mitch McDonald is one of the finest architects in the country."

"I played bridge with Marian McDonald for years," said his mother. "Isn't their daughter named Melanie?"

"Mellie, for short," Ken confirmed. "How come I didn't know her when we were growing up?"

"Probably because she *was* younger than you, and a girl as well, Ken. Well, well, well. Little Mellie's going to be our daughter-in-law. I couldn't be more pleased!" Grant's voice reflected the smile that Ken couldn't see.

Their conversation was interrupted by the pounding on Ken's door and Charles' voice calling out urgently.

"My neighbor's at the door, Mom. Gotta go. I'll call you on Saturday to fill you in on the wedding plans."

Ken put the phone down and heaved a sigh, wishing he could be nearly anywhere on earth but where he was at the moment. He knew he had to face Charles, and after all, it wasn't all Charles' fault. Ken had to take responsibility for the relationship, too. He hoped they might be able to remain friends, but given Charles' attitude, it didn't seem likely. Probably better to make a clean break so there was no chance of a leak. Mellie wouldn't understand and her parents would be horrified if they heard even a whisper about his affair. He was beginning to wish he'd never met Charles at all.

Within minutes, his fears threatened to suffocate him. "That weasel!" he cried. "No! He can't do this to me, not now! Oh, God, how did I get into this mire?"

"It was your dad's letter that got them in a snit, Ken," said Charles. "Why did he change his mind?"

"From the sound of it, he didn't really change his mind on the subject of cooperation, just on this one issue. Defense contracts are pretty touchy stuff and account for a whole lot of money changing hands. My guess is that the American contractors want their piece of the action and the Japanese are making it difficult for them to get it." Ken stopped talking, his mind racing in an effort to find a way out.

"The only thing we can do is make a clean break, Charles," he continued, fearing the reaction he was sure lay ahead. "If they have nothing to blackmail us about, they can't get anything from us."

Charles proved predictable. "No!" he cried as he sank into the chair across from Ken. "There must be another way!"

Ken felt sorry for Charles in spite of himself. "There's something else you don't know, Charles. I've been a coward about telling you, but I can't hide it any longer. You were right when you thought I was seeing someone else. I didn't want to tell you because I knew you'd take it badly, and no matter what you may think, I still don't want to hurt you."

Ken rose and crossed the room to where Charles kept his scotch, turning his back so he wouldn't have to look into Charles' eyes. "I'm getting married on Thanksgiving weekend."

For what seemed like an eternity, the only sound in the room was that of ice cubes clinking in the glasses as Ken stirred the drinks. Then a low moan as Charles acknowledged the truth he'd been trying desperately not to hear.

Ken's stomach lurched at the sound. Speaking softly and deliberately, he went on, "I've been thinking of moving most of my stuff into my parents' house in Pacific Heights over the next month or so, but if Morita is threatening us again, maybe I should do it right away and stay there myself until the wedding. Since Dad took the cabinet post, there's only the caretaker living there anyway, and I'm sure Mom would okay it. If we're not living so close together, they can't prove anything and if they do spread any rumors, we can just deny them." He was doing his best to keep the conversation from deteriorating into an emotional encounter. "It would be Morita's word against ours, and who'd believe someone we know only casually from a bar?"

Over the next few days, Charles could hear Ken carrying boxes of books and suitcases down the stairs. Then the movers arrived to load up the furniture Ken had decided to store until he and Mellie had found a place to live. The agony seemed endless, and yet it seemed to happen overnight. Charles didn't go into the office and refused to answer his phone at home. He drank himself to sleep at night and stayed in bed until noon each day, repeating the pattern again soon after his morning coffee woke him up.

It was dusk of the third day when Ken knocked on his door to say he was ready to leave for good. He was carrying a bottle of Chivas Regal and asked if Charles would join him in a farewell drink.

"I'm sincerely sorry that I've hurt you, Charles. I've never had such a close friend and I hope someday you'll be able to forgive me."

Charles wasn't sure whether he was hung over or still drunk from the night before, or maybe on his way to getting drunk again. But then, what difference did it make? He accepted the drink that Ken poured for him and raised the glass in a toast.

"To friendship. And love, wherever you may find it," he said. Downing the amber liquid in one long swallow, he held out his glass for another.

Ken filled the glass slowly and deliberately. "Charles," he began, "I don't think you're seeing this in a reasonable perspective. We got on so well together in the beginning. It was a relationship built on the kind of understanding that men don't always have in the competitive business world today. We trusted each other. We seemed to reinforce each other's self-worth. Maybe we needed the physical relationship to cement the bond."

He paused, searching for the right words to say what he had just begun to realize. "It's okay for women to share their emotions, their secrets, and to talk about pretty much anything they feel like talking about. It's also okay for them to touch each other, to be physical in their attitudes toward one another because they're the ones who nurture. Males are brought up to be comrades, share jokes, shake hands, pound each other on the back, but never let the other guy see you confused or uncertain, or, God forbid, cry. In some ways, that's the unnatural behavior. You and I became true friends and then went beyond proscribed behavior. Being lovers seemed to be a logical step because our feelings for each other weren't what we've come to expect they should be."

Charles stared at him, befuddled by his days of drinking, hearing but not really assimilating.

Ken went on, "Once we began the relationship, we didn't want to think of it as being temporary because we were going against society's mores and the only way to justify that was to consider ourselves committed to the relationship. Don't you see? I don't think you're really gay, any more than I am. We don't have to be lovers to love each other."

He stopped, intrigued and mildly excited by his own ideas, and seeing their friendship in a new light. His pleasure was short-lived, however, as he took note of the dullness in Charles' eyes. Defeated, he realized that he had to leave before Charles fell apart completely. For now, he could only hope that time and sobriety would help Charles find his way back.

"I hate to leave you like this, Charles. You don't want Morita to expose our relationship any more than I do, and if he sees you like this, it will confirm everything. Please," he implored, "you have to pull yourself together and get on with your life!"

Charles swayed drunkenly. "Yeah, yeah. Don't worry 'bout Morita. He won't see me like this 'cuz I'm not going anywhere."

"At least take a shower and eat something, then get a decent night's sleep. And get back to work before somebody starts checking up on why you're not there!" Ken began to edge toward the door, afraid that Charles might be on the verge of making a scene. He paused to look back at the wretched man who had meant so much to him. The golden head was disheveled, the blue eyes were vacant. Ken's own eyes burned and he longed to turn back to comfort Charles. Knowing that would only make it harder, he closed the door gently and went down the stairs.

As Ken's footsteps faded, the silence was overwhelming and tears ran from Charles' eyes as the feeling that he had nothing left swept over him. He stared into the crepuscular light of dusk, squinting at the little dust motes illuminated in the waning sun. Tiny little invaders, he thought, sneaking in without so much as a by-your-leave.


It was the first week of October, but who in San Francisco would know that it was fall? There was no visible sign, no leaves turning color, drifting from the trees. No curbside fires, carefully tended, to dispose of the piles of leaves that had so recently been crackling beds for children's games. No gleeful shouts as small arms flung bundles of red, gold, yellow and brown skyward, their faces turned upward in simple pleasure as the leaves fell to earth again. Only the fog slowly obliterating the sunlight, a preface to winter, turning everything cold and grey.

Charles wept for his childhood and longed to be a kid again, playing in the leaves, running from his father's feigned ire as he brandished a rake, the sweet smell of cider wafting from his mother's kitchen. Why do we have to grow up? Why is the world such a complicated place to be?

Even as a teenager, the most difficult thing he'd had to face was the prospect of poor grades on a history test. There had been so much to look forward to. He'd known very early on that he would follow his father's footsteps in the field of finance. Given Bill Stuart's position and reputation, Charles had had a foot in the door before anyone knew that he'd knocked. At seventeen, he'd been a player in foursomes on the golf course that included some of the most important men in the world of money and banking.

Charles had never considered being 'gay' and probably would have had to stop and think about what the intricacies of being gay meant. He had never been turned on by men's bodies, either. He'd spent more time in the men's locker room at the country club than he had in the boy's locker room off the gymnasium. The men who used the one at the country club didn't make smarmy jokes about females like the boys at school had. They'd talked about more important things, things that really mattered.

Ken had been the first person who didn't expect anything from him other than his companionship. The first who didn't need a reason to brag about a son, husband, or employee. The first who didn't set standards for him to live up to. The first to like him for himself. Oh, God. He couldn't live without Ken. He needed Ken more than air to breathe or food to eat.

Charles picked up the bottle of Chivas that Ken had left and poured another drink, downed it and poured another. He peered at the air where the little creatures of the dusk had been hovering and saw that they had vanished. Had they followed Ken, sticking with the winner, abandoning the loser?

If it hadn't been for that rat, Morita, none of this would have happened. People like him shouldn't be allowed to live among decent people. Or at least they should have to wear a sign that identified them for what they were. He'd be doing the world a favor if he eliminated Morita.

He was swirling the scotch in his glass, seeing the face of his enemy reflected in the liquid, when his phone rang as though cued by some invisible prompter.

"Chuck? You've been a naughty boy, Chuckie. You haven't done what you were supposed to do and you haven't been answering your phone. I might have to make another call and you don't want me to do that, do you Chuckie?'

Charles' lips curled in a snarl at the sound of the familiar voice. He seethed at the vicious use of the nickname that no one had ever used in addressing him. Staring at the receiver with unbridled malice, what he had to do became startlingly clear in an instant. He hid his anger and proposed that they get together at the bar where they'd met several weeks earlier. They could discuss the matter over a drink.

His brain clouded as it was by alcohol, Charles still knew that to convince Morita he was in control, he had to clean up. He showered and put on jeans and a baggy sweater, then looked at his face in the mirror and decided not to shave. He grabbed a cap to cover his blonde hair and was ready to leave. His head had cleared just enough to conceal the effects of the scotch, but not enough to chase away the demons that made him dangerous.

He drove carefully, not too slow, not too fast. Wouldn't want to get stopped by the cops. Each red light seemed to detain him longer than he thought necessary as he made his way out Geary Street to Morita's hangout. It would be perfect. No one knew him there, and certainly no one would expect a Federal Reserve Bank economist to be frequenting such a place. He passed the place once and drove around the block, checking out the traffic, pedestrian as well as auto. He chose a spot to park on a side street well away from street lights, and made his way back to the bar.

His nose wrinkled involuntarily as the smell of stale beer invaded his nostrils. An arm went up in the gloom and he moved toward it, assuming it was Morita. As he approached, Morita got up from the stool where he'd been sitting and motioned for Charles to follow him to a booth near the back of the bar.

"Your lover's daddy is being very uncooperative, Chuckie. He wrote another letter, but this one worries my friends. They liked it better when he and your daddy were telling the politicians that protectionism was bad. What happened?"

Charles glanced over his shoulder to see if there was anyone close enough to hear their conversation. "Don't call him my lover," he hissed. "And why don't you ask the secretary himself what his policies are? Or ask *his* son, not me?"

"Because it's more fun this way, Chuckie. I like your lover boy better than I like you, so it gives me a jiggle to put the screws on you. Now what are you going to do about this? Or have you decided to 'fess up and tell daddykins that you're getting it on with another guy, though why a guy like that would do it with you is beyond me."

Charles was beginning to sweat. It was all he could do to keep from reaching across the table to turn Morita's face to pulp with his fists. He forced himself to breathe.

"Why don't we get out of here?" he suggested. "Is there a back door?"

Morita chuckled. "What's the matter? Don't want to be seen with me anymore?"

"You got it," Charles said, rising.

"Okay, okay. My car's out back anyway. We can talk there, but don't get too long winded. I'm thirsty and this bar doesn't provide curb service."

Charles followed the little man through a curtain and down a hallway to a back door that led to the alley beyond. Neither man spoke until they were in the car. Morita turned so that he was leaning against the door on the driver's side, his left arm looped around the steering wheel. In the darkness, he failed to see the knife that Charles had removed from his belt. Sure that he had the upper hand, he was supremely confident. His death was quick as stabbings go because Charles was lucky and plunged the knife into his heart on the first try.

Later, it would all seem a bit surreal to Charles. He watched Morita's eyes widen in shock as the knife came out and blood began to ooze from the wound. He hadn't touched anything but the door handles. He was careful to pull the sleeve of his sweater down before opening the door from the inside, removing his fingerprints. Wiping the outer door handle, he took a last look at the eyes that remained open in surprise, the hand that clutched a bloody chest.

"So long, Billy," he said.

The knife had surprisingly little blood on it. Charles walked to a dumpster a few steps down the alley and picked up a fast food bag that lay on top. Concealing the knife inside, he left the alley and turned away from Geary Street to make his way back to where he'd left his own car a block away.

When he got back to his apartment, he dumped the bag into the sink, pushed the decaying food into the disposal and washed the knife clean. No one would think to look for a murder weapon in his kitchen since no one knew he'd been anywhere near Morita. Better to know where it was than chance the cops finding it and tracing it back to him. He held it up to the light and smiled before putting it back in the drawer where it belonged. Carrying the paper bag and food wrappers into the living room, he tossed them into the fireplace and watched as they disappeared in the flames.

Sure that he'd done everything that needed to be done to conceal his crime, he picked up the glass that was still on the table beside his reading chair, carried it to the kitchen, rinsed it out and filled it with fresh ice. He went back to the living room and poured Chivas Regal to the rim. The more he drank, the more convinced he became that he had taken the only course open to him.

Morita had been a menace in his life and he had eliminated the menace. Now Ken would have no reason to leave him. All he had to do was say that he had taken care of things, can't say how, but Ken would realize that his friendship was far too valuable to lose. Even if he did go through with the marriage, eventually he'd realize that Charles was more important to him than any woman could be.

It never occurred to him that whoever was behind Morita's actions might retaliate. He thought only of Ken as he sipped from the glass until it fell from his hand when he passed out.

# CHAPTER TWENTY ONE

"**S**hit!" The Secretary of Labor bellowed, slamming the phone down following the latest threat of a permanent plant closure as strikes lingered on with no settlement in sight. Without exception, his calls throughout the morning had been decidedly unfriendly in nature as union representatives and company managements alike called for government intervention. Labor leaders were no longer able to define negotiation points and workers were growing more and more unruly. Plant owners saw profits disappearing and angry stockholders were raising hell.

To make matters worse, non-union construction projects in California had suddenly been halted as loans were inexplicably called in by lenders when contractors were unable to meet payment deadlines due to strike related slowdowns and their inability to get necessary materials from suppliers.

The secretary wiped beads of sweat from his brow. What the hell was going on? It certainly wasn't in anybody's best interest to call loans on projects that were at least keeping *some* of the work force on the job. He scribbled the names of the construction projects affected on a yellow pad and buzzed his secretary.

"See what you can find out about the lenders on these projects," he directed, "and make notes on any similarities you find."

Late that afternoon, she knocked on his door and handed him a neatly typed page divided into columns with the companies affected in the first, the type of project in the second, and the lenders in the third. The companies were all mid-sized outfits and the projects were office buildings, apartment complexes and shopping centers. Each of four banks appeared repeatedly in the third column. Two had Japanese names, one was a Canadian bank that had recently been purchased by Japanese interests, and sixty percent of the stock in the fourth was under Japanese control.

The labor secretary picked up his phone and punched in the number for the vice president's office. Maybe *he* could shed some light on why The President was dragging his feet. Upon hearing the vice president's voice, he wasted no time on pleasantries.

"We have a serious problem here! Japanese banks in California are suddenly calling loans on construction companies! I thought we were all palsy-walsy with them again since the bond boycott rumor. With teamsters and farm workers out on strike and construction coming to a screeching halt, half the country is out of work and the other half can't buy anything because there's nothing being delivered to the stores!"

"Are you sure this isn't just another threat to get us to toe the line on protectionism?" The vice president couldn't believe what was happening on his watch.

"The way I understand it, it's a done deal. The loans have actually been called. We have to find out what's going on in the inscrutable oriental mind and do some fast talking or we're facing total disaster!"

The vice president's mind was racing. Another damaging blow to the administration. If he didn't get a handle on things, the election was lost before the campaign even started, and if the election was lost, so was his career. He could kiss the presidency goodbye.

"I'll get back to you," he said tersely and pressed the disconnect button with his finger, lifting it again to dial Zach Templeton's office. If anybody could get some swift answers, it would be Zach. He'd grumbled about the number of ministries that had to be consulted during the auto plant negotiations, including the Ministry of Finance. Maybe he could get through to the right people.

As the vice president waited to be connected, it occurred to him that developing a good rapport with Zach could lead to substantial support from the grass roots political organizations in Tennessee. Minutes later, he had Zach's promise to find out whatever he could. In less than twenty-four hours, Zach was reporting his conversation with Vice Minister Nobuya Saito.

"He seemed surprised to hear about it and stalled with the usual evasions, to wit: it was probably coincidental and the banks do have a professional obligation to protect their stockholders and depositors from losses, and considering the unsettled conditions that were affecting so many Americans, it was only prudent that they maintain sound fiscal policies." Zach let the sentence run on intentionally as he cited Saito's equivocations.

"When I asked point blank whether it might have been a directive from his ministry, he was emphatic that it was not and said he'd discuss it with his associates, whoever they might be," Zach finished.

In Japan, Saito was puzzled. As he always did when he needed a moment to think about things, he removed his glasses, pulled a handkerchief from his pocket and rubbed the lenses absentmindedly. He recalled the conversation he'd had with Vice Minister Tokumura in recent weeks during which they had discussed the idea that construction loans in California meant higher returns for Japanese stockholders, and would serve a secondary goodwill purpose through the notion that funds on deposit would be inserted back into the local economies.

He had no idea why the loans had been called so abruptly. What had he missed? He put a note on his secretary's desk asking her to please make an appointment for him with the vice minister at MITI at his earliest convenience. A short time later, she informed him that unfortunately, Vice Minister Tokumura's calendar was exceptionally full. It could be a week or more. If it was important, perhaps one of the vice minister's deputies could discuss the matter and submit a report for consideration.

Saito pondered the dilemma and decided to seek answers elsewhere for the time being. He hesitated to call the Minister of Finance, Hideki Watanabe, as such a call might indicate that he was not doing his job adequately. He would go directly to the officers of the banks in question, he decided. As with most things Japanese, it would take time, but he was sure there must be a logical answer, so he put aside his concern.

He was, however, possessed of a niggling little doubt as to just what part Vice Minister Tokumura might have in this. A power play, perhaps?

Washington, D.C., was awash as the tail end of Hurricane Edna blustered like the wicked witch of Oz. The storm that had ravaged cities from Puerto Rico to North Carolina was winding down in gales of wind and rain over the nation's capital. Anyone not of strategic importance to his or her employer had been urged to stay at home as traffic already gridlocked by the strikes grew worse in the abominable weather.

The President was in his study upstairs in the White House private quarters. The First Lady, terrified by the thunder and lightning, had been sedated and slept in their darkened bedroom. He didn't want to be too far away to hear her call should she waken, and most of the staffers weren't in. Government had stalled like the cars that couldn't get through flooded intersections. He was grateful to have this time alone.

The vice president was insisting that it was time for presidential intervention in the strikes, saying that he must declare a national emergency under the Taft-Hartley Act and call for an injunction requiring strikers to go back to work. It had already gone too far. The vice president couldn't understand why The President was hesitating and The President couldn't tell him. It was an impossible situation.

The troubled auto plant in Tennessee had been targeted by the United Auto Workers union. Some of the plant employees had formed an Associates Alliance to oppose the union, claiming that the Japanese owners, who took the position that plant workers were a family and as such, would look out for each other, had given them so much in the way of benefits that they didn't need a third party interfering.

Others were still angry about the layoffs and had raised questions about the death of the local plant manager, Tommy Durand. It could be an explosive situation and Tennessee politicians were afraid that the plant might close altogether, taking all of the jobs back to Japan. Both Governor LaFarge and Congressman Templeton had expressed the opinion that government intervention at this time would anger workers and management alike.

Another call had come from Satoshi Yoshida on behalf of the Japanese plant. Yoshida had indicated that the company was convinced that they could restore order with the least amount of inconvenience if they were allowed a little more time, say thirty days, before an injunction forced the issue.

"By the way, how is your lovely wife?" Yoshida had asked, going on to say that the research and testing on the new drug for Alzheimer's was nearly complete and it would no doubt be ready for use at about the same time. Of course, since it had not yet been presented to the American Food and Drug Administration for testing, it could be years before it was available in the United States.

"But don't worry, we'll work something out that will allow access to it indirectly," Yoshida had told The President.

The implication was clear. He was being held an emotional hostage by the Japanese industrialist. If he hoped to obtain the medication for his lady, he would have to delay intervention in the strikes. How could he justify that kind of action, or non-action? And yet, could that little bit of time be so important that he must jeopardize his wife's future?

The President hated unions. They had far exceeded their original intent. Greedy employers and abuse of workers had been replaced by greedy employees and power-mad union bosses. What would happen to the army if generals had to submit to collective bargaining with privates on KP duty? And what would happen to the nation if enlisted men went out on strike with demands for higher wages and more benefits? And God help the military base controlled by a union local under the thumb of organized crime!

The President swiveled around in his chair and reached out to run his fingers over the well-worn military strategy books on the shelves behind his desk. Try as he might, he couldn't seem to find viable applications for military strategy when it came to ruling the country. Especially a country in which every citizen was endowed with so many inalienable rights.

'Benevolence and righteousness may be used to govern a state,' said Sun Tzu in The Art of War, 'but cannot be used to administer an army. Expediency and flexibility are used in administering an army, but cannot be used in governing a state. Order and disorder depend upon organization, courage or cowardice on circumstances, and strength or weakness on dispositions.'

Benevolence and righteousness? Had the rugged general become a kindly grandfather? The general must see the obstacles in the terrain and guide his soldiers through dangerous territory with wisdom and courage. Benevolence had nothing to do with it. Benevolence could get them killed.

Government didn't run the way the military did. A guffaw escaped The President's lips at the thought. It'd be a damned sight better off if it did!

Bureaucrats and politicians with fragile egos couldn't be ordered around just because he outranked them. Grown up little boys playing super spy who kept secrets even from each other couldn't be scolded just because he was the boss.

Now that communication was instant and nations held summit meetings instead of war councils, men had to find new reasons to kill each other. Mostly it was religion. The strange thing about that was that the goal was not conversion, but separation. Neighbors who had spent centuries in symbiotic dwelling were suddenly threatened by each other, usually because somebody with personal motives initiated rumors calculated to instill fear.

General or president. He couldn't be both and he had lost the desire to be either. The vice president was the one who should be president, leading the nation with absolute confidence in his own judgment. What twist of fate had directed the two of them to act out parts that suited neither of them?

The President must play his part for now, however, and find an acceptable alternative to intervention. Suddenly an old strategy occurred to him, one he didn't like to think about because it seemed dishonest.

Deception. Create changes in the situation, moving only when it is advantageous. Subdue the enemy without fighting. He would take the position that presidential intervention was justified only in the event that the strikes were a threat to public health or safety. Since police and firefighters had not walked out, the strikes were an inconvenience, an annoyance, but not life threatening. And since the party platform included the call for less, not more, government, it was too soon to resort to a presidential injunction.

He would have to believe that his was the truth and pray that the treatment he was so desperate to acquire would be available before the little voice that questioned his honor for the first time in his life got too loud to ignore. Without honor, he was nothing.

The President gave very little thought to what Yoshida's interest in the Tennessee plant might be, speculating only momentarily on the vastness of the industrialist's holdings.

# CHAPTER TWENTY TWO

In Tokyo, Yoshida allowed himself a small smile. If you were good at it, and he was, you could manipulate anyone. The old saying that everyone has his price applied universally. The President of the United States had been easily coerced into agreement by the mere suggestion that his wife's future could be dependent upon his cooperation. He would even risk the welfare of his nation for her. Yoshida's disdain for Americans was reinforced once again. They deserved to suffer.

The longer the strikes went on, the more chaos they created and the greater the diversion from recent occurrences in the American economic climate. When the thirty days were up, he would delay the injunction a few days at a time until the end of the year when the strikes would be trifling compared to the pandemonium that followed the introduction of the computer virus.

Yoshida turned his attention to another project that gave him great pleasure: the orphanage near Kyoto that was his second obsession. Only pure Japanese children were in residence there. No mutants, no mixed blood of any kind. These children were receiving the best possible education, the most healthful diet, and a strict exercise regimen that would produce the most perfect human beings ever to live. When the children reached adulthood, they would be ready to assume leadership of the near perfect society that was his dream.

He would be responsible for the establishment of such a society. That fool, Hitler, had assumed that Yoshida agreed with the premise that Aryan Caucasians were a superior race. The only conviction Yoshida had in common with the erstwhile Fuehrer was that there *was* a superior race. It certainly was not Aryan, however. Hitler simply had been eliminating some of the less acceptable inhabitants of planet Earth, so the sensible thing to do at the time had been to support his efforts.

Nothing was too good or too costly for his children. They were given only the best and were very carefully taught. Those who exhibited a talent for the arts were trained in the ways of the ancient artisans. Some would be potters, some would excel in calligraphy, some in book binding, some in drama, and some in poetry. Others would be mathematicians, economists, historians, writers, businessmen and politicians. Females were taught the essential art of maintaining serenity in the home. Some would be allowed to become primary school teachers.

Each child was subject to regular examination so that each was placed in classes that made the best use of his interests and skills. Some of the less intelligent ones often showed an aptitude for gardening or other outdoor work. No ability went unnoticed in his children, as he thought of them. There were now more than a thousand of them in the secluded compound on the shores of Lake Biwa.

A few of the most beautiful girls had been raised in the tradition of the geisha and were reserved for his private use. He had personally taught each of them the ways of pleasing a man. Sometimes when he really enjoyed one of them, he brought her to his penthouse in Tokyo. When he tired of her, she was returned to Kyoto where she might concentrate on her artistic talents or assume the duties of teacher to those who would follow.

Yoshida had had a wife long ago, before the war. She had been killed along with his parents in a bombing raid. There one day, and poof, gone the next. He hadn't wasted much time mourning any of them. He'd already made his first few million and had an agenda of his own for the future.

He had started the orphanage in 1955, a couple of years after his release from prison. There had been so many children without families, many the offspring of heroes killed in the war. Yoshida's theory had been that since they were relatively unspoiled by prior learning, they had nothing to unlearn and could be trained from their earliest years without interference.

He called his institution simply The School, never the orphanage. Very few people knew of Yoshida's association with The School, and those who did were cautious about what they said. Most of the earliest alumni remained there as teachers. Soon now, there would be enough graduates to begin inserting them into business, politics and academics.

Once Nito Ryu had completed its mission and the United States had fallen, the orphans would be useful in directing bilateral trade between the two nations. The Americans would be subjects of the true master race, governed by those trained to perfection. Perfect order on both sides of the Pacific Ocean. It was such a glorious vision that Yoshida hardly had need of a woman anymore to bring on a climax of explosive proportions. He occasionally ejaculated sitting at his desk with the files that now indicated how close he was to realizing his vision. He was still robust, but the sheer numbers in his age suggested that time was no longer his ally, and patience had never been one of his more obvious qualities. In a matter of months, the dream would be reality and he would be recognized not only for his wealth and power, but for his patriotism as well. The man who epitomized the master race would lead it nobly into the twenty-first century.


George Hagura pulled his pickup over to the side of the road and turned off the ignition. He stared out the window for a few moments, then got out and climbed down a small gully and back up to the barbed wire fence that surrounded a field of rotting lettuce. It caused him physical pain to see the dead crops and know that he was at least partially responsible for them. He clung to the wire, his fingers curled tightly, his eyes burning.

His years as a laborer in the California valley had been made bearable by the scent of the earth as it nourished the plants, the color of the leaves that grew from the seeds, the buds that became fruit. Now miles and miles of fields throughout the valley lay decayed and brown. Had he been so busy organizing the march on Sacramento and accepting the laurels as they were heaped upon him that he failed to notice the death and destruction in the fields? Had he gone too far?

The news that reached his desk for publication in The Wage Earner was increasingly bad. A company in Ohio had closed ten plants because of losses caused by the strikes, putting several thousand employees out of work permanently. It had been rumored that the company would be sold to a conglomerate and most of the operation moved to Nebraska to be reopened with non-union workers at lower pay. That kind of job loss wasn't what George wanted.

And despite the great number of people around him, he was still lonely. When the cheers ended and the marchers went home to their families, George spent the night alone in a hotel room with only the TV for company. He had begun to realize that he was no longer a young man, over forty actually. In his quest for respectability, he never had time left over to get to know a woman well enough for a long-term relationship. Now not only was he respected, he was loved by thousands who saw him as their savior. But he was still alone when he went to sleep.

His shoulders slumping, he turned away from the rotting field and climbed back into the truck. Driving back to the office, he watched the sun as it sank quickly behind the hills to the west. By the time he unlocked the door and reached in for the light switch, it was dark outside. The day's mail lay on the desk and he opened it methodically. Not much of interest. He stacked it in neat little piles and was about to leave for the day when the door opened and the Japanese businessman who had taken him to lunch several months earlier walked into the office.

The man explained to George that responsibility for publication of The Wage Earner was being moved to a facility in the Midwest to be closer to the more heavily concentrated union membership. George's services as publisher would no longer be required. The issue now at the printer would be his last. His value as a spokesman for the farm workers was unquestionable, however, and the company wished to compensate him handsomely for his dedication so that he might continue to serve those who were in need.

George was at a loss for words and mumbled something polite about accepting what must be. The man left as unobtrusively as he had entered and it was several seconds before George looked at the check in his hand. It was for $50,000, more money than he had ever earned for years of backbreaking toil. He dropped it on the desk in shock, sure that he must have read it wrong, then picked it up again to examine it more closely. The second line read, 'Fifty thousand and 00/100 dollars.' No mistake. He fell back in his chair and stared at the check for several minutes.

It was more than enough to pay his expenses for quite some time, maybe even entertain a lady now and then—if he knew any. He squinted at his reflection in the glass that covered a framed print on the wall and decided that at least he wasn't ugly. With his new respectability, there must be a nice woman somewhere who would like to be with him.

He folded the check and put it carefully in his shirt pocket.

# CHAPTER TWENTY THREE

Diane Manchester stepped through the sliding glass door to the balcony that went around two sides of her apartment and crossed to the railing. The view was nothing short of stupendous and the air that touched her face was cool and invigorating, the kind that inspires a gusto in those who inhale it, giving rise to thoughts of tackling long put off projects that were quickly discarded in favor of flying kites. It was a glorious day in San Francisco. Diane took a sip from the coffee cup she held and squinted at the light reflected on windows across the bay. If not for the reflection, she thought, I could see right into their living rooms.

The Sunday newspaper lay spread out on the sofa in her own living room, spilling onto the floor as sections that had been read were carelessly tossed aside. Diane ambled back from the balcony and picked up the business section of the Chronicle. A photo on the first page showed a Japanese man at a podium, holding up two toothbrushes as though comparing them for some unseen audience. Puzzled, Diane read the accompanying article and began to laugh.

The speaker, a representative of the Japan External Trade Organization, was giving a pep talk on how to sell American made toothbrushes to the Japanese. The handle must be slimmer and shorter for the slightly smaller hands of the average Japanese, he told them. A hole in the handle allows the brush to be hung for storage, and the bristles must be harder than those offered to Americans. Additionally, the package has to have a window so that discriminating Japanese can see what they are buying.

The message that, contrary to widespread perceptions in America, the Japanese market was open to foreign competition, but the American manufacturer must offer products that are acceptable to the Japanese consumer. The formula for success, said the spokesman, was called the 'Five A's.'

Added Value: the product must offer something extra.
Appearance: aesthetics were important.
Availability: market research was important.
After-sale Service: assurance that it would work properly.
Atmosphere: labeled 'Made in California' wouldn't hurt.

Diane wondered how many American manufacturers would be willing to retool their equipment to make the obligatory improvements to their products in order to crack the Japanese markets. Even if they did, chances were the Japanese would find another obscure reason for denying access to picky consumers. In the short time she had been employed by Habatsu, she already knew that they were masters at evading a difficult issue. Were Americans really that gullible? Yes, she sighed, they probably were.

Sandwiched in on the last page of the business news, along with the obituaries, was an article about an employee of the San Francisco branch of Yamasu Securities who had been mysteriously murdered. The article suggested that the man had been thought to associate with members of the local Japanese underworld and it was suspected that his death was gang related. Hmmm, thought Diane, I didn't know there *was* a Japanese underworld. She put the section aside and forgot about it.

The front page of the Metropolitan section of the paper was devoted to the march on Sacramento by supporters of the United Farm Workers union. A large photo showed the organizer of the march, George Hagura, being embraced heartily by former governor, Jerry Brown. The crowds were thought to have exceeded fifty thousand people. What a different world she lived in now, Diane mused. Farm workers, lettuce boycotts, marches on the state capital. She couldn't recall ever hearing of a march of the New York capital in Albany. She wondered if she should stop buying lettuce, if she could find any in the store.

A breeze from the open door to the balcony riffled the pages of the paper and Diane decided she'd read enough. Gathering up the scattered sections, she left them in a pile on the coffee table and went through her bedroom to the bathroom. Dropping her robe and pajamas on the floor, she stepped into the shower.

It had been obvious to Diane from the moment she hung her meager wardrobe in the closet of her new luxury apartment that it was hopelessly inadequate for her new lifestyle. Surveying the frayed cuffs and waistbands of drab jackets and skirts, she had come to the conclusion that a shopping expedition was most definitely in order. A foray into the colorful world of Macy's California had left her overwhelmed by the seemingly endless supply of bright hues and rich fabrics available to the shopper. She discovered that she loved the loose fitting styles that felt great on her body. She'd even thrown caution to the wind and bought a few really kicky things that she was sure she wouldn't have the courage to wear.

Each time she looked at herself in the mirror, she was startled by the change. Her dark eyes, formerly distant and preoccupied, now sparkled. Her smile made people turn to see if she might be smiling at them, wondering if they knew her and wishing they did. She had blossomed in the California sun and was now a confident, almost beautiful woman who looked much younger than her thirty-some years.

One thing had not changed, however. The social naiveté that went with years of burying herself in computers had yet to be dispelled. But that only added to her appeal.

Rubbing herself briskly with a towel, Diane thought about what she might do on this glorious Sunday in San Francisco. A bus to Golden Gate Park? A visit to the deYoung Museum? All the way to the ocean to dig her bare toes into the sand? No, she felt more like being with people with whom she might strike up a conversation and share the exhilaration of this wonderful fall weather. The Buena Vista Café, the BV to those in the know, was always crowded with people sharing tables on Sunday mornings. Suddenly ravenously hungry, she couldn't wait to devour a hearty breakfast of corned beef and eggs while watching Sunday strollers along the waterfront near Ghirardelli Square.

A few minutes later, she was at the corner waiting for the Powell and Hyde Street cable car that would creep up steep hills, pausing for breath at the top before plunging down the other side, clanging merrily all the way to the end of the line. Now that summer was over and the tourists had thinned out, it was easier to get a seat on the outside of the car.

Diane jumped up easily, holding tightly to the pole beside her as the car began to move. Clang, clang, clang went the motorman's bell as he signaled the presence of the little trolley that might or might not be able to stop if something got in its way.

Turning toward the man seated next to her, Diane grinned. He grinned back and reached up to tip his hat, a narrow brimmed green felt with a jaunty feather in the band. It went well with the tweed jacket he wore.

"Isn't this one of the most magnificent days in the history of the world?" She just couldn't resist asking the question even if it did sound a bit banal.

"It's a lovely day today and whatever you've got to do, you've got a lovely day to do it in, that's true," the man sang out in a rich baritone voice, making heads turn in their direction throughout the car.

Diane giggled, and then laughed wholeheartedly as the other passengers joined in and conversations began between strangers who let San Francisco's spirit turn them into friends.

"Visiting?" the man asked.

"No, I live here. I just moved from New York a couple of months ago and I can't believe how lucky I am! Are you visiting?"

"No, I was even luckier. I was born here and have lived here all my life. My name's Jack Mercer." He stuck his hand out toward her. "And you are . . . ?"

Taking the hand he had extended, she said, "Diane Manchester."

"Welcome to San Francisco, Diane Manchester. If we'd gone to school together, you'd have been seated in front of me in the classroom and I'd have dipped your pigtails in the ink well—if there'd still been ink wells, that is. Where are you off to on this fine day?"

"I thought I'd have scrambled eggs, corned beef, and an Irish coffee at the BV," she told him.

"Well, now, there's another coincidence. I'm on my way to the BV myself. Will you and your flashing brown eyes join me for a cup?"

"My eyes and I would be delighted, Mr. Mercer." Diane didn't hesitate. She had already decided on her destination so why not walk in the door with a native San Franciscan? He was well dressed and friendly to boot. She smiled in anticipation.

The cable car came to a halt, brakes squealing, at the foot of Hyde Street. Jack Mercer jumped down quickly, holding out his hand to help her descend. Several voices called out to him as they entered the pub.

"Hey, Jack!"

"Hi there, Jack!"

"Where've you been, Jack?"

Someone raised an arm, beckoning him to join the large round table by the window midway down the length of the bar. Jack took Diane's elbow, guiding her through the mass of people who stood shoulder to shoulder, sometimes closer, from one end of the bar to the other and beyond. There was a momentary scuffling as chairs were rounded up and passed over heads to the table where Jack introduced Diane to his friends as they squeezed in together.

She soon discovered that Jack was a staff writer for the Chronicle, as were a couple of the others at the table. One of the women, whose graying hair and horn-rimmed glasses were deceptive, wrote steamy romance novels. Another, who wore nondescript sweats, turned out to be a buyer for I. Magnin evening wear. It was impossible to tell whether any of them were couples or if they were all singles.

Jack made no secret of the fact that he and Diane had just met on the cable car, explaining that he had been drawn to her because of her smile and her eyes, and had to know more about her since she was obviously meant to be a very close friend. The observation that she was so young to be such a high ranking executive in such a prestigious company was not a new one to Diane, but she did acknowledge that recent attitude and wardrobe changes contributed to her youthful appearance. Always up front, Diane was never secretive about her age.

The afternoon would be one that altered Diane's life forever as she sipped Irish coffee with congenial new friends and the man who would teach her that the love between a man and a woman could be more than the traditional relationship she had always assumed it to be. With him she would discover a connection that made them one in mind, heart, body and spirit; a connection that superseded the limited personal self; a connection that took her beyond the ordinary into a higher consciousness and gave her an almost mystical sense that she was one with God.

When the group began to break up, going their separate ways as evening began to emerge, Jack and Diane boarded the cable car that would carry them back up Russian Hill. Stopping at a corner deli to pick up sandwiches and beer, they headed toward Diane's apartment.

"Holy moly!" exclaimed Jack as she inserted the key and opened the door. "Are you sure you don't rob banks for a living? I didn't know that computer programmers, even high level ones, made this kind of money!"

Diane confessed that she had been as stunned as anyone might be, but that she had been actively pursued by the company. "I'm still not sure why they wanted me so badly, except that they want the system enhancements I had designed for IBM before they fired me. Of course, they had to be restructured to meet the specifications for Habatsu equipment, and they'd like to be able to market a product that offers something more than the IBM system, too, so I guess they really do need me."

In the hours they spent finding out about each other, Diane learned that Jack had been married to the girl who had been his college sweetheart, mostly because it had been expected.

"We discovered early on that once everybody else went home, we really had very little in common," he told her. "The divorce was amicable and there were no children. Since then, I've been cautious about relationships based on surface attraction and haven't had any serious attachments for several years. How about you?"

Diane was embarrassed to admit that she had been too absorbed in her work to have had any serious relationships.

Jack smiled. "I find that a very agreeable quality," he said.

Have you always wanted to be a journalist?" Diane asked.

"I've always been fascinated by the written word," he replied, "but what I really wanted to do was write commentaries on the state of the State, or maybe observations about the way things are, like what Herb Caen does in the Chronicle. I've done a number of columns on some of the world's hot spots over the years, and I really enjoy covering foreign news, but the wire services make it so readily accessible that only the giants in the business send their own reporters nowadays. Someday

I'd like to write a book, or maybe several books, on the lesser known effects of culture and tradition on international diplomacy."

"Sounds like a major project. I've always lived in the world of math and science where everything is proven and tradition is an unknown. Where did you go to college?"

"The University of Missouri. I have to admit that that was a real culture shock to someone who was raised in California. There's a different value system in the Midwest, not that it's wrong or anything, just different. Probably because of the distance from either coast. They're in a cocoon of sorts and neighbor helping neighbor is more of a requirement."

By the time the evening ended, they had explored politics, religion, movies, television, food, their expectations and their dreams. Diane liked everything about him: the way he dressed, the way he talked, the way he listened, the way he cared. She respected his opinions and his integrity. Most of all, she liked the way he laughed.

They did not sleep together that night, but each of them knew that when they did, it could be magic.

# CHAPTER TWENTY FOUR

The newly appointed Secretary of Commerce, Grant Williamson, was also enjoying San Francisco's clear October weather that day. He and his wife had flown in from Washington the night before and he was scheduled to fly out again the next day on his way to Beijing where he would discuss American business ventures with the Chinese. His wife planned to remain in The City for the next several weeks so that she could help with their son's wedding plans. Recalling their daughter's wedding, Grant was very glad he had good reason to be left out of the pre-wedding chaos. At least he wasn't paying for this one.

The bride's family had invited the groom's family to their home in Los Gatos for a Sunday afternoon by the pool. Though the coals in the brick barbeque had been fired up, the only thing that would be cooked by the host or hostess were the steaks. The rest of their 'little dinner' had been prepared much earlier by the family cook and waited in the refrigerator for the hostess to remove the Saran wrap and carry it outside.

The outdoor bar was amply stocked, but Grant Williamson resisted repeated offers of libation, anticipating the very long plane trip to Beijing. He did accept a glass of champagne, however, for toasts to his son and Mellie McDonald and their endless happiness together.

The vice president would be joining Grant in Beijing for talks on the proposed openings of an American securities firm in Beijing and

Shanghai, as well as the purchase of American tires for Chinese air force jets. These issues were mostly an excuse for representatives of the two powerful countries to get together, but they had to tell their respective press something other than 'we're just sniffing around.'

While the Secretary of Commerce and the vice president were in China, the Secretary of Defense would be visiting Singapore to discuss Singapore's invitation to base American warships there. The addition of such military strength in the Pacific, along with Clark Air Base and Subic Bay in the Philippines, would secure American dominance of Asian sea lanes.

The development of new markets for American products and increased American naval power in the Far East were parts of The President's plan to prepare for possible losses in the European market when and if the communist states collapsed. The plan was the one thing on which The President and his second in command agreed.

The President's military background made him cautious about the inevitable fallout when political power changed hands. The vice president's background in economics had taught him the pitfalls that beset fledgling governments when restructuring of the magnitude that would be required in the Soviet Union and Germany occurred.

Other cabinet members and key trade negotiators were investigating the possibilities in Indonesia, Malaysia and India as well as those with current trade allies such as South Korea and the Philippines. A brainstorming summit was scheduled for the end of January. Each participant would present findings and offer proposals for long-term goals at that time.

The junior senator from Ohio could hardly wait for the vice president to leave Washington. The two men had been at odds for months and the junior senator hoped to avoid the grief he knew he'd get when he introduced his knock-your-socks-off legislation. It was common knowledge that you had to sponsor bills that made news or you were doomed to obscurity and probably wouldn't get re-elected. His bill was guaranteed to headline the evening news, and if it passed and became law, it would put those little yellow bastards in their place. They'd been getting away with too much American money for too long, what with the trade imbalance and the American tax dollars spent on their defense. His bill would put an end to that.

In Tokyo a few days later, Sunao Tokumura was livid. He had just read the translated text of SR 182, introduced into the United States Senate by the junior senator from Ohio.

"The stupid little bastard," he said aloud. "He's living proof that they're all barbarians!"

The proposed legislation asked for a tariff on all Japanese imports in an amount equal to the difference in percentage of the GNP spent by the U.S. on defense and the percentage of the Japanese GNP spent on defense. In other words, if the U.S. spent ten percent of its GNP on defense and Japan spent only five percent, the tariff would be five percent. The argument in favor of this outrageous proposal was that it compensated the U.S. for defending Japan.

As if the vice minister didn't have enough on his mind already. He had been working day and night on a long-range plan for the development of Asia for Asians, a blueprint for survival once the economic superiority of the U.S. had been at least temporarily extirpated. Japan must have adequate alternative markets as the world balance of power was restructured, and a healthy relationship with her Asian neighbors was essential.

The initial stages of the plan had already gone into effect. Emphasis had been placed on the need for greater domestic consumption rather than the traditional Japanese penchant for saving. Directives had been agreed upon urging the people to spend more now that their savings earned increased returns.

To compensate for the Japanese lack of raw materials, the plan also included the development of cooperative production ventures with neighboring countries such as China and Malaysia. Yoshida's company, Nippon Heavy Industry Corporation, had established a venture of this nature with China in building ships and manufacturing arms. A regional trading block would be in place soon. A glitch had appeared, however, upon the arrival in Asia of the American vice president and two cabinet secretaries.

Tokumura was well aware of Singapore's standing offer to the United States of port space for American warships. He had not considered it a serious threat in view of the fact that the offer had been made repeatedly since World War II, and had yet to be acted upon by the U.S. government.

Why should the Secretary of Defense suddenly appear in Singapore? Once Nito Ryu, the Two Sword plan, had accomplished its goal, the Americans would no longer be in a position to limit Japanese military strength to defense forces created during the occupation. Japan would be able to increase the size of its army and navy, providing security for its Asian allies. The timing could be disastrous if the United States and Singapore were to enter into an agreement now.

The same was true of Chinese-American agreements. Though many new luxury hotels had appeared recently throughout China, most were European ventures and catered to the tourism that the Chinese government encouraged in an effort to erase the memory of so many failed schemes initiated by Chairman Mao.

The Great Leap Forward, for instance, had been an attempt to industrialize the vast rural population by moving them from the land into communes where they were instructed to devote themselves to steel production. Every piece of iron or steel that the peasants could lay their hands on had gone into smelting pots—hammers, hoes, axes and buckets. To fuel the fires, every tree on every hillside had been cut down, causing erosion that had yet to be corrected.

There had been no time for planting or harvesting and most of the implements required had been tossed into the pots anyway. An estimated twenty million lives had been lost as the people starved while party secretaries lied about the success of the movement, fearful of Mao's retaliation should they admit to failure.

If the Americans lifted restrictions and entered into joint manufacturing deals, the Japanese position could be severely jeopardized. The Vice Minister of International Trade and Industry would be held accountable for any reversals suffered, and no matter how noble his intentions, he would be unable to take credit for the destruction of the U.S. economy. His career would be at an end.

Tokumura was in frenzy at the thought. His ability to meditate, to transform his spirit into that of the warrior of a previous incarnation, had been grievously challenged. Nito Ryu *must* succeed, and quickly, before the Americans had time to establish new alliances in Asia. The junior senator from Ohio must be stopped from passing his racist legislation.

Tokumura considered himself an honorable man, one who would normally avoid violence. Though he didn't often allow himself to think about it, he knew that Yoshida's connections extended well into the world of organized crime. If he were to be really honest, he also knew that much of the progress with American labor had been a result of those connections. This, however, was an unacceptable situation that justified radical measures. He picked up the phone and arranged to meet with the industrialist the next morning. The junior senator must be made to see the error of this legislation, or suffer the consequences.

"In large scale strategy, it is beneficial

to strike at the corners of the enemy's

force . . . the spirit of the whole body

will be overthrown."

The Fire Book

Book of Five Rings

Miyamoto Musashi

# CHAPTER TWENTY FIVE

The calling of loans by Japanese banks in California had been as much a surprise to Stan Mitsunari as it had been to the American construction companies affected by it. If only one bank had been involved, it might be unusual but not particularly startling. But actions such as this would not be taken without some sort of directive from one or more of the ministries. And the ministries did not issue directives without weeks of discussion and subsequent proposals that were altered repeatedly as everybody who wanted part of the credit, or wanted to avoid any of the blame, made suggestions. And in the process, Stan's office knew about it. What, or who, could be behind a maneuver that was already sending some of America's borrowers into bankruptcy?

Stan's phone had been busy and messages calling for information from colleagues around the world were spilling from the fax machine. He had spent the afternoon trying to reach Tokyo based officers of the two Japanese banks whose branches in California had called loans, growing more and more frustrated as he was deferred from one to another with no one admitting anything.

The terms 'interest rates' and 'negative compensation' had been repeated, as had phrases about encouraging domestic spending. What domestic spending had to do with loans to California construction companies escaped him. Just months before, these same banks had been urged to extend the loans, justified by the argument that deposits recycled into local economies created good will toward Japan. Now there was a lot of mumbo jumbo about increasing domestic consumption. None of it made sense, and no one seemed to know what was going on, or if they did, they weren't telling.

Stan was reaching for the phone to call Nobuya Saito in the Ministry of Finance when it rang. Since his hand was already on the receiver, he picked it up quickly.

Even after many years, he recognized the voice and was taken aback by the anger in her tone.

"How could you do such a thing?" she demanded.

"Maggie," he said. It was a statement rather than a question. "What have I done?"

"You know damned well what you've done. Is this your way of getting back at my father?"

"I have no idea what you're talking about, Maggie. I heard that your father passed away, and I knew that you had taken over as CEO, but what is it that you think I've done?"

"The twenty percent of Davidson stock. Did you think I wouldn't find out who bought it? It took a little time, but that's what attorneys get paid to do. How did you know that Buzz would sell? And is the 'M and D Corporation' your way of saying Mitsunari and Davidson?"

"I still have no idea what you're talking about, Maggie. I assume you think I coerced Buzz into selling me twenty percent of your company, but I didn't. Why would I want to buy into Davidson Hotels?"

"Revenge? And don't lie to me, Mitsu." She used the nickname his fraternity brothers had given him without thinking. "Your name came up as sole owner of an obscure company in the Caribbean that does business with an estate planner, also obscure, who serves clients who wish to remain anonymous. Why all the subterfuge? What are you planning to do with the stock? I still control eighty percent, so you can't affect the decision making. Just tell me why!"

"Maggie, I swear to you that I have not spoken to Buzz or anyone else, nor have I coerced anyone, nor have I bought any Davidson stock. There must be some mistake."

"No mistake. It's definitely your name, and as sole owner of the stock. Why would anyone else buy it in your name?"

"I can't imagine who or why," Stan said truthfully. "How did Buzz happen to have twenty percent? I knew your dad had rewarded him and the other two managers with stock options, but I thought it was less than that."

"It was in Daddy's will that they each had the option to buy an amount equivalent to what they already had, which doubled the amount that's out of the family. Of course, Daddy never dreamed that Buzz would pull such a double-cross. But then, he never dreamed that I'd take over the hotels, either."

"I saw you in Hawaii, Maggie. It was quite a shock after all these years. It looked like you were planning to take over the Kaimana Surf and Sand. Have you?"

Maggie was puzzled. "I didn't see you," she said. "Where were you?"

"My wife and I were sitting in the cocktail lounge when you came out of an office and went up in the elevator. You looked stunning. Much more sophisticated than you were in college."

"Your wife? I wondered if you had married. Were you there on vacation?"

"No, I was scheduled to speak at a conference in Honolulu, so we took the opportunity to go a little early and enjoy the beach for a couple of days."

"You should have let me know that you were there. I'd like to have met your wife. Perhaps now that you're a business associate of sorts, we'll meet in the future." Maggie's tone had only a hint of sarcasm in it. She wanted to believe that he really didn't know anything about the stock.

"My wife was killed in an accident shortly after we returned to Japan, Maggie," he said softly. "A tour bus full of Americans hit her."

"Oh, Mitsu, I'm so sorry. Of course, I didn't know. Americans haven't always been good to you, have they?"

He ignored the question. "I heard from friends who keep in touch that you married several years ago. Someone your father found acceptable, I gather."

Her laugh was bitter. "Yes, he was acceptable. But he's no longer acceptable. We're divorced. He found someone he liked better than me."

"My turn to be sorry, Maggie. Why don't I see what I can find out about that stock and call you back? There has to be a record of the transfer and as the new owner, however unaware, I should be able to trace the broker. I hope you believe me, Maggie," he said quietly. "It was painful, all those years ago, but revenge wasn't something I considered."

"I want to believe you, Mitsu. I'll hold off on judgment until I hear from you." She hung up.

The use of his old nickname brought the memories flooding back. Memories he had deliberately scorned since Akiko's death. Just when he'd thought he could be wholly Japanese, using his anger to thoroughly demolish the part of him that remained American, in the blink of an eye—or the ring of a telephone—it had all come back to haunt him again. Destiny perhaps?

Who could be responsible for his ownership of the Davidson stock? Could someone be setting him up for blackmail? He had no political aspirations, he didn't gamble, he wasn't an alcoholic, and he had no kinky sexual tendencies. In fact, he'd been faithful to his wife since their marriage—not so much because of his devotion to her as because of her willingness to fulfill his every need. He'd had no reason and no pressing desire to look elsewhere.

Ownership of stock in a profitable American company was not cause for blackmail in and of itself. It had to have been someone who wanted a favor, or more likely, a number of favors. And it had to be someone who knew a great deal about his past. Stan frowned. It also had to be someone very rich.

The answer came to him suddenly, though it seemed so unlikely that he shook his head, denying it as impossible. Vice Minister Tokumura. Still . . . it had been the vice minister who encouraged the anti-American sentiments that had become the meat and potatoes of Stan's columns in recent weeks. And as innocuous as it had seemed at the time, there had been hints that his patriotism would not go unrewarded.

Had his rage so blinded him that he allowed himself to become a political dupe? Was something expected of him that he had yet to discover? Something worth the price of the Davidson stock?

Vice Minister Tokumura was known to be well off, but most of it was tied up in the property said to be worth many millions. If it *was* him, there had to be someone else behind it as well, someone with a lot of ready cash.

The California bank loans temporarily forgotten, Stan reached for the phone and dialed the number for MITI. It was urgent that he reach the vice minister, he told the secretary, and left his name.

Otsu Tokumura peeked through the shoji that led from the dining room to the garden, watching her husband as he slashed at empty air with the sword he had removed from the wall of his study. It was a very old sword, the blade beaten, folded and tempered by a master swordsmith of the fourteenth century when weapons of this kind were prized as objects of great beauty and spiritual force—the soul of the samurai.

Otsu had never seen him like this. As dedicated to his career as any Japanese man, her Sunao had always been rational. In recent weeks, however, he had begun to frighten her. He rarely spoke to her except to growl when something displeased him, and had taken to spending the few hours a week that he was at home and not sleeping, either in the garden with the sword or in the little teahouse. Even the Three Shouts during lovemaking had become increasingly violent as he attacked and conquered enemies she could not see.

As she watched him on this crisp fall evening, she began to fear the fury she saw in his eyes, fury that grew more demented with each passing day. Did the madness she saw at night disappear during the day, she wondered. What had caused so much anger? The words he muttered in his sleep told her that it had something to do with Americans. She shuddered and closed the shoji softly, retreating noiselessly on cloth slippered feet.

# CHAPTER TWENTY SIX

etween construction layoffs and the strikes that affected every labor union, the state of California was in chaos.

Dusty Jurgens pounded the steering wheel of his pickup truck impatiently as traffic on the San Diego freeway moved a few feet and then stopped again. He had spent most of the afternoon at the unemployment office, and he wanted to get home by six o'clock for Monday night football. It was about the only pleasure he got out of life since the construction company he worked for had stopped work on both of the big projects they had going. The foreman had told him that they planned to file bankruptcy by the end of the week, and that meant the layoff would be permanent.

Dusty had trouble with the forms the unemployment office said he needed to fill out. He had finished high school, but like so many kids, he really couldn't read all that well. The only reason he'd progressed through the grades and graduated was that teachers had to keep as many kids in class as they could in order to claim federal funds that were allocated according to the number of students. So even though Dusty had cut a lot of classes and paid little attention in the ones he did attend, he had been moved along in the system with everyone else.

It hadn't mattered a lot to Dusty, however, because he knew he could make good money in construction. He'd had to get a job right out of school since he and Cindy hadn't been too careful about protected sex and she was three months pregnant on graduation day. That had been three years ago and the monumental medical bill still wasn't paid off. Cindy had started having problems with the pregnancy soon after the wedding and had to stay off her feet, which meant that she couldn't work like they'd planned. The birth itself had been difficult, too, requiring a lot of extra medications and procedures.

Cindy still couldn't help out because it would cost more to hire somebody to watch the baby than she could earn since she didn't have any more skills than he did. All in all, it was a dead-end life, and now that fat pig in the unemployment office had told him his benefits would be limited all because the company had paid him under the table, claiming him as a part time laborer so they saved and he took home a lot more cash than he would have if all the stuff like social security and taxes were deducted from his paycheck. It had sounded like a good idea at the time, but now he was up shit creek without a paddle.

By the time he finally reached the driveway of the little house they'd rented, Dusty was tired and angry. He slammed the door of the pickup, not bothering to lock it—who'd want to steal it anyway?—and walked around to the back of the house. As he inserted his key in the lock, he wondered why it was so dark inside. Cindy never went anywhere and usually left lights on in every room of the house. He was surprised to find her sitting at the kitchen table in the gathering gloom and indicated as much on his way to the refrigerator to get a beer before turning on the game.

"What's the matter with you?" he asked, then exclaimed, "What the hell?" when the light failed to go on in the refrigerator as the door opened.

"They came and turned off the electricity," she said dully.

"Why? Didn't you pay the bill?"

"With what?" she asked. "I thought we'd have more time and the baby needed stuff and there were groceries to buy, and you only gave me fifty dollars last week."

Dusty reached for a beer and swore as he realized that it was already getting warm. Pulling the tab from the can, he swallowed half of it before taking a breath.

"That's not all," Cindy said.

"What? There's more? That's all I need to finish a perfect day. Know why it was a perfect day? Because *nothing* went right, not a goddamn thing!"

176

"We got a notice that the phone will be shut off Friday unless we pay something on the bill, and the hospital turned our account over to a collection agency. A guy called and said we'd better pay up."

"Fuck," said Dusty. He strode into the living room to turn on the game. When the set remained dark, he realized that without electricity, it wasn't going to work any better than the refrigerator did. "Fuck, fuck, fuck!" he bellowed. Standing in the middle of the living room, he finished the beer, then went back to get another.

"Might as well drink 'em before they all get warm," he said. By the time he finished the second one, Cindy was on him about their money problems.

"What did you do that you got laid off?" she whined.

"I told you, I didn't do nothin'—the company just quit building. Somethin' to do with their loan at the bank. They're going bankrupt and that means no more job, period."

"Did you go to the unemployment office?"

He crushed the can and opened another before he told her about the benefits he wouldn't be getting. When she started to cry, he hit her across the mouth and yelled for her to shut up.

"Where's the baby?" Dusty had just noticed that he hadn't heard any noise from the bedroom.

"I took him over to Janie's next door. She said she'd take care of him until you came home and we could figure out what to do about the electricity." Cindy was gulping between words, holding one hand against her bruised cheek.

The more he drank, the madder Dusty got. It just wasn't fair. He'd been a real hot shot in school. Really cool—Somebody with a capital 'S.' If Cindy hadn't gotten herself prego, he wouldn't be in this mess. He'd be drinking with his buddies in a bar, cheering for the Raiders instead of drinking warm beer in a dark house with a whiny wife. He opened the last can, drank a few swallows, and glared at Cindy.

"Don't we have any candles?" he asked. "It's almost clear dark. We can't stay here in the dark."

She began to cry. Something inside Dusty snapped. He slapped her again and again, harder each time as her tears turned to sobs and then screams. When she fell to the floor, he yanked her back up by the hair and hit her again. This time she cracked her head against the edge of the table as she fell. He kicked her in the ribs as she lay on the floor, then slammed out of the house, got into the pickup and squealed the tires backing out of the driveway.

He didn't get far. Police estimated he'd been going in excess of eighty miles an hour up the on-ramp to the freeway before he lost control and flew over the concrete abutment, rolled twice and landed upside down on the pavement below. It took the wrecking crew more than two hours to remove his body from the truck and he died without knowing that Cindy hadn't felt the kick to her ribs. Her skull had cracked when she hit the corner of the kitchen table, and she was already dead.

Neighbors described the couple to police as quiet and well mannered. Janie was a heroine of sorts for a week or two as she located the address for Cindy's parents up the coast and accompanied their grandchild to their home. She told the grieving parents that their daughter's death must have been an accident and that the loss of his job had no doubt been responsible for Dusty's deep depression and anger over his inability to pay the bills.


Dan Whiting drove slowly but deliberately east on Ogden Avenue in Chicago. He knew he shouldn't be doing it, but he was delivering a load of fresh meat to a supermarket in an area not friendly to outsiders under normal circumstances and certainly not friendly now that tempers were flaring over five pound sacks of flour. But Dan also knew that the regular drivers hadn't delivered anything fresh to the area in weeks and he felt sorry for the people who were going without.

A television crew had done a story on how the strikes were harder on some areas than others, citing ghetto neighborhoods where even non-union drivers who sometimes crossed picket lines to deliver essential supplies refused to go. One interview with a mother of two small children had particularly touched Dan's heart. So he'd decided to play Good Samaritan.

Careful to seek out the safest time, he had concluded that mid-morning would see the fewest people on the streets. Those with jobs would be away, teenaged gang members might be in school, and housewives would be at home. The only markings on the truck were on the driver's side door, but a vehicle as large as his would stand out now that there were so few on the streets. He hoped to attract as little attention as possible so he made a right turn off Ogden as he reached the predominantly black neighborhood, and stayed on back streets.

Dan had planned his route on a map, memorizing the street names in advance. As he drove, he counted the blocks, and then made a left turn onto the street that should lead to the supermarket a half mile beyond. Many of the street signs were missing and he hoped the route he had worked out really did lead to the store. He breathed a sigh of relief as it came into view.

Going directly to the loading ramp at the back of the store, he jumped quickly from the cab. The store manager had been alerted and was watching for him. Three very large young men appeared as if by magic, silently reaching for the refrigerated boxes the moment Dan unlocked the rear door. Dan carried a box with him as he entered the store and followed the manager to the office where paperwork awaited. Within minutes, the truck had been emptied and the manager was handing him the clip board that held signed packing slips acknowledging delivery.

What Dan didn't know was that the manager had told just a few of his best customers and one or two of his relatives that there would be a delivery that morning, and if they were to come very early, he'd let them in and then lock the store. As is the human thing to do, most of the people who had been told had whispered the secret to only their best friends, and as Dan reached for the clip board, he looked through the one-way glass window into the store proper and saw people coming toward the front entrance.

Within seconds, a few people had become dozens and then an angry mob that broke the plate glass windows to gain entry. It was hard to tell where the first gun shot came from. Dan tore the packing slips from the board and raced out the back. He was reaching for the door handle to the cab of the truck when several pairs of hands pulled him to the ground.

There was no logical explanation for what happened as frustrated, hungry humans beat the man who only wanted to help them. They stopped short of killing him, leaving him lying beside the truck in a pool of blood, his face unrecognizable. An elderly couple, too frail to compete with the crowd that swarmed the market, watched from down the street. As the mob disappeared inside, they approached the injured man cautiously. Together, they lifted him into the back of his vehicle, then got into the cab and drove to the hospital about a mile away.

As orderlies arranged the tattered body on a gurney and moved through the door to the emergency room, the couple vanished as silently as they had appeared. Dan Whiting came out of his coma a few days later, remembering nothing beyond the time he parked the truck behind the store. He had no idea who had saved his life.

Doctors and nurses put Dan's body back together as best they could, but he would be forever troubled by aches and pains that often made themselves known at inconvenient times. He would walk with a slight limp, and one side of his face would refuse to match the other when he smiled. The scars faded as time went by and eventually he no longer noticed them when he looked into a mirror, but others noticed and eyed him with pity before they turned away.

Union leaders were unhappy with his actions, hinting that he'd gotten just what he deserved for taking it upon himself to make an illegal delivery during the strike. His position as president of the union local was awarded to another man, explained away by the need for leadership in his absence. As he convalesced, his visitors came less frequently until the television set became his only company.

The worst part of the whole thing had been that most of the meat he delivered had been spoiled as frenzied consumers fought over it, tearing it to bits before it was even packaged by the store's meat cutters. Some of it reached dinner tables through black market hoodlums, but many of the people who ate it suffered later, the result of contamination caused by too much time in the trunk of a car. The same hospital that treated Dan Whiting's battered body also pumped the stomachs of some of them.

In his solitude, Dan began to wonder just what the strikes were all about. The truckers in his union had walked out in sympathy for the laid-off Tennessee plant workers. When union leadership reacted quickly, sending a team to the auto plant to organize laborers, they had met with strong resistance on the part of those who sided with Japanese plant owners.

The sympathy had extended to farm workers in California as slowdowns began in the fields. Slowdowns, Dan thought. Not actual strikes. It had been the Teamsters who initiated the strikes. Some of the union locals had been approaching contract renewal time and obscure issues were raised to justify walk offs. Emotions were running high, and the issues had become clouded, if not forgotten entirely.

Many of the truckers were experiencing personal hardships as time passed without a settlement. Incomes were in jeopardy and empty shelves in stores affected everyone. An underground movement had been established as drivers took turns making runs from Kansas and Iowa to pick up beef and vegetables that didn't make it beyond the company yards. The potential for unlimited violence seemed just around the corner. Dan began to wonder if the strikes had outlasted their usefulness. Perhaps the time had come for someone to introduce a little rationality into the situation. But how?

About thirty miles south of San Francisco, on the suburban peninsula, Marian McDonald was beginning to have spells of anxiety over her daughter's upcoming wedding to Ken Williamson. The prices quoted by the caterer for smoked salmon and caviar were increasing daily since even ordinary things like carrots and potatoes were difficult to get, and luxuries nearly impossible. Marian had been planning Mellie's wedding since the day they brought her home from the hospital. It would be the event of the decade, something Mellie would remember all her life as the most romantic of days.

Marian wanted this perfect day more than she had ever wanted anything. Though she couldn't really have explained it, it was something that was the fulfillment of dreams that began generations earlier with grandparents who came from the old country, had too many children and struggled to give each of them a dream to work toward. Most were now well educated and instilled in the eldest of the children the notion that they had a responsibility to help the younger ones. Many in that generation grew up to be over-achiever types like Marian's husband, Mitch, who expected *their* children to reach for the moon.

Marian's own wedding to Mitch had been held in her parents' living room, made sweetly romantic by the candlelight that hid threadbare furniture and the lack of crystal glasses for the champagne that was the only extravagance the budget would allow. But Mitch had worked long and hard to be successful, and now these dreadful strikes might deny his daughter the wedding that Marian thought of as her absolute right to have.

She could hardly keep from crying at the very idea.

# CHAPTER TWENTY SEVEN

Sumio Masabe was bent over his microscope, absorbed in his work, and did not hear the laboratory door open. The two men in dark suits were standing beside him before he was aware of their presence and he knew immediately that they were not scientists, nor were they authorized personnel. His heart leapt into his throat even as his head told him he no longer need be afraid. The taller of the two asked politely if he would please accompany them from the laboratory, his demeanor making it quite clear that Sumio had no choice in the matter.

Removing his apron, he took his jacket from the hanger where he had hung it carefully, put it on and followed the men through the door, jiggling the doorknob to make sure it was properly locked behind him. Outside, he was surprised to see that they intended to take him wherever they were going in a long, black limousine with very dark windows.

"Where are we going?" he ventured.

"For a short visit with the man who has subsidized your research," replied the man who was apparently the spokesman. "Do not worry. He only wishes a report on your progress. You will be back at work in a couple of hours."

"But the weekly reports I prepare are picked up regularly. What more can I tell him?"

"Perhaps he wants a more personal review. He will tell you shortly." The man leaned back and closed his eyes, making it clear that further conversation was unwelcome.

Half an hour later, the limousine stopped and Sumio was blindfolded for the remainder of the journey. He knew only that they were in Tokyo's business district and that meant very little to him. Led from the car through the back entrance of the Nippon Heavy Industry Corporation headquarters, he was aware of rising in an elevator and heard a door close firmly before the blindfold was removed and his eyes began to adjust to the dimness of a conference room.

"Ohayo gozaimasu, Masabe-san. Sit down, please," said a voice from the far end of a very long conference table.

Sumio stood uncertainly for a moment, unsure whether to go toward the voice or sit at the end where he stood. The voice solved the problem by gesturing toward a chair near where he stood. He sat and looked in the general direction of the voice as his eyes adjusted. The only light in the room came from a fixture recessed in the ceiling above and a little forward of his chair. Once seated, it shone on his face, but the man at the other end remained in deep shadow.

"Bring me up to date, please, on your research," the voice ordered.

"Ummm," Sumio began, confused as to whether or not this man had read his weekly reports.

"Your reports are excellent, Masabe-san, but as I am not a chemist, I would like more personal instruction, as well as an estimated date for completion of the project."

Sumio began to speak, hesitantly at first, then with conviction as he warmed to his subject. "The problem," he said, "is in finding just the right balance in formation of the calcium channels. Too much calcium triggers enzymes that eat proteins called 'tau' that normally bind to the microtubules within the nerve cells. Without tau, the microtubules fall apart and die, and the ability to relay signals is challenged. The brain is unable to transmit the messages that affect motor skills, sensory processes and memory." Anxious to please his benefactor, he hoped his narration was informative without sounding condescending.

"How close are you to establishing the proper balance and thereby realizing a completion date? In other words," said the voice, "when will a drug be ready for use on humans?"

"Very close. A matter of a few weeks at most."

The voice urged him to do all possible to speed up his research and hinted at making a formal announcement of his success.

"The Nobel Prize in chemistry could be awarded for a breakthrough such as this. But timing is essential."

Sumio hardly noticed when the blindfold was put on again and he was led back to the limousine. Nor did he pay any heed to the scenery dimly perceivable through the smoked glass windows of the car when it was removed. He was thinking of the money and prestige that would be his when he received the Nobel Prize for chemistry.

He began to compose his acceptance speech.

Storms that had doused the state of Texas for over a week had cleared miraculously just in time for the gala grand opening of Victor Buchanan's presidential library. Red coated parking attendants opened the doors of Lincolns, Cadillacs, and even a Ferrari or two as politicians, dignitaries and movie stars arrived for the celebration. Victor's popularity crossed party lines and had brought out the most stellar of stellar personalities.

Guests entered the building by way of a red, white and blue carpet that lay between velvet ropes attached to shiny brass posts. A receiving line that included Victor and Pamela, and their two daughters, welcomed the glitterati.

Among the first to arrive were the Douglas clan—Kirk and Anne and their son, Michael and his wife. The very lovely Anne Douglas looked positively ethereal in pale blue satin.

Not far behind them was designer Oleg Cassini, who had been responsible for most of Pamela Buchanan's wardrobe when she was First Lady. The story had circulated that she had asked a number of dress designers to create something special for her to wear, but when Cassini was asked, he turned her down, saying that he would be delighted to create a 'look' exclusively for her, but that if too many designers put forth their own designs, her life would be a frenzy of fittings and she would end up with no style of her own. Pamela had been immensely impressed and wore nothing but Cassini designs from that moment on.

As the evening wore on, Frank Sinatra was seen chatting with Bobby Short, and the governor of Tennessee, Rusty LaFarge, apparently charmed Liza Minnelli. Rusty's wife, Anne, didn't feel well and spent most of the evening huddled over a cup of hot tea, fighting the flu bug that would keep her in bed the following week.

As the biggest single contributor to the library, Satoshi Yoshida was an honored guest. He had flown from Tokyo to Dallas in his private jet the previous day and planned a quick and quiet side trip to Andrews Air Force Base before the return trip to Japan. During a very brief stopover, he would tell The President that the medication so vital to The First Lady's life would be available within a few weeks—in time for the Christmas holidays—and assure him that the chemist who had discovered this critical breakthrough was working night and day to finish his research.

He would be supremely gracious in his thanks to The President for his cooperation in the effort to stabilize an enduring relationship between the United States and Japan. Yoshida thought that perhaps it was time to add that history would remember The President as a man of great stature for his ability to see the advantages in resisting political pressure. The Tennessee plant was very close to resolving the issues that confronted it, and discussions were ongoing in the Japanese community regarding the possibility of several additional facilities in the States. And after all, the striking workers were no doubt in need of regular paychecks so settlements would be reached soon in any event.

Pamela Buchanan watched her husband as he circulated through the room pointing out special exhibits of events in his presidency to some of the guests, most of whom seemed to be the youngest and most beautiful in attendance. She wondered if he would ever outgrow his seemingly insatiable passions and considered divorce for the millionth time.

The Thursday after Victor Buchanan's library opened was Thanksgiving and Ken Williamson was surrounded by his loving family at a table laden with roast turkey, cranberry sauce, mashed potatoes and pumpkin pie. He marveled at his mother's ability to provide the feast under the circumstances, but then, money and connections spoke with authority.

Ken was happier than he'd ever been. Mellie was every man's dream. She was smart, loved her job as the west coast editor for a women's magazine, could put food on a table that made him want to swoon, and she was sensational in bed. Ken had yet to discover any flaws. They even enjoyed talking to each other and shared the same opinions on most of the important things in life. Their honeymoon would be a two-week cruise in the Mediterranean and then a week in Venice, arriving back in San Francisco just before Christmas.

Ken had managed to keep his affair with Charles a secret so far and the only blip on the horizon was his fear that Charles might drink too much and make a scene at the wedding on Saturday. They had agreed to meet at the bar in Maiden Lane for a drink earlier that week and though Charles had been more or less reasonable, Ken sensed that there was something very wrong beneath the façade. Charles had been overconfident one moment and morose the next, though not excessively. Curious, Ken had decided to let well enough alone and resisted the urge to ask questions.

They had touched briefly on Morita's death when Ken mentioned that he'd seen it in the newspaper. Too bad, he'd said, not really meaning it, but the grin on Charles' face had been almost evil. Now that Morita was no longer a threat, maybe Charles would get on with his life, realizing that their friendship had exceeded the acceptable only because they had taken such pleasure in discovering their shared interests.

Unfortunately, one of the fundamental ingredients in the casserole of life is the surety that what can go wrong will go wrong—Murphy's Law.

On Friday morning, Ken's mother awakened him with a breakfast tray that held orange juice, black coffee, a sweet roll, a cordless telephone and an urgent message from Charles. He sighed as she closed the door on her way out and swallowed the orange juice in three long gulps. Pulling up the antenna on the phone, he dialed Charles' number.

As he feared, Charles was on the verge of hysteria and insisted that they meet one last time before the wedding. Ken had no choice but to agree when Charles said, "It's either now or tomorrow at the church. You decide."

An hour later, Ken climbed the stairs to the floor he had shared with his good friend. He heard music coming from his former lodgings across the hall from Charles' apartment and had a momentary twinge of homesickness for the old place. It was dispelled quickly when Charles opened the door following his knock.

Unshaven since before the holiday, his eyes bloodshot, and holding a glass of light amber liquid that Ken assumed was scotch, Charles appeared on the edge of insanity.

"My God, man, what's happened to you?" Ken blurted.

"I did it for you, you know," Charles said. "But you left me anyway."

"What are you talking about?"

"Morita, of course. I took care of him so he wouldn't bother us anymore."

"Took care of him? He's dead, Charles. You know that. The police think it was gang related because of his association with what they called the Japanese underworld. What do you mean, you took care of him?" Ken frowned, seriously concerned that Charles' mind may have snapped.

Charles simply stood there, his eyes dull and half closed. He began to laugh humorlessly. Suddenly Ken began to understand.

"Oh, my God, Charles. *You* didn't do it, did you? How? Why?" Ken turned away, doubling over as bile rose from his stomach to his throat.

"He called the day you moved out. He said his friends, whoever they are, didn't like the letter your dad wrote to the Secretary of Defense about the FSX talks and that I wasn't doing what I was supposed to be doing, which was to keep both our dads under control. He threatened to tell them about us and I knew it wouldn't end until he was dead. I told him I'd meet him at the bar out on Geary, and then I said we needed more privacy, so we went out to his car and I stabbed him. He was so vile." Charles shuddered.

"Oh god, oh god, oh god," Ken repeated. "What have you done?"

"I thought that would be the end of it, especially when the paper said it was probably gang related. But this morning when I went out to get some sweet rolls, two men came up on either side of me. They were so close that I could feel their arms against mine. One of them said, 'You didn't really think you'd get away with it, did you, Mr. Stuart?' At least they didn't call me Chuckie like Morita did."

"Did they say what they want? Could they have any proof that you did it?"

That they had no proof was one thing Charles was pretty sure about. "What difference does it make if they have proof or not," he asked rhetorically. "All they'd have to do to ruin us is make the claim. They disappeared as fast as they showed up. Just dropped back and when I turned around to look, they were gone. My life is a mess, Ken. You have to help me!"

Ken sank into a chair, his elbows on his knees, and covered his eyes with his hands. "What can I do?" he asked. He could think of nothing he could do to erase the terrible problem Charles had created. He considered briefly, then said slowly, "If you're sure that they have no proof it was you, there's be no reason for them to tell anyone it was you. It's just a threat and in time, it will just fade away, Charles."

"But you can't leave me here alone now!" Charles cried.

"Think about it. If I called off the wedding at this late hour, it would look suspicious if they made any claims about us, but if I'm married and away on a honeymoon, no one would believe them. You're inviting trouble by over-reacting like this! This destructive behavior has to stop!"

Confused by days of alcohol abuse and unwilling to let go of the idea that Ken must come back to save him, Charles reiterated, "What about Morita? What if they tell the police that it was me?"

Trying to be patient, Ken said, "You said that they couldn't prove anything. Does that mean there's no fingerprints or weapon, and that nobody saw you?"

"I parked on a side street away from the bar and I killed him with a knife from my kitchen that I brought home with me. I wore old clothes and a cap, I didn't shave and I made sure I didn't leave any fingerprints. So yeah, no proof, right?"

I can't believe I'm having this conversation, Ken thought. Have I made some sort of quantum leap through the looking glass?

Anxious to please Ken, Charles managed a tentative smile and Ken couldn't help feeling a mixture of sympathy and horror. Part of him wanted to comfort the man with whom he'd spent so many happy hours, but the vision of Charles stabbing Morita made him ill. Self-preservation demanded that he shove the memories into an abyss and convince Charles that they must carry on as if nothing untoward had happened. There were no acceptable alternatives.

# CHAPTER TWENTY EIGHT

Charles descended the steps leading to the street from the foyer of the church, his vision blurred by the emotions that raged in his heart. The wedding had been even more beautiful than his own to Maggie, he reflected. Vases of white flowers among huge potted ferns crowded the altar. The ferns would be rushed to the country club for the reception and then taken to the newlyweds apartment in San Francisco.

Ken had not asked Charles to be a member of the wedding party and Charles had not expected it. Though he remained devastated at losing the companionship and yes, love, that he had shared with Ken, he really couldn't wish Ken and Mellie anything but happiness in their future together. It was almost a relief now that it was a done deal.

The comradery between Ken and his fraternity brothers from Stanford brought back memories of the kinship Charles had known at Dartmouth. In some ways, it seemed a lifetime ago and in others only yesterday. They'd had their whole lives ahead of them back then—dreams and expectations, the promise of excitement as they began their voyages on yet to be charted seas, the conviction that they were destined to make a difference. How could he have sunk into the depths of self-destruction instead?

Mellie and her sorority sisters reminded Charles of Maggie and her college chums as well. Maggie had been so lovely, floating down the aisle on her father's arm, her blonde hair swept back from her face and flowers woven into her curls. He had thought she was as close to perfection as a man dared hope to find. And still he had betrayed her. Left her, his home, his job, and even his own family, for a life with Ken in San Francisco. He watched Ken and Mellie laughing as they ran to the limousine that would take them to the country club. A terrible nausea began to creep into his belly. He turned away from the other guests, sure that his shame must be evident to anyone who glanced his way.

It was not the love he felt for another man that made him ashamed, it was the manner in which that love had consumed him, changed him into a whiny, drunken, self-absorbed sot who wallowed in degradation and even committed the most horrendous of sins—murder. How could anyone stand to be near him, let alone love him? Afraid he might be sick right there on the church steps, he strode toward the parking lot where his car waited. He could not go on to the reception with the others. His presence would be an affront to friendship and decent people.

His hand shook as he tried to unlock the car door and the keys fell to the pavement. He leaned against the vehicle, absorbed in the contempt he felt for himself, and so was unaware of the Asian man in the dark suit and sunglasses who moved quietly to his side, bending to retrieve the fallen keys.

"Are you unwell, Mr. Stuart?" The man's voice was low and raspy, a little like Jimmy Durante with a cold, Charles thought spontaneously. He straightened and looked into the man's face, realizing that this stranger had used his name and that the meeting had not been accidental.

"What do you want?"

"Why nothing, Mr. Stuart. For the moment anyway. We have not yet decided how to handle your mistakes. You see, Mr. Morita was not really one of us, though he had hoped to be accepted into our brotherhood. He was not temperamentally suited for our kind of work, too abrasive, too volatile. But he was on an assignment for someone we respect a great deal, nevertheless, and we cannot allow you to go unpunished for his murder. Quite a dilemma, as you can see."

"You have no proof that I was anywhere near Morita. Why don't you just leave me alone?" Charles attempted to bluff his way out of the confrontation.

"We don't need proof, Mr. Stuart. Proof is what the police require if there is to be a trial. You need not fear that your crime will come to trial in an American court. Your punishment will be determined by our organization, though you may eventually wish that it was the other way around. For the moment, however, we will simply keep an eye on you." With that, the man handed Charles the keys that were still in his hand and bowed slightly as he turned away.

Charles watched as the man got into a car. He waited for the sound of the engine turning over, but heard nothing as the man sat behind the wheel regarding Charles from behind his dark lenses. He's just trying to scare me, Charles thought. It's their way of terrorizing people. All I have to do is stay calm and keep my wits about me. Don't do anything stupid. Mustn't let him see any fear.

Charles took a few deep breaths, then unlocked the car and slid in behind the wheel. He deliberately ignored the other car as it followed him from the lot and up the road to the 280 freeway entrance. Half a mile north, the car passed him, its driver staring straight ahead. Forty minutes later, Charles came to the end of the freeway and swore aloud as traffic slowed to a crawl on Nineteenth Avenue. Regular Saturday afternoon shoppers at neighborhood stores in the Sunset district competed with Thanksgiving weekend shoppers for their place in line at each stop light.

Reminding himself that it hardly mattered since he had no urgent destination anyway, only a date with the scotch bottle in his lonely apartment on Russian Hill, Charles did his best to relax. He followed traffic through Golden Gate Park and turned right on Geary Street. He was only a block away when he realized that his route would take him past the tavern where Morita had had his last drink.

Gripping the wheel firmly, he forced himself to concentrate as he sped up and changed lanes. Sliding between two cars on his left, he narrowly missed the rear fender of the car that had been in front of him. He maneuvered in and out until he reached Franklin Street where he swung to the left and breathed a sigh of relief. Suddenly anxious to reach the safety of his own apartment, he focused his attention on driving. His hands and forehead were clammy as he turned his key in the lock and strode to the kitchen where he reached for his old friend, the scotch bottle.

Looking back on the past few months, he found it hard to believe how drastically he'd changed. The man who had been Phi Beta Kappa at Dartmouth, the man who had been smiled upon by Chicago's old money bankers, the man who had married the lovely Maggie Davidson, daughter of the founder and CEO of the Davidson Hotel Group, the man whose own father was chairman of the board of the Federal Reserve Bank, the man whose mother thought the sun came up only to shine on him. The man who was now a murderer.

He was facing a life of perpetual torture from mysterious sources that he might never be able to identify. If, in an effort to eliminate the constant fear they promised, he confessed to his crime, he would bring shame to everyone he loved, and he would be lucky to escape the electric chair at San Quentin.

He was startled to discover that he no longer thought of Ken as a lover, but as someone whose friendship and respect he valued. In fact, he could hardly recall moments of intimacy. Ken had known all along that it was not meant to be a permanent lifestyle. Would Charles have been able to accept that had Ken made it clear in the beginning? He began to feel an all-consuming shame at his behavior. Had it not been for the jealousy that had ravaged his brain, Morita would have been almost laughable. Certainly not the dangerous threat that Charles had perceived him to be. Even the hatred was suddenly gone. But that wouldn't bring the man back to life and the choices remaining were all loathsome.

Charles knew that if he went over the edge again, Ken's future would be jeopardized and that was as unacceptable as the knowledge that he was a disgrace to his beloved parents. He stared at the glass in his hand, knowing that if he kept company with the bottle as he had been doing, it was more than possible that harassment from his new enemies would push him into committing additional foolish acts in a fit of passion. There was really only one choice left.

Tears began to form in his eyes, spilling over and down his cheeks as despair wracked his being. He began to sob uncontrollably, hugging his sides in agony. Slipping to the floor, he curled up in a fetal position and cried until he had no more tears, then rocked, moaning, until he was too tired to go on. He lay there until he slept, and when he woke an hour later, he knew what he had to do.

He wrote a short letter of resignation to his office, adding that he planned to end his life and would appreciate it if someone would make sure that his parents were notified if the authorities failed to do it for one reason or another. He spent the rest of the evening gathering up the things that were special to him, keepsakes from years past, and putting them in carefully marked boxes. He packed his clothes neatly, selecting a dark blue blazer, light blue turtleneck shirt and grey flannel trousers to wear the next day. Looking at the bookcases that lined the living room, he decided to leave a note to the effect that Ken should take any of the volumes that he might like to have and that his father should dispose of the rest.

The last thing he did before he went to bed was to write another short note, this one to his parents. There really wasn't much he could say other than how sorry he would be to hurt them and that he hoped they'd forgive him. He left the note beside the other ones in the living room. When he finally got into bed, he fell asleep almost immediately and slumbered undisturbed until morning.

# CHAPTER TWENTY NINE

Charles felt a rather remarkable sense of well-being as he dressed, and wondered if that was normal for someone who was planning to die that day. It was certainly a far more pleasant state of mind than the drunken tirades had been. That thought seemed to indicate that he had made the right decision.

The weather was exceptionally fine as he drove toward the Buena Vista Café where he planned to have at least one Irish coffee with a nice hot breakfast. He glanced at his watch and noted that it was nearly nine o'clock. He stepped on the gas pedal, hurrying to arrive before the usual Sunday crowds began to show up. It was impossible to get a seat if you didn't get there by nine o'clock. He laughed at the idea that he was in a hurry to beat the crowds when time would soon be completely unimportant to him. At least time as he now knew it.

Miraculously, he found an empty parking space just around the corner from the BV. The air was crisp and chilly, and he threw back his head, breathing deeply to fill his lungs. He entered the already noisy café through the back door and made his way to a seat at the bar, ordering an Irish coffee before he picked up the breakfast menu.

Raucous laughter erupted as a group of people at a nearby table shared a joke. Charles eavesdropped more or less unintentionally and came to the conclusion that they were regulars who gathered there weekly. At least one or two journalists, he surmised from the conversation. He recognized the name of a local columnist, Jack Mercer, who was apparently on a Hawaiian vacation. A woman with salt and pepper hair speculated on just what their friend might be doing at that moment.

"Contemplating the grains of sand running through his toes?" suggested someone else.

"More than likely ravishing Diane repeatedly in a room that hasn't seen sunlight since their arrival," said another.

"At his age?" scoffed a young, preppy-looking man. The others regarded him disdainfully, murmuring among themselves that he obviously had much to learn.

Charles swallowed the last of his Irish coffee and signaled the bartender for another. A sudden pain in his chest brought a lump to his throat that threatened to force embarrassing tears from his eyes. Everybody was so happy, nourished by the bonds of friendship and exuberant about life. Everybody but him. But then, he didn't deserve it, did he?

The sun was almost directly overhead by the time he drove across the Golden Gate Bridge and took the winding road down into Sausalito on his way to another of his favorite bars. Gatsby's, located a block over from the main drag, was a hangout for locals that tourists usually failed to find. The dark, smoke filled bar was home to any number of jazz greats such as Al Jarreau, and Charles wanted to hear a little mellow music, even if it came from a juke box.

He ordered a scotch and soda—what difference would it make if he did get drunk, he wasn't planning on driving far—and asked the bartender for quarters for the juke box. He carried his drink with him as he crossed the room to pick out tunes. The first one he selected was the Kingston Trio rendition of 'Scotch and Soda.' He leaned against the box to listen for a moment, humming along, then punched in the numbers that would bring up Wes Montgomery and 'Goin' Out of My Head,' then 'Tequila' and several others. He still had more than half of the quarters left, but his glass was nearly empty, so he went back to the bar to have it refilled.

An hour or so later, he had listened to a little Oscar Peterson, a lot of Dave Brubeck, and the Four Freshmen singing about the things they did last summer. Feeling remarkably sober despite the amount of liquor he had swallowed, he attributed it to a heightened awareness brought on by the knowledge that he no longer had to pretend to be anything but what he was.

Time to move on, he thought. He paused at the exit to say one last farewell to Gatsby's, and drove back up the hill to the view area that was situated just north of the bridge. Opening the glove compartment, he withdrew the kitchen knife that had ended Bill Morita's life, put it inside his jacket and then left his wallet in its place. He got out of the car, stretched and inhaled the fresh air, and walked toward the bridge span. How beautifully clear it was. The view was so often obscured by fog. And it was so much warmer here than in The City.

A pair of red and white buses lumbered past and Charles was startled to feel the roadway tremble beneath his feet. The sun was lower on the horizon now, leaving the north end of the bridge in shadows while the center span remained in the light. The City shone in the distance, Alcatraz was but a lump in the bay, and dozens of little white sails on the water seemed suspended in time. Charles felt curiously at peace as he went past the concrete tower at lands-end above a rocky point that guarded the entrance to the bay.

Afraid at first that he might stand out among the bridge walkers, he soon realized that no one was paying him the slightest attention. Humanity of all varieties strolled the sidewalk: families with toddlers, college kids wearing school sweatshirts, elderly couples holding hands. There were faces of many skin colors. None of them even glanced his way.

Confronted by the self-absorption of his fellow man, Charles found that rather than being reassured, he was lonelier than ever. He stopped to lean on the metal railing. Shadows had begun to creep into the crevices in the San Francisco skyline. Lights were coming on in the tiny buildings that tumbled down the hillsides like children's toys. Charles pulled up the collar of his jacket and turned away from The City, looking out cross the roadway to the west. There were fewer people on the bridge now that evening was coming on.

Heading further toward mid-span, he reached the north tower and was gratified to find that the sidewalk went around the back side of it, creating a shelter from the ocean breezes. He stood in the shadows there, watching as a large freighter came around the far side of Angel Island, making its way under the bridge into the endless ocean beyond. Tiny sailboats taunted it, even raced across its wake as it blasted warnings.

Containers filled its deck, four or five high and of several different colors.

As it approached, he read the words Yang Ming Line on its bow. Chinese, he thought. Hong Kong? Taiwan? Maybe even Shanghai? He wondered about the crew. Were there people waiting on a faraway shore for them? Did they look forward to happy reunions after long months at sea? The ship passed under the bridge and disappeared into the light that still shimmered on the Pacific.

The water below was green and murky as Charles stared down at it. He began to feel an almost cosmic connection with the darkness that beckoned beneath him. Mesmerized, he watched as the waves played little games of tag.

If I stare at the water long enough, could I see the face of God, he wondered. Does God have a face? If I could see it, would he be angry with me, or would he be sad that I've chosen to die rather than face my transgressions?

Charles had never given much real thought to God, taking him for granted. Now that the answers sought by so many people would soon be his, he found a certain comfort in the knowledge. If this was indeed the end, it didn't matter, and if there was a hereafter, it had to be better than life on earth. He'd rather face the judgment of God than that of men.

As he stared into the water, swaying slightly in tune with the movement of the waves, he saw Maggie's face. Would she mourn him? Probably not, after what he'd done to her. A vision of her beside their Christmas tree appeared. Christmas had been her favorite holiday. Charles had been touched by her memories of Christmas Eve as a child.

Her mother had worn a long black taffeta skirt that rustled when she walked and her father had worn a red sweater that was soft against Maggie's cheek. Dinner was always New England pot roast that had simmered for hours on the stove and smelled better than anything in the world, the next day's turkey dinner being the only possible exception. After dinner, Victoria took Maggie to her room to wash her hands and comb her long curly hair before they opened their presents. As the last of the tangles were being brushed from the little girl's hair, the doorbell would chime and Maggie would hear her daddy's voice booming, "Well, hello Santa! Come on in!"

Maggie would struggle to free herself from Victoria's firm grasp and race down the hall to see Santa, but every year her father would be leaning out an open window, waving and calling out to a disappearing mythical sleigh, "Bye, Santa! See you next year!" Michael would explain hastily that Santa had to hurry to visit children all over the world before the night was over, saying, "Look what he's left here for you!"

Charles smiled tenderly at the picture of a small Maggie tearing at packages, finding new clothes on all her dolls, or the white colonial doll house that was still in her old room.

Maggie's face in the water was replaced by Ken's face. Would he be sorry that Charles was dead? Probably. But not because he'd be devastated by the loss. He'd feel sorry for Charles, consider him a pathetic creature. Pity him.

Only his parents would truly mourn his passing. And if they knew the truth about the past year of his life, even they would find disgust mingled with their sorrow. Regret that all the magnificent accomplishments they had anticipated for his future would never be realized. Charles had always known that he could never achieve the success his father had. Maybe that was because he'd known all along that his was a soul of lesser quality.

Would his body be recovered, he wondered. Somehow it didn't seem very important. If the person known as Charles Stuart ceased to exist, then his body wasn't important anyway. And if his soul was a separate entity that had resided temporarily in the physical body of Charles Stuart, it wouldn't want the body that had failed it so miserably. Would it leave his body before or after the moment of death?

Would there be pain in dying? Probably not much unless he was still conscious when he hit the water, and since that would be like hitting cement, it wouldn't last long.

Dusk was turning into evening. Charles glanced around, but saw no one nearby. He pulled the knife from inside his jacket and examined it closely. No trace that he could see of the evil it had done, but still, it was the only link between him and the death of Bill Morita. Sliding his hand over the rail, he let it fall into the water, watching as it tumbled end over end, taking its time to reach a final resting place. He couldn't remember—did everything fall at the same speed regardless of weight? He lost sight of the knife.

Charles looked out once more at the city that had brought him so much pleasure and so much anguish, and at that moment he saw himself as only one small part of an enormous universe. He backed up, then sprinted to the rail and vaulted over with one last agonized cry that no one heard.

# CHAPTER THIRTY

I t was Saturday and Zach Templeton was not in his office when the mail was delivered. The secretary who was there to sort it and give exigent matters at least a perfunctory glance was not in the mood to spend the day inside. It was a holiday weekend, what with Thanksgiving, and the building was deserted except for those junior staffers like herself who had drawn the duty. She couldn't imagine what could possibly be important enough to warrant attention at such a time. Most of what crossed her desk at any given time carried negligible weight in her opinion. She had thought that working for a congressman would be exciting, but in the three months she'd been employed by Zach Templeton, she had yet to come across much that qualified. Mostly it was complaints from old ladies in Tennessee or boring communiqués from other congressional offices. She hadn't even seen the vice president in person, never mind The President. It was really a ho-hum job, but then, you never knew so she'd decided to stick it out for awhile.

In a preliminary inspection of the pile on her desk, she tossed everything with bulk rate postage in the trash, piled the magazines in one stack, the oversized material in another, and left only personally addressed letters in front of her. She slit open the envelopes and separated their contents into two more piles—one for constituency mail with Tennessee post marks and another for business mail.

In a game of eeny-meeny-miney-mo, she selected the official stack and began looking over the correspondence. The third letter was from the Japanese company that owned the Tennessee auto plant that was the congressman's pet project. At first glance she thought it was just more of the polite mumbo jumbo that the Japanese were so fond of sending, but as she read the second page, she realized that the letter was officially announcing that the plant would be closed immediately and that all employees would be placed on indefinite leave.

The secretary frowned. Surely if the congressman knew about this, all hell would have broken loose around the office and he wouldn't be off on a family holiday. Should she phone him, she wondered, deciding quickly that disturbing his holiday would be preferable to taking chances.

She was unaware that Zach Templeton had already been disturbed by the new plant manager who had just discovered that all the locks on plant doors had been changed and a sign had been posted at the main entrance informing anyone who came close enough to read it that the plant was closed until further notice. The personal notices that had been mailed to each employee were lying in a large canvas tub in the Jackson post office. The Japanese clerk in Tokyo had been unaware of the American devotion to the Thanksgiving holiday and that delivery of mail might well be delayed a day or two.


In Hawaii, Diane Manchester and Jack Mercer spent most of Saturday lying on the beach in front of the Colony Surf where they were lodged in a luxury condominium owned by Diane's Japanese employers. Diane had arrived the week before and considered herself practically a native by the time Jack got there. She had checked out the Kaimana Surf and Sand next door and loved the beach bar. She had met the new owner, Maggie Stuart, and was eager to introduce Jack. Maggie was in a frenzy over the grand opening party planned for the following week, however, and had been nowhere in sight when they stopped by on Friday evening.

Jack had been talked into spending ten days there—his first real vacation in many years. Diane still had two weeks of her three week holiday, a vacation time span beyond Jack's comprehension, and considering her relatively short period of employment, a bit of a surprise to Diane as well.

Accustomed to the pace in San Francisco, Jack was having trouble adjusting to laid back Hawaii. Up at dawn each morning, he had discovered a newsstand several blocks away in Waikiki Beach that carried the Chronicle and that kept him occupied for a couple of hours. The fact that the paper was a day old by the time he got it was a temporary annoyance, but at least he felt connected.

By Saturday, he was sufficiently relaxed to sleep on the warm sand and admitted that there was a slim chance he might get used to this lifestyle after all. They enjoyed a magnificent dinner at Michel's, and then went next door to Maggie's place, as they had begun to call the Kaimana Surf and Sand. They had just ordered brandies when Maggie stepped off the elevator and came toward their table.

"Maggie, this is Jack Mercer," Diane began. She stopped, noticing that they were staring at each other, their mouths open in surprise. Jack was the first to recover.

"Maggie Davidson! Sweet, beautiful Maggie Davidson!" he exclaimed. "I had no idea that Diane's friend Maggie Stuart would turn out to be the girl who had most of Stan Mitsunari's fraternity brothers thinking up ways to do him in so they could take his place! How could your name be Stuart? Surely the romance of the century didn't end badly!" Jack's arms opened wide to enfold Maggie in a great bear hug.

"You two know each other?" Diane was stunned.

Maggie was laughing as she returned the hug. "Dear, dear Jack! You always were good with the blarney. I heard through the network that you'd gone back to San Francisco after . . ." her voice trailed off.

"You can say it, Maggie. After the divorce. Somebody should have told us that football games and sorority dances aren't study courses for marriage. But you and Mitsu? That was different. What happened? Or isn't it any of my business?"

"I'm not really sure what happened, Jack. We went to Chicago so that he could meet my folks and discovered that they weren't as broad minded as I'd always thought they were. The sad part of it is that Mitsu bought into it and went back to Japan. Eventually, I married the yuppie that my dad approved of, but that didn't work out either." Maggie looked away, then changed the subject by reaching for Diane's hand.

"You didn't tell me that your Mr. Wonderful was my old friend from our college days," she said.

Diane blushed as Jack laughed and took her other hand.

"I'm the lucky one in this relationship, Maggie," he said. "I'd begun to think that an old curmudgeon like me would be unlikely to find a woman who was not only my dream girl, but who loves me in spite of my peculiarities. Diane's genius mind keeps her oblivious to my more odious faults. Did she tell you that the company she works for is about to release a new computer storage system that she designed? Or that the IBM system that's in test stages is also her design?"

Maggie laughed along with him. "She's been modest about her accomplishments, but she *has* been trying to convince me that I don't have to carry everything around with me, and that it would be perfectly safe entrusted to the hotel computer system. As you can see, however, I'm a hard case." She held up a file overflowing with papers of varying size that was always in her possession. "It's a little academic right now anyway, since our whole system has been shut down for the installation of a new program. As a matter of fact, I think we're installing one of the new test programs you just mentioned. I'm not really sure how the hotel happened to be included in these test cases—somebody knew somebody, I think—and I'm so clueless about computers that I haven't paid much attention. The night auditor is due to check it out this weekend.

Releasing Diane's hand, Jack said, "Well, Diane will have you converted by the time she leaves here. If I'm not being too nosy, have you kept in touch with Mitsu at all? Since we're both in the newspaper business, I do know that he's an executive with the Japanese financial paper. I don't think he's been back to Mizzou, or for that matter, even comes back to the states very often."

"It's curious that I should run into you like this, Jack. I hadn't heard from him in years until recently when I discovered that he had somehow acquired stock in my company. I phoned him and accused him of taking revenge on my family, but he claims to know nothing about the stock. He's supposed to look into it and get back to me."

"Revenge isn't Mitsu's game, Maggie. Do you believe him?"

"I think I do, but I can't imagine how the stock came to be in his name. It's all very mysterious—a Caribbean holding company with an elusive manager who specializes in clients who wish to remain anonymous."

"Could it have been someone who wanted the stock for some other reason and knew of your past relationship with Mitsu?" Jack asked, then speculated, "Could your husband be seeking some sort of retaliation?"

"Charles?" Maggie scoffed at the idea. "No, if anyone were to seek retaliation in that relationship, it would be me. Besides, it isn't Charles' style any more than it's Mitsu's. In any event, I hope Mitsu comes up with a good explanation," she responded, dismissing the issue.

As his old friends were getting reacquainted in Honolulu, Stan Mitsunari was still trying to understand the story he'd been given the previous day. Sunao Tokumura had admitted that the stock in Davidson Hotels had been purchased as compensation for his loyalty to Japan. But the vice minister had been deliberately vague when pressed for the name or names of whomever was behind it. He had alluded to an agreement between powerful men, nationalists of the highest order who were duly appreciative of other patriots. Tokumura had gone on to cite the need for absolute discretion and confidentiality, urging Stan to accept the reward without further questions.

In compiling a list of Japanese who had access to the kind of money it would take to give 'gifts' of this magnitude, and who were known to be fanatic nationalists, Stan had come back repeatedly to the same name: Satoshi Yoshida. Though it would be beyond the means of most men, the sum required to buy the Davidson stock was a drop in the proverbial bucket for the billionaire industrialist, and it was common knowledge that the man despised the United States. Could he be plotting some kind of revenge against the country that had considered him a criminal over forty years ago?

And how did Sunao Tokumura fit into it? The Ministry of International Trade and Industry was undoubtedly the most powerful of all the ministries, more so than either Foreign Affairs or Finance when it came to the economic well-being of the country. The influence wielded by the vice minister was mighty, and no doubt crucial to any plan to damage the United States.

Stan suddenly recalled the meeting several weeks earlier during which Tokumura had told the story of his father's anguish at the

Japanese surrender, and the promise he had made that he would make it right. A chill ran up Stan's spine as he remembered what Tokumura had said: "It seems that opportunities may have arisen that will enable me to fulfill my old promise."

At the time, Stan had assumed he meant some sort of spiritual redemption in the old samurai tradition, and had dismissed it. Now that he thought more carefully about it, however, the old samurai tradition was one of violent retaliation in many cases. Surely another Pearl Harbor was out of the question! Military action would be too obvious and require too many other people involved to be kept a secret.

What else could Tokumura have meant? Some sort of economic retaliation? Strategically planned, it might be a possibility. Reaching for a yellow pad, Stan began to make furious notes. The United States was reaching a state of crisis because of the labor strikes that were crippling the country. How had they begun? Stan turned to the computer keyboard and punched in the topic, watching as a list of related articles from various news services appeared on the screen.

Initial releases dealt with farm labor in California and proposed work slowdowns. Later releases told of sympathy walkouts by other unions, most notably teamsters who cited the massive layoffs at the Japanese auto plant in Tennessee.

Two hours later, Stan had several pages of notes. One name stood out: George Hagura, revered leader of the California farm workers. An inflammatory labor publication, The Wage Earner, had popped up shortly after the first signs of labor unrest, with George Hagura as its editor and publisher. A background search brought forth the information that Hagura had been born in an American detention camp during the war. Were his motives as noble as his followers believed, or did they include some sort of revenge?

The telex began to rattle and Stan rose from his desk to tear off a paragraph reporting the closing of the Tennessee auto plant. The same plant that had laid off hundreds of its employees without notice and started the teamster walkouts. Collusion? Didn't seem feasible . . . not with the teamsters at any rate. But sympathy strikes were reasonable. Had some master strategist known that this could happen? Even planted the seed and helped it to grow?

A sense of foreboding began to cause twinges in Stan's stomach. He turned his attention to the construction loans that had been called recently by Japanese banks doing business in California. In his urgent need to find out how his name came to be on the Davidson Hotel Group stock, he had delegated the loan question to one of his research staffers. It didn't take long to find the file on it that held several pages of telephone inquiries.

The head of the loan department at the main office of the Bank of Tokyo had recalled a conversation with the executive vice president of the bank who had referred to the ten-year plan that called for increased domestic spending versus saving. When questioned, the executive vice president said that he recalled seeing a directive urging that funds be recycled back into the Japanese economy. His memory failed him when asked where the directive had come from.

Calls made to the branches in California yielded little in the way of explanation. Loan officers said that clauses that were often included in loan documents but rarely activated, had been exercised at the request of the board. The trail was impossible to trace with reliable accuracy. No one is better at covering his ass than a Japanese businessman, Stan thought. He reviewed the editorials he himself had written in recent weeks. The first had urged cultural unity and hinted that Japan was doing the U.S. a favor by refining technology for them. Then had come one that could be construed as blackmail, suggesting that if Japan were to deny semiconductors to the Americans and sell them to the Russians, she had the ability to change the balance of world power.

Good god! He'd played right into their hands! If in fact a conspiracy did exist, that is. How far had it gone? What didn't he know? And worst of all, how deeply was he implicated as a co-conspirator through ownership of the Davidson stock? He spent most of the day reviewing the scribbles on the growing pile of yellow pads, then decided he must see Maggie in person and quitclaim the stock back to her.

A call to her office in Chicago informed him that she was in Hawaii for the grand opening of the most recent acquisition of the Davidson Hotel Group. In a matter of hours, he was on a plane to Honolulu, arriving shortly before noon Hawaiian time.

Front desk personnel at the Kaimana Surf and Sand were polite, but tense as they explained to him that their computer system was down and they hoped he'd be patient while they checked with housekeeping to ascertain the availability of rooms. When he asked to see Mrs. Stuart, he was told that she was unavailable at the moment, but they would see to it that she received a message.

Somehow it seemed that the problem might be greater than a computer that was down. Stan wondered what it was.

# CHAPTER THIRTY ONE

In a smallish room behind the front desk, Diane Manchester was working with the hotel's computer operator to restore the IBM system that had been installed and loaded only days earlier. The system had been powered up by the night auditor shortly before midnight the evening before, and as he watched the screen, everything that had been entered since Maggie's takeover had vanished. The resulting chaos was threatening disaster. All future reservations had been wiped out, as had credit card deposits, food and beverage inventories and orders, and accounts payable and receivable. Maggie was on the verge of hysteria.

Diane had offered to help since she was responsible for the original program design. She had discovered that most of the data was stored on floppy discs and could be reloaded in a matter of hours. There were files or correspondence that had been scanned and discarded, but all in all, it wasn't hopeless as far as Diane was concerned. What bothered her was the reason for the failure in the first place. She conferred with the man who had been on duty when the problem occurred, urging him to go back to the moment when he sat down to power up the system.

"What was the first thing you did once the power was on?" she asked.

"I was about to bring up the accounts payable data when I noticed that the date was wrong. Instead of November 27th, it said December 27th. Since it was only a few seconds before midnight, I waited for it to turn over before I changed it back. When it automatically turned over, everything just disappeared," he recounted.

"Hmmm . . . let's see what happens if we enter those dates again." She set the clock for a minute before midnight on December 27th and as the date rolled over the screen went blank and the data that had been re-entered vanished once again.

"Holy Jehoshaphat!" she exclaimed. "There must be a virus installed that's set to activate as the date rolls over to December 28th! How could such a thing happen?"

The implications of a virus began to dawn on her as she realized that IBM might be about to release a whole MVS system that had been infected. Had it not been for the early release of a limited number of test versions, and had the date not been incorrectly entered when Maggie's system installed it, all data on all of the computers using it would have been wiped out. Who would do such a thing? Since the system was not yet widely available, it couldn't be an ordinary hacker. Someone had to have infected the system intentionally. Suddenly, it hit her that she might be blamed for it in view of the fact that she'd been fired only weeks before the system was released. The company might think she'd done it as an act of revenge. She had to get in touch with IBM at once. Should she call Harry Cesnick? Surely he wouldn't have done such a thing. For that matter, he wouldn't know how to do it anyway and he wanted to take credit for the system in the hope that it would advance his own career.

Since it was apparently not scheduled to activate for another month, Diane decided to think it over and hope that she could figure out who might be responsible and why before she made a mistake by moving too quickly. She left the computer operator busy reloading the system again and went to find Maggie to reassure her that everything would be all right in a matter of hours.

Maggie was huddled with the food and beverage manager and the executive chef in a windowed cubicle at one end of the kitchen. They were going over menus, checking for the odd items that might not be on regular orders and may have been overlooked. Her own office was too accessible to other staff members, most notably the front desk and housekeeping people who were getting crankier by the minute as they coped with the loss of computerized information. She had vowed that she would be the essence of leadership, suppressing the panic that hovered just below the surface. It was crucial to her future relationships with hotel personnel that, as the new company CEO, she put forth a positive image. There were always those who would love to say I-told-you-so, even her own mother, if she didn't handle her position not only with as much ability, but more ability than her father had done.

She left the kitchen a short time later, having made sure that each man had a list of necessary supplies for which they were personally responsible. As she crossed the lobby on her way to the banquet manager's office, she was thinking about room set-ups, extra chairs and buffet tables. She wished she hadn't authorized a brief trip to Maui for the new general manager she'd stolen from one of the resorts there, but he had left his family behind and might not see them for awhile once the hotel was officially under the Davidson banner. But then, no one could have predicted a potentially disastrous computer failure. God, she hoped that Diane had it under control! A guardian angel must have been perched in a palm tree when Diane showed up, bringing Jack Mercer along as well!

Maggie heard her secretary calling to her from across the lobby. As she turned, she heard another voice, this one masculine, say her name. Her heart skipped a beat, then did flip flops. She reached out for the support of a nearby table, her knees weak and threatening to buckle. Afraid to look, she waited.

"Maggie?" He was so near she could almost feel his breath. It was the same voice that had said her name so many times, so long ago, and the feelings that bubbled in her chest were the same as those she thought long forgotten. She turned and looked into the eyes that she would always love.

He was standing there looking uncertain. Tears sprang to Maggie's eyes as the years of separation fell away and passion surged into her heart. Her arms reached out to him and the uncertainty vanished from his face as he, too, relived the fire of their youth. His arms enfolded her and they clung to each other, oblivious to the glances of hotel staff and guests. The resentment and anger of many years were wiped out in a moment.

A gentle cough nearby brought them back to reality. Maggie's secretary waited to be acknowledged, then said apologetically, "There's a message for you, Mrs. Stuart. I was told that it was important, so I thought you should have it right away."

Maggie unfolded the slip of paper, read it and laughed.

"It says that Stan Mitsunari is here in the hotel and wants to see me as soon as possible."

She thanked the young woman for her diligence, then said, "May I introduce Stan Mitsunari?"

The secretary smiled and said, "Since you found each other without any help, I'll just get back to work."

"Have we found each other, Mitsu?" Maggie asked softly.

"I hope so, Maggie," he replied.

Diane leaned back in her chair, ran her fingers through her dark hair and grinned triumphantly. The computer had been almost entirely reloaded, and was functioning again as it should. There was still plenty of time to contact her old employer and perhaps even help them develop a vaccine to be emergency released to all clients using the system, but for now, she was eager to get out of the cramped space behind the front desk and back into Jack's arms. She picked up the phone and pushed the button for an outside line, savoring the thought of a tall, cool drink as she waited for Jack to answer.

A few minutes later, Jack strolled through the double doors from the street that were closed only in the worst weather, and went directly toward the beach bar, intent upon finding Diane. He stopped short, stunned to see Maggie Stuart and Stan Mitsunari seated with Diane at a table for four.

"Now this is really too much!" he exclaimed as he approached. "First I find that Maggie Stuart is really my old friend Maggie Davidson, who tells me that she hasn't seen my old fraternity brother in years, and suddenly here they are together, looking like they've never been apart! Have I flown into a time warp of some sort?"

Stan rose and the two men greeted each other with a handshake that quickly became an enthusiastic bear hug.

"No time warp," Maggie laughed, "and I was as surprised as you are. It's all happened in the past few minutes and I'm still in shock myself! One minute I was frantic about the computer failure that Diane assures me is no longer a problem, or at least won't be when some sort of virus is deleted, and the next minute I was looking into eyes I thought I'd never see again."

"How did this happen, Mitsu?" Jack looked at Maggie meaningfully, wondering if he should let on that he knew about the Davidson stock.

Maggie postponed the need for an immediate explanation by suggesting that they order a bottle of champagne for a celebratory toast to both old friends and new friends. Once the initial shock of seeing each other had been overcome, both Maggie and Stan found themselves unexpectedly shy and glad of a temporary diversion. They avoided eye contact for several minutes, each afraid that the intensity of their emotional reunion might have been premature.

When the toasts had been offered, Jack brought the conversation back to Diane's part in solving the computer crisis. "So you saved the day, did you? What was the problem?"

"It seems there might be a virus in the system, programmed to activate on December 28th," Diane began. She went on to tell them about the operator who had noticed the discrepancy, adding that when they re-entered the same date, the data that had been re-entered disappeared again.

"What worries me most is that if there is a virus, I might be blamed for inserting it," she said quietly. She turned to Stan to explain that she had been fired by IBM just before the new enhancements were released to a limited test group.

Stan suddenly remembered why her name had sounded vaguely familiar when they were introduced. "I wrote a column on the implications of IBM's new operating system right after I saw a telex about it being released as planned in spite of the loss of the project leader. In fact, I suggested to the vice minister of MITI, our Ministry of International Trade and Industry, that you might be invaluable to a Japanese company, given your expertise in the field." Even as he spoke the words, Stan realized that here was another link in the chain that connected Sunao Tokumura to the increasing problems in the states, though it seemed more than outrageous to consider.

"Who do you work for now?" he asked Diane.

Jack spoke for her, saying, "She does have a fantastic job with an exceptionally generous Japanese company, as a matter of fact. The condo we're using next door belongs to them and the use of it for three weeks of every year is included in her contract."

Stan stared at him, the gremlins in his stomach doing more flip flops as he added still another coincidence to the succession of coincidences that seemed to be turning up too rapidly to ignore. How far would Sunao Tokumura go to keep his promise to avenge his father's shame? Could the IBM virus have been inserted by using Diane without her knowledge? Had she been enticed into cooperating?

"Is there someplace we could go where we can talk privately?" he asked.

Noticing his sudden pallor, Maggie was alarmed. "Aren't you feeling well?"

"I came here to explain things to you, Maggie, but more and more, I have the feeling that it's even bigger than I suspected. If it's even remotely connected with what I think it is, we cannot chance being overheard."

"That sounds pretty ominous, buddy," Jack commented.

"It could be," Stan asserted solemnly.

Maggie put her hand over Stan's and told him that she had mentioned the stock to Jack. "It came up when I said I'd spoken to you on the phone just recently," she said. Then it occurred to her that Stan must have found out who had bought the stock. "Is my stock involved in something illegal?"

"I don't think it's directly involved, unless they want something that will link me to their plan," Stan said.

"This is beginning to sound like some sort of espionage, Mitsu." Jack's nose for news had begun to smell a story.

Stan looked around, unwilling to say anymore until he was sure they wouldn't be overheard. Maggie stood up and suggested that they all go up to her suite.

# CHAPTER THIRTY TWO

As the elevator purred upward, Stan wondered just how well Jack knew Diane. He felt sure that she was probably innocent of any part in a conspiracy, but could he be sure that she hadn't inserted the virus as an act of revenge against the company that had fired her? If that was the case, the virus would have nothing to do with the plot he attributed to Yoshida and Tokumura.

Once in her suite, Maggie poured coffee from the urn that was kept filled by an attentive housekeeping staff, and three faces turned expectantly toward Stan. He suddenly felt a little foolish as he tried to think of a way to reveal his suspicions without sounding like a total idiot. After all, he had no proof of anything, just a series of coincidences that might be just that—coincidences.

He decided to begin with Diane and questioned her about her job. "Did you apply for the job or were you approached by the company?" he asked.

"As a matter of fact, they must have seen the same news release that you saw because I got a call less than a week after IBM let me go. The salary and benefits they offered me were phenomenal. As Jack told you, I have the use of the condo for three weeks each year and they're paying me double what I earned before. I was stunned by how valuable my knowledge seemed to be. I knew, of course, that they wanted me to give them the program enhancements that I designed and I even told them that I had back door access to the IBM project. But I always made sure that I was alone when I made use of it. No matter how angry I was at that fool, Harry Cesnick, I wouldn't deliberately sabotage the company."

"What is it that you suspect, Mitsu? Aside from getting a serious career boost, Diane doesn't have anything to do with whatever it is that you're suggesting," Jack said emphatically.

Stan sighed. "I'm not sure I'm actually suggesting anything, Jack. It's just that there are too many coincidences to ignore."

The phone rang. Maggie stood up and crossed to the bar to answer it. The others were silent so that she could hear. Mitsu scowled when he heard her say, "Yes, Mother? It must be quite late in Chicago. Is something wrong?"

They all watched as her hand went to her throat and she sank into a nearby chair. Replacing the receiver a few minutes later, she was ominously still for what seemed an eternity. Finally, she lifted her head and said, "It seems that my former husband has killed himself."

No one moved, each of them waiting for some clue as to how they should respond. What was the right thing to say in this kind of situation? As a long-time friend, Jack was inclined toward a desire to comfort her; Stan's interest was a little more personal. Diane was the new kid on the block with less in the way of personal references, but given her natural penchant for openness, she was the first to speak.

"What happened?" she asked artlessly.

"Apparently, he jumped off the Golden Gate Bridge sometime Sunday afternoon. Someone saw him from a distance and reported it to the bridge authorities, but the body wasn't recovered until this morning. They suspected who it was when they found his car in the view area lot, but in the absence of any evidence of 'foul play,' and no obvious note in the car, they had to wait for something more definitive. When they finally got into his apartment, they found the notes he left for his parents and his . . ." Maggie's voice dropped as she hesitated, then finished, "friend."

"How do you feel about it, Maggie?" Stan asked apprehensively.

"I'm not sure yet. Angry. Sad. And maybe a little indifferent."

The others tried to hide their surprise at the word 'indifferent,' and Maggie herself realized that though it might be unusual, it was true.

"Do you want to talk about it?" Jack was, by now, slightly uncomfortable, but at the same time he wanted to be supportive.

"I don't want to go into the details, but I guess I should explain my indifference. I'm not sure I can put it into the right words, but I'm angry because he hurt me deeply and then didn't stay around to face the consequences. I'm sad because he must have been terribly confused and unhappy, and in the long run, I'm indifferent because it's behind me now and I'm getting on with my life. Before anyone asks, I don't really feel the need to go back to Illinois for the funeral. My mother thinks I should, but she's not aware of the circumstances surrounding the divorce."

Stan and Jack looked at each other. Should they go on with their earlier conversation? Diane stood up, preparing to leave.

Maggie, realizing their discomfort, eased the situation by urging them to make themselves at home while she made a couple of calls from the phone in the bedroom.

"It won't take long, but I have to speak to Charles' parents, if I can locate them, that it," she said. "Judging by the fact that you made a trip all the way to Hawaii, Mitsu, whatever you were going to tell us must be important. I'll be back in a few minutes."

Diane dropped her shoulder bag again and went to get the coffee pot. She refilled cups while the two men spoke quietly about some of their old friends and caught each other up on what they, themselves, had been doing over the years. Stan had been an undergraduate while Jack was studying for his master's degree, so their close friends in the fraternity had been in different groups.

Maggie returned shortly as promised, saying, "I'll apologize in advance in case I'm distracted now and then, but I'm anxious to hear what you have to say, Mitsu. What does my hotel stock—or should I say, your hotel stock—have to do with international espionage?"

Stan took a deep breath and began, "I think the only relevance may be to involve me in their plot, if there really is a plot. It involves at least two very prominent, very powerful men and the mere thought of it sends chills up my spine. I don't want to believe what I've begun to suspect, but recent discoveries make it impossible for me to ignore the implications."

"Who are these men?" Jack wanted to know.

"I hesitate to name them, but one is an exceptionally wealthy industrialist and the other is a powerful bureaucrat from an old samurai family."

"A powerful bureaucrat?" Maggie repeated. "Isn't that a contradiction in terms? I thought bureaucrats were the little people who scurry around making life difficult for the rest of us."

"There's an entirely different system of business and government in Japan, Maggie," Stan responded. He frowned, thinking of how best to explain it to them. "In Japan, the government is responsible for the well-being of the economy, which makes it only logical that it have the right to dictate to industry. Additionally, a very low percentage of industry is owned by individual stockholders—less than twenty percent—and most capital is obtained through loans that are backed by the government. This means that there is a low degree of influence on the part of stockholders, quite the reverse from American business. This is possible for a number of reasons. The Bank of Japan is an arm of the Ministry of Finance and a government run postal savings system gives competitive interest rates that encourage workers to put their savings into it. The money goes directly into Ministry of Finance accounts and therefore is available to be reinvested according to government plans.

"The post-war alliance with the United States is extremely beneficial as well. There is ready access to a significant export market, ready access to technology, and very little defense expenditure which allows funds to be diverted according to the latest government directives.

"The Ministry of International Trade and Industry, MITI for short, has the power to approve technology, any joint ventures between countries, patent rights and trade agreements. The ministries draft pretty much *all* legislation and are the source of all major policies, not to mention in control of the national budget."

As Stan paused to take a sip of his coffee, Jack asked, "Can you be more specific? I mean, I know that Japan is run by the bureaucrats, but the U.S. budget is allocated essentially by bureaucrats, too, only they call themselves congressmen." The irony was not lost on the others.

"Well . . . , in the U.S., the congress is elected by the people and those representatives are responsible to the people. The congress has final authority over the national budget and can approve or disapprove any or all portions of it. In Japan, the ministers themselves are politicians and are elected, but the vice minister of each ministry is a bureaucrat who has achieved his status through a career that often begins as early as kindergarten. The right schools, carefully cultivated friends in the right circles—all of these things are of utmost importance in the achievement of power. In America, retired businessmen often run for office or assume appointed positions in government. In Japan, the reverse is true. Japanese bureaucrats retire at an early age, most in their fifties, and then assume senior management positions in private enterprise. They already know how things get done and who to call upon, so are very valuable in the private sector. This kind of knowledge is considered completely acceptable to the Japanese businessman who sees no conflict in making use of what westerners might call insider information.

"Changes in American politics occur through election battles. If government principles are unpopular, the government is simply voted out of office by the people. Industry dictates to government through the use of lobbyists and campaign contributions, and quick profit for stockholders is the bottom line.

"In Japan, change comes about through internal battles within the ministries and Japanese industry is content to wait for profit margin to increase through long-term effectiveness. Now do you see how dangerous a powerful bureaucrat could be?" Stan looked at each of them questioningly.

"The ministers have the international prestige, but the career bureaucrats have the power?" Jack's eyes narrowed as he concentrated.

"Well, yes, but the bureaucrats who make it to the top possess significant stature as well," Stan replied. "There are other factors that contribute to the success of the Japanese system, too. For instance, most workers depend upon a lifetime of employment with the same company and a seniority wage plan. Unions are formed within the enterprise rather than by job description. The well-being of the company, therefore, is paramount to the well-being of the individual."

"I had no idea that there was such a difference between the Japanese and American political systems," Maggie commented. "I guess I've thought only in terms of democracy versus communism and things like liberty and justice. Pretty naïve, huh?"

"I've had my head buried in computers for so long that I don't think I've actually thought much about it at all," Diane added. "Mostly what we think about when the subject of Japan comes up, if it comes up at all, is that they don't play fair when it comes to the balance of trade."

Jack responded with a cynical guffaw. "And most Americans probably couldn't explain what balance of trade means!" He went on to bring the discussion back to its original objective by asking, "What are these discoveries that make you suspect a plot of some sort, Mitsu?"

Stan looked at each of them, then down at the table. He picked up his coffee and sipped at it, stalling for time. Jack understood his hesitancy and said, "You can trust us, Mitsu. I'm sure we all agree that what we hear will go no further than this room."

"Let me begin with the Davidson stock. I assure you, Maggie, that I had no idea it had been purchased and I had no idea that it had been put in my name. It wasn't until you called that I knew anything at all about it. I remembered that the vice minister I spoke of earlier had said something to the effect that my loyalty to Japan would be rewarded at the proper time, so I questioned him about it. He admitted that the stock had been acquired and urged me to accept it without questioning it further, alluding to an agreement between what he termed powerful men, nationalists of the highest order, who were duly appreciative of other devoted patriots. He also said that discretion and confidentiality were crucial."

Stan paused to take a deep breath, then continued, "I should add here that for many years, I felt somewhat alienated in my own country because of my American education. When my wife was killed by a bus full of American tourists, I was angry and made up my mind that my loyalty was to the country of my birth. It was not long after that that I began a series of editorials that played right into their hands. I called for cultural unity and suggested that criticism of Japan was racially motivated. I went so far as to suggest that Japan could affect the balance of power between the Soviets and the Americans by selling semiconductors to the Russians and denying them to the U.S. In my own defense, I can only say that at the time I had convinced myself that I truly believed what I was writing."

"I think both Jack and I know you well enough to agree that your motives were genuine," Maggie said, "but why the Davidson stock?"

Stan avoided looking at her as he responded, "Saving face still holds a notable place in Asian culture, Maggie. It wouldn't have been difficult for them to look into my past. In fact, it would have been a necessity if they were recruiting men who might have reason to hold a grudge against Americans. When you asked if it was my idea of revenge, you weren't far from the truth except that it wasn't my idea. They must have guessed that I'd been rejected by your family and rationalized that owning a portion of the family business would be suitable retribution."

Tears sprang to Maggie's eyes. "Oh, God, Mitsu, I knew you had good reason to feel personally insulted by my parents' attitude, but I never realized that it could be construed as an insult by an entire culture. I'm so sorry!"

Stan reached for her hand. "It was a long time ago, Maggie, and it wasn't your fault. We were both young and naïve. To get back to the question of how the stock was acquired, I knew that the vice minister himself did not have the kind of cash it would have taken. He is, as I mentioned, a member of an old and highly respected samurai family, and lives on the estate that has been theirs for a couple of centuries. The land is worth millions and on paper, he's very wealthy, but he wouldn't have access to that amount of cash.

"In an earlier conversation with this man, he spoke of 'opportunities to fulfill an old promise.' The promise he meant was one he made to avenge his father's shame at the Japanese surrender in 1945. I dismissed it as some sort of traditional samurai idea at the time, and it wasn't until the issue of the stock came up that I began to put it together.

"The next step was to figure out who had the kind of money it required. I started making a list of those who were not only rich, but obsessively nationalistic as well. I kept coming back to the same name. This man has motive in that he was imprisoned as a war criminal for several years after the war. An alliance between the two men, unthinkable as it may be, could have been forged in an effort to destroy the country that they both hate, probably economically."

Three sets of eyes widened in shock.

"I know. It's too far out to consider. That was my first reaction, too. But then I made a list of recent developments in the U.S. that were causing havoc, like the labor strikes that have half the country immobilized and the construction loans that have been called by Japanese banks doing business in California." Stan paused again.

"How could two Japanese men possibly affect American labor?" Jack wanted to know.

"I'm still not sure that they did," Stan replied. "But in researching it, I discovered that the strikes began with farm workers in California.

223

Do you know who their leader is?" Without waiting for a response, he went on, "A man named George Hagura who was born in a detention camp during the war. I'm not saying he actually knew anything about a plot—he could have been used in the same way that I was, without knowing it."

Maggie and Diane stared at him in disbelief, but Jack had begun to realize that if there was any truth to the possibility, Diane might have been used in the same manner. His mind raced as he thought of the consequences involved in the loss of data from the nation's computers in the event of a massive failure.

"Oh, my God," he said aloud.

"Stan . . . Mitsu, I'm not sure what to call you," Diane said. "Which do you prefer?"

"Actually, I've grown used to hearing 'Stan,' or rather 'Stan-san,' but many of the memories recalled by my nickname are happy ones." He smiled at Maggie.

"Well, Stan-san, if this plot does exist, how does the computer virus fit into it?" Even as she spoke, Diane realized the impact that he loss of information would have on American businesses. "Wait a minute. It's apparently scheduled to activate on December 28th. That would be when most places are closing out their books for the year. It would be disastrous for the whole country, or at least a major part of it that had installed the IBM system. Stock market transactions, banking records . . ."

Jack was putting the pieces together. "There's been a lot of talk lately on the subject of why The President doesn't end the strikes by declaring a national emergency under the Taft-Hartley Act and calling for an injunction that requires strikers to go back to work. You can't possibly believe that The President of the United States is deliberately stalling? He's a retired military man, as nationalistic as anyone in the world! That's what got him elected!"

"If he is, Jack, it's because he's being manipulated just as I'm sure Diane may have been, and George Hagura as well. The two men I believe may be responsible for such a plot, if there is one, are brilliant men who would consider such actions heroic and feel that they're serving their country with honor. They may well have found a way to use even The President of the United States. The money, power and resources available to them are phenomenal."

The discussion continued for some time as Stan responded to questions. Finally, Maggie was the one who asked the question that stumped them all.

"If there really is a plot to destroy America, what can we do about it? Who'd believe us?"

"From one thing, know ten thousand things.

When you attain the Way of strategy,

There will not be one thing you cannot see."

The Ground Book

Book of Five Rings

Miyamoto Musashi

# CHAPTER THIRTY THREE

Stan was floating on an interim plane, neither awake nor asleep. The long flight from Tokyo, the time change, the hours of discourse, and the joy of discovering that the passion of his youth still lived had combined to toss him into a sphere of marginal reality. He couldn't be sure whether or not it had all been a dream. Physically exhausted, he stopped struggling and slept.

He woke to the miracle of Maggie beside him in the huge bed. Her blond hair was tousled, curls tumbling unrestrained against her cheeks. He stared at her, still afraid it might be only a fantasy that would dissolve at any moment as the spirits of the night snickered gleefully at his disappointment.

The vision remained. The miracle was real. He gazed at the curve of her cheek and laughed aloud. She stirred, opening her eyes part way to smile sleepily. Neither of them moved, willing the rapture of waking in the other's arms to go on forever. Maggie's fingers crept tentatively toward Stan's and his responded involuntarily, the tips stroking hers in a whispered caress. She watched in awe, holding her breath until she realized that he was holding his as well.

The spell was broken as they laughed together.

Soon after Jack and Diane had departed the night before, Stan and Maggie had given in to the desire they had hidden even from themselves for so many years. They had reached out to each other shyly at first, then eagerly. There was no need to talk; they knew that fate had smiled on them, intertwining their karma once again, and yin and yang melded in ecstasy. All the uncertainty vanished and they became the college sweethearts they had once been, the maturity gained during the years between making it that much sweeter.

Stan reached out to stroke her arm as the sun peeped over the volcanic mountain that was Diamond Head. Her skin was soft, so soft that the slightest touch of his finger left a tiny indentation that disappeared as quickly as it had appeared. His eyes preceded his fingers over her body, randomly seeking hidden crevices. She was intent upon her own exploration as she discovered a joy in loving and making love that she had never known.

Their eyes met again and he said, "Have I ever told you how much I love chocolate?"

The question, which seemed so out of place, astonished her. "Chocolate?" she repeated.

He laid back against the pillows and guffawed. "I know that seems like a completely irrelevant tidbit of information at the moment, but I was thinking how soft and creamy your skin feels, like chocolate that melts in your mouth. Just touching you makes me feel as though I've fallen into a vat of creamy chocolate and been told that I can wallow there as long as I please."

She laughed with him. "May I join you there? We'll wallow together . . ." Her words were lost as her mouth found his earlobe and her lips journeyed to his throat, then down to his chest. He quivered, his arm moving to enfold her as her tongue flicked the inner side of his elbow, leaving feathery little kisses in its wake. Time lost meaning as they loved and made love.

Sometime later as Maggie lay satiated and wishing she didn't have to get up at all, something occurred to her and she bolted upright.

"Charles' father!" she exclaimed.

"Charles' father?" Stan repeated dumbly. "What about him?"

"He's Chairman of the Board of the Federal Reserve Bank! Why didn't I think of that before!" She turned excitedly to add, "He might be just the person to talk to about the possibility of a Japanese plot!"

"Maggie," Stan began, "the man's son just committed suicide. I doubt he'd be receptive to the idea that your old boyfriend thinks that there might be international chicanery afoot. And what makes you think he'd believe it even if he listened?"

"Because he's an honorable man. I'm absolutely sure of that, Mitsu. And he'd certainly be tuned in to any economic problems that the country might be having. Oh, Mitsu, it's worth a try!" She sat up, swinging her legs over the edge of the bed.

"I'll find out when the funeral service is and we'll both go to Illinois. No, no," she assured him, "you don't have to go the service itself. We'll fly into Chicago and you can wait there while I go down to Beardstown. I'm sure that I can talk him into stopping over in Chicago before he goes back to Washington."

Stan looked dubious until she finished with, "Unless you have a better idea?"

The vice president was beside himself. The trip to Beijing had been frustrating and only mildly productive. Dealing with the Chinese was even more difficult that dealing with the Japanese. At least you knew that the Japanese had the capability of carrying out agreements. With the Chinese, you weren't sure whether or not the hotel elevators would be working, never mind long-term promises of functional office space.

On his return to Washington, the vice president had been dismayed to find that not only had the labor problem not been resolved, but that The President had gone off to Los Angeles to accept an honorary degree from some university. Things were going from bad to worse as he examined the proposed legislation in front of him.

It seemed that in his absence, the junior senator from his state had introduced a bill that imposed outrageous tariffs on Japanese imports, and while the senate was still picking itself up off the floor where it was collectively rolling around in hysterical laughter, the little bastard had introduced *another* bill proposing that bond be posted equal to the amount off-loaded at customs by the Japanese that would be cleared only when an equivalent amount of American goods had been cleared into Japan. Well, that was *one* way to achieve a trade balance.

The state of Ohio was becoming a laughing stock and the vice president feared that his own reputation would suffer by association. How had that nitwit managed to get elected? More to the point, how could he be stifled?

First things first, however. If the rest of the country was suffering as badly as Washington was, it was time for presidential intervention

229

in the on-going strikes. Way past time, in fact. How the hell could the man have left Washington?

The vice president wondered if maybe he should get in touch with labor leaders himself, appealing to their sense of honor and urging that the strikes end for the good of the country. The more he thought about it, the better the idea sounded. If he could arbitrate a settlement without the intervention of The President, he'd be hailed as the great savior, a true statesman that the voters would remember. And certainly he'd have the grateful support of the party when the primaries came around. It was definitely worth a shot—another few weeks and the citizens of the U.S. would be at war with each other in battles over the barest necessities.

He supposed he'd have to include the Secretary of Labor in any talks that might come about, and probably the Secretary of Commerce, Grant Williamson, as well. Grant had been with him on the trip to Beijing, but had taken time off on their return to marry off his son in San Francisco. He was no doubt just as troubled by the lack of strike settlements.

Well, I can still claim credit for initiating the process, the vice president thought.

It occurred to him that the leader of the farm workers, George Hagura, had been getting some heavy support from California's former governor, Jerry Brown. As a public figure of some repute, the governor would surely see reason. He buzzed his secretary and told her to get Governor Brown on the phone if she could locate him.

She came into his office a short time later to say that while the governor was indeed in his office in San Francisco, he could not be disturbed. He would call back in an hour or so.

"He's meditating, sir," she said.

The vice president looked up. "Meditating?" he repeated, his eyes wide.

"Meditating, sir."

The vice president looked down at the papers on his desk, hoping to conceal a sudden desire to giggle.

# CHAPTER THIRTY FOUR

It was unseasonably warm in Beardstown, Illinois, as Bill Stuart and his wife prepared to bury their only son. The early snow that had fallen over Thanksgiving had melted quickly, leaving the pavements damp. Though it was warm enough to go without the layers of clothing usually donned at this time of year, the sun had not come out to dry things off and drops of moisture fell from the bare branches of the trees, landing in little plops on the heads of those who passed beneath them. Squirrels scampered over the ground in search of winter provisions.

Bill felt very much alone in his grief. Charles' mother wept openly, as a mother should, blaming some unknown influence for the loss of her son, some unidentified somebody or something that was ultimately responsible for his death.

But Bill did not have the benefit of that kind of solace. He simply did not understand why a young man with the world on an oyster shell, every advantage on his side, would suddenly find life unbearable. To Charles' mother it was simple. Something or someone had made Charles so miserable that he couldn't go on. She would get through this by being angry and her anger would sustain her. Bill felt separated from humanity. How could the sun go on rising and setting, the seasons change, the world go on as though nothing untoward had happened when the mahogany box on the ground in front of him held what was left of the son for whom he lived?

Visions of Charles on the tennis court, Charles grinning as he held a soccer trophy aloft, Charles as he received his diploma from Dartmouth, Charles at the altar on his wedding day—the years, happy years, moved in front of Bill's eyes like a video tape on fast forward. Suddenly everything he'd worked for and achieved meant nothing. Everything that had seemed so utterly important only days earlier no longer mattered.

He moved by rote, his wife clinging to him, depending on him to carry on, doing the things that had to be done, and he would do them as expected. He would thank people for their expressions of condolence; he would pay the undertaker, the cemetery and the florist, and no doubt go back to Washington and carry on with the job he'd been so proud to accept a few short years ago. But he would never be whole again.

Someone touched his sleeve gently and he turned, anticipating the sympathy of another family friend. He found himself looking into Maggie's eyes, and though he had been told she would not be in attendance, he was not really surprised to see her.

He was surprised, however, by the tears that came to his own eyes at the sight of the lovely young woman who had been his daughter-in-law. He had never understood Charles' decision to leave Maggie and move to San Francisco so suddenly, and had thought that Maggie was probably bitter, deservedly so. Looking at her now, he saw only sorrow and compassion. She took his hand and they stood silently for several moments until a soft rain began to fall and someone nearby raised an umbrella over their heads.

At a gathering of friends and relatives at the Stuart home following the graveside service, people spoke quietly in small groups, munching on little sandwiches made by well-meaning neighbors. It was difficult for most of them to find words to say to the bereaved family. What could you say? Sorry your son killed himself? So most didn't stay long, leaving with hugs and handshakes that involved the use of both hands rather than the useless phrases of condolence.

As she came from the kitchen with another tray of sandwiches, Maggie was startled to see Ken Williamson speaking to Charles' mother.

"We shared some very special times, Mrs. Stuart. Charles was one of the best friends I've ever had."

"It was so kind of you to delay your honeymoon to be here, Ken. Both Bill and I appreciate it and I know it would mean so much to Charles to know that you were here," Mrs. Stuart replied, stroking Ken's cheek gently. "Please come back to visit us again so that we can get to know you better."

Maggie stood transfixed, hardly able to contain her loathing for the man, as she listened to the exchange. Looking over Mrs. Stuart's shoulder, Ken caught her eye. Unable to bear the thought of making polite conversation, she fled back to the kitchen. Of course, the Stuarts could not know it, but Ken's marriage was probably responsible for Charles' decision to end his life. Maggie hoped they'd never find out.

It was late afternoon, already dark outside, when she was finally able to speak privately to Bill Stuart. She had decided to say as little as possible about her reasons for wanting him to stop off in Chicago on the way back to Washington, telling him only that she had discovered crucial information regarding the labor strikes and that it was imperative that he meet privately with someone she would identify later.

Bill had no trouble changing their plane reservations since people were not traveling much these days. Although pilots were still flying and many airlines still had cabin service, most of the baggage handlers were on strike so passengers either had to struggle with their own luggage or wait for long periods of time, hoping that it would appear sooner rather than later.

The Stuarts had rented a car at O'Hare Field rather than try to make airline connections to Beardstown, so getting to the Davidson Chicagoan was not a problem.

Late the next afternoon, Maggie and Stan waited in the conference room that adjoined her office. When Bill Stuart joined them, they began by explaining the Davidson stock transfer and Stan's subsequent investigation into the mysterious Caribbean company that he had been stunned to find he owned. Describing his initial concern that the stock had been given to him, Stan went on to tell of the vice minister's comment regarding an agreement between powerful men who considered themselves patriots of the highest order.

"I began to realize that the stock was intended to represent some sort of revenge against the Americans who had insulted me because I was Japanese," he said.

It wasn't until Maggie reached out to cover Stan's hand with her own that Bill realized that the two of them had been more than friends in college. He withdrew instinctively, then slumped slightly in his chair as he thought, what did it matter anymore, anyway? It had been Charles who left Maggie, the girl that they all loved. He wondered if her parents had forbidden an interracial marriage. Looking more closely, he understood their feelings for each other and was happy for them.

"You said that you had information regarding the strikes, Maggie. What does the Davidson stock have to do with that and what is it that you're suggesting?" Bill asked apprehensively.

Stan and Maggie glanced at each other, their eyes saying well, here we go, ready or not.

Stan began, "As much as I hate to even think such a thing, I believe that there may be a conspiracy between two, and quite possibly more, Japanese men of wealth and power." He went on to share his suspicions regarding the strikes, the calling of bank loans in California, and the computer virus.

"It would appear that December 28th may be the projected culmination of their plan, since that's the date the virus is scheduled to activate. As you know, it would be disastrous to businesses and government agencies using the new storage system, particularly if there is no disc backup. With the country already in chaos because of the strikes, and the Christmas holidays diverting attention, it could be catastrophic." Stan paused, looking intently at Bill Stuart.

"There's one more thing," he said. "Do you remember a couple of months ago when there were rumors of a Japanese boycott of long-term treasury bonds?"

Bill nodded and Stan continued, "The same rumor has begun to circulate again in the Japanese financial world. So far, no one seems to be taking it seriously, but if a conspiracy exists within the ministries or if some are being manipulated by others who have their own motives, you can see the potential for disastrous effects.

"The loss of Japanese support for U.S. bonds could trigger an international loss of faith. Interest rates would have to skyrocket to attract buyers and that would mean big losses on Wall Street. Coming on top of the other problems, it could very well bring America to its knees—which is probably what this is all about."

Bill shook his head in disbelief. "Why would anyone in his right mind want to do such a thing?"

"Please understand, Mr. Stuart, I don't believe this is in any way attributable to the Japanese government or the Japanese people, but rather, it is being carried out by a few fanatic nationalists . . ." Stan's voice dwindled to hardly more than a whisper and after a short pause, he finished, "If it is a reality, I can hardly believe it myself."

He squared his shoulders and went on, "You must understand the Japanese mentality. The Japanese are obsessed with the need to excel and to that end, will sacrifice self and family for the good of the company or the country. It's a mass psychology brought about in part by population density. Japan has an estimated 830 people per square mile. Of the developed nations, only Hong Kong exceeds that number.

"There are four cultural concepts that provide a guideline: the first is kokutai, national essence; the second is the national religion, Shinto—the way of the gods; the third is bushido—the way of the warrior, and the fourth is called Tenno Heika, which, when translated, gives divinity to the emperor.

"With such strict parameters, it is not difficult to understand the Japanese belief in racial purity, though the idea is sometimes carried to extremes. Someone, a former prime minister, I believe, said that the Japanese are more capable than a mixed nation like America because their genes have not been adulterated by inferior strains."

Stan paused again, a little embarrassed by his own words. Bill Stuart was quick to put him at ease, saying, "Please. Go on. If more Americans took the time to understand cultures that differ from ours, we'd all be better off!"

Stan looked askance, but continued, "Most of the people are followers rather than leaders and competition among those who lead is fierce. The people are incapable of defying their superiors and take the expectations of their peers very seriously as well.

"I tell you all of this to perhaps explain the motivations of the men I believe may be responsible for what I have suggested. I have heard stories about one of them—the bureaucrat. It is said that he believes himself to be the reincarnation of a seventeenth century warrior called Musashi."

"Musashi?"

"A folk hero to many Japanese."

"Ummm, well, young man, much as I admire you as a journalist and your courage in coming forward with your suspicions, it really boils down to a couple of simple things. Can you prove any of it? And if so, what can we do to stop it?"

"The computer virus can be stopped, in fact is already in the process of being stopped, thanks to the presence of the system designer at Maggie's hotel and a mistake in entering the date by the operator. Presidential intervention could stop the strikes, and the right approach to the right person or persons might bring about a strategic change in attitude regarding the bank loans and the possible bond boycott. The trouble is, I can't be sure who might be involved. If I'm wrong about it and word got out that I had even whispered such a thing, my career would be at an end, and quite possibly my life as well."

"If I didn't know Maggie as well as I do and trust her as much as I do, I might have thought that you were some kind of lunatic, Mr. Mitsunari, but if I can confide in you as you have confided in me, I have wondered for several weeks if there could be some conspiracy afoot. Not that I suspected anyone specific, you understand, and I dismissed the idea almost as quickly as it came to mind. I am aware of your reputation in the financial community, and I will consider what you've said. Now, my wife will be wondering what's become of me, so I must leave. We'll be in touch."

With that, Bill Stuart stood up. As the door closed behind him, Maggie and Stan could only stare at each other as the enormity of what they'd done by giving voice to such inflammatory suspicions began to sink in.

"I feel like a traitor to my country," Stan said morosely.

"But you have two countries, Mitsu. And you did the only thing you could do. The honorable thing," Maggie replied gently.

# CHAPTER THIRTY FIVE

Bill Stuart was lost in thought as he sat beside his wife on the plane back to Washington. His wife thought it was because he was thinking about their son and slipped her arm through his comfortingly.

"It was nice to see Victoria Davidson again," she said, hoping to ease his pain by diverting his attention. She had visited with her son's former mother-in-law while her husband attended to the business she neither knew nor cared about in Chicago.

"She's very concerned about that Japanese boy that Maggie was interested in when they were in college," she continued. "Apparently, he's suddenly shown up again after all these years and is staying at the Davidson Hotel. I don't suppose you happened to run into him, did you?"

"What?" Bill asked absently.

"That Japanese boy," his wife repeated. "Did you happen to see him at the hotel?"

"Oh. Yes, I did meet him, and he's no longer a boy, any more than Maggie's still a girl. He's a very highly respected journalist in Japan. Editor of the Japanese version of the Wall Street Journal, in fact." Bill put his head back and closed his eyes, hoping to eliminate the need for further explanation.

"I suppose now that Maggie is running the hotels and is . . ." she paused, a catch in her voice, "available again, he thinks he's got another chance with her."

"I believe it's pure coincidence that they've seen each other again, though they do seem . . ." Bill stopped, wishing he had not said the last four words aloud.

"Seem what?"

"To be good friends," Bill amended his original sentence. "I think I'll take a little nap while I still can. God only knows what Washington will be like. We may have to walk home from the airport if the limo doesn't show up and the taxis are still out on strike."

His wife knew that he was avoiding the issue, but also knew that it was useless to push it. She'd bring it up again when the opportunity presented itself since it was obvious that Bill knew more than he was telling her. She hadn't been married to him for all these years without learning something about how to get the information she wanted. It was just a matter of timing. She settled back in her seat, determined to stop thinking about her son's death, or at least try. For a little while, anyway.

Bill kept his eyes closed to continue the ruse, hoping his wife would forget her questions about Maggie's relationship with Stan Mitsunari, but he was far from sleepy. His thoughts were tumbling over one another as he considered the possibility of a scheme that even the most dedicated Japan bashers would scorn as preposterous. Stan had nothing to gain, however, and everything to lose by telling such an outrageous story. His life wouldn't be worth a plug nickel in Japan and certainly no one in America would trust him, so there was no advantage in deception.

What worried Bill Stuart the most was not the manipulation of American labor, nor was it the bank loans. It was the possibility of a Japanese boycott of the next Treasury auction.

The time for a firm stand on the strikes, with intervention if agreements could not be forged, had come, and The President must realize that. The Christmas holidays were nearly upon them and the spirit that accompanied the season should be conducive to cooperation among union members without paychecks. They would probably welcome a direct order to return to work.

The calling of California bank loans was disastrous to that state's economy and might remain a mystery for all time, but emergency low interest loans, guaranteed by the government, could be arranged through a little diplomatic maneuvering.

There was no proof that any of these admittedly serious problems had been deliberately initiated by the Japanese, and to publicly suggest that there was some sort of heinous plot being carried out would cause international shock waves of massive proportion.

But the loss of government revenue and subsequent stock market decline caused by a boycott following on the heels of these distractions could be the fatal blow.

Americans would be horrified if they took the time to examine how the monumental government debt was financed. Every three months, the government was borrowing more money to pay off existing debts—notes and bonds sold years earlier and interest on current ones—and adding an extra few billion dollars to fund current expenses that mounted with each new social program, each addition to agency staffs, each cost of living adjustment to entitlement payments. The money it "borrowed" was really only paper issued by the Treasury Department and sold to the highest bidder at auctions conducted by the Federal Reserve Bank.

It made no difference to the spenders in Washington who bought the debt that, after all, was only paper, as long as somebody continued to foot the bill for the budget that defied balancing. Since the government kept no definitive statistics on who bought and owned its bonds, it was easy to be lured into a false sense of security by ignoring the dangers in allowing the debt to be financed by foreigners.

The November issue had seen a record investment by the Japanese, with eighty percent going to Japanese interests at the high interest rates offered to lure buyers when rumors of a boycott threatened. Everybody had breathed a collective sigh of relief and gone about the business of spending as usual.

The *really* frightening part of it, Bill thought, was that American bond traders had become accustomed to the Japanese pattern of selling off a previous issue to participate in the current one. Many of them were ready to sell short in anticipation of a new issue in February. Selling what they did not yet own. Should the Japanese actually boycott the February auction and retain bonds already in their possession, most of the American traders would be bankrupt and the government would be unable to pay off debts it had guaranteed years earlier.

If Bill had been aware of a conversation that was taking place in Tokyo at that very moment, he'd have been more than just worried, he'd have been completely unnerved.

"They have condemned us repeatedly! Enough! Do they think we are complete fools?" The Minister of International Trade and Industry glared at Sunao Tokumura, the bureaucrat who ran his ministry. They were closeted in an after-hours meeting to discuss the effects of recent legislation introduced in the American House of Representatives.

"These proposed solutions to the trade imbalance are worse than idiotic. Tariffs equal to the difference spent on defense! Impound accounts! Foreigners required to register with the government if they plan to invest more than five million dollars in American business or property!" The minister's eyes blazed with anger.

Tokumura's eyes reflected his own outrage. "There is only one way to put them in their place," he said. "The decline of the American dollar has allowed the yen more purchasing power, it's true, but it has also wiped out much of the profit on their bonds. We had hoped that by participating heavily in the November auction, we might prove our willingness to cooperate. But this legislation is clearly racist and aimed at Japan. It cannot be ignored."

"What do you suggest?"

"That we encourage Japanese investors to keep their current holdings at the high interest rates already in place, and put off further participation in Treasury auctions until such time as an agreement can be reached regarding this continuing harassment." As angry as Tokumura was, he was also secretly delighted by the stupidity of the Americans. It couldn't have come at a better time.

"They think we have no place else to put our money," the minister reflected, "and that we are grateful for interest rates that are four to five percent higher than here at home."

"Ah, but they fail to realize that to a Japanese, country comes before profit. And the argument can be made that excessive profits result in higher taxes as well." Tokumura knew that his words were having precisely the effect on which he planned.

"Yes," agreed the minister. "I'm sure that the Ministry of Finance will concur. Watanabe-san hopes to be elected prime minister next spring. His devotion to Japan in this case is sure to be seen as inspired."

At another meeting later that night, Tokumura assured Satoshi Yoshida that the final stage of Nito Ryu, the Two Swords plan, was in place and that success was assured.

# CHAPTER THIRTY SIX

Sally McNamara stood in front of the medicine chest mirror in her little bathroom trying vainly to pull a hairbrush through her tangled red curls. No matter how hard she tried, the battle to achieve a smooth, sophisticated look was one she had yet to win. She shook the brush at the ceiling and wailed at God, asking why me, Lord, why me? Why couldn't you have given me shimmering golden locks and alabaster skin like the heroines in romance novels instead of this red mop and freckles?

Sally was trying especially hard to look her best. The three Japanese men who were visiting the bond trading room at the Wall Street firm where she worked had asked her to dinner as a reward for her help in teaching them the ins and outs of the bond trading market. Their firm had applied for primary dealership status and had appealed to the American firm for guidance in the computer trading system. Sally was in charge of the voluminous and confidential manuals that were the bible for company traders.

She had been given strict instructions that much of the material was considered classified and only certain portions were to be copied for the three men. She thought it was all a little silly and that the company was being overly protective. Besides, the Japanese men were such darlings, bowing to her and smiling and thanking her so profusely for every little thing. So polite. Why couldn't she find a guy who'd treat her that way? Ha! Fat chance among the Irish cops she dated. A couple of beers after a movie was all she got from most of them, and then they whined when she didn't invite them to spend the night!

Sally surveyed her closet despairingly. She couldn't very well show up wearing a skirt and sweater, and the bridesmaid dress she'd worn for her cousin's wedding was definitely out. Then she remembered the soft green cashmere sweater that went with the dark green palazzo pants she'd bought ages ago at a Saks Fifth Avenue spring sale.

Even on sale, the outfit had been expensive, but she'd fallen in love with it and visualized herself making a grand entrance into an elegant party on the arm of a man who looked very much like Mel Gibson. Well, Mel Gibson they weren't, but this was a close as she'd ever get to making an entrance, she thought, and lifted it lovingly from the bottom drawer of her dresser.

The three men called for her promptly at seven, waiting in a limo in front of her building. All three jumped out as she came through the door, bowing and smiling and helping her into the car while the American driver ignored them. They rode uptown for several minutes as Sally wondered where they were going. She was thrilled when the driver pulled into the semi-circle in front of the Plaza Hotel and a doorman reached in to take her hand.

At dinner, Sally ate things she had only heard about, things like escargot and caviar. Who'd have thought that a snail could be so delicious in garlic butter? And the fish eggs that she put on tiny crackers along with a little chopped onion were salty, but oh, so good. She was surprised how much these oriental men knew about ordering in such a fancy restaurant and at how well they spoke English, too. It made her a little ashamed of the times she'd agreed with her brawny Irish brother when he badmouthed foreigners.

As the four of them sipped cognac after dinner, the older gentleman, obviously their leader, handed her a flat velvet box, urging her to accept 'this small token of our esteem.' When she opened it, she was dazed to find a necklace of the most perfect pearls she'd ever seen.

"Are they real?" she blurted, and blushed nearly purple when the man assured her that they were quite real, but only a poor token for someone as generous as she had been. The maitre d' helped her with the clasp and Sally thought she'd died and gone to heaven.

She got her chance to make a grand entrance at the Carlyle Hotel where they ended the evening listening to Bobby Short at the piano.

She was absolutely sure that nearly every head turned to watch as the redheaded American girl walked in with three very well dressed Japanese men. She could imagine the conversations that were taking place and smiled what she hoped was a worldly smile as she lifted her chin a couple of inches.

The next day at the office, Sally walked on air, daydreaming about being swept off her feet by the youngest and tallest of the three men. And then, of course, she would return with him to his historic family estate in Japan where she would live in luxury for the rest of her days.

When he came to her office late in the afternoon, she hardly heard him when he said he wished he could borrow the manuals, just overnight, of course, so that he could study them more closely. He wouldn't want to embarrass his American instructors by making mistakes, he told her.

That night, the three men stayed up all night bent over Xerox machines as they copied every page in each of the ten volumes, saving their company hundreds of hours in the development of their own bond trading manual.


George Hagura stroked the soft leather of his seat in the first class section of the airplane that was carrying him to Washington, D.C., to meet with the president of the United States. He could hardly believe he was awake. Seated beside him was the man who had stood beside him at the rally in Sacramento, and who had once been governor of the state of California, Jerry Brown.

George was wearing all new clothes. Even his underwear was new, though he was sure he'd have been more comfortable in the old and tattered stuff that was soft from so many washings and molded to fit his shape. More new clothes were packed in the brand new luggage that had replaced the cardboard box he'd carried around for years. Reluctant to see it disappear down a chute where someone would put it aboard the plane, he had watched until it was out of sight. At least it was supposed to be put aboard the plane. He had trouble believing he'd ever see it again and wondered morosely if he'd have time to get another suit if the one he'd just bought didn't show up.

He had a new truck, too. He'd looked at a couple of snazzy cars, but then admitted to himself that he was so used to his old pickup that he wouldn't be comfortable in a regular automobile.

When he thought about the reason for this trip, his mood alternated between pride and fear. Pride in that he was respected by the people who mattered in the world and paralyzing fear that made him tremble at the thought of making an utter fool of himself in front of those same people. Sometimes he wondered what it was that had made him do the things that had put him where he was. Were his motives really as noble as he'd been given credit for or was he just pulling off the biggest scam of all? He had more money than he'd ever dreamed of having, though he wasn't sure just where it had come from. And though he'd achieved much in the way of garnering the respect he so agonizingly craved, he still went home to an empty apartment and slept alone. Worst of all, his people still were no better off.

He was avoiding visits to the fields. The guilt he felt when he looked into the tired eyes of suffering workers who had gone on strike at his recommendation left him with a heavy heart. Lives that had never been easy had become outright miserable. He wished he could tell them to forget it and go back to work, but how could he do that when so many other unions had initiated sympathy strikes on their behalf and were suffering the same as the field workers were? Well, maybe not quite the same. Most had a roof over their heads. Some of the growers had thrown out whole families who refused to work, leaving them to put up makeshift tents or huddle under bridges.

George hoped with all his heart that Mr. Brown and The President would find an honorable way to end it.

Sumio Masabe's hands were sweating as he clutched the envelope he was delivering to the pharmaceutical association that published a quarterly review of new developments in the field of medical research. He had worked very hard on the paper he was submitting, often until he nearly dropped from fatigue after a long day in his laboratory. But he was sure that his project would stun the industry.

He wasn't quite as sure that his benefactor would approve of his independent action, but what little contact he'd had with the mysterious man had been initiated by the man himself and Sumio didn't even know his name, so how could he ask for permission? Certainly such a generous humanitarian would agree that the findings should be recognized so that the new medication could be made available to those who suffered from this distressing disease.

Wouldn't he?

In his elegant office several miles from where Sumio Masabe stood at the entrance to the pharmaceutical association building, Yoshida couldn't help himself. His usually crumpled face broke into a smile. He pursed his lips and tried to frown, but couldn't do it. He had just spoken to a contact in the bond department at the Bank of Japan and been told that the bank had decided to keep its current holdings of twenty billion dollars worth of American bonds temporarily, and probably pass on the next issue.

Yoshida hadn't felt this good since . . . well, he couldn't remember. He removed his glasses, reached for a tissue in one of the overstuffed pockets of his sweater, and began to polish the lenses.

The timing was crucial. To avoid catastrophe when the U.S. economy collapsed completely, bond holdings must be sold piecemeal and only to American interests just prior to the next auction. It could be managed. It *must* be managed. There were around forty American primary dealers who would be eager to grab whatever they could get their hands on after a few anxious weeks of selling short. Yes. A word or two and rumors would begin to circulate. The bonds would be snapped up and put into house accounts where they'd stay as their value diminished or ceased to exist altogether when the U.S. government failed to meet its obligations. Since the bonds would be from Japanese interests, no one could cry foul or suggest conspiracy.

Sunao Tokumura brushed his forehead with a handkerchief, trying in vain to wipe away the sweat that dribbled from his hairline down to his chin with unrelenting perseverance. How did these people manage to get anything done, he wondered. The heat never seemed to let up.

Well, they didn't really accomplish much and that was the reason for his visit to Indonesia. He intended to obtain agreements whereby Japan provided technology, electronic equipment and financial aid to the Indonesian government in return for the partially refined oil, liquefied natural gas, tin and timber that Japan lacked.

In spite of an abundance of raw materials that could make the country a major world exporter, most Indonesians were still tied to agriculture and fishing. Following near bankruptcy, a series of five-year plans had been put into effect aimed at increasing employment opportunities and establishing a more equitable distribution of wealth. Declining prices had limited annual growth to a modest five percent, however, but with Japan's help, Indonesia would prosper. More to the point, new markets would open up for Japanese manufacturers.

Time was of the utmost importance and these people moved so slowly. The pro-western government must be convinced that its future lay with Japan, as must other nations allied with the Association of Southeast Asian Nations (ASEAN). The independent countries of Southeast Asia had formed this regional alliance in 1967 as a safeguard against the spread of communism in the area and one of its principal objectives was to promote regional peace and stability.

Now that communism had won in Vietnam and was established in China, the ASEAN countries must be convinced that the West was basically racist and that their economic futures were in the Asian marketplace.

The potential for sales in China and Vietnam was astronomical and these small, hot weather nations must be made to see that.

Months of negotiations had left the vice minister only weeks in which to cement agreements. The Philippines was growing tired of American military presence and was leaning toward an Asian alliance, but Malaysia was dragging its feet. Singapore and Thailand still did not trust the Japanese, but would have to come around when their American markets were either jeopardized or non-existent.

Sunao Tokumura sighed inwardly and tried to concentrate on the gong and drum ensemble that was performing in his honor. It was difficult to appreciate as each gong and drum played individually, some offering short, continuously repeated patterns, while others played many melodic and rhythmic variations. His eyes began to glaze as he retreated into a meditative state where he was alone with his reincarnated spirit.

# CHAPTER THIRTY SEVEN

Diane stared out the window of the jet into the inky blackness that was broken more often than was comfortable by jagged flashes of lightening. She considered praying, but dismissed the idea as being quite possibly more harmful than beneficial after so many years of silence. God might well be aggravated into plunging the plane to earth in fiery retribution should He hear a plea for intervention from her.

She pulled the shade down and reached up to switch on the light over her seat. Her concentration was limited, however, and after rereading the same page of the airline magazine for the third time, she gave up. Checking her watch, she computed the time in California and wondered what Jack was doing at that moment.

Her skin tingled at the thought of his touch and she longed to be back in Hawaii sharing the big bed where they'd discovered a passion that neither of them had known before. She'd found it difficult to believe at first that Jack had not loved someone with as much hunger as she felt. After all, not only was he older than she, he was a man and she'd always thought that with men it was pretty much the same no matter who the woman might be. He'd convinced her that it was not as he gradually overcame the shyness that went along with her lack of experience. The body that she had thought of only as housing for her mind had awakened to the joy of physical pleasure.

Being with Jack was like savoring a full bodied wine, she thought, then giggled at herself for giving in to such a silly cliché. Funny how living in California had changed her life so much. Her previous experience would not have included knowing a full bodied wine from a glass of grape juice, never mind savoring it, had she not discovered the wineries that were only an hour from San Francisco.

After talking it over and then talking it over some more, she and Jack, and Maggie and Stan had decided that she should go to New York and speak to IBM management personally about the virus.

Her old bosses hadn't believed it initially, but when she suggested that they scan the software on the already released system, they saw that they had a serious problem. Late night discussion had produced the only solution. Disclosure must be made along with an emergency release of new software for customers who had already installed the system.

Harry Cesnick had been frantic, fearing that he'd be blamed for what might have been a disaster. Apparently, he'd sipped a little too much from the bottle in his drawer and gulped too many of the tranquilizers he ate like candy. His car had hit a tree at what police described as a very high rate of speed and Harry had been killed instantly. No one had seemed very surprised at the news. One senior vice president had muttered under his breath that the only surprise was that it hadn't happened sooner.

Diane had been gratified when the division president not only offered her Harry's position, but practically begged her to come back. There was a certain amount of satisfaction in receiving the offer and knowing that her reputation had been restored, even enhanced. She'd told them that she was flattered, but no. She had to remain at Habatsu until somebody found out who was behind the evil deed. If she left now, just as IBM announced the discovery of the virus and offered a vaccine, they'd be sure to know that she was onto them.

It was hard to believe that Habatsu management could have done such a thing deliberately. Stan had suggested that there might be cameras in her office that had picked up her back door entry code to the IBM system, indicating that it could have been anyone, even a night watchman or cleaning personnel who had infiltrated the company. It would be best if she stayed on and acted like nothing had happened, at least until they made sure that the virus had been eliminated without further complications.

The Gang of Four, as they had begun to call themselves. It was a take-off on the designation given to the Chinese quartet made up of Chairman Mao's widow and her co-conspirators who had attempted to take control of the government following Mao's death.

"Let's hope we don't end up the way they did," Jack had said wryly.

And now she was on her way back to San Francisco. She still had a few days of vacation left and wished with all her heart that she and Jack could spend them at the beach condo, but she knew he'd be immersed in his job again. She was lucky to have had him to herself for as long as she had.

A voice announced to the passengers that the captain had turned on the seat belt sign and that they were beginning their descent into San Francisco. Diane raised the window shade to look around for lights below, but saw only grey, wispy fog that curled around the wing of the plane like a slippery ghost.

She heard the landing gear go down, then watched in the eerie light as the flaps lowered on the wing beside her. The huge plane seemed to be going so slowly that it was about to settle on some extraterrestrial field. Suddenly, rain slick pavement appeared and the wheels touched the ground. Passengers began to applaud in gratitude to either the pilot or God—she wasn't sure which.

And then she was in Jack's arms again.


The file on The President's desk contained reports from each of the members of a special board appointed to look into the issues involved in the ongoing labor disputes. He had been astonished by the lists of minor grievances. The truck drivers claimed that tires on their vehicles were not replaced often enough, that the logs they were required to keep took too much time, and that they were not allowed extra time on runs where traffic lights were excessive. Auto workers said that they were required to spend too much time in meetings. Taxi drivers resented non-smoking rules.

There wasn't a principle among them that justified the continuation of the strikes. It was apparent that what had begun as a solidarity movement had taken on a life of its own that no one seemed able to control, much less understand. The President shook his head. He should have appointed the board long before he had. How could he have allowed himself to ignore the well-being of his fellow countrymen for so long?

The Attorney General had been alerted and was prepared to issue an eighty day injunction that would require employees to return to work for that period of time. After sixty days had passed, the special board would report again and workers would be given an opportunity to cast secret ballots on proposed solutions to the grievances.

The President sighed heavily and wondered how the conference arranged by the vice president was going. A short, informal reception was planned for those who were participating in the talks that included union representatives, a congressman or two—or three—and former California governor, Jerry Brown.

The President was to present commendations to the farm labor man, George Hagura, and to Dan Whiting, a Chicago union leader who had been badly beaten trying to deliver meat to a suffering neighborhood. The courage and integrity of these two men deserved recognition.

The President had awarded many such commendations during his career, but never had he felt as unworthy to do so as he did today. While he dragged his feet, Americans had paid the price. The mortgage market had nearly ceased to exist as lenders limited their commitments; companies affected by the strikes had defaulted on loans and filed bankruptcies; insurance companies and unions had been forced to sell property, much of it to the Japanese.

Perhaps the most heartbreaking of all were the empty shelves in toy stores at Christmastime. The President could only hope that it wasn't too late to rally the people and celebrate a merry Christmas after all.

He rose from his desk and made his way up to the private family quarters where he found his wife at her dressing table brushing her hair. The First Lady's condition was a mystery. She had not wandered off in recent weeks as she had done before, but just a few days ago, she had forgotten his name. She had known that he was her husband, she just couldn't remember what he was called. That she would forget the name of someone of importance at a diplomatic function was a sure bet for the near future.

The President stood behind her, stroked her hair, leaned over to kiss the top of her head gently, and made a decision. He would release a statement immediately after Christmas to the effect that he would not seek re-election. Leaving the room as quietly as he had entered, he returned to the oval office to await word from the conference participants.


Congressman Zach Templeton had the floor.

"At this moment, gentlemen, hearings are taking place regarding the imposed tariffs on certain Japanese products that are necessary to American manufacturers. As you know, the auto plant located in the great state of Tennessee was closed indefinitely by its Japanese owners. I have here a letter listing specific examples of imposed tariffs that are in good part responsible for the plant closing." The congressman paused to look around at his colleagues, waving the pages above his head.

He went on to explain that tariffs imposed on equipment necessary to the assembly line had taxed the company out of profit to the point where they saw no other solution until the matter could be resolved.

"Of course, other industries are affected as well. In Indiana, for instance, a Japanese appliance maker uses a compressor imported from the company's factory in Japan. Tariffs on the compressors may well close that factory as well, putting another two hundred Americans out of work!"

Again, Zach paused, warming to the task. He leaned into the microphone for effect and continued, "Law enforcement agencies from other states have sent representatives to testify that these tariffs could add millions of dollars to the cost of computerized equipment essential to identifying criminals! Are you prepared to let these criminals roam the streets, stalking your children? I don't think so.

"Hospitals and research laboratories need microscopes made in Japan. These tariffs were initiated in response to a dispute over the failure of Japanese companies to stop selling semi-conductors for less than the cost of production, but we have over-reacted and will suffer the consequences if repeal is not imminent!"

Zach lowered his voice, speaking sincerely to his audience. "Once our esteemed congressional leaders respond to this over-zealous reaction, the Tennessee plant will reopen and layoffs that were in part responsible for the sympathy walk-outs will be a thing of the past. Teamsters can be reassured and thereby encouraged to cooperate in putting an end to the strikes that are endangering the American way of life." Zach allowed a small catch in his throat as he finished.

A few days later, the early editions of the nation's newspapers nearly all carried huge headlines announcing the end of the strikes.

## IT'S OVER! ! !

Americans celebrated, then buckled down and gave new meaning to the Christmas spirit. Freight forwarding companies offered rates that hardly paid their costs to every toy manufacturer in the country. Every major grocery chain had trucks on the road before the papers hit the stands, many of the drivers volunteering their time for the first runs, perhaps humbled by pictures of Dan Whiting, leaning on his cane, proudly accepting his commendation from The President.

Only those in Silicon Valley offices really noticed another article buried in the business sections that warned of an impending computer virus designed to wipe out everything on the new IBM MVS operating system on December 28th. IBM urged all users of the system to contact their New York office for emergency adjustments.

Satoshi Yoshida noticed. His anger at the combination of news caused great distress to the twelve-year-old orphan from Kyoto who had been pleased by the summons to Tokyo for his attentions.

# CHAPTER THIRTY EIGHT

Maggie looked in the mirror and decided that she looked like a Chia Pet on steroids. The excessive amount of traveling in such a short time had left her frazzled and exhausted almost beyond endurance. She and Stan had turned around immediately after their meeting with Bill Stuart, returning to Honolulu for the grand opening of the Kaimana Davidson Hotel, as she had renamed it. Then it was back to San Francisco, then a quick trip to New York to interview the candidates for Bob Mattheson's job. All of it in only a little over a week.

She surveyed the stacks of boxes that were still waiting to be unpacked in the apartment she had rented, but hadn't had time to make into a home. She vowed she'd do so before the holidays that were only a couple of weeks away. The furniture she'd chosen to keep from the suburban house had been left haphazardly in the rooms, cartons of dishes made it difficult to get to the kitchen sink, and she didn't even want to think about her clothes.

What she needed most, she realized, was a hot shower and one night of uninterrupted sleep. She had spoken to her mother only briefly on her one day in Chicago and knew that Victoria would be anxious to hear from her.

"Oh, God," she said to the ceiling, "she's going to go straight over the edge when she hears that I'm planning to marry Mitsu." That thought alone was enough to convince Maggie that the emotional confrontation could definitely wait and it wasn't long before she was sound asleep.

She phoned Victoria the next morning, postponing the inevitable by inviting her to dinner at the new apartment that evening.

"But Maggie, dear, your apartment is still a shambles. Why don't you come over here where it's homey and comfortable?"

"I know I'm not settled yet, Mother, but I promise you'll be quite comfortable. I'm taking the day off to do some organizing and by dinner time I hope to have things under control." At least I hope I will, she added to herself.

By mid-afternoon, she had arranged the furniture, unpacked most of the dishes, set the table and prepared logs for fires in both the living room and the bedroom. A quick trip to the little convenience store around the corner on Division Street yielded an adequate supply of food and by five o'clock, the aroma of spaghetti sauce mingled with the smell of pine in the fireplaces. A nice cabernet sauvignon was open and breathing, and her mother's favorite cognac and crystal snifters were on a silver tray on the hearth.

The buzzer rang, signaling Victoria's arrival downstairs. Maggie took a last look in the hall mirror and was pleased to see that she'd lost the Chia Pet look. Her curls were held firmly in place with combs and even her mother should consider her appearance suitable, if not ideal. She pressed the button on the intercom, said hi-come-on-up, and pushed the button that would release the lock on the outer door.

"Well, here goes nothing," she said to her reflection in the mirror.

"Darling, you can't be serious!" Victoria said later. "I thought you had come to your senses long ago!"

"No, Mother, it has taken me all these years to come to my senses, as you put it, and marry the man I should have married when we graduated from college. I would never had had to go through what I've gone through in the past year had I been a stronger person back then."

"Poor Charles is dead, Maggie. You can't be saying that you're sorry you married him. Why, his mother and father are charming people, and so well connected, too."

"I agree that his parents are fine people, Mother. But Charles had some very serious emotional problems, as you should be able to tell from the fact that he's dead by his own hand."

"The poor man was devastated when you divorced him! His mother hinted that she thought he moved to San Francisco because he couldn't bear not being with you. I can tell you, I had no idea what to say to her. I was ashamed of my own daughter for causing such heartache in such a fine man that he couldn't face living!"

Maggie didn't know how to argue the point. She couldn't tell her mother the truth about Charles, and wouldn't consider letting *his* mother know that he'd died because he could live very well without her, but couldn't live without his male lover—the man who'd had the effrontery to show up at his funeral with his brand new wife on his arm.

"Mother, I cannot tell you everything, but I *can* tell you that although I'm the one who filed for divorce, Charles was the one who left me, not the other way around. I was never what most people would call 'happy' with Charles, but I didn't realize until I saw Stan again that I was simply stumbling through life without a prayer of knowing what happiness was. We can argue about it until hell freezes, though I'd rather not, but you will not change my mind about marrying the one man I truly love."

Tears formed in Victoria's eyes as Maggie had known they would, but she gazed back steadfastly, holding her ground until Victoria pulled a handkerchief from her purse and dabbed at her face. Lifting her chin, she looked at her daughter and said resignedly, "Well, if you're determined to make more mistakes, I guess I can't stop you."

"If you'd just give yourself a chance, Mother, you might see what a fine man Stan is. I hope someday you'll do that."


When Maggie walked into the Davidson Chicagoan the next morning, she found everyone in a jubilant mood, with newspapers being handed around as everyone pointed to the headlines:

### "IT'S OVER! ! !"

Taxis were lined up at the cab stand outside, dining room personnel rejoiced in the knowledge that they would once again be able to offer guests a full menu, and everyone was smiling.

Maggie grabbed a paper and hurried to her office. Shrugging out of her coat, she flipped through the pages until she reached the business section. She cheered aloud at the article announcing the IBM computer virus and subsequent emergency adjustments being made available. It seemed that it might be a very merry Christmas after all.

The President looked up from his desk as the Chairman of the Federal Reserve Bank was announced. He stood to come around the desk and shake hands with Bill Stuart, indicating that they might be more comfortable having coffee at a table across the room.

Bill decided to come right to the point.

"It has come to my attention that there may be trouble ahead when the February issue of thirty-year bonds are offered," he said.

"Oh, come now, Bill, we've heard those rumors before and they haven't been carried out. What makes you think it will be any different this time?"

"I have reason to believe that this time there may be a deliberate plan in place," Bill began.

The President's eyebrows shot up. "Are you saying that someone, presumably Japanese since these rumors are generally attributed to them, is planning to sabotage the auction?"

"Possibly, sir. As you know, the Japanese own a major portion of the U.S. debt, about $65 billion worth, and that we are dependent upon them to continue financing it. If they do not, interest rates will rise significantly to lure buyers and that could rupture the stock market."

"Surely you aren't suggesting that the Japanese government would approve such a move! They need American markets for their own products and to jeopardize those markets would be disastrous to their own economy!"

"That's true, Mr. President, but what if they had acquired new markets in Asia through agreements with developing nations?"

"Do you have information that would confirm that?"

"Not specifically, but it's a real possibility. I believe that the Japanese government itself may not be aware of the situation. There are so many committees within the ministries, many of which confer before decisions are made, and it might not be difficult for a small number of people to create an atmosphere of financial distrust in our Treasury bonds."

The President frowned, understanding that one of his chief advisors was actually suggesting a dangerous plan to deliberately damage the country.

"What about the profit they'd be giving up? Surely the, what is it, five percent or so, higher yield on American bonds is incentive enough to encourage investment!"

"The Japanese are not as dedicated to profit as Americans are, Mr. President. They don't need it in the same way we do and are really just looking for a place to put their money. Japan is a very nationalistic country, devoted more to long range goals than we are. If they were to be convinced that this country could not guarantee continued stability, they would not hesitate to deny their financial support."

"And why would they doubt our continued stability?" The President was wary.

"The chaos that's resulted from the strikes that have plagued us for months and the failure of American technology on a massive scale may have been deliberate," Bill said matter-of-factly.

"The strikes? The strikes are over. Where is this coming from, Bill?"

"I apologize, Mr. President, but I'd rather not say who told me until we know more. I was astounded myself and almost disregarded it as unthinkable, but if it turns out that there's even a remote chance of it, we must act quickly."

"Is your source a reliable one, Bill? I'm the president of the United States, for God's sake! Why can't you tell me who it s? Surely you don't believe I'd knowingly do anything that would put this country at risk!"

"Of course not," Bill assured him. "My source is highly respected, but has requested that he remain anonymous for his own protection."

"Is he Japanese?"

"Yes."

"Is he in a position to have reliable information?"

"Yes."

"What do you think we should do with this information?"

"I think we should make every effort to find out more about how extensive the boycott of the February auction might be, as well as what's going on within the ministries. There's something else that could make a bad situation worse, sir."

"What's that?"

"Bond traders have acquired the habit of selling short on an existing bond issue in anticipation of Japanese purchases of the next one. In other words, since the Japanese usually sell their existing holdings to participate in the next one, American traders often sell what they don't yet own. If this happens and the Japanese don't sell, it would be ruinous on Wall Street."

"How much time do we have?"

"Hard to say, sir. No more than a few weeks."

The President was silent for a moment. Then something occurred to him. "We might have just the person right under our noses, Bill. Former President Victor Buchanan."

"President Buchanan?"

"Yes. He's pretty chummy with the Japanese, spent more time over there than at home this past year. He and Pamela were included at a White House dinner for the Japanese prime minister a couple of months ago for just that reason. Satoshi Yoshida, the industrialist, contributed a great deal of money to Victor's presidential library, as a matter of fact."

Alarms began to go off in the minds of both men. The President rose from his chair and crossed to the window overlooking the White House lawn. Bill Stuart his looked down at his hands.

The President began to speak almost to himself. "Yoshida was considered a war criminal back in the forties. He spent a few years in prison before he was pardoned. Did you know that, Bill?"

"I think I may have heard something about it," Bill replied carefully.

"Do you think he might have been carrying a grudge all these years? Waiting for his chance to get even?" The President turned back suddenly. He leaned on his desk, his hands folded into fists. "You do, don't you?" he demanded.

"I think we must be very cautious, Mr. President. Yoshida may have reason to dislike the United States, but if he does, why would he support President Buchanan's library?"

"As a diversionary tactic? To thumb his nose at us, saying in effect that he can afford to buy us? To gain an ally among us?"

Recovering from the momentary shock at the mention of the Japanese industrialist who had to be the one Stan Mitsunari had referred to, Bill said, "Possibly any or all of those."

"You referred to a failure of American technology. What does that mean?"

"A virus that was scheduled to activate on December 28$^{th}$ was inserted into the new IBM system that has been marketed as the most advanced and fastest MVS system in the world." Bill went on to elaborate on the horrific probabilities had the virus not been detected, adding that the system's designer had been hired by a Japanese firm immediately following her departure from IBM. "They apparently found a way to insert the virus without her knowledge," he finished.

The President nodded. "Hmmm . . . and what did the strikes have to do with this supposed plot?"

"Well, sir, they seemed to take on a life of their own once they began in sympathy for the California farm workers and . . ." Bill paused. "Then the Teamsters walked out when the Japanese auto plant laid off two hundred workers. It could be a coincidence, but I'm inclined to agree with my source that they might have been encouraged for two reasons: one, to create an atmosphere of antagonism, American against American as commodities disappeared from shelves; and two, to divert attention from the ultimate blow to the American economy: the February bond auction."

"Give me a day to think this over, Bill. I'll get back to you tomorrow morning." The President came around the desk to offer his hand, indicating that the meeting was over. When the door closed behind the banker, The President left instructions that h was not to be disturbed. He sat down at his desk and whispered, "My God, what have I done?" He put his head in his hands and wept with shame.

The man whose life had been devoted to honor and country knew that Yoshida had manipulated him, but he had let himself believe that it was because of the Tennessee auto plant. Now he had to admit to himself that it might well be part of a much more dangerous plan. How could he have let himself be deluded by a man known to the world as a war criminal, however long ago? A man rumored to have connections that reached into the darkest alleyways. A man who could not be as rich as he was without being ruthless.

The President realized that he had let his devotion to his wife supersede his devotion to his country and that was unacceptable to a man who considered his honor sacred. The worst of it was that the breakthrough medical treatment he had been promised had yet to be delivered.

He reached for a yellow pad and began to draft the resignation he would submit in January.

# CHAPTER THIRTY NINE

Snow was falling on Washington in little white clumps. It managed to give the city a look of virginal neatness, though anyone who wasn't from another planet knew that beneath the layers of maidenly dress lived a harlot of insatiable tastes.

The vice president stared out the window of his office. Things were looking up for the man who would be king—or president—the terms were pretty much interchangeable in view of the American position in the world. He had just received the news that the former general who currently held the office planned to resign immediately after the Christmas holidays. The President had admitted that though he might be an expert at leading troops, he was not cut out to lead a nation. He had come to realize that his devotion to his wife was a priority he could no longer ignore, and since the next election was still nearly two years away, the vice president would be in a far more advantageous position if he were to hold the office in advance.

The vice president was sure that there was more to it than the general was admitting. After all, the country had nearly gone to hell while he dithered in indecision.

A short distance away, Bill Stuart looked out another window, contemplating the wisdom of assigning the designation of detective-ambassador to another president. Victor Buchanan had been understandably reluctant to believe that his good friend in Japan might be harboring iniquitous intentions, but he had agreed to reconnoiter in an unofficial capacity.

It seemed that fortune was smiling on the United States for a change. Victor and Pamela had been invited to sail with Satoshi Yoshida to a tropical island in Micronesia over the New Year holiday. Bill couldn't help wondering if Yoshida had timed the trip intentionally to alleviate any suspicion of collusion on his part in the computer failure that had been scheduled for December 28th. He must know by now, however, that the virus had been discovered and the vaccine made available. What reasons other than fun in the sun might there be for this timely vacation?

Once the yacht had returned to Tokyo, Bill and the Treasury secretary would join Victor for some emergency diplomacy at the Japanese Ministry of Finance—a sort of G-2 conference. For the time being, the secretary would be told only that another rumor had surfaced regarding the upcoming Treasury auction.

If all else failed, the United States would call for an emergency meeting of the G-5 countries in an effort to force a disclosure of Japanese intentions. The G-5 alliance between Britain, France, Germany, Japan and the U.S. had originated as a forum for facilitating cooperation between the world's economic powers through discussion of national policy, the reasoning behind it being an elimination of surprises. If ever there had been a need to do just that, it was now, Bill reflected.

Bill was almost as weary of Washington as was The President. His wife was emotionally torn between the desire to be among friends in Illinois and the need to be somewhere where each face she saw did not display sorrow and concern at the loss of her son. Bill knew how she felt.

He glanced at his watch and remembered that Grant Williamson would be arriving at any moment. Another expression of sorrow and concern to get through, he thought. Coming on the heels of his own son's wedding, Charles' suicide was sure to be troublesome for Grant. Bill wondered if Ken might have told his father anything that would shed some light on the reasons for Charles' unhappiness.

"No," Grant said a little while later, "Ken had almost nothing to say about it. I admit that my mind wasn't on Charles at the time, but he seemed to be in good spirits at the wedding. My wife and I were surprised that he didn't come to the reception, and we had returned to Washington before . . ." he stopped.

"It's all right, Grant. Before they found Charles' body in the bay," Bill finished the sentence. "I guess we'll never know. The divorce, maybe. Remorse at having left Maggie so abruptly. It was kind of Ken to delay his honeymoon to attend the funeral service. Did he get the books he wanted from Charles' apartment? I didn't get a chance to ask him."

"He didn't mention it, Bill. Sorry."

They moved on to the reason for their meeting. The chairman of the Federal Reserve Bank wanted to discuss international trade with the Secretary of Commerce.

"The policy committee has agreed that the dollar has fallen farther than we anticipated," Bill said. "There's evidence that the loss of profit in conversion to other currencies may result in a lack of participation in the next treasury auction."

"Lack of participation? Another rumor that the Japanese are going to boycott? Maybe the time for words has passed, Bill. Have you heard about their latest moves? Since the release of Habatsu's version of the new IBM MVS system, they've been dumping their outdated stuff in developing Asian countries."

The term 'dumping' referred to selling products at below manufacturing cost, a practice considered morally reprehensible in America. The Japanese government had signed an agreement saying that Japanese businesses would refrain from doing it, but couldn't enforce the commitment. When the practice continued, the U.S. congress had responded by imposing the tariffs that had been the subject of Zach Templeton's address to labor leaders.

"But that's not the worst of it," Grant went on. "A division of Nippon Heavy Industry Corporation has sold equipment to the Russians that makes submarine detection nearly impossible."

The alarms went off again in Bill Stuart's mind.

"Nippon Heavy Industry? Isn't that Satoshi Yoshida's company?" he asked.

"The old curmudgeon himself," Grant replied. "It's my personal opinion that trade sanctions are in order. That young pup from Ohio who introduced the trade legislation may be a laughing stock now, but for my money, he's on the right track! Yoshida's up to his old tricks again, supporting the enemy."

"It wasn't long ago that you and I wrote a joint letter to congress about unfair trade legislation, Grant," Bill said slowly. "Have you changed your mind?"

"That letter was written to encourage a spirit of cooperation that we haven't seen," Grant said angrily. "They're pushing us against the wall and it's time we retaliate!"

"And what if they react the same way they did in 1941?"

"Surely you're not suggesting that they'll bomb Pearl Harbor again, are you?"

"There are less violent measures available that would be just as destructive," Bill observed.

"Like the bond boycott? They threaten that every time they want to rattle our cages, Bill. In the end, they don't follow through."

"The money they insert into our economy helps make up for the trade deficit. The U.S. has to generate sixty billion dollars annually just to repay the *current* interest and principle due on its foreign debt. What do we do if it isn't forthcoming?"

"Look, Bill, *every* issue has become a fight with them. Agricultural products, cigarettes, even baseball hats, for Christ's sake! They claim that the Japanese bone structure doesn't adapt to American caps or some such idiotic thing! We have construction companies that want to bid on projects like the Osaka airport and can't. Are we supposed to just lie down and take it?"

"We have to find a solution to the problem that is at least mildly satisfactory to everybody before it's too late," Bill said quietly.

Grant Williamson heard the apprehension in the banker's voice and wondered aloud, "Has it ever occurred to you that they might be holding a grudge because we won the war that they started?"

"As a matter of fact, it has," Bill replied.


Pamela Buchanan stretched languorously in the huge bed and looked around the stateroom. God, she could really get use to this kind of luxury, she thought. Old Satoshi-san sure knew how to spend his money. The boat—ship?—was moving slowly and Pamela could hear the waves lapping against the sides.

Both she and Victor had been exhausted from the long plane trip the day before, and had retired very soon after they boarded the yacht in Tokyo Bay. It had sailed as they slept. At first, she'd thought that she was dreaming when she felt Victor's hand on her breast. She had turned to press her body against his, willing the dream to go on forever. It wasn't until she arched her back as he entered her that she realized she was awake and her husband was really making love to her. Remembering it in the grey light of dawn, she got chills up and down her spine.

Victor was stupendous in bed. Probably because he got a lot of practice, she thought wryly. Usually not with her, however. She thought a lot about divorcing him, but could she live through the scandal that was bound to accompany such a move? A former president of the United States getting divorced? At their age? Oh hell, she still loved him anyway and had since they met and probably would for the rest of her life.

Pamela was glad that the Christmas holidays were over. Victor had been particularly jumpy this year. He was always chaffing at the bit to get back into circulation, but this year he seemed to have something on his mind beyond his next romance. He'd bounded out of bed earlier, showered quickly and hurried up on deck as Pamela was still trying to get her eyes open. She had stopped trying, hugged her pillow and gone back to sleep.

That must have been two or three hours ago, she thought. It would be hot up on deck, but the air-conditioned stateroom was cool and comfortable. There was even a fireplace in it, presumably in working order. A crystal chandelier with a rheostat hung from the ceiling and wood paneled walls held original oil paintings that created a perfect background for the exquisite European antiques. It was obvious that the very large cabin had been decorated expressly for Yoshida's frequent western guests.

Old Satoshi-san's stateroom across the way was a bit on the austere side from what Pamela had seen through the door. Very oriental, in muted shades of grey with a combination of western furniture and sit-on-the-floor kind of stuff. Well, he was oriental, after all. Give me this decadent featherbed any day, she mused.

Since they had boarded so late the day before, Pamela hadn't really had a chance to find out who else was on this cruise. She'd caught a glimpse of Hideki Somebody, the Minister of Finance, and wondered if he had a wife with him this time. Did these Japanese men ever take their wives anywhere?

There had been a map posted in the lounge that indicated their course and Pamela knew that they were headed straight south from Tokyo to some island just north of the equator. Probably one that old Satoshi-san owned. He had more money than God as she'd been told more than once, and without him Victor's library would still be scrounging for funds.

Well, time to crawl out of my cave and spelunk my way up toward daylight while there still is any, Pamela supposed.


Victor Buchanan was watching two of the young staffers who had come along with their bosses. The black sunglasses that had become his trademark hid his eyes, allowing him to observe without calling attention to the fact that he was doing so. His wife would have been astonished had she known what was going on in his mind.

Not only was he finding that he felt no desire for either of the two young ladies, he was recalling the lovemaking of a few hours ago with a happy heart. Even though she was past what most people would consider her prime, Pamela was a fine woman. Her skin was still soft to the touch and her figure had rounded edges that were far more pleasing than the angles of the hard bodies that women today struggled so hard to achieve. He really enjoyed putting his hands around her breasts, squeezing them gently until the nipples hardened, then tasting their sweetness.

When had he changed, he wondered. Or had it always been Pamela he wanted? Had he been so hung up on his reputation as a lover that he overlooked the obvious? My God! I love my own wife, he realized. Is it too late to let her know? Do I even know how?

He unfolded the copy of the guest list that had been left in their stateroom and glanced through the names. The Japanese Minister of Finance, Hidecki Watanabe, was assigned to Stateroom Three. Yoshida occupied number one, he and Pamela had number two across the corridor, so that meant that Watanabe must be next to Yoshida.

There were ten large cabins for guests on what was called the main deck and another ten smaller ones on the aft end of the deck above for staff members of guests who couldn't leave home without them any more than they could be without their American Express cards. A large lounge and a formal dining room were forward of those cabins with the captain's quarters and the bridge above that. Deck hands, stewards and galley personnel had small cabins below the guest deck. The boat accommodated well over fifty people quite comfortably.

Though it was a sailing vessel with three tall masts, it did have engines that could be put to use in calm seas or bad weather. The hull was constructed of steel and met the highest safety standards. Anyone lucky enough to be invited aboard could not help but compare it to the opulence usually reserved for expensive cruise ships, and declare it far superior to anything afloat.

A uniformed steward appeared with a tray carrying a choice of orange juice, tomato juice, or mimosas. Victor selected a mimosa and carried it with him to the rail where he stood gazing toward the island that had appeared on the starboard side of the boat. Just one of the thousands that made up Micronesia, Melanesia and Polynesia. You really couldn't tell one from another as white sand glistened and the leafy fingers of tropical palms beckoned to passersby.

Victor chose a deck chair and sat down to look over the guest list again. The Chinese Minister of Development, Chen Yutang, was in Stateroom Four. Though only the men's names were shown, Victor assumed that Chen's wife, Li-ming, was with him. A very controversial figure in the Chinese political world, Li-ming had been educated in England and was not shy about voicing her views regarding what she considered the abominable position of Chinese women. She was known to travel, excessively in the minds of some, to European countries where she bought the designer clothes she wore.

A Japanese banker whom Victor had not met, and the publisher of a respected financial journal in Singapore occupied cabin numbers Five and Six, and old Norbert Wardley, the British bachelor who was the corporate head of Hong Kong's biggest insurance company, was listed in number Eight. A real Who's Who of international figures, Victor noted. Wonder where I fit in? Yoshida's pet American?

Could any or all of these men be involved in the scheme that Victor still found pretty hard to swallow? The Chinese minister was no doubt aboard because of the cooperative agreement Yoshida had recently forged. He would be invaluable in cutting through the Red tape, pun intended, that could drive a sane man over the brink in China. He would have no reason to want to see economic disaster in the United States. To the contrary, his government had fought for recognition and needed the west.

The banker might be in on it, but where would a journalist from Singapore fit in? And Bert Wardley was the epitome of a British stereotype, stuffy and old world. He more than likely handled Yoshida's colossal insurance needs and was aboard as a result of a long-standing association.

The cabins on the lounge deck were only half occupied. There were two American Secret Service men, and conveniently, the banker and journalist had each brought a secretary who kept them up-to-date with information patched through quickly on lap top computers and fax machines. They must be the ones he'd seen earlier. Two or three members of Yoshida's own staff who were so unobtrusive they were nearly invisible completed the list.

One of the cabins had an occupant whose presence was entirely unknown to the other voyagers. Her cabin had been deliberately sound-proofed and a narrow twisting staircase led from it down to a secret panel in Yoshida's luxurious stateroom. She was twelve years old and had shown great promise as a musician at the orphanage. She was also very beautiful, with blue-black silky hair and a flawless complexion. Her breasts were little more than buds on the tiny figure that made hardly a dent among the futons where she was learning the intricacies of intimacy from the man who knew them all.

Hideki Watanabe, accompanied by another Japanese man whom Victor assumed was the banker, appeared on deck and paused to take a glass from the tray held by the steward. Following on their heels like lap dogs were two slender women who were speaking energetically, their conversation punctuated by high pitched giggles.

Not far behind the foursome was a lone woman in a brightly colored sarong who could only be Chen Li-ming. She, too, paused to pick up a glass from the tray, remaining motionless for just the right length of time to draw every eye before she continued across the deck to a chair next to the one where Victor sat mesmerized.

"Good morning," she said in flawless English.

Victor peered at her through his dark glasses, taking just the amount of time she had known he would to respond.

"Good morning," he said.

She held out a hand with long, tapered nails that were enameled in a soft coral color and introduced herself.

"I am Chen Li-ming, or to Americans, Li-ming Chen. I believe my husband and I are in the stateroom next to yours. Is your wife recuperating from the long flight? I look forward to meeting her and perhaps learning more about how American women have been able to gain so much independence."

Victor recovered his aplomb and took the hand that she offered, saying, "How nice to finally meet the lady who promises to be such a positive force in aiding China's entry into the twenty-first century."

She laughed. "Oh, you are a charming man, Mr. Buchanan. I had heard of your diplomatic skills and wondered if such artful sensitivity could be possible in an American politician."

Further pursuit of the dialogue at which Victor excelled was cut short as the two Japanese couples strolled their way. Hideki Watanabe introduced the banker, Shijiro Koyama, and then the two women, explaining that neither of them spoke more than a few words of English. Both bowed politely, and then stood aside as their husbands forgot their presence.

Li-ming Chen surprised everyone by saying, "Ohayo gozaimasu, good morning, hajimemashite, how do you do?"

Stunned by the Chinese woman's use of Japanese language and slightly embarrassed at being addressed so directly, both women blushed and said in unison, "Doozo yoroshiku," in reply.

Li-ming laughed again and admitted that she had just about used up her Japanese vocabulary. "Pretty much anything beyond that and I have to say, 'wakarimasen'—I don't understand," she told the three men.

"Your excellent English makes it possible to converse well with most nationalities, Mrs. Chen," said Watanabe. "While many Japanese men are bilingual or multilingual, our wives do not have the same abilities."

"Abilities, Mr. Watanabe, or opportunities?" Li-ming retorted. She either failed to notice or was unabashed by the frozen smile on the finance minister's face.

Fortunately, Satoshi Yoshida chose that moment to shuffle across the deck, welcoming his guests expansively.

"Now that you have had time to rest a little after your journeys, we will be better able to get acquainted leisurely," he began. "A buffet has been set up in the dining area and you are welcome to enjoy it whenever you wish. If there is something you would like to have that is not there, please feel free to ask the steward. I find it pleasant to keep the first day at sea a casual one, and hope that you will each partake in whatever activity you may find agreeable."

It occurred to Victor that he would find it very agreeable indeed to rejoin Pamela in their stateroom, provided she had not yet left their very agreeable bed.

# CHAPTER FORTY

The White House physician used the week between Christmas and New Year's to catch up on all the medical journals he had stacked up in his office. He was always on the lookout for articles that pertained to Alzheimer's disease, though he didn't think there was much hope that anything would develop in time to help The First Lady. She was such a lovely woman. It was hard to understand how a disease as debilitating as this could be creeping so insidiously into her brain.

He came across two short articles in rapid succession that linked Alzheimer's with Down syndrome, considering the possibility of a genetic connection. The National Institute of Health reported that an extra copy of a gene responsible for the production of the protein amyloid had been found in both Down and Alzheimer patients.

The doctor picked up a publication that had been sent to him by a former colleague who was now in Japan. He liked to keep up on what other countries might be doing in the way of research and development, as well as what treatments were available overseas that could take months, even years, to be approved in the United States. Skimming through the table of contents, he saw that a paper written by a Japanese chemist on his discoveries in the field of Alzheimer's had been included. The doctor flipped the pages quickly and was soon absorbed in his reading.

Victor and Pamela held hands in the moonlight. The humidity that seemed to cling to everything, turning ordinary objects into slippery demons, was especially heavy that evening. The tropical mystique was compounded by the pulsating rhythm of drums and dark skinned figures dancing in the light of several beach fires. As they watched from the yacht, anchored offshore and swaying lazily, their eyes met and Pamela's heart began to pound. Drawing her into the shadows, Victor kissed her urgently, his tongue probing, his fingers caressing the delicate material that covered her breasts.

They were alone in the tiny outdoor area located in the stern on the guest deck, having found that hardly anyone ever ventured out there. Staircases on either side led up to the lounge deck behind the staff cabins, but the guests always used the elevator or the stairs located amidships that led directly into the lounge. It was their secret place and they felt wonderfully decadent making love in a place where they could be discovered at any moment.

We're acting like teenagers, they told each other. But it felt so good that they simply couldn't help themselves. Victor had told her, almost shyly, that he had been a fool for too many years, and that he hoped to make it up to her if she could find it in her heart to let him. How could she do otherwise, she'd thought to herself. That he had come back to her made life pure joy. She shuddered involuntarily as his hand tugged at the hem of her skirt.

A lazy agenda had developed as the boat made its way south. The captain had been sailing the sun drenched waters of the South Pacific for more than thirty years and knew every hidden cove in the area. Mornings were usually spent anchored off a sandy beach, with picnic lunches of fruit and fresh seafood provided. As it became too hot to stay in the sun, everyone came back to the boat where the men had fallen into the habit of playing poker in the air-conditioned lounge for most of the afternoon.

An umbrella set up by a steward shaded Li-ming and Pamela from the afternoon sun as they sat outside nibbling on fresh fruit. The juice of a mango dribbled down Li-ming's chin and somehow it made her look sexy rather than sloppy, Pamela thought. How does she do it?

The two women had become friends of a sort since neither of them could communicate with the two Japanese women who stayed indoors much of the time anyway, modestly covered as required by their husbands. The wife of the publisher from Singapore, Nelson Yu, had been noticeably hostile to Li-ming, a result of her family history with the Chinese communists.

As the wife of a former U.S. president, Pamela had tried to remain neutral in the interest of international politics, but it was difficult. She was so happy with Victor, and Li-ming was such fun to be with while Victor hung out with the men. She peered through the glass and wondered what they talked about during these lengthy card games.

Victor had been patient for several days as conversation had been limited to the heat, the rain that seemed to come from nowhere at times, the food, and cards. He was anxious to get down to some serious talk about money and politics, and was forming his thoughts into an introduction of such a discussion when Nelson Yu did it for him.

"Are you ready for the change of power in 1997, Bert?" he asked the British insurance mogul.

Aware of the presence of the Chinese minister, Bert Wardley was cautious in his reply. "My company has always believed in the diversification of assets, so we don't anticipate any serious problems," he began. "We have considered moving cash assets into both real estate and government bonds in the United States, particularly since the interest rates became so appealing at the last Treasury auction. Nine and a half percent is better than we could hope to do in other investment areas. If Japanese investors don't buy out the store, that is." He came as close to smiling as his very British demeanor would allow.

Hideki Watanabe responded genially, "We wouldn't dream of leaving you out, Bert. In fact, with the foresighted vision of the Japanese people, we may let you have a significant portion of the next issue."

"That sounds suspiciously like you know something that the rest of us don't," Victor said, matching Watanabe's geniality.

"Not at all, Victor, it's just that the current problems in the states may be diverting the attention of the government, and a wait-and-see attitude might be in order. Nothing definite, you understand, just prudent business policy."

Victor turned to Shijiro Koyama and asked, "Has the Bank of Japan taken a position on this?"

"We would have to agree that a watchful attitude is justified," replied the banker. "In my position as head of the securities division, it is my responsibility to ascertain the risk factors involved in our investments."

The usual double talk, thought Victor. Nobody will give you a straight answer until half the country has been consulted.

Satoshi Yoshida interrupted the discussion to suggest that they might all enjoy a cool drink outside before it was time to change for dinner. He rose from the table and signaled to a steward.

Victor busied himself shuffling cards as he watched and wondered if his friend had deliberately chosen to end any examination of Japanese policy on the upcoming bond auction. I must find a way to speak privately with Watanabe, he thought to himself. Unless something unforeseen happens, the man will soon be prime minister and the U.S. needs to know if his attitude would be antagonistic in nature. The supposed conspiracy is being attributed to Yoshida and someone within the Japanese bureaucracy, presumably the powerful MITI, but does it extend beyond that? Surely Watanabe recognizes that the two countries are mutually dependent on each other in the international marketplace, and that a blow to the U.S. economy would affect the sale of Japanese products to Americans. His comment about a wait-and-see attitude before Yoshida ended the discussion seems to indicate that a bond boycott could be a reality!

Victor followed the others outside and ordered a tall scotch and water from the steward. The sun was low on the horizon and about to disappear in a dazzling red glow when one of Yoshida's aides appeared carrying a fax and looking decidedly shocked. He headed straight for his boss, handing over the paper with trembling hands.

Yoshida fumbled through pockets looking for his glasses, then found them on top of his head where he had shoved them as he led the group outside. He read quickly through the page in his hand, stood up swiftly, took two steps forward and fell to the deck. There was a moment of stunned silence as his guests and the aide stared disbelievingly at his inert form. Li-ming Chen rose from her chair and knelt beside him.

"I believe he's had a stroke," she said, taking his wrist in her hand to determine a pulse.

Norbert Wardley, who sat closest to them, bent to pull the paper from Yoshida's clenched fist, anxious to see what news could have been responsible for such an intense reaction. He looked down, then back up, his eyes directed toward Victor Buchanan. "It seems the president of the United States has announced his resignation, effective almost immediately," he said.

Victor leapt to his feet, crossing the deck in long strides. Reaching out to grasp the communication, he read it aloud to the group.

"In an astonishing announcement today, the president of the United States revealed his pending resignation, telling reporters gathered at a hastily called press conference that his wife's health had led him to the decision. The discovery of a new treatment for the debilitating Alzheimer's disease that has begun to affect the first lady, available only in Japan at present, has given the president hope for her complete recovery. The couple will leave for an extended stay in Tokyo as soon as an orderly transition of leadership can be achieved. The vice president, asked for a comment, said . . ."

"Upon my soul," whispered Bert Wardley.

"Dear me," said Nelson Yu's wife.

"Holy shit," murmured Pamela Buchanan.


Two hours later, Pamela and Li-ming sat by a window in the lounge. The captain had decided to head directly for the U.S. military base on Guam where the best medical care would be available. The sails had been taken down and the engines were running at full speed, making the journey considerably rougher than it had been for the past several days. It had been determined that they would arrive sometime in the wee hours of the morning.

Victor was closeted with Hidecki Watanabe and had been for quite some time. Pamela was trying not to speculate on the urgency he had exhibited in commandeering the finance minister's attention.

In his stateroom below, Satoshi Yoshida had been made as comfortable as the crew had been able to make him since he was unable to speak or move on his own. His aides took turns looking in on him, though it seemed there was little they could do other than peer into his glassy eyes and take his pulse.

In the cabin directly above Yoshida's, the little girl who was accustomed to being summoned each evening was growing sleepy as she waited. She opened the door to the narrow staircase and listened, but heard nothing. One by one, she crept down to the lower end and pushed on the release panel. The room was dim, lit only in one corner, but she could see that Yoshida-san lay in the bed, so she moved silently across the floor toward him. When he did not respond to her whispers, she decided to let him sleep and wake to find her waiting. She removed the obi sash from around her waist and let her kimono fall to the floor. Pulling the quilt aside just the slightest bit, she slid underneath and moved his arm gently until she lay close in his embrace.

Since he was completely helpless, no one knew that Satoshi Yoshida was fully aware of what had happened to him and his anger was a terrible thing. The apparent release of Sumio Masabe's research and The President's discovery of it had been more than he could bear. He drifted in and out, able to hear those around him as they planned his immediate future, but unable to bellow his refusal of American medical attention.

Though his struggle could not be seen by those who had watched as he fell, he writhed inwardly, desperately battling his body in a futile attempt to regain control. If he didn't, the Americans had won again and he would be at their mercy in the hospital on Guam.

An hour later, a bewildered aide found the tiny slip of a girl sound asleep beside him. The aide backed out in haste. He was hurrying down the corridor in search of help when he bumped into the steward entrusted with her meals who had discovered her absence and hoped to find her before anyone else did. As the two men woke her, Pamela returned to the stateroom across the corridor. She watched in amazement as the naked child was carried from Yoshida's bed. In all her years of public life, never had she met with so much intrigue.

She could hardly wait to tell Victor.

Victor was anxious to get to Guam and find a secure telephone line, though he wasn't absolutely sure just who he should call. The President had requested his cooperation in finding out who might be behind the acts of sabotage against the United States, but could he be sure that The President himself wasn't involved? Victor was sure that it was impossible, but with his resignation and pending trip to Japan announced in the same breath, Victor decided he should exercise caution.

Yoshida's reaction and subsequent stroke seemed to indicate that he'd had no prior warning, and since he'd been even more upset than any of the others by the news, it could be that The President had outwitted him somehow.

The former president had spent more than an hour with Japan's finance minister, questioning him carefully about his knowledge of the pending bond boycott, and finding that Watanabe had been irritated by the use of the word.

"Boycott is a severe term, Victor," he had said, "and implies widespread collusion on the part of Japanese investors. I assure you that no such conspiracy exists. The possibility of removing Japanese support of U.S. bonds temporarily is only that—a possibility, in response to the labor unrest that America has suffered over the past few months."

"Do you recall where the suggestion originated?" Victor had asked.

Watanabe had responded that although he couldn't be positive, he thought he might have discussed it with the minister of International Trade and Industry, and quite possibly with the vice minister of his own ministry. Word tended to spread quickly in the financial community, he'd gone on, and it would be difficult to be specific as to where it had begun. It was entirely possible that a bank or insurance company had expressed concern about the stability of the American government to someone, and it had simply been passed on in the ministries.

When asked about his relationship with Yoshida, the finance minister had said simply, "Money talks, Victor, as you well know, and Yoshida-san has a great deal of it."

"Would it be possible for him to, shall we say, significantly influence policy?"

"You mean 'bribe' someone, Victor?" The tone of Watanabe's voice suggested that he was beyond irritation and moving toward outrage. Victor hastily assured him that he meant no offense, and that the question only reflected his concern about the rumors that seemed to surface repeatedly at auction time.

Watanabe had sighed deeply and agreed that it must be distressing to the American government. He had gone on to say that it was virtually impossible to bribe anyone at the civil service level that would be required in order to influence policy within the ministries. It would not be quite as impossible, however, for someone to have his own agenda, but to ascertain the identity of such a person would be like trying to reverse the tides in the ocean.

Victor had been gratified by the offer, made freely, to look into the origins of the rumors.

"I could not inform you of my findings, you understand, but I will pledge to you that if I discover anything improper, I will remedy it myself. Does that reassure you, Victor?"

It had, indeed, reassured the former U.S. president. He felt sure that the man who would soon be prime minister of Japan would not risk dishonor, even if he were the only one who knew it.

Victor returned to the stateroom where Pamela regaled him with the tale of the naked child in Yoshida's bed, then did her best to get him to tell her about the obvious urgency of his meeting with Watanabe.

He deflected her questions by remarking, "The Japanese-American relationship is crucial, as you well know, Pamela. I am simply acting as an unofficial goodwill ambassador in light of The President's surprise resignation."

Pamela was not fooled by his off-handed dismissal and watched as her husband paced the floor of the cabin impatiently, preoccupied with his own thoughts.

The yacht was met by a U.S. Navy launch as it entered Guam's territorial waters, and escorted to the dock where an ambulance awaited. The two secret service agents had wired ahead for an automobile to carry Victor and Pamela directly to the base commander's office. Victor disappeared into an inner office, emerging shortly thereafter only to hurry off to a communications center where he would have access to a secure line to Washington.

Pamela was entrusted to the commander's aide and escorted to private visitor quarters where a steward was directed to see to her every need. Her husband would join her shortly, she was told.

A few minutes later, another phone call was made from Washington to the Virginia headquarters of the CIA, and moments after that an agent in Tokyo received orders to investigate the origins of the paper recently published in the pharmaceutical journal and the laboratory of its author as well.

In less than twenty-four hours, a report was faxed to Washington with the information that the author of the paper had submitted it himself. A visit to the chemist's laboratory had made the man tremble in fear of his unknown benefactor's wrath at the unauthorized release of his findings. Tracing the identity of the benefactor would take a little longer.

Victor and Pamela, still enjoying the hospitality of the navy, were dining at the officer's club when a folder marked 'Top Secret' was delivered. Victor's relief at whatever news the folder contained did not escape his wife's observation. Stealth and furtiveness seemed to follow them everywhere, she thought ruefully. Would they never be able to escape the madness? Now that they had rediscovered each other, she wanted nothing more than to spend the rest of her days enjoying uninterrupted ecstasy in some tropical paradise with her husband. But once a politician, always a politician, she supposed.

They paid a courtesy call on Satoshi Yoshida prior to leaving the island. His prognosis was not good. They were warned that he had not regained his ability to speak, nor was there any movement in his limbs. He probably wouldn't even know they were there. But Victor insisted on seeing the old man anyway.

As they stood by his bed, Pamela was taken aback by the look in his eyes. If she hadn't known his condition and if he and Victor hadn't been such buddies before the stroke, she'd have said that what she saw reflected was pure hatred.

Following their return to Washington, Victor spent much of his time closeted with the resigning president and the chairman of the Federal Reserve Bank.

# CHAPTER FORTY ONE

In Tokyo, Nobuya Saito sat behind his desk nervously cleaning his glasses. He stared at the phone he had just put down, suddenly fearful for his own future. In a surprise call, Hidecki Watanabe had questioned him regarding the rumors of a bond boycott of American Treasury bonds.

"I told Victor Buchanan that the Japanese were simply being prudent in considering the stability of the American government," Watanabe had said, "but now that the strikes are settled and a more forceful leader has replaced the indecisive president, I have begun to wonder if the cause for concern hasn't been eliminated. After all, that market is the only one big enough to absorb the excess cash in our own economy."

Saito reached for the phone again, intending to get in touch with his counterpart in MITI. He was told by the secretary who answered that the vice minister was unavailable. Saito recalled his inability to reach Sunao Tokumura when the question of the California bank loans had arisen. Once again, he wondered just what part Tokumura might play in all of this.

Sunao Tokumura was not in his office. He was pacing in his garden at home, trying in vain to calm the panic that had begun to rise at the news of Satoshi Yoshida's stroke. Nothing was going as planned. The

American strikes had been settled, the computer failure so carefully orchestrated had been discovered, and it had just been announced that the U.S. would be accepting Singapore's longstanding offer to base American warships there. China had announced the opening of an American securities firm in Beijing, along with the news that contracts had been signed for the purchase of American tires for Chinese military planes.

The Indonesians were dragging their feet and it looked like they weren't buying the 'Asia for Asians' idea. With Yoshida bedridden in an American hospital in Guam, of all places, the Two Swords plan appeared doomed in its effort to destroy the American economy, bringing his old enemy to its knees. One sword had been rendered useless, the other severely disabled.

The only part of Nito Ryu that still had any chance of success was the proposed Treasury bond boycott. That by itself would at least cripple the U.S. economy. It *must* succeed.

Driven by a well of angry energy, Tokumura strode from the garden to the house and headed for his study. He rarely used the room for business purposes, but it was the one place where his privacy was assured. Thumbing through his personal directory, he wrote down a short list of names and began dialing.

His first call was to the investment manager at Japan's largest insurance company. When questioned about the company's intent regarding the approaching bond auction, the manager voiced the same opinion that Hidecki Watanabe had presented to Saito that morning.

"We are already heavily committed to the U.S. stock and bond market," he said, "and not only are interest rates on the bonds higher than we could get in Japan, but the anonymity of ownership is beneficial. With all the publicity that surrounds Japanese purchases of real estate and corporate stock, the lack of public information on who buys American debt is one way in which we can make money without enduring criticism."

"Have you considered the variance in inflation rates between the U.S. and Japan?" Tokumura asked. "It is too early to tell how high the American inflation rate may go under the new administration. Even with higher yields on long-term bonds, the profit may disappear. The lower inflation rate in Japan may offset lower interest rates in the long run. I am simply suggesting that you may want to adopt a wait-and-see attitude."

A few more calls and the seed had been planted. As Tokumura had known would happen, the seed would be nourished as telephone lines buzzed with shared information.

Bob Sanborn prided himself on his excellent physical condition, gained primarily from frequent games of racquetball with business acquaintances. A former assistant secretary of the U.S. Treasury, now a bond specialist in New York, Bob found that he killed any number of birds with one stone through his racquetball games. It helped him maintain a physical image that belied his age, it boosted his energy level tremendously, and best of all, he never left the court without gathering some small tidbit of information from his opponent. He was definitely on top of the world, raking in money what with a hefty salary and great commissions earned through bond sales to the serious players, and he had every intention of retiring early to partake of the pleasures of the world.

Bob planned on making a real killing in the next few weeks as participants in the upcoming Treasury auction sold off previous issues. He had gone all out this time, selling short to the max, and he couldn't help but dream a little about the fifty foot cruiser he'd already picked out. Another five years, maybe less, and he'd be in a position to put it all behind him and sail off to the Mediterranean, the Greek Isles, and Monte Carlo.

Sweat dripping from nearly every pore on his body, he grabbed a towel from the bench and held open the door to the locker room for the tall Japanese man he'd just allowed to win. They went through the usual polite maneuvers as the Japanese man declined to pass through the door first, saying, "Doozo, doozo," and urging the American to go ahead. As usual, Bob ended up doing as the man wanted.

"Great workout, isn't it?" he asked rhetorically, stripping quickly for a shower. "I'm ready for a tall cool one—how about you?"

Bob's companion, the same man who had recently been the object of Sally McNamara's dreams, agreed. He had spent nearly every waking hour since the dinner with Sally memorizing every page of the manual, and was quite sure that he now knew more than most of the American traders. It never hurt to schmooze—a silly word he'd picked up from the New Yorkers—with the competition.

The two men made small talk over their first drink, and it wasn't until he was half way through his second one that Bob said, "Your clients should be about ready to unload some of the November issue of thirty-year bonds. I know I have a shitload of people eager to pick them up."

Knowing that Bob had probably already recorded the sales, the Japanese man took his time in answering. He tilted his head back, moving it in a circle as if to ease kinks in his neck, then picked up his glass and sipped leisurely.

"Can't really say. The question of lower interest rates, combined with a higher inflation rate in the U.S. than in Japan, has made them a little nervous about selling."

Bob's eyes narrowed. "Oh, come on, not the old 'maybe we'll boycott' line again! Your clients *always* sell their previous holdings to get in on the next issue!"

"I assure you there is no intent to boycott. Our financial analysts have merely pointed out that if interest rates go down from over nine percent to seven and a half percent, profit begins to disappear when an inflation rate two percent higher here than in Japan is taken into consideration."

Bob was beginning to sweat again. "How soon will you be in a position to know for sure?" he asked, trying his best to hide his burgeoning anxiety.

The Japanese man hid his enjoyment at the American's discomfort with far more finesse. "Soon, perhaps . . ." he said vaguely.

When several days passed after the public announcement of the February bond issue was posted and still no offers to sell had come in, Bob really began to sweat. If he couldn't cover his sales, his anticipated commission would vanish and he'd also be responsible for monumental losses for the company. He didn't even want to *think* about the amount, and in any case, his name would be mud on the Street. He began to pray in earnest.

Hidecki Watanabe was playing golf with his wife's brother. It was a game that he'd discovered only a few years ago and now thoroughly enjoyed. Courses in Japan were not yet up to the standards of those in America, but this was due in part to the lack of adequate space in which to put them. Perhaps his friend, Victor Buchanan, would invite him to play at his country club the next time he visited the states.

Watanabe's brother-in-law was a tiresome man, pedantic and boring, but duty required that they get together now and then. The Finance minister had chosen this particular day because of Makoto-san's position as manager of a pension fund that held enormous quantities of American investments. It was a pleasant way to spend time with his relative—they were only in close proximity as they teed off on each hole and putted on the green—and he could get information as well.

"The Americans have announced the quarterly auction of their thirty-year bonds," Watanabe said diffidently. "I suppose you will be participating as usual?"

"Maybe, maybe not," Makoto replied non-commitally.

"Oh? Why is that?" Watanabe pretended to be only marginally interested as he concentrated on a long putt.

"Lower interest rate than on the last issue, combined with the discrepancy between Japanese and American inflation," Makoto said brusquely.

"Where did that idea come from?"

"Word gets around," came the reply. "It seems prudent to wait and see."

Watanabe was annoyed. "Word gets around from where? You and I should be able to speak frankly, Makoto-san. If you can't trust me, who can you trust?"

"Hmmm . . . yes, well . . . I had a call from the vice minister at MITI. He said a wait-and-see attitude might be judicious."

"Sunao Tokumura? That's odd. There's been no directive from either MITI or Finance regarding the idea. Perhaps he and Saito have learned something that escaped my attention." The finance minister returned his concentration to the game, intentionally ending the conversation.

# CHAPTER FORTY TWO

Bill Stuart frowned. The auction was only days away. Non-competitive tenders, submitted by small investors, had maintained the usual level of activity, but competitive bids from primary dealers representing the big investors were conspicuously absent. It was not yet cause for panic, since bids were accepted up until 1:00 P.M. on the day of the auction and this kind of delay was not unusual, just stressful under the present circumstances. The bids were sealed and confidential until after the deadline when they were opened and listed at Federal Reserve Bank branches throughout the country.

Usually, Bill had a sort of sixth sense when it came to the movement of money, but it was failing him this time. He'd heard the latest reasoning: the disparity between the inflation rates in the U.S. and Japan—what would they think of next?—but a half percent increase in interest rates would compensate for that if it was really the influencing factor.

Immediately following his return the U.S. from Guam, Victor Buchanan had reported his conversation with Hidecki Watanabe, saying, "It's my feeling that the man is above reproach. I pushed him to the point of insult and he reacted with what I believe was sincere indignation."

Satoshi Yoshida's stroke had been the subject of a lengthy discussion between Bill Stuart, Victor Buchanan, Stan Mitsunari, and the resigning president. The four men speculated on the future of any plot he may have masterminded.

"The stroke seemed to be in response to the news of your resignation and proposed trip to Japan for the Alzheimer's treatment, Mr. President," Victor had said. "Why would that cause such an intense reaction?"

The President was noncommittal. "He had mentioned the existence of research on the disease when he was here for the White House dinner, but said the drug might not be available for quite some time. It was the White House physician who saw an article in a pharmaceutical journal about it. Since it's still experimental, it probably won't be available in this country for months, if not years. My wife needs it now which is what prompted my decision to resign."

Stan had remarked, "News of a medical breakthrough would be beneficial to the public image of his country. Surely he wouldn't have reason to withhold it." The comment was a statement rather than a question and avoided the inference that the Japanese industrialist might have ulterior motives for keeping such news from the president of the United States.

"At any rate, he certainly won't be masterminding any sinister plots in the near future," Victor said quickly, ending speculation as well as the need for a response from The President. The implications had not escaped anyone, however. Had the American president deliberately delayed action in ending the crippling strikes in return for personal favor? Impossible!

"If there really is a plot, I'm inclined to believe that Yoshida and one other man were entirely responsible for it," Stan had said. "The only portion of it that may remain in place is the boycott, if we're correct in our analysis. In the event that this is the case, the other man involved is still a threat."

Rumors reached the Fed chairman just as they reached everybody else, and Sunao Tokumura, vice minister of the powerful MITI, appeared to be the culprit behind the inflation rate idea. Bill thought it a safe bet that he was the other man.

Victor had volunteered to get in touch with Norbert Wardley in Hong Kong to stimulate British participation and Stan had indicated that he'd see what he could find out in Tokyo. The resigning president had been oddly silent.

The night before the auction, Bob Sanborn was playing racquetball with a savagery of awesome proportions. Offers to sell previous bond issues had begun to come in piecemeal, but Bob was still seriously overextended. He'd heard that several bond traders had sealed bids on the next day's auction, but had been instructed by their clients to hold onto them until the last minute. Never had he encountered so much secrecy. No one was talking, probably because they were as overextended as he was and feared for their own careers. No, that wasn't quite true, he admitted to himself. He'd been so sure of himself that he'd gone out to the very end of the limb while the thirty or forty other traders who did the same thing had stayed closer to safety.

Bob swung viciously at the ball, and then swore as pain erupted in his wrist. He dropped his racket and bent over, holding the wrist with his other hand. Offering a gruff apology to his opponent, he strode toward the locker room without a backward glance.

By noon the next day, offers to sell previous issues of the thirty-year bonds had increased, but bids on the current issue were still sluggish. There was a flurry of activity with only minutes until the one o'clock deadline, and shortly after one o'clock when the sealed bids had been opened and listed, traders cheered at the news that though participation by Japanese interests had declined, sales to British, Dutch and Hong Kong interests had stepped up significantly. The results were encouraging. A collective sigh of relief was audible up and down Wall Street and politicians began calling for a balanced budget amendment before settling comfortably back into spending as usual.

Bob Sanborn's absence was hardly noticed throughout the morning and it wasn't until late afternoon that someone thought to call him at home. The phone was answered by Bob's attorney who provided the reason why he hadn't been in his office on such an important day. He'd been speeding on the beltway when his car hit a cement retaining wall and Bob had died in the ambulance enroute to the hospital.


Warm sunshine and a profusion of cherry blossoms made spring in Tokyo a magic time. The new president of the United States, formerly the vice president, stood beside the former president once removed, Victor Buchanan, at the outdoor reception that followed the swearing-in ceremony of Japan's new prime minister, Hidecki Watanabe. A spirit of international cooperation prevailed at the event as the three men shook hands all around.

In his newly acquired capacity as elder statesman and ambassador of goodwill, Victor had flourished. He was, after all, only in his sixties and in robust health. Representing the United States in confidential talks, he had almost singlehandedly brought about a new era in world trade in a matter of months.

Unencumbered by the prearranged agendas that were the norm in high level conferences of an official nature, Victor had formed solid relationships with other world leaders—relationships that now served his country well. Agreements that would significantly increase available markets for American manufacturers were being signed regularly.

The new American president was already campaigning for re-election on a platform that called for a balanced budget. His chosen running mate, Tennessee congressman Zach Templeton, was enjoying a resurgence of popularity following the reopening of the Japanese auto plant in his state. Economic expansion in the region was one of the benefits of lower unemployment, and Zach didn't hesitate to exploit his advantages by claiming direct responsibility.

"In the void is virtue and no evil.

Wisdom has existence, principle has existence,

The Way has existence, spirit is nothingness.

Book of the Void

Book of Five Rings

Miyamoto Musashi

# CHAPTER FORTY THREE

In the garden outside his ancestral home on the other side of Tokyo from where the reception was in progress, Sunao Tokumura meditated in the teahouse that had been his refuge for more than fifty years. He had failed to fulfill his promise to his father to avenge the shame caused by the Japanese surrender in 1945. He had also failed as the reincarnation of the ancestor who had been his inspiration, seventeenth century warrior, Miyamoto Musashi.

Nito Ryu, the Two Swords Plan, had ended in disaster, its strategists defeated. It was only a matter of time before the steps he had taken on his own initiative were questioned by his superiors. He would be exposed, considered a trouble maker, his resignation demanded. Although his motives had been honorable and success would have restored Japan to its former glory, failure meant personal disgrace and shame to his family, and that was unacceptable.

He rose and walked slowly into the house that had sheltered so many of his forebears. The black cherry wood passageways that connected each wing, the treasures that would remain for Mineo and Sachiko to care for in future years, the stone basin that served as a reminder to all who entered that anxieties should be left outside—all were reminiscent of the traditions he was sworn to uphold.

The children were away with school friends and only Sunao and Otsu remained in the house. He was loathe to leave Sachiko and Mineo. They were just entering the world beyond the sheltered environment of their studies. They needed his guidance, whether they knew it or not. Mineo's obsession with rock music was disturbing, and Sachiko's desire for a business career even more so. But to fail in his obligation to carry out the code of the samurai would be to leave a tainted legacy. He would have to believe that his dedication to honor and duty would set the example for his children.

He had planned the ceremony with great care. Otsu waited for him in the bedroom they had shared for nearly twenty-five years. Though he had not yet told her of his intentions, he was sure that his wife knew him well enough to suspect that they had reached a crisis in their lives. He would tell her as they bathed together, then she would help him dress after he made love to her one last time.

A trusted childhood friend would prepare the teahouse for the ritual as he and Otsu spent their last moments together. A raised platform would be covered with red carpeting and the two swords, one long, the other short, that had been lovingly tempered by a master swordsmith five hundred years earlier, would be laid out. The two men would share a cup of sake as they bid each other farewell.

Walking softly through the house, he found Otsu kneeling in front of the small shrine in their bedroom, her hands together, her head bowed in prayer. He touched her shoulder gently and helped her to her feet. They undressed silently, showered, and stepped into the large tub that was separated by a glass window from the pool just outside where silver and gold carp swam lazily among lush greenery. Lotus flowers blossomed sweetly on the surface of the water, adding to the ambiance intended to bring peace and serenity to the bather inside.

Sunao was particularly tender with his wife as they lay on the bed they shared and she employed the subtle techniques she knew would please him as their lovemaking commenced. This would be the last time the Three Shouts of his passion would echo in her ears. There was no need for words when they rose and so they did not speak.

Otsu helped her husband don the robes that were once worn by his grandfather, then bowed to the man she had honored and loved. She knelt again by the shrine, her eyes lowered, and remained there long after he had left the room.

The sun had nearly set as he entered the small round teahouse and greeted his friend, nodding his approval of the preparations. They spoke of their memories for a time as the moon replaced the sun and then Sunao rose from the tatami mat and crossed to kneel before a small wooden Buddha. In a final prayer, he asked for the forgiveness of his family and for Right Understanding and Right Aspiration on the pathway toward Enlightenment.

His spirit was still, already entering another realm as he moved to the platform where he knelt again, his back to the mortal world, and grasped the short sword in both hands. Holding it firmly, he bowed, then straightened as his right hand extended until the tip of the blade touched a spot just below his breastbone. He breathed in and out several times in deep meditation, and then plunged the blade into his body, drawing it down and across until he slumped forward.

The old friend who had vowed his loyalty in Sunao's ultimate gesture of devotion came to his side, the long sword raised, and in one sweeping motion, slashed Sunao's neck, beheading him. He took the short sword from Sunao's hand and wiped the blood from both weapons before carrying them outside. He would clean them thoroughly and return them to their places on the wall where they had been for many years, to be honored by generations to come.

Logs and kindling had been prepared and the man struck a match to light the fire that would destroy the teahouse along with the body of Sunao Tokumura, scholar and nationalist whose allegiance to his country and emperor were boundless.

Otsu watched from the house as flames reached toward the stars in the sky above. She would not dishonor her husband's memory with tears. As she peeked through a crack between the shojis, the tall slender figure of a man appeared silhouetted against the flames. He carried a cup that he lifted to his mouth, his head back as he swallowed the last of the liquid that it had held.

The moon disappeared behind a cloud as flames consumed the vines that crept up the walls of the little teahouse. Soon there was nothing left but ashes.

No blossoms and no moon

And he is drinking sake

All alone.

Matsuo Basho

1644—1694

# EPILOGUE
## SIX MONTHS LATER

**M**r. and Mrs. Stan Mitsunari were snuggled in the big bed in their apartment in Chicago, a cozy fire burning in the fireplace. It was a Sunday morning in early October and sections of the impossibly thick Chicago Tribune lay scattered around them.

"Oh, look at this," Maggie exclaimed, pointing to an article on page three of the front section. "It says the former first lady has made remarkable progress during her treatment in Tokyo and that the scientist who developed it has been nominated for the Nobel Prize in chemistry. She's such a lovely person, and so brave to try medical treatment in a foreign country."

"Not so foreign to me," Stan asserted.

Maggie laughed. "You're more American than I am in some ways, Mitsu, and I tend to forget that you have two countries. Do you miss Japan?"

"Sometimes. But since I'm still reporting on global economics, I'm in touch with former colleagues who keep me posted on what's happening. And I'd rather be here with you than anywhere else on earth!" He leaned over to kiss her cheek.

Stan and Maggie had been married in late spring, having finally won over Victoria Davidson. As a respected journalist in the financial arena, Stan had been welcomed first as a guest columnist, then as financial editor at the prestigious Chicago Tribune when the post became unexpectedly available.

Diane Manchester and Jack Mercer had been married in San Francisco in June, with Stan and Maggie as their witnesses. The Gang of Four was looking forward to getting together for a barge trip down the canals of France, with a stop in Lyon to consume as many gourmet meals as possible, and another in Provence where Jack owned a farmhouse. They would end the trip with a week at the gaming tables in Monaco.

Diane had left her job at Habatsu and was now gleefully designing computer games. Jack had finally begun writing the book he'd dreamed of writing for years. They had exchanged the penthouse for an old Victorian in Pacific Heights that they were restoring, a project that promised several years of hard labor.

Ummm," Maggie murmured as Stan's kiss lingered, "tell me again why I remind you of chocolate."

His fingers caressed her face as he nibbled at her ear, then nuzzled her throat, whispering, "Milk chocolate, creamy and delicious . . ." By the time he got to rich, dark chocolate, she was moaning in anticipation.

In the fertile San Joaquin Valley of California, George Hagura woke each morning in joyous expectation of the day ahead. Not only had his status as a leader of men improved with each passing day, he had also found a woman who shared his passion. She was the daughter of one of the major growers, and had learned of the abominable conditions of the itinerant workers during an epidemic of smallpox that had threatened the lives of dozens of families. Appalled by the discovery that little children often went hungry while she lived in pampered splendor, she had become an ardent crusader.

Together, George and his new love were building housing with the aid of Habitat for Humanity. Though he had received a number of awards since his visit to Washington, George was most proud of the one that had been presented to him personally by the former president. He, too, was pleased to see the article in the Sunday paper about the former first lady's recovery.

Above Los Angeles, a Japan Air Lines jumbo jet was circling, waiting its turn to land. Seated in the first row behind the bulkhead were Mineo and Sachiko Tokumura, with their very frightened mother between them. It was Otsu's first experience on a plane and she had huddled in her seat most of the way, silently berating herself for having agreed to accompany her children.

She still had trouble believing that her son's rock band had been invited to record at the studio he assured her was the best in America. Nor could she believe that her daughter planned to produce a video to be released along with the recording. No amount of cajoling had convinced either of them that they should not do such a thing. So she had agreed to accompany them to the jungles of America. Otsu tried not to think about what her husband would say if he knew.


In a private hospital on Lake Biwa near Kyoto, the man who had once been a vital force in industry lay unmoving in a room that looked more like one in a luxury hotel than in a hospital. He had never regained the use of his body and no one was sure whether or not he was cognizant of what went on around him. Unable to feed himself, he had lost weight until his arms and legs were mere sticks with flesh that hung in ugly wrinkles.

Though assured of continued financial support by Yoshida's personal attorney, the orphanage had fewer children now. A new administrator had allowed television and movies to be shown, so those who remained were learning about the outside world. Some of the older ones were quite vocal about their eagerness to see it for themselves. Without the iron hand of its benefactor, the institution had grown significantly more liberal in a very short time.

The new administrator was proud of those who were now being interviewed by some of Japan's foremost corporations. With their superior education, they could not help but be successful. One of them might even become prime minister some day!

Though his strength had ebbed away and he didn't stay awake for very long at a time, Satoshi Yoshida was still aware of his surroundings. His anger might well have been what kept him alive, though he yearned for death to take him.

Only a few Americans were aware of how close the United States had come to economic disaster and those who were quickly forgot. The following Christmas season saw record spending as Santa filled the stockings of American children to the brim and average citizens and members of congress alike continued to pursue the American Dream with gusto.

## THE END

# ABOUT THE AUTHOR

Novelist Geri Bennett is also the author of Send Me Safe My Somebody, a novel, and The Silent Sailors, in Their Own Words, a non-fiction account of six American submarines in the Pacific during WWII. Her third novel is scheduled to be released sometime in early 2012. Though she considers San Francisco her home, she presently resides in Tennessee.